This book is dedicated to five wonderful women:

Carol Celano Mazza.....Lorraine Celano Menist.....Frances LaRocca Celano
Margaret "Peggy" Kavanagh.....Christina "Tina" Kavanagh Parisi

ANTHONY CELANO

THE CASE OF THE HUNTED WOMAN

1

<u>Revenge Is Sweet</u>

SARAH INCE EMERGED FROM prison looking healthy.
Incarceration, in a way, had been good for the twenty-three
year old. Confinement provided the young woman the
opportunity to eat regularly, sleep well, and acclimate herself to
a disciplined daily routine.

Released from the grip of an institution that choked her off
from the rest of the world, Sarah entered the open air eagerly.
Once beyond the prison walls, she began inhaling deeply. Her
exhales were loud enough to be heard by the two people in the
waiting car. Sarah looked up at the blue sky and stretched her
arms apart as far as they would go.

"FREE!" she announced loudly.

"C'mon, get in the car, will ya?" cried out Fats after tooting the
horn of his Toyota.

"Give her a minute," said his girlfriend, Greta. "Let her enjoy
the moment."

Responding to the honk, Sarah began waving to her best
friend. The broad smile on the face of both women was an
indication of their fondness for each other. Sarah got in the
back seat, hardly acknowledging Fats, who she didn't care for.
Greta's boyfriend physically resembled Sarah's stepfather, who
she detested. Her mother's second husband had ordered Sarah

out of his house after the death of her mother. "Get out! You're dead to me," were his parting words. His farewell still stung.

Detecting two distinct fragrances inside the car, Sarah sniffed loudly. The pleasant scent came from the perfume Greta wore; the pungent odor came from Fats, who had always smelled of rotten fish.

Sarah rolled down the car window a few inches to neutralize the foul body odor that her friend Greta had gotten used to. She placed her head back against the headrest, pretending to be listening to Greta, who chatted away about the latest doings. As her friend talked, Sarah was thinking of ways to make money now that she was back in circulation.

##########

SARAH WORKED OUT THE DETAILS of the robbery on her own. Since she knew the victims, she had to restrict her role to driving the getaway car. Spotting their intended victims exiting Italo's Restaurant, Fats exited the vehicle while Sarah drove around the corner and double-parked on a side street just off Cross Bay Boulevard. Finding talk about the fast-approaching Y2K millennium bug a distraction, she shut the car radio off. "Another scam," Sarah muttered under her breath, believing that the scare was a scheme cooked up by the computer geeks. It didn't make sense to her that the changing of the year 1999 to 2000 could cause the havoc being predicted.

Fats has gotta have the drop on them by now, thought Sarah, who was filled with anticipation. Her only lament was not being able to personally witness Judge Fatima West squirm. Facing the business end of a gun was sure to rattle the woman who had sent Sarah to jail.

Although she was missing out on the real action, Sarah nevertheless recognized the upside to driving the getaway car. Since the victims would never see her, they couldn't identify her. As a result, if something went wrong, it would be Fats who would take the fall. If he had the misfortune of getting caught at the scene or later identified by some witness who appeared out of nowhere, it would be his tough luck.

Sarah focused her attention on the vehicle's rearview mirror. Expecting that her cohort would soon be rounding the corner, Sarah double-checked the passenger side door to ensure that it would be open for the fleeing felon. This preoccupation caused her not to immediately see the woman crossing in front of her car.

When Sarah finally noticed the pedestrian, they made eye contact. Sarah stubbornly refused to look away; she merely pulled down the brim of the black baseball hat she wore. Her wealth of blond hair was long and worn in a ponytail that extended midway down her back. When the woman kept walking, Sarah dismissed her as a potential problem.

The thrill connected to carrying out the armed robbery she masterminded caused Sarah to squirm in her seat as the tension mounted. Turned on by perilous criminal behavior, the buildup to the moment brought about a sexual climax for Sarah. In a sense, it could be said that she was being rewarded for living dangerously.

Sarah jumped up in her seat when she heard what sounded like a shot being fired. She knew better than to think it was a car backfiring. She was sure that Fats must have let a round go from the revolver she had armed him with. Sarah immediately put the car in drive. Steeled for whatever was to follow, her lips were now taut as she awaited the return of her criminal associate.

"What the hell happened, Fats?" she asked once he got in the car.

"Get moving, will ya?" he shouted. "This ain't the time for questions!"

Sarah drove off as directed. Her protruding eye condition gave her a sleepy look that did much to conceal her inner excitement. Once a safe distance from the crime scene, Sarah again posed her question.

"So what happened?"

"The judge gave me a hard time," replied Fats. "I thought you said that this job would be a pushover."

"The bitch actually put up a fight?"

"Yeah, she put up a fight!" barked Fats. "She made a play for my gun," he explained. "Next thing I know, a round goes off." Fats went on to be less than accurate in his account of what had transpired. "I think she shot herself in a bad place."

A smile crossed Sarah's face as she envisioned the scenario. What she was being told exceeded expectations. Sarah's euphoria over the shooting of the woman whom she had yearned to get even with was a delicious moment.

"Are you sure she got hit, Fats?"

"She went down like she had her legs chopped out from under her. What do you think?"

"Was she scared?" queried Sarah, who was starved for more details.

"How the hell do I know if she was scared?" replied Fats, adding, "I didn't stick around to ask her!"

"She must have been scared shitless!" commented Sarah with satisfaction. "How much did we get?"

"I'm not sure. I gotta count it."

"Well, count it," ordered Sarah. "What are you waiting for?"

"We got about fifteen thousand," Fats informed her after conducting a fast count.

"I told you the judge's husband would have that kind of money on him!" Sarah reminded him. Her words came with great satisfaction. The accuracy of her prediction supported her belief that she was destined to be a criminal Einstein.

"Yeah, well, we got fifteen grand in cash and a million bucks in trouble if that judge croaks," noted Fats pessimistically. "Where exactly was she hit?" asked Sarah.

"In her gut," barked Fats. "Let's just hope she lives."

"Why should we care if she lives or not," commented Sarah coldly. "Look at the bright side. We made a good score. I told you her husband would be carrying big money," she again mentioned.

"I got some jewelry off the guy as well," noted Fats.

"Great!"

"Yeah, well, all I know is shooting a judge is gonna come with big-time heat."

"You were the one who shot her, Fats," she answered. "So don't cry to me—I had nothing to do with that end of things."

"What was I supposed to do? She went for the gun!"

"So, forget about it then. She had it coming."

"All right, all right, enough with this bullshit….keep driving," ordered Fats. "Our talking about it ain't gonna change anything. Just go find us a place to whack up the score."

Sarah resented his telling her what to do. "Just remember, it was me who brought you into this deal as a favor to Greta," she reminded him. "It's my job all the way, so I'm the one who gets to call the shots."

Fats was astonished that Sarah was concerned about who was boss. "Can't you appreciate the situation we got here, Sarah? This ain't no rolling of some drunk. If that judge croaks, they'll have a posse out looking for us that'll really make those eyes of yours pop. I need my head examined for letting Greta talk me into working with you," complained Fats.

"Don't worry about my friggin' eyes!" shot back Sarah, sensitive to the condition that caused her eyes to bulge.

"And another thing, why didn't you tell me that the bitch was as big as a mountain?" asked Fats.

"Are you gonna ever stop whining, Fats?"

"Yeah, well….just so you know, that bitch was a powerhouse."

"All right, she was Godzilla," said Sarah curtly. "So tell me exactly what else happened?"

"What more can I tell you? I took the money and jewelry off the husband with no problem," explained Fats. "When I turned to the judge, she made a grab for the gun. She had the barrel with both hands and twisted. She almost got the gun from me. It came down to either me or her. I think she might have even had her finger on the trigger….the more I think about it, she probably shot herself."

"Yeah, she was attempting to commit suicide," said Sarah sarcastically.

"What do we do if this judge dies?"

"Will you stop about the judge already," said Sarah sternly. "If she dies, she dies."

"Well, what are you gonna do if she does?"

"Nobody saw me do anything."

"No, you were smart. You stayed in the car," said Fats derisively. "What a freakin' laugh. It's you and Greta who got me into this swindle, and I gotta do all the sweating!"

"Chill out, will ya...."

"That's easy for you to say. You were out of sight in the car....MY CAR!" shouted Fats. "That's another friggin' thing....what happens if someone got my plate? That'll lead the cops right to me!"

Sarah acknowledged that Fats had a valid point. "So we'll ditch this car and play it safe."

"But I need my car...."

"You'll buy another with the insurance money."

"What insurance money?"

"You're gonna report this car stolen."

"I am?"

"That's right, genius."

"Now, ain't that just grand," said Fats, sounding disgusted.

"What kind of jewelry did we get, Fats?"

"I got the husband's Rolex watch and his pinkie ring."

"Did you get anything off the judge at all?"

"I never got that far with her—she grabbed for my gun, remember?"

"That's right," acknowledged Sarah.

"So where are you driving to, Sarah?" asked Fats, noticing that they were departing Queens County.

"We're going to Staten Island."

"What's in Staten Island?"

"We're gonna ditch this car there."

Fats turned on the radio to listen to the news. When it was aired that Judge Fatima West was shot and killed during a robbery in Queens, there was a hush in the car. As the felons

7

made their way over the Verrazano Bridge, it was Fats who broke the silence by punching the car ceiling.

"Now we're really in for it," thundered Fats.

"You have nothing to worry about. I've got it all worked out," Sarah assured him with a calmness that even surprised Fats. "You do?"

"Like I said, we're gonna ditch this car and you'll report your car stolen when you get home, Fats….and that's all there is to it."

"I'm taking off once the insurance pays off," said Fats. "What about Greta, your girlfriend? You do remember her….my best friend."

"You can keep your best friend. I'm tired of traveling with baggage."

"You do what you have to do, Fats," conveyed Sarah calmly. His attitude was going to make Sarah's change of plans easier. "Where in Staten Island are you driving to?" he asked.

"Don't worry. I know a place where we could dump this car and catch a ride at a nearby car service. Oh, and let me have my gun back."

"I was gonna get rid of it by tossing it in the drink."

"No, Fats, it's mine. Let me have it back."

"Here, take the damn thing," said Fats, passing the weapon to Sarah.

"Do me a favor, Fats, take the wheel," she said, pulling the car over. "You drive. I'm starting to feel a little nauseous."

"Sure, now you're starting to realize the spot we're in." "C'mon, let's switch seats," Sarah said, feigning an ailing look. "We're not far from where we need to go."

Once Fats parked at the secluded destination Sarah had selected, she placed her gun against her crime partner's temple and fired once.

"That was for Greta, you fat bastard," Sarah said icily, after executing Fats. She went on to let out a purr of pleasure as she paused to watch the blood ooze from the hole made by the bullet.

After letting out a sigh, the murderess wiped her gun clean with a hankie. Using the hankie to grasp the gun, she placed the weapon in the right hand of the dead man. Once that was done, she released her hold, allowing the gun to drop not far from his hand. Before leaving, Sarah wiped down the car so that her own prints couldn't be detected.

Prior to departing, Sarah relieved Fats of the money and jewelry he had on him. The money was for her boyfriend, Mickey, so that he could make payment on a debt he owed to a dangerous man. Sarah walked off after recording the license plate of the getaway car on a piece of paper.

Sarah thought things over as she proceeded to the car service. *I'll call the detectives in Howard Beach to let them know that it was Fats who killed the judge,* thought Sarah, *and I'll give them the plate to his car.*

Sarah was correct in her assumption that the Staten Island cops would figure Fats a suicide. She also correctly assumed that they would know that Fats killed the judge once they figured out that the gun found on him was the same one that had killed the judge.

It'll be that simple, thought Sarah. *All I need to do now is convince Greta that Fats was suicidal.*

2

Laying Down The Law

JUDGE FATIMA BRADFORD WEST was a highly competent, no-nonsense judge with a strong work ethic. Of that, there was no question. Easily irritated, she was known to be vindictive when things didn't go well. With her reputation of running hot and cold, people assigned to her court walked on eggshells.

When working her way through college, Fatima was employed part-time at a Manhattan-based property management firm. It was there that she met Amos West, a politically connected real estate attorney. He took an interest in Fatima, and the two began dating. West convinced the young student to go to law school. Upon Fatima's graduation, West assisted her in securing employment as an assistant district attorney in Queens County. Fatima eventually went on to become a bureau chief. It was shortly after receiving this promotion that she and West got married. Unbeknownst to Fatima, a few years later her husband placed a bribe in the hands of a member of the Mayor's Advisory Committee on the Judiciary. This consideration led to Fatima's appointment as a criminal court judge.

Physically, Judge West cut an impressive figure. She stood close to six feet, her shoulders broad from her passion for swimming several times a week. Fatima wore her thick black hair long with a center part. When on the bench, attired in her black robe, the judge projected an imposing figure. One of the few who refused to be intimidated by her authoritative presence was a fearless young defendant named Sarah Ince. The fair-skinned Sarah, at seventeen, was in court facing robbery charges. The teenager had been arrested by a passing police officer for her role in luring a drunken man to a secluded location, where he was rolled by accomplices who managed to escape apprehension.

At her arraignment the defendant began to nonchalantly twirl her long blond hair while standing before the bench. This relaxed behavior annoyed Judge West, who considered the defendant's conduct to be disrespectful. The fact that the defendant had an affliction that caused her eyes to bulge mattered little to the Judge West, who exhibited no empathy. "Is there something about this proceeding that you take not to be serious, Ms. Ince?" the judge asked sternly.

"No," replied Sarah, who yawned, projecting a bored look. Her response only served to annoy the judge.

"I assume that you do understand the grave nature of the charges you face. Am I correct in that assumption Ms. Ince?"
"Yeah, I do," replied Sarah, who rolled her eyes and stared down at the floor.

"I'm going to set your bail at five hundred...." said the judge, suddenly pausing mid-sentence after noticing the eye-rolling. "I will not tolerate this kind of behavior in *my* courtroom, Ms. Ince!"

"What's your problem, now?" asked Sarah, who was displaying signs of temper.

The remark caused the judge to respond harshly. "You are hereby sentenced to serve six months for contempt of court!" ruled the judge, bringing her gavel down so hard that the sound echoed beyond normal throughout the courtroom.

The jacked-up bail got Sarah's attention. "You're giving me six months before I'm even convicted?" asked the angry defendant. "You can kiss my friggin' ass, lady!" she added. Sarah had now worked herself up into a state where it took two court officers to remove her from the courtroom.

"Hold it," ordered the judge. "Bring the defendant back here right now!" The court officers again returned the defendant to face Judge West. "Let's make that 364 days!" voiced the judge. The smirk on Judge West's face made it clear that she was more than willing to make matters worse for Sarah. At this point, the defendant, to the satisfaction of the sentencing judge, wisely heeded her court-appointed attorney's advice to hush up.

While incarcerated, Sarah came to reconsider her foolish courtroom behavior. Her conversation with an older inmate, who was jailed for stabbing her common law husband, did much to set her straight.

"Everybody knows that you can't get testy when you go before Westy," said the older inmate. "That's one judge who you never play around with,"

"I found that out," acknowledged Sarah.

"You can't ever let them see you be too strong in court. Whenever you go before a judge, you gotta look sorry, girl," counseled the more experienced woman. "You gotta make it look like they broke you."

"I wouldn't give that bitch the satisfaction."

"Then no judge is ever gonna be lenient with you. You gotta make them feel like they won."

After thinking about it Sarah had to admit that the advice she received was sound. "Whatever," she said with a shrug, resigning herself to serving her sentence. "But don't think she's getting away with this. I'll get even with her one day, that's something you can bet on."

"Damn, girl....I think you really mean that."

Sarah had a long memory. Years later she proved that she did mean what she said.

##########

JUDGE WEST WAS LOOKING FORWARD to her time off. Her plan was to meet her husband for dinner at Italo's, a popular Italian eatery, prior to embarking on their vacation. The childless couple, who resided in the upscale Forest Hills section of Queens, intended to head to the airport after dinner to catch a late flight. Since she had dictated where their last vacation would be, it was now her husband's turn to select a travel destination. Amos, who enjoyed gambling, selected Las Vegas. Fatima's preference would have been to spend a week in Puerto Rico. She believed that the mountains and waterfalls and the El Yunque tropical rainforest would all contribute to a wonderful experience. The judge felt that San Juan, known for its hotel strip, beach bars, and casinos, would more than meet the entertainment needs of her husband. However, Amos was adamant in his choice of their destination.

On the ride over to Italo's, Judge West read aloud to her husband the newspaper article that featured an old case she had presided over. Amos politely smiled and nodded approvingly as he pretended to be listening. Inwardly he was pondering ways to propel his wife's career to greater heights. Operating within a highly competitive industry had taught Amos that in the real estate business, one needed to be ruthless in order to attain great success. Experience had taught him the importance of having access to those of influence. Amos understood the correlation that existed between political access and superior earning capacity. Armed with this awareness, Amos had every intention of doing his utmost to further Fatima's success, for she was his conduit to further riches.

Under average height and wiry, Amos exhibited no indication of inadequacy from being married to a much larger spouse. In fact, walking alongside the towering Fatima bolstered his ego. Amos was astute enough to be careful in how he comported himself publicly. As the husband of a criminal court judge, he knew that negative publicity needed to be avoided. A scandal could potentially derail the big plans he had for Fatima. Yet, despite being attuned to this, the judge's husband continued to satisfy his vices. Unbeknownst to Fatima, Amos was an aficionado of illicit gambling locations and bordellos.

As a man with an active libido, Amos relied on supplemental intimacy to meet his needs. Wary of entangling himself in a relationship that could lead to a messy situation, he restricted himself to pay-for-play dalliances. Such interactions had little chance of causing problems.

Amos engaged in weekly outings to a bordello with his friend/business associate, fellow attorney Marvin Butterworth. Both men didn't mind paying the premium fee required for the satisfaction they received each Friday afternoon. The lawyers took the position that they were paying the women not only to service them but also to go away. They viewed their involvement as business transactions that came free of commitments, demands, or expectations.

Marvin, who was many years older than Amos, was a man with varied business interests. He owned buildings located in the garment center, represented high-end clients and, like Amos, was not above getting involved in less-than-above-board deals. Their Friday routine consisted of doing some business, having a drink with lunch, and then heading over to a brothel on the Westside of Manhattan. Marvin could be relied on to provide the Viagra when necessary.

At the sex emporium Amos and Marvin would be greeted by a madam who collected money in advance at the door. Once payment was made, the sex workers were summoned to come out into the main room, where they stood in negligees before their clients.

Marvin favored variety, trying out a different woman each week. The judge's husband, on the other hand, was a creature of habit. Amos preferred to engage regularly with one particular woman, a blond girl who suffered from an eye affliction. When they coupled, the sex worker's eyes protruded in such a pronounced way that it made Amos feel as if he was performing in herculean fashion. The illusion of being a man who excelled sexually kept Amos a loyalist.

As Amos and the sex worker got to know each other better, they began to exchange personal information, which included Sarah's true identity. Sarah revealed her checkered upbringing and spoke of a wheelchair-bound mother and an alcoholic stepfather. Listening to her story caused Amos to take pity on the young harlot. It turned out to be a case of his heart overruling his common sense. Believing that something more than a professional bond existed with Sarah, Amos put forth details of his own life. Among the things he confided was the identity of who he was married to.

3

Ruffy Shea

SARAH AND GRETA, FRIENDS SINCE CHILDHOOD, shared an exceedingly strong bond in that both were products of a troubled home life. When Sarah was put out of her home on her sixteenth birthday, Greta decided that the time had come to leave hers. The two women pooled their money and took a small apartment in a rundown building in Coney Island. In order to get by, they engaged in unsavory activities that included taking advantage of intoxicated men in the local bars.

While seeking opportunities on the boardwalk one afternoon, the women came to meet Fats, a Queens man who was ten years their senior. Fats took an immediate liking to Greta. He subsequently won her over with big talk of his involvement in incidents that had never occurred.

Sarah, who was less impressionable than Greta, formed an altogether different impression of Fats. She saw that beyond the braggadocio was a not too bright, small-time criminal operator. However, Fats did represent a lifeline of sorts.

The dubious trio formed an alliance and began engaging in criminal activities together that proved to be profitable. Shortly after, Greta moved into the Queens flat where Fats resided. Sarah, now on her feet financially, moved into a nearby apartment house to be near her friends. Things moved along steadily for the crime team until Sarah was arrested and sent to prison for five years. She never let on to Greta that she held Fats responsible for her bad luck.

During her incarceration, Sarah's bitterness toward Greta's boyfriend only grew. She was unable to forgive Fats for neglecting to step up and fight off the officer who had arrested her. Aside from being the only one of the trio to serve time for a crime all three were involved in, her animosity was enhanced by the shabby way Fats treated Greta. She found his abusive behavior toward her friend infuriating.

Upon her release from prison at the age of twenty-three, Sarah tried to dissuade Greta from continuing her intimate involvement with Fats. It was to no avail. Unable to gain traction in convincing Greta to break off the relationship, Sarah was forced to accept her friend's choice of companionship for the time being.

When Fats learned from a friend that there was a need for young women to work a stag party, he immediately thought of Greta. Inspired at the thought of receiving a commission for his effort, Fats persuaded Greta that the opportunity was sure to be a financially rewarding one. He then asked Greta to see if Sarah could be induced to also work the party.

When Sarah inquired as to the type of work they were expected to do and what the related wages were, Fats was vague. When pressed for specifics, Fats conveyed that the job called for two ample-bosomed women willing to serve drinks while topless. Once Fats had assured them that the compensation would be generous, both Greta and Sarah were more than willing to sign on.

During the course of the stag party, Sarah came to notice the special treatment that partygoers were affording a man who appeared to be in his mid-fifties. He was the tough-looking type, the sort of hoodlum that Sarah found interesting. Sarah made it her business to acquaint herself with the seemingly important man.

During the course of the evening Sarah flirted shamelessly with Ruffy Shea, eventually slipping her telephone number and address into the breast pocket of his sport jacket. The organized crime hit man wasted no time in taking advantage of the opportunity presented to him. He made arrangements to see Sarah the following evening for dinner.

Ruffy dispatched one of his minions to Sarah's apartment the following day to transport her to the chosen restaurant. Ruffy's errand was run by Miltie, his longtime criminal associate. Sarah's first impression of Miltie wasn't favorable. He reminded her of a weasel.

During the drive, Miltie, as instructed, went on a flowery discourse as to the virtues of Ruffy. Sarah listened politely, knowing well that Miltie had been put up to spewing the accolades he put forth.

These guys must think I just got off the boat, thought Sarah.

As things turned out, the date ended with a romantic interlude at a midtown hotel. Ruffy and Sarah were in agreement that they should continue to see each other, without any expectations of commitment. As long as Ruffy remained generous, and Sarah readily available, the arrangement suited both parties just fine.

At some point after the stag party Fats approached Greta and Sarah with what he believed to be another good money making opportunity. This time Greta's boyfriend knew of a Brooklyn brothel in need of part-time sex workers. Since the financial projections were impressive, both Sarah and Greta agreed to give such work a try. Fats wasted no time in introducing the women to the people who oversaw the operation at the bordello he secretly frequented himself on occasion.

Because the financial gain was not what it had purported to be, Greta and Sarah quit after one day. They learned from another unsatisfied sex worker that a high-end Manhattan house of ill repute was currently in the market for young sex workers. They responded to the location and met the madam, a woman named Queenie, who operated the house. Queenie was an attractive auburn-haired woman in her late 30's.

Unbeknownst to Sarah and Greta, the bordello was owned by the madam's longtime boyfriend, who happened to be Ruffy

Shea. Ruffy, who never micromanaged Queenie, had no idea who was employed at his brothel at any given time. Since Ruffy didn't involve himself operationally, neither Queenie nor Sarah knew that they were sharing the same man.

The fearsome reputation of Ruffy made it obvious to all that knew him that Queenie was off limits to other suitors. When it came to Sarah, the hit man was equally protective. Despite the terms they had originally worked out, Ruffy expected exclusivity. Had he known that Sarah had been hired to work at the bordello, he'd have hit the ceiling.

4

All In The Family

MICKEY WALKER AND HIS SISTER GREW UP IN a one-family
house in Queens. His parents, who took their religion seriously,
made sure that the family of four attended Mass together each
Sunday. As good parishioners, the Walkers supported their
church by making the expected donations. They also sent their
children to parochial schools. Life for the Walkers changed
unexpectedly when Mickey's father accidentally fell into the
drum of a spinning cement mixer while at work.

The tragedy left Mrs. Walker alone to assume the sole
responsibility for raising her children. Financially challenged, the
matriarch was compelled to take on two jobs to make ends
meet. Her children were encouraged to take on after-school
work.

The red-haired Mickey grew up a thoughtful, introverted youth
who never did anything to attract attention. If a stranger
happened to look at Mickey twice, he'd withdraw, as if he had
been caught doing something naughty. Not one to amplify his
voice, Mickey was the sort of youth who was often overlooked.
If something struck him funny, he'd cover his mouth with one
hand to suppress his laughter.

Mickey's fair-skinned sister, who was a year younger, was very
different from her brother. She was an outgoing, spirited social

butterfly who made friends easily. When the siblings were together, more often than not, Mickey's sister carried the conversation.

Not having much of a social life, upon graduating grammar school Mickey gave serious consideration to the priesthood. After discussing the matter with his mother, it was decided that Mickey undoubtedly had a religious calling.

Mickey attended a Roman Catholic high school and seminary in order to pursue his religious inclination. At some point during his senior year his spiritual aspirations were abandoned. The cause of his defection was his sister's girlfriend, whom Mickey met at a birthday party.

"Why does everyone call you Mickey if your real name is Michael?" asked the daughter of Ruffy Shea.

"Mickey is just a nickname my mother gave me."

The young woman was no stranger to people having nicknames. Her father Ruffy and his cohorts all had much more colorful nicknames than Mickey. Ruffy's daughter, an innocent girl, looked up at Mickey's wavy red mane and smiled softly. "Well, I'd have nicknamed you Carrot Top," she said playfully.

"Carrot Top!"

She laughed at Mickey's reaction. "I'm just kidding. I'll just call you Mickey if that's all right with you."

"That's just fine with me," Mickey answered softly. His tiny trace of a smile matched hers. Having found each other, the two followers of their faith became inseparable.

##########

MICKEY'S MOTHER HAD RESERVATIONS about her son's new girlfriend. The ugly rumors surrounding her father were troubling. Consumed with work obligations, the widow lacked the energy required to launch a campaign with the effectiveness necessary to undo her son's romantic entanglement. All Mickey's mom could do was bide her time in the hope that her son's relationship would run its course. This proved to be a losing strategy.

Mickey's mother was in her kitchen having a cup of coffee when her daughter announced that she had been chosen to be the maid of honor at her brother's wedding.

"What wedding?" asked the mother, who was stunned by the news.

"Mickey and his girlfriend are getting married, Ma....didn't he tell you?"

The older woman closed her eyes and lowered her chin downward. She began to slowly shake her head disapprovingly as things began to register. "That boy never even mentioned a word of this to me," she answered. "No wonder he dropped out of college to go to work."

"What's wrong, ma? She's a very nice girl and they've been together for years now."

No response was given. The troubled woman just gazed out the kitchen window. Her face reflected a sadness that only a mother can have when worried about her child. She'd lived long enough to know that she'd have to make the best of it.

##########

THOSE WHO KNEW MICKEY'S MOTHER BEST often said that her bladder was in her eyes. This was never more evident than when her son Mickey got married. As she sat in church witnessing the ceremony, a wagon train of tears journeyed down her cheeks. The weeping finally began to cease when the time came to file out of the church.

The liquid flow resumed when the groom's mother danced with her son at the reception. In front of over two-hundred guests they waltzed to the tune of *Boy of Mine.* Her leaking abated when it was the turn of the bride and her father to take the dance floor. This time the song was *Daddy's Little Girl*, as sung by a prominent recording artist.

As Mickey's mother watched the broad-shouldered Ruffy dance with his daughter, he somehow didn't appear to be quite the brute he was purported to be. *Maybe I'm judging this poor man wrongly*, thought Mickey's mother, taking an optimistic stance. *After all, how bad could a man be who pays for a wedding of this magnitude?*

When Mickey's mother turned her attention to the wedding singer she wondered if what she had heard were true. Was he really working the party for free, as a favor to some big shot the bride's father knew? *That can't be true,* she thought, *or could it?* By the end of the night the matriarch had modified her opinion of Ruffy Shea. Exposure to the gangster's civil side caused the groom's mother to amend her feelings toward him. She even began to find Queenie, Ruffy's girlfriend, to be likable. Mrs. Walker's impression of Ruffy's two most trusted associates was less favorable. She found Joe Bullets to be sinister and Miltie to be something of a sleazebag.

##########

RUFFY TOOK AN ACTIVE INTEREST IN the future of his new son-in-law. The hit man/mobster viewed being a lineman for the telephone company as an unimpressive occupation for someone married to his daughter. Ruffy took it upon himself to do something about it. He sent Miltie to notify his son-in-law to be at his social club that evening.

Mickey reported to the club as directed. Like others in the area, he was aware of the club's questionable reputation. When he arrived, he proceeded to the front door cautiously. When challenged by an older man at the entrance, he wasn't surprised.

"Where are you going, Johnny?" asked the man in the ill-fitting silver wig. He spoke in a clipped, not very friendly fashion.

"I'm supposed to meet my father-in-law here," replied Mickey softly.

"And who might that be?"

"Ruffy Shea...."

"Ruffy's ya father-in-law, is he?"

"Yes, he told me to meet him here," answered Mickey.

"Why didn't ya say that in the first place, kiddo?" asked the man, brightening. "Come on in, you're among friends, Ruffy's inside."

Ruffy was seated at a round table in the rear of the club having a beer with a member of his crew, Joe Bullets. Joe, who was ten years younger than Ruffy, was Ruffy's protégé. Both men were attired similarly in sport jackets and slacks. Both were clean shaven and styled their hair in the same fashion.

"Let's go in the office, Mickey," said Ruffy. Once alone with his son-in-law Ruffy pointed to a chair. "Take a load off, kid." As directed Mickey took a seat. "I called you in to have a man-to-man talk."

When Ruffy asked Mickey if he wanted anything to drink, Mickey declined the offer. "No, thank you," he politely replied. "What did you say?" asked Ruffy, who could hardly hear his son-in-law. "Speak up."

"I said no thank you, *sir*," repeated Mickey, thinking he hadn't been respectful enough.

"Take it easy. You were just talking too low. We ain't in the army over here, so forget that sir shit."

"I thought...."

"Yeah, I know," said Ruffy, short-circuiting Mickey's attempt to explain. "Now pay attention, kid. You know I like you. If I didn't, you'd have never gotten permission to marry my daughter."
"Thank you, I really appreciate....

"Stop with the ass-kissing, will ya?" said Ruffy, displaying a flash of frustration. "I wanna help you, kid. But I can't if you keep acting like some sissy. That won't float in my world."

"I don't understand...."

"Then let me educate you. First off, you can't go around looking like a rag picker. I got an image to maintain. The people I do business with have to see me in a certain light....and you indirectly reflect me."

"I understand," said Mickey, who remained grim faced as he continued to listen.

"Ever since my old lady died, I've been spoiling the hell out of your wife."

"I understand," said Mickey, repeating himself.

"I know you help out your mother, and that's a good thing, kid. A boy must never forget his mother. But let's get to the point here. Whatever money you're pulling down at the telephone company ain't enough. I ain't looking to put you down, kid, I'm just stating facts."

"I know."

"You *must* have heard by now that I've got powerful friends, right?"

"I don't really pay attention to that kind of talk."

Ruffy looked at Mickey in a way that made it obvious he was evaluating his sincerity. Once Mickey passed Ruffy's sniff test the gangster continued. "That's a good answer, kid. You'd like to make more money, I imagine. Wouldn't you?"

"Yes, of course," replied the son-in-law.

"Good, so here's what we're gonna do. You're gonna quit that job you got and go to work for me. I'm gonna start you out by paying you double what you're making now....how does that sound to you, kid?"

Mickey was taken aback by the offer. "What will I have to do?" he asked cautiously.

"You'll be learning to do a lot of different things. I got money out on the street, so I'm gonna start you out by keeping track of my collections."

"I don't understand...."

"Boy, are you green," said Ruffy, shaking his head at Mickey being so naïve. "I loan money to people and they pay me back a little each week until they save enough to pay off the whole loan in one shot. Sometimes they never get enough to pay it off in one shot, which is the best kind of loan you could make. It means they pay forever."

"You want me to go out and get the money for you?"

"No, no, no. They come to you with their payments and then you give me the money. All you gotta do is keep track of what I got out there and who's falling behind on their payments. When it looks like things are getting out of hand, we let Joe know. He'll go out and do the heavy lifting when it comes to deadbeats."

"I understand."

"Sure you do. You'll learn, kid. You got the right attitude. I'm also gonna see a very dear friend of mine and see if he could get you a job on the books at a big electrical company. That job will give you a weekly check and medical benefits."

"What hours will I be working there?"

"There are no hours to work with the electrical company. It's a no-show job. You only go in on paydays to get your check."

"We can do that?"

"We can do a lot more than that, kid. Just remember, you'll be kicking back to me half of that check money, understand? I keep half of what you give me and then kick the other half upstairs to my dear friend. So, you see, we all get to eat. Understand?" Mickey nodded timidly in the affirmative. "Good. I can see that we're gonna get along real good. Now you can thank me, Mickey."

"Thank you."

"Oh, there is one other thing, Mickey. Not a word about any of this to my daughter. She's a good girl."

##########

MICKEY'S INTRODUCTION TO LOANSHARKING came with a limited understanding of just who his father-in-law was. It was Miltie, after the two got comfortable with each other, who explained to Mickey that Ruffy's *"dear friend"* was Philly Rava, boss of the Rava organized crime family.

"I had no idea of that," said Mickey.

"Are you kidding? They're as tight as you can get," advised Miltie. "Your father-in-law is Philly's main torpedo."

"I don't follow you, Miltie."

"Ruffy's a shooter, kid, explained Miltie. "He's Philly's personal assassin."

"He is?" asked the wide-eyed Mickey, who was now gulping. "Now look, Mickey....remember, you didn't hear any of this from me. If Ruffy thinks I'm talking out of school, I'll be in the trick box, which ain't a healthy place to be." It was at this point that Mickey came to fully comprehend the circle he was traveling in.

After Mickey's wife gave birth to their son, Ruffy became even more of an influence in Mickey's life. The grandfather, who doted on his new grandson, decided that the child needed a backyard. He was so adamant in this belief that he gifted his daughter the money necessary to purchase a home near his in Howard Beach.

When Ruffy's daughter later indicated to her husband that they could use an in-ground pool in the yard, Mickey balked at the cost connected to such a luxury. The following day Mickey heard from Miltie that Ruffy wanted to see him at the club. "So, Mickey, I think it's time you start making a little more money so you can get that pool my daughter wants," began Ruffy. "I'm in a new business with my dear friend. He's a silent partner. The business is in Manhattan, and it's doing great. I'm gonna give you a piece of my end as a gift."

"What kind of business is it?"

"It's a cathouse. I got my girl Queenie in there managing the place. She gets a nice salary, so she's happy."

"What about my regular work?"

"You still get to do that, kid."

"What are my duties gonna be?" asked Mickey.

"You show your face and collect our money from Queenie. She does everything else.

"I don't know....my wife might not like the idea," said Mickey. "Whoa....hold it right there, Junior," said Ruffy, holding up his hand to signal a halt. "Are you forgetting the golden rule already? You don't say anything to your wife, your priest, or anybody in your friggin' dreams about our business! You got that?"

"What if I talk in my sleep?" asked Mickey, who wasn't trying to be funny.

"You won't be doing it twice because your tongue will be wrapped around your neck," replied Ruffy coldly.

Mickey was taken by surprise at how quickly Ruffy switched

lanes. Seeing Ruffy's vicious side was insightful. "When do you want me to start?" he asked.

"You'll start working there Wednesday. Queenie pays off the girls at the end of the night, and then she'll give you the rest of the money. Your job is to bring the rest of the cash to me."

"What do I do if there is a problem?"

"You call Joe Bullets if you run into ball-breakers. In two minutes, help will be there."

"Who is responsible for paying the bills?"

"That's Queenie's department."

"What about the police?"

"You don't have to sweat it. All you have to worry about is me getting a fair shake with the money. I trust Queenie, but you never know."

##########

RUFFY SHOULD HAVE REALIZED THAT exposing Mickey to a brothel was bound to be a disaster. The closest Ruffy's son-in-law had ever come to anything remotely close to infidelity was his occasional browsing of a naughty magazine. Now, amid the temptations connected to the flesh industry, Mickey was destined to weaken.

The brothel was located on an upper floor of a commercial building. A small elevator transported Mickey up to the fourth floor, where three offices were located. The print on the door to 3-C reflected the business name *Tobias Textile, Inc.*

When Mickey entered the bordello, he was warmly received by Queenie, who sat at a desk just off the entrance door. Attired in a green pants suit, Ruffy's girlfriend appeared presentable enough to work at any legitimate office. It would be fair to say that the slender Queenie was as attractive as any of the sex workers she oversaw.

"Hi, Mickey," greeted Queenie.

"Hi," he answered, walking toward the desk.

"You'll find this place a piece of cake," advised the madam. "C'mon, let me show you around."

The main part of the room had a sitting area where several customers waited their turn. A blue curtain separated the main room from the rear bedrooms where the working girls plied their trade.

"Are all these guys waiting to be serviced?" asked Mickey. "Yeah, they'll sit there quietly and wait their turn like good little boys. We never have any trouble here, Mickey," said Queenie. "Our customers are mostly married men who don't want problems. Even the hoods we get in here watch their step. You can thank your father-in-law's reputation for that."

"Do you serve drinks?"

"No, there is no drinking allowed in here and I don't let in anybody drunk or high. That's a strict rule."

"They cause trouble?"

"Not just that. A lot of times, it takes them forever to get off. Time is money around here."

"I never thought of that," admitted Mickey. "What about the girls....how are they?"

"Every so often, they can act up. But I can handle them. If a girl comes in high, I usually send her right home. I just warned this girl Greta about coming in high. If these men thought we were serving up junkies, they'd never come back. They'd be afraid of bringing something home."

The working girls at the brothel were all between twenty and thirty-five. When word got around to the staff that Mickey held an interest in the brothel, he became quite popular with the sex workers—none of whom were more interested in the new boss than Sarah Ince.

########

THE UNUSUAL EYE CONDITION OF SARAH intrigued Mickey so much that he clumsily began sneaking glances at her. Sarah was fast to pick up on his interest. Whenever their eyes happened to lock, the two exchanged smiles.

Sarah found Mickey's shyness to be amusing. What she didn't realize was that Mickey didn't view her purely in a lustful way, as did everyone else who patronized the brothel. Still influenced by his early religious training, Mickey saw Sarah as someone to be pitied because of her eye affliction. In time he came to learn that Sarah was not only a soiled dove but also someone with a criminal propensity.

As Sarah got to know Mickey better, she found him to be the sort of man she probably was best suited for. While her sexual preference leaned toward the macho sort of man, she knew that such men were incapable of meeting her needs beyond the bedroom. What sold her on Mickey was his ability to make her feel as if she were in charge. Adding to Mickey's appeal was his not minding taking a back seat to her likes.

Since Ruffy insisted that his connection to Sarah remain a secret, his name was never uttered by Sarah. All Sarah really knew about Ruffy was that he was a generous bigshot thug with whom she went out with on occasion. She had no knowledge that he was an owner of the brothel or that he was Mickey's father-in-law. She was also unaware of Queenie's connection to Ruffy.

"Are you hungry?" asked Sarah, one evening when Mickey was at the bordello.

"I could eat."

"I'll be leaving in a little while. Wait outside for me, and we'll grab a bite."

"Sure," replied Mickey.

Mickey pulled into the parking lot of an all-night diner. Sarah requested that they be seated in a booth near the front entrance. After they had satisfied their hunger, Sarah devised a scheme to avoid paying the bill.

"Go get the car, Mickey, and pull up out front," she said. "This is my treat."

"You don't have to do that, Sarah."

"I insist, I'll take care of this and be right out." It was a gesture that encouraged Mickey to believe that he was influencing Sarah in a positive way.

When the waitress passed by the table Sarah informed her that her husband was in the restroom and that he would be paying the bill as soon as he finished his business. When the waitress became occupied elsewhere, Sarah slipped out unnoticed, leaving the bill unpaid. Success in carrying out such small larcenies was considered to be an accomplishment by Sarah.

As Sarah grew to be more comfortable with Mickey, she began to ask probing questions. When Mickey conveyed that his partner in the bordello was Ruffy Shea, Sarah was stunned. She became really shocked after learning that Ruffy was Mickey's father-in-law.

"I can't believe this!" expressed Sarah. "Ruffy Shea is really your partner and your wife's father?"

"Yeah," acknowledged Mickey. "Do you know Ruffy?"

"Only by reputation," answered Sarah untruthfully.

"Ruffy is the only reason why I'm here. He likes to keep things in the family."

"I can see that."

"Queenie is his girlfriend."

"Well, what do you know about that," said Sarah, shaking her head.

The sex worker was appalled at her inability to put things together on her own. Sarah was now more determined than ever to play her own cards close to the vest. She had no intention of revealing her relationship to Ruffy.

The subsequent affair that went on between Mickey and Sarah couldn't remain a secret forever. Their interactions at the brothel made it evident to Queenie that the two were involved. The madam knew that such a reckless romance would come with a steep price to pay once Ruffy got wind of it.

As Ruffy's girlfriend, Queenie found herself in an awkward position. Not immune to experiencing Ruffy's dark side, she felt herself in a quagmire in that she'd be expected to inform Ruffy of Mickey's amorous antics. Yet, by alerting the hot-tempered Ruffy, she knew that she'd also be facing his wrath. He'd surely blame her for allowing such a thing to occur in the first place.

Ruffy's gonna just have to get wise some other way, thought Queenie. If questioned, she'd tell Ruffy that the wayward pair conducted themselves discreetly. All she could do was hope that, if Ruffy confronted her, he would swallow her fib.

After a night's sleep, thanks to disturbing dreams, Queenie felt the need to minimize her exposure. She decided that she might have to terminate both Sarah and her friend Greta. In the event of Mickey lodging a protest, Queenie believed that she could neutralize him by threatening to take the matter up with Ruffy.

5

No Time For
Scratching Itches

MICKEY BECAME SO FOCUSED ON SARAH that he made the huge mistake of failing to take into account the needs of his wife. Usually, when returning home late, Mickey would find Ruffy's daughter in bed fast asleep. It never occurred to him that his wife could deviate from this norm.

Having read several chapters of a spicy novel one evening, Mickey's spouse decided to wait up for her husband. Feeling in a loving way, she liberally applied the perfume she used to convey her desire for intimacy.

When Mickey arrived home, he tiptoed into his bedroom. The scent of the sweet fragrance that permeated the air caused his nose to tickle. He knew that this could only mean that his wife was in the mood for a command performance. Having just left Sarah, Mickey frowned at the thought. Physically drained, he simply lacked the stamina for encores.

Pretending not to pick up on the signal sent by his wife, Mickey purposely took his time preparing for bed. Hoping that his wife's desire would pass, he took a long time changing into pajamas in the dark. He was even slower brushing his teeth. When he ran out of ideas on how to further stall, he sat on the edge of the bed thinking.

When Mickey felt the inevitable touch of his wife's long nails gently scratching his back he froze. Receiving no response from her husband, Mickey's wife began to explore other areas in an effort to ignite Mickey's frisky side.

"Mickey...." she finally said, finding his lack of interest frustrating.

"I'm sorry, but I'm very tired," said Mickey in a low voice. "I need to get some sleep." He then put his head on the pillow while facing away from his wife. "Good night, honey."
Mickey's response was very unlike him. As a rule, Mickey had always been up to the task when called upon. His wife thought it possible that he might not be feeling well.

"Is everything all right, Mickey?" she asked. "Are you sick or something?"

"Go to sleep. I'm fine. I just need some rest."

Mickey's reply caused his wife to become suspicious. Searching for a reason that would justify Mickey's cooling, she could arrive at only one conclusion. *He must be getting it someplace else,* she thought. *Of course, what else could it be?*

Determined to get to the bottom of things, Mickey's wife turned on the lamp that rested on the night table next to the bed. Then, in an accusatory tone, began to interrogate her husband.

"Where have you been?"

"I've been working," replied Mickey.

"I've been waiting for you."

"I know that, but I'm too tired. Will you please let me go to sleep?"

"Wait a minute, not so fast. I want to talk to you."

"Let's talk in the morning," he said, placing the pillow over his head to shut her out.

Mickey's wife sat up straight in bed. She pushed her husband's shoulder roughly to get his attention. Mickey rolled over to face his wife. "What is the problem?" he shouted.

Now facing Mickey, Ruffy's daughter saw something of interest on Mickey's neck. To see better she adjusted the lamp to maximum illumination. The sight of a hickey on her husband's neck caused her to explode.

"What the hell is that on your neck?"

"What?" asked Mickey, trying to come off as innocent as possible.

"Where did you get that red mark on your neck?"

When his wife tried to put her finger on the area in question, Mickey pulled away from her. "It's just a pimple," he answered, rubbing his neck.

"Don't you dare tell me that's a pimple!" his wife shouted, escalating the matter. "That's a hickey!"

"If it is….you must have given it to me."

"Me? Now tell me, who the hell were you with?"

Knowing that he couldn't very well fess up to his infidelity, Mickey struggled for a credible explanation. Ruffy's daughter had been led to believe that her husband worked nights at a private sanitation concern.

Under relentless grilling, Mickey's defenses finally collapsed. Cornered, he admitted to a single infidelity. He invented a tale that emphasized that his indiscretion was with a hooker. He thought that his spouse would find this to be the most palatable explanation.

Mickey's explanation only further stimulated his wife's curiosity. She stepped up the pressure and subsequently extracted more false information from her husband. Fearing Ruffy, Mickey was determined to hold his tongue concerning the brothel.

"Promise me that you won't say anything to your father," pleaded Mickey, realizing the precarious situation he was in. "I know that I was wrong, and I'm sorry. It'll never happen again."

"You disgust me!" exclaimed his wife. The bitterness in her voice made it clear that she was unwavering in her outrage. "You've betrayed me and gone back on your vows."

"Are you going to tell your father?"

"He'll know, because I'm divorcing you, Mickey."

"Divorcing me? Please, you're overreacting. We should try to work this out...."

"There is no working anything out, Mickey. You betrayed me, so it's over between us. Go to your whore!"

"What are you going to tell your father?"

"I'm not going to lie for you, Mickey."

Now desperate, Mickey was willing to try anything to salvage the marriage and save his own neck.

"We could try going for counseling....nobody has to know."

"Forget it, Mickey. It's over," voiced Mickey wife. Her tone conveyed a coldness that he had never seen in her before.

##########

WHEN MICKEY'S WIFE NOTIFIED her father telephonically that she was filing for a divorce, she refused to offer an explanation as to why. Ruffy, who didn't believe in divorce, found the news disturbing. He immediately went to his daughter's house in an attempt to reverse her decision.

"Look, honey, don't be hasty about this," said Ruffy. "What the hell did he do? He didn't beat you or anything, did he?"

"I wish that was all it was."

"Well, what exactly did that bastard do?" asked Ruffy, now thinking something worse had occurred.

"He violated the sixth commandment."

"The sixth commandment—what the hell did he steal?"

"He committed adultery! Stealing is the seventh commandment," she corrected.

"Who was he with?"

"He went with a prostitute behind my back!" the daughter advised angrily.

In the scheme of wayward behavior, Ruffy didn't view this as an unforgivable offense.

"Who is the whore?"

"Someone he picked up on the street, or so he says. I don't know who she is."

"What else did he tell you?"

"Isn't that enough?"

Relieved at not being exposed as the owner of a bordello, Ruffy breathed more easily. "Your husband is still wet behind the ears. Think of the baby...."

"I'm sorry, but I'd have no respect for myself if I took him back. I took *my* vows seriously!"

"Sure you did, but believe me, it's no fun going it alone. I should know. Can't you see how I've been struggling since I lost your mother?"

"It's no use. I've made up my mind!" said Ruffy's daughter adamantly. "I lost my respect for my husband, and without that, there is nothing to salvage."

Ruffy could see that he was left with little choice but to go along with his daughter's decision.

"You hitched your wagon to a no-good sneaky rat bastard!" Ruffy bellowed, putting on a good show of outrage. "Just wait until I see him!"

"I don't want you getting involved in this. I'll handle it."

"All right, maybe you're right. Just do me one favor, consider this alternative ... "

"What?"

"I can see to it that Mickey is taught a good lesson, one he won't ever forget. It's guaranteed to keep that son of a bitch flying straight in the future."

"No, that won't do. I told you, he's lost my respect. I don't want him. As it is, he's sleeping on the couch now."

"He is?"

"Yes, and I've decided to sell this house. I can't stand being here."

"What do you mean you're selling the house?" asked the shocked father.

"I can't stay here any longer," replied Ruffy's daughter with definiteness.

"That'll pass, keep the house. Besides, I don't want the money."

"I'm glad to hear that because you weren't getting it."

"What are you talking about? I gave you the money!"

"It was a gift," reminded the daughter. "I'm going to invest the money I get from the sale."

"You're *not* selling the house," declared Ruffy firmly.

"Yes, I *am* selling this house—*and* I'm calling in an investment adviser."

"What investment adviser? What are you talking about?"

"I'll need to know how to invest the money I get from the sale of my home."

Ruffy went ballistic after hearing this. "That's *my* money, you're talking about," bellowed the father. "I want it back if you sell this friggin' house!"

"How is it your money? You gave it to me as a gift! It's mine!" protested Ruffy's daughter, with equal emphasis. "I'm using the money from the house to finance your grandson's education." Ruffy backed off. A realist, he admitted to himself that he had hit a dead end when it came to getting his money back from a daughter who was as strong-willed as he was. Ruffy could see that he'd have to resort to other tactics in order to recoup his money.

"You do whatever you want to do," finally voiced her father, accepting defeat. *I'll make that son-of-a-bitch Mickey pay me back every dime,* he thought.

###########

QUEENIE PLACED THE TELEPHONE RECEIVER away from her ear to avoid the sting of Ruffy's shouting. She had been with him long enough to know not to interrupt him when he was angry. "So, answer me, have you heard from that son-in-law of mine?" he demanded to know.

"No, I expect to see him later when he comes by to collect. Is there a problem?"

"Yeah, he's been screwing around on my daughter. He gave her some song and dance about being with some whore. That's gotta be bullshit, he ain't the type. He's just dumb enough to have a friggin' steady squeeze tucked away someplace."

"Oh, Ruffy, I had no idea," said Queenie, hoping her lie was acceptable.

"You don't know anything about this?"

"Not a thing, Ruffy, I swear it," replied Queenie, using her most guiltless voice. "If I had any inclination, I'd have called you, you know that."

The sound of Queenie's proclamation of unawareness raised a red flag. Ruffy recognized her tone for the camouflage it was. "Cut the crap, Queenie—I can tell by your voice that you knew," he accused.

"I didn't know a thing, honey," said, Queenie, refusing to admit Ruffy was right. "How would I know about anything?"

"We'll talk about *that* later. You call Mickey and tell him to get his ass over to the club right away. Tell him I understand his situation—you know, make it like I'm sympathizing with him."

"Did you try calling him?"

"He's not picking up for me."

"I'll call him."

"You do that. If he says that he's too scared to come to the club, just tell him his punishment is gonna be not working with you anymore."

"Okay, Ruffy. But what if that doesn't work?"

"If he don't buy that, then tell him that me and Joe Bullets are gonna go looking for him. I don't think he's gonna want that."

"No, he's definitely not going to want that."

"Now I gotta start looking for a replacement to work with you," lamented Ruffy.

"Don't worry, honey, you'll find somebody. And if you don't, it's no big deal. I can take care of everything until you do."

"All I know is that the dumb bastard screwed his way out of a good thing!"

"Don't do anything hasty—"

"Relax, Queenie, nothing is gonna happen," Ruffy assured her. "Mickey ain't even getting the beating he's got coming to him. I got reasons for wanting him healthy. But I'll tell you one thing, I'm not forgetting about that girlfriend he's got someplace. I'm gonna find out who she is, hunt her down, and go to work on her but good for causing me this grief!"

Queenie cringed at the thought of Ruffy finding out that it was one of the bordello girls who had taken up with Mickey. When Queenie later spoke to Mickey telephonically, she conveyed Ruffy's message.

"You better not waste any time getting over to the club, Mickey, Ruffy is pretty steamed at you," she advised. "Why didn't you pick up the phone when he called you?"

"I was afraid to talk to him. I know he's pissed off at me. What do you think he'll do?"

"Well, I can tell you one thing, Mickey. He told me he wasn't going to lay a finger on you."

"Do you believe that?"

"Yeah, I really do. He's got plans for you, but hurting you isn't one of them."

"I guess I better get over to the club then," said Mickey."

"I would. And Mickey, I wouldn't count on you coming back here. Ruffy put me on notice that he's declared you out."
"Did he say why?"

"You'll have to take that up with him," advised Queenie, adding, "I think you already know why."

"Have you seen Sarah?"

"I'm thinking that I might have to let her go."

"You are? Why?"

"That's another thing that I think you know the answer to, Mickey."

Mickey now knew that Queenie was aware of his relationship with Sarah. "Did you tell Ruffy about me and Sarah?"

"What's to tell?"

"About me and Sarah—"

"Don't go putting me in the middle!" shouted Queenie, catching an attitude. "As far as I'm concerned *nobody* knows a thing about anything. If Ruffy thought I knew about you two, he'd blame me, and my ass would be in the street next to you and Sarah."

"I understand. When you see her, just let Sarah know that I'll call her."

"No dice, Mickey. I'm not getting involved in your problems."

##########

MICKEY'S MEETING WITH RUFFY at the club couldn't have been more stressful. Ruffy's son-in-law didn't know whether or not he'd be walking out of the club in one piece. When Ruffy began pressing Mickey about the woman he had taken up with, his son-in-law tried his best not to implicate Sarah Ince. Mickey lied and said that his fling was a woman he met while shopping in a department store.

"My daughter told me you said you were screwing some hooker. Now you're telling me that you were with someone in a department store—which is it?"

"She was just shopping like I was. We got to talking about men's shirts and one thing led to another—"

"You know what? Cut the shit. I don't want to hear any more of your bullshit. Every time you lie to my face, it makes me want to hurt you!"

At this point, there was no stopping Ruffy from unleashing his aggressive side. He picked up a glass ashtray off the table they were sitting at and bounced it off his son-in-law's head. Stunned by the blow, Mickey winced upon impact. He placed his hand where the sting was coming from. When he removed his hand from the injured area, he saw blood on his fingers.

"That's just a sample," said Ruffy. "If you want some more, then keep up the bullshit. Now who is the girlfriend?"

Mickey knew he had to fess up or face further consequences.

"Her name is Sarah."

"What's the last name?"

"I don't know her last name," he fibbed, still looking to protect the woman with whom he had taken up.

Ruffy picked up a large gray stapler. "Do you want me to close that gash in your head with this?"

"No, hold up—"

"What's the name?"

"I don't know—but Queenie probably knows her last name," answered Mickey, without thinking.

"Where does she fit in?"

"Sarah works for us at the house."

"SON OF A BITCH!" shouted Ruffy. "Did Queenie know about what was going on between you and this Sarah?"

"I don't really know," fibbed Mickey, looking to protect the madam. "She never said anything."

Ruffy had little choice other than to give Queenie the benefit of the doubt. Strange as it might seem, it never dawned on Ruffy that the Sarah who took up with Mickey was the same Sarah with whom he'd taken up himself.

Ruffy gave Mickey twenty-four hours to move out of his own home. The terrified son-in-law was warned that he'd better agree to whatever terms Ruffy's daughter demanded, and that included visitation restrictions concerning his own son.

The hoodlum made it abundantly clear that Mickey was washed up as a member of his crew. Lastly, Mickey was told in no uncertain terms that he owed Ruffy the money he and his wife had received for their house. Ruffy emphasized this by pointing his thick index finger in Mickey's face.

"Hear me good, Mickey," warned Ruffy menacingly. "This is *your* debt—nobody else's. Get me?"

"Where am I gonna get that kind of money?" asked the harried Mickey. "Have a heart. I don't have a job."

"I'm having a heart by not cutting yours out!" barked Ruffy. "You're gonna pay me fifteen hundred a week until you get even—and I want it *every* Sunday after the last Mass, even if you gotta rob the collection basket to come up with the money."

"Where am I gonna get the money to make that kind of a payment?" Mickey again asked.

"Go see your mother. Tell her to sell her house. Or go see that sister of yours. Better yet, go out and steal like a man!" shouted Ruffy. "I want the first payment one week from this Sunday—and you better not disappoint."

"But—"

"No buts! You miss a payment, and I'm gonna chop off one of your fingers. If you miss ten payments, you got no more fingers! After that, I go to work on your toes." Mickey gulped and nodded weakly. "Now go to your whore and get the hell out of my sight!"

##########

SARAH HAD LITTLE REGARD for the men she serviced. She saw the Johns as chickens to pluck. Amos West, her regular Friday afternoon trick, was no exception. When Amos had let it come out that he was the husband of Judge Fatima West, Sarah's interest in the attorney skyrocketed. Never forgetting her treatment in court at the hands of the judge, Sarah was just waiting for her chance to get even.

Servicing Amos behind the back of his unwitting wife provided just limited satisfaction. Her animosity was so intense that she wished there were a way to infect Amos with a venereal disease so that he could pass it on to the judge.

As usual, Amos arrived at the brothel with his friend, Marvin, who was also his business associate. Both men were in exceptionally good spirits. Amos was so upbeat that he gave Sarah a hefty bonus after their weekly matinee. As Amos peeled money from his thick bankroll, Sarah couldn't help but notice. "Where are you off to with all that money?" she asked.

"I'm going to Vegas to do a little gambling. Do you like to gamble, Sarah?"

"I'd be willing to take a risk—with your money." Amos found her remark funny.

"Well, I'll have to keep that in mind. I can't do anything now. I'm taking a late flight to Vegas after dinner."

"You're not taking me?" asked Sarah in a childlike way. She was feeling him out to see if he was amenable to such a thing. "No, sorry, I can't bring you along on this trip."

"You gonna bring me back a present?"

"Sure, I am. You can count on it."

"Will it be something nice?"

"It'll be nice," answered Amos, who chuckled at the question.

"Do you promise?"

"Sure, I promise, and if I win big at the tables, trust me, you'll be a happy young woman."

Clearly satisfied, Sarah smiled broadly. "Are you going with your friend, the old man?"

"Marvin? Hell no, I'm going with my wife."

"You're taking her?"

"It's our winter vacation."

"Oh, how domestic," Sarah replied sourly. "So, how is *she* doing?"

"She's doing okay."

"Going on vacation with your wife must be a real blast," said Sarah sarcastically.

Amos laughed, "I know she stuck it to you that time in court. But we spoke about that. That's what a judge is supposed to do. They're not social workers, you know."

Sarah had a smart answer for his comment but held her tongue. "So, how much do you gamble?" asked Sarah, changing the topic.

"Sometimes too much, I suppose."

"So, you're a high roller?"

"That's what some would say, but what can I tell you? It's what I enjoy."

Through further conversation, Sarah got a general idea as to how much money Amos must have drawn from the bank to finance his trip. She further learned where and when he and his wife were having their dinner prior to heading to the airport. "Can I ask you a personal question before you go, Amos?"

"Sure, what's the question?"

"How is the judge in bed?" asked Sarah, trying to envision Fatima West in moments of passion. "Is she as good as me?"

"She's not as good as you, I can tell you that."

"I bet she likes to get on top—right?"

"She does. How did you know that?"

"And I bet you feel like you're under a bed of cement."

"Oh, c'mon now, Sarah, you're being too much!"

"Do you think of me when you do it with her?"

"Of course I do."

"What makes me so special?"

"You want the honest truth?"

"Sure...."

"I get turned on when I see your blue eyes about to pop out of your head when we do it. They're so—expressive."

"I've heard that before."

When Sarah finished with Amos, Queenie entered her room to have a word with her. She was stunned when she was informed that she was being terminated.

"We'll see what Mickey has to say about that when he comes by," said Sarah.

"He won't be coming by, Mickey's out, Sarah."

"He's out? What are you talking about? He's an owner here."

"No more."

"What happened?"

"All I can tell you is that Mickey doesn't belong anymore."

"We'll see about that."

Sarah telephoned Mickey, who enlightened her as to the situation. The briefing included Ruffy's demand for money. Sarah's mind raced in an effort to determine what to do. It only took her a short while to formulate a plan of action.

"Satisfied?" asked Queenie. "You better get your things and go now, Sarah."

"I'll leave, Queenie," said Sarah, holding her temper.

"Take Greta with you. She's through here as well."

"What did she do?"

"Goodbye, Sarah."

"No problem."

Before leaving the brothel with Greta, Sarah turned to ask the madam a question.

"What was I supposed to do?" she asked. "Mickey was an owner. I was supposed to deny him?"

"Queenie looked at Sarah icily. "All I know is what you two girls are supposed to do now, honey."

"And what's that?"

"Leave. And if you're smart, you'll stay scarce."

Sarah immediately went to meet Mickey. When Mickey finished talking, Sarah responded.

"So, you admitted to Ruffy my being with you?" Sarah asked.

"I had to tell him," answered Mickey, pointing to the wound on his head.

"We're dealing with a dangerous man, Mickey, so there is only one thing to do," replied Sarah. "Do you love me?" she then asked, straying off topic.

"What?"

"Answer me. Do you love me?"

"Well, sure I do," he replied, fearing he would be abandoned totally if he answered otherwise.

"Then we'll do what we have to do," said Sarah, without emotion.

"What's that supposed to mean?"

"We're making a quick score tonight. It'll be enough for you to pay Ruffy and buy us another week before you have to come up with the next payment. I just need to call Greta."

Sarah now had to work fast. She saw the gunpoint robbery she had concocted as a solution that came with an upside.

"Greta, is Fats there with you?

"Yeah, we just got in. What's up?"

"I got a score lined up for us. It'll mean big money."

"He'll love that. Hang on. I'll put him on the line."

After finalizing her arrangements with Fats telephonically, Sarah turned to Mickey. "We're all set, Mickey."

"Do you need my car?"

"No, it's all good. You know something, Mickey, this is gonna kind of work out nice in a few ways."

"How is that?"

"I'm gonna help you with the money situation, get to square the account with a black robe-wearing bitch I've been looking to get even with, and do my girlfriend Greta a favor."

"But what about Ruffy? He's not going away, you know."

"You think not, sweetie?"

"What do you mean?"

"You'll see. We're taking things one battle at a time."

6

The Last Supper

ITALO'S RESTAURANT WAS exceptionally crowded when the judge arrived with her husband. The crowdedness was something they didn't mind because, as expected, they were immediately assigned a table. While the food was excellent, it wasn't all about the meal for the couple. The fact that they were treated specially was of equal importance. The ego-feeding recognition connected to being able to jump ahead of people waiting to be seated had an uplifting effect.

Once settled in, Amos excused himself to use the restroom. In his absence, Fatima took the liberty of ordering drinks. After placing their order, she perused the room in search of notables who may have noticed the special attention she received.

When Amos returned to the table, he came energized with an idea. "You know, Fatima," Amos began. "With the sort of exposure you've been receiving, we should think about running you for some political office," he proposed. "There are many big advantages that come with political office."

"Funny you should say that. I've been thinking the same thing."

"But understand, getting elected to any office is going to require an investment of money, Fatima."

The cost didn't deter the judge. "How about we shoot for a mayoral run, Amos? City Hall would be a nice place to live."

"Well, now that's an ambitious thought, Fatima."

"Are you worried about the money, Amos?"

"No, not really. I suppose I could arrange for the necessary funding. The question is identifying the right position for you."

"What's wrong with mayor?"

Amos chuckled at his wife's delusion of grandeur. "I was thinking more along the lines of President Clinton's job," replied Amos, attempting to bring the judge back to reality.

"Perhaps mayor is too ambitious," she conceded. "What do you think would be an appropriate position?"

"Something that provides me with an unobstructed path to city properties would be nice. That would make the big developers fall all over themselves to get close to me."

"I suppose access is important," said the judge, sounding lukewarm to the statement made by her husband. "Did I mention to you that I've been approached by a magazine that wants to profile me?"

"I hope you told Playboy that posing nude was out of the question."

"Oh, please," Fatima said with a wry smile.

"You never know, there is probably a lot of interest in what's beneath the black robe."

"Italo is coming," said the judge, noticing that the owner was approaching their table.

Italo, at forty, was the restaurant's owner of record. His silent partner was his older cousin Ciro, a soldier with the Philly Rava crime family.

The cousins were also partners in a gambling casino, located on the top floor of a building located just a short distance from the restaurant. It was Ciro's responsibility to oversee the casino operation, while Italo concentrated on the restaurant.

"Buona sera," said Italo, bowing politely before the judge.

"And good evening to you, Italo," greeted the judge. "You know my husband, Amos, don't you?"

"Yes, I think we've met," answered Italo, smiling cordially. "And how are you, sir?" he asked.

"I'm doing fine," replied Amos. "I see business is doing well."

"Yes, business has been good since we hired the new chef."
After some additional small talk, Italo excused himself.

When the waiter arrived to take their order, Amos ordered
another round of drinks. Midway through dinner, Italo again
stopped by their table. "Is everything satisfactory, Judge?"
"Yes, the food is excellent, as usual."

"You know, Judge....we got these kids hanging around outside.
They get loud sometimes, and some of my customers have been
complaining."

"Have they accosted anyone?" asked Fatima.

"No, no, it's nothing like that. They're just annoying."

"I can call the precinct captain for you," offered the judge.
"Thanks, Judge, I appreciate it. Something has to be done
before these kids have to answer to some serious people," said
Italo, expressing himself by placing his index finger against his
nose. The gesture indicated that he was referring to members
of organized crime. The restaurant owner then nodded his head
knowingly and walked off.

"He shouldn't be saying such things in my presence," said the
judge, "let alone directly to me!"

"He doesn't know any better, Fatima," answered Amos.

After finishing dinner Amos called for the check while his wife
went to the restroom. He was surprised to be informed by the
waiter that the bill was already taken care of.

"Who took care of it?" Amos asked.

"Italo took care of it."

"Where is he? I'd like to thank him." When Italo came to the
table, Amos extended his thanks. "You didn't have to do this. It
wasn't necessary."

"Don't thank me, Amos. Thank my cousin."

"He's here?"

"No, Ciro never comes here. You know how it is. He doesn't
want to give the place a bad name."

"But why did he pick up the tab?"

"Ciro knows you took a haircut over at the casino the other
night. He just wants to do the right thing," explained Italo.
"Oh, I see. Tell him I said thanks."

"Shhhhh—here's your wife," warned Italo. "We ain't looking to get the joint raided."

"Thanks again," said Amos, dropping the subject.

"Thanks for what?" asked Fatima, who joined her husband as Italo walked off.

"He treated us to dinner, Fatima."

The judge flashed a broad smile. She believed that she had been treated because of her official capacity. Amos took the opportunity to further swell his wife's head. "It's good to be the judge," he commented.

"Even better to be mayor," replied Fatima smugly. The judge was totally unaware of the familiarity that existed between her husband and the shady cousins.

##########

THE JUDGE WASN'T HAPPY AT having to walk to her car. She made that point very clear to Amos as they hoofed their way to where their vehicle was parked.

"I don't know why you just didn't have them park the car for us," she complained.

"I thought this would be quicker," answered Amos.

"Well, it isn't," the judge said snippily.

"You know, I can't get over how dark it is with that streetlight out," advised Amos, as he looked ahead in the distance.

"Of course, it's going to be dark with the streetlight out."

"Shhhhh—be quiet!" said Amos suddenly. "I don't like the looks of this character walking toward us. Stand closer to me."

"What is he drunk, Amos?"

"I'm not sure—"

"AMOS!" shouted the judge. "HE HAS A GUN!"

"All right, shut ya trap!" ordered the corpulent stickup man. "You," he said, addressing Amos, "make with the cash. And give me that ring and your watch."

Facing the barrel of a gun, Amos complied without argument. Fatima stood by, watching as Amos handed over his property. Running through her mind was the notoriety she'd gain by thwarting the holdup man. *He's so out of shape,* she thought. *I could take that gun off him easily.*

"Now, let me have your driver's license," ordered the holdup man. After taking the license, he turned to the judge. "C'mon, lady, now it's your turn. Shower down," ordered the armed man.

"What?"

"Don't argue, give him your money and jewelry," injected Amos.

"Listen to him, momma, and remember, I know who you are and where you live," warned the holdup man. "So, do yourself a favor and forget my face."

It was at this point that Judge West acted foolishly. Her poor judgment proved costly. After intentionally dropping her purse to the floor to distract the stickup man, she lunged forward in an attempt to seize control of the gun that was now trained on her. Her decision to make a fight of it had fatal consequences.

A second after the round was discharged, the judge sank to the ground. Amos stood by his wife helplessly as Fats dashed off to the waiting getaway car. He moved with a speed uncommon for a man of his size.

"FATIMA!" screamed Amos, once he'd realized that the judge had expired.

Long after the gunman made his escape, Amos sat on the sidewalk with his wife's head cradled in his lap. He watched helplessly as the red dribble of claret continued to ooze from Fatima's wound. The flow reminded Amos of lava coming from a volcano. All he could do at this point was to rock his wife as he held her tightly. The soothing back-and-forth motion did more to comfort Amos than Fatima, who was beyond comfort.

7

Cleopatra

STORM WELLS WAS LESS THAN HAPPY WORKING for the law firm founded by his father and uncle. Storm had only become a lawyer after succumbing to the pressure placed on him by his father. Although it was a struggle, Storm eventually gained qualification to practice law. His finishing at the bottom of his class was something never discussed.

The law firm of Wells & Marino specialized in criminal defense work. Based on Queens Boulevard, over time the firm expanded to include other areas of law. It was hoped that Storm would be able to build upon their small employment law presence. This proved a challenging aspiration.

Storm's lack of enthusiasm translated into an anemic work ethic. Complicating matters further was the attorney's poor judgment. The combination was a formula that resulted in an ineptitude that exhausted the patience of the founding partners. The situation reached a point where everything Storm did wrong became a big deal.

On this day, the problem was Storm's appearance. The young attorney's work attire was more suited for an academic setting. His brown corduroy sport jacket with elbow pads, solid knit maroon tie, jeans, and two-tone brown saddle shoes, caused his father and uncle to cringe. Adding to their displeasure was

Storm's long hair and Merlin-like beard.

Things came to a head with Storm when his father noticed that he was now sporting a gold stud in his ear lobe. For the founding partners, this was the last straw. A meeting was promptly held in answer to this perceived embarrassment. "Son, your uncle and I are appealing to you not as family, but as colleagues," began Storm's father calmly. "We are in agreement that you need to do improve your appearance."

"What's wrong with my appearance?"

"It runs contrary to the firm's culture," answered the uncle.

"What culture? Our firm is a rinky-dink mom-and-pop business."

"Is that so?" asked Storm's father, who took exception to the remark. "Exactly what part is rinky-dink? Is it the part that financed your education? Or the part that overpays you? Tell us which part is rinky-dink!"

"I didn't mean to insult you. I'm appreciative. But don't forget, you were the ones who insisted that I go to law school," conveyed Storm.

"Can't you see that you're embarrassing us, damn it!" said the father to the son, emphasizing his displeasure by pounding his fist on his office desk. "Now, take that stupid thing out of your ear!"

"What's the big deal? Nobody cares if I choose to wear a stud," protested Storm.

"Well, I care, and your uncle cares, so take the damn thing out! And while you're at it, shave off the whiskers. You look like one of the Smith Brothers. This practice isn't about selling cough drops, for Christ's sake!"

"C'mon, man, lighten up. That kind of thinking went out with hula-hoops!"

The reference to hula-hoops really set off Storm's father. At this point, the uncle exited the office, not wanting to be around if things escalated further.

"Stick out your tongue, damn it!" shouted the father.

"What for?"

"I want to see if you got a stud there too!"

"Are you through?" asked Storm, who had enough of the conversation.

Not wanting to give up on his son altogether, the father aborted his bullying tone. He attempted to reason with his son using milder tactics.

"Storm, listen to me," said the older man softly. "Think like a businessman for a minute. Do any of the people we represent look or dress like you?"

"C'mon, Pop, most of the people we represent are freaking racketeers!"

"Yeah, perhaps they aren't of the highest quality. But you need not lose sight of the fact that hose racketeers keep this firm fluid. Their money feeds us, clothes us, and sent you to law school without your having to take out a loan."

"There you go again with the money. I never wanted to go to law school in the first place," Storm reminded him.

"Do you know what your problem is, Storm?"

"Tell me, what's my problem?"

"You're spending too much time around that airhead girlfriend of yours!"

"I'm out of here!" Storm said abruptly, bolting from the office. "Now I know why you graduated law school at the bottom your class!" shouted the father to his son's back. "It's because you're a moron!"

Seeking solace, Storm spent the night with his girlfriend at her home in Howard Beach. Part of his duties, when there, was to do the dishes, put out the trash and walk Cleopatra, her 150-pound Saint Bernard.

Storm wasn't overly fond of Cleopatra because the hound could be difficult to walk. Whenever the massive canine had a notion to proceed in a direction of her own choosing, it required all of Storm's strength to control the leashed animal. It was not unusual to see the attorney stomping along behind Cleopatra as she pulled him along the street.

Cleopatra's favorite place to do her business was at the foot of a massive London plane tree located not far from Italo's Restaurant. When Cleopatra reached her sweet spot, she came to an abrupt halt. Storm waited patiently as the dog sniffed the dirt around the tree. It was Cleopatra's custom to do this prior to relieving herself. When the dog took too long to go, Storm grew impatient.

"Come on, let's go, Cleopatra. Stop procrastinating and take your dump," said the dog walker.

Cleopatra answered Storm's command by rapidly walking in several small circles as if chasing her tail. This signaled to Storm that Cleopatra was preparing to unload. When the Saint Bernard finished, Storm kicked the dog's leavings toward the street, soiling the tire of a parked 1966 powder-blue Cadillac.

"Hey, cut that out!" The gruff sounding voice wasn't close by. Storm turned to where he thought the voice might be coming from. Seeing no one, he shrugged.

"Hey, I'm talkin' to you down there!" said the locksmith who resided in the apartment above his shop.

Looking upward, Storm made eye contact with the man who was stationed at the upper floor window.

"Clean that up!" ordered the locksmith.

"I forgot my pooper scooper," replied Storm. "I have nothing to pick it up with."

"Just stay there, I'm coming down."

Seconds later, Storm found himself face to face with the locksmith, a hefty man of middle age. The stranger was built along the lines of a square box. The long unlit cigar protruding from the mouth of the locksmith made him seem more formidable than he probably was. Sensing an argument, Storm profusely apologized for failing to pick up after Cleopatra. "Here, take this and clean that tire," ordered the locksmith, handing over the rag he produced from his pocket.

Storm did as instructed while the brutish man looked on. When Storm finished, the locksmith returned to his building. Before shutting the door behind him, he turned to issue Storm a warning.

"Next time you do that, it'll be more than just my car that gets messed up."

Storm, who believed the man quite capable of carrying out his threat, continued on his way. After traveling a few feet, he suddenly heard the piercing sound of a woman's cry. Cleopatra was the first to react, cutting loose with a barely audible growl. "Easy, Cleopatra," said Storm, tightening his grip on the leash. At a distance of about a dozen car lengths, Storm witnessed a heavyset man pointing what appeared to be a gun at a man and a woman. Once it became apparent that he was witnessing a robbery in progress, Storm took cover by crouching down low behind Cleopatra. Using the dog as cover, the lawyer hugged Cleopatra's massive body, bringing himself closer to her. Shielded by the dog's torso, Storm peeked over Cleopatra's back at the crime taking place.

Storm witnessed the struggle that occurred between the armed man and his female victim. The physicality of the confrontation concluded when a shot was discharged. The sound of the gunfire caused Cleopatra to start barking wildly. Storm, who had again ducked his head behind Cleopatra's torso, waited a second or two before again peeking over the dog's back. He did this in time to see the armed felon flee the scene. To his surprise, Storm recognized the stickup man. It was Fats Plummer, a client his father had represented in criminal cases. Not wanting to get involved, the young attorney hastily made tracks. Somehow Storm found the strength necessary to drag Cleopatra away from the scene.

By the time Storm arrived at his girlfriend's house, he still wasn't over the shock of what he had witnessed. Aside from the psychological anguish, his back, arms, and shoulders ached from muscling the powerful Saint Bernard along.

"What's wrong?" asked Storm's girlfriend, detecting her boyfriend's discomfort.

"The damn dog fought me tooth and nail coming home," complained Storm.

"Why?"

"I suppose it was because we took a new way home."

"You've never had a problem with Cleo before."

"I've *always* had a problem walking Cleopatra. I just never said anything. I need a drink—what have you got around here?"

"Do you want soda, juice, or water?"

Storm shook his head, conveying his disappointment. "Why don't you ever have anything in this house that could take the edge off?"

"I'm sorry, but we drank the last of the wine the other night."

"Oh, for God's sake, I can't believe you don't have any alcohol around," complained Storm, who began glancing around. Under a small Christmas tree, he found the relief he was looking for in the form of a gift-wrapped bottle. "What's that, chopped liver?" he asked, pointing to the holiday gift.

"That's a bottle of scotch for my uncle."

"Let's open it up."

"We will not. That's his Christmas present," protested Storm's lady friend.

"So, I'll buy him another one," answered the attorney abruptly. "We have plenty of time to replace it."

Storm was obviously jumpy. His normally docile behavior was so altered that his girlfriend believed that something terrible must have happened when he was out walking Cleopatra. "What occurred out there?" she asked.

"Nothing," he replied.

"Oh, come on, Storm. Tell me...." When her boyfriend remained tightlipped, she offered Storm an alternative to alcohol. "Do you want to smoke a joint?" she asked.

"Yes, and I want to open that present as well."

Storm's romantic interest relented to his demand for the scotch. After receiving her blessing, he tore into the packaging and prepared himself a stiff cocktail. Once the drink began to settle Storm, the weed was introduced. The combination of alcohol and marijuana eventually made the attorney amenable to questioning.

"So, are you going to tell me what really happened?"

"Nothing good happened," replied Storm.

"C'mon Storm, we have no secrets. Tell me what happened." Storm let out a sigh before communicating what he witnessed in the street. "And you saw it all?" she asked.

"Yeah, and let me tell you, it was scary."

"Did you notify the police?"

"Are you crazy? I can't talk to the cops!"

"How could you not tell them what you saw?"

"Because I know the man who shot that lady, for Christ's sake, that's why!"

"Even so, you can't protect him. He's liable to hurt someone else."

"Look, there is more involved here than you think. My firm represents this guy in criminal cases. He's a dangerous dude."

"Who is he?"

"Fats Plummer, and from the stories I've heard, he's a real head case."

"But Storm...."

"You don't get it. You just don't know how things work."

"I'll never get it if you don't explain things to me."

"What I'm trying to tell you is that the guy is a dangerous psychopath. Besides, when it comes to our clients, they live by only one rule."

"What rule is that?"

"Snitches get stitches." Storm could see that his girlfriend was taken aback by his words. "Let me try to explain things to you. First of all, my father and uncle would have a fit if I took a role in putting away one of their clients. They'd look to bounce me from the firm altogether or maybe even disinherit me."

"But you don't work for criminals."

"Yeah, I don't—but the rest of the firm does. You got no idea how many bad guys we have as clients."

Storm's girlfriend nodded with some degree of understanding. "So, this guy is a member of organized crime?"

"I don't know that for sure, and I don't want to know." Storm sank deeper into his cushioned chair after inhaling a deep drag of the joint he was smoking. "I wouldn't put it past Fats to come to the office looking for me if I snitched on him."

"Do you think he actually would do that?"

"Why wouldn't he?"

"Oh, my God!" she said, expressing shock by placing her hand to her face. "You better not tell anyone about what you saw."

"You think?"

Storm's girlfriend walked to her bedroom. After a minute she returned with two more joints. "Did anyone follow you here?"

"I don't think so. But somebody might have seen me. That dog of yours isn't exactly invisible."

"I hope no one followed you here."

She was now wondering if she herself was in a precarious position. She nervously lit her joint and took three long tokes. In her perturbation, she never thought to pass the weed to her boyfriend.

8

Waldo The Boss

FROM DETECTIVE LIEUTENANT WALDO REALE'S perspective, he was perfectly suited for the position he held. As a precinct detective squad commander, he possessed tremendous influence over matters being investigated by his detectives. From an economic standpoint, Waldo recognized the value of his power.

Waldo had the authority to ensure that a complaint was addressed by his staff with expediency or not. He could upgrade a crime, downgrade one, or rectify a dispute by orchestrating a predetermined outcome in favor of the preferred party. Some cases ended up in the trash basket, and some cases Waldo signed off on the day the complaint was filed without any action taken.

If adequately incentivized, Waldo was willing to compromise his ethics. Among other things, he'd use his leverage to discourage a complainant from pressing charges. The list of benefits that he could bestow was lengthy. It was clearly in the interest of lawbreakers—and those who walked a thin line between right and wrong—to be on good terms with the squad commander. Simply put, Waldo was a valuable resource to those residing or doing business within the confines of his Queens precinct.

########

REJECTED BY HIS FATHER, WALDO HAD BEEN BORN out of
wedlock in a tenement on the Lower East Side of New York City.
At the time, the neighborhood was riddled with negative
influences that made exposure to the trappings of the gutter
inevitable.

Waldo learned to navigate the ways of the street early on. His
urban education came with little attention paid to sensitivity.
His being called a bastard child by his peers only served to
toughen Waldo's skin. He began to turn rogue in his early teens
when he was recruited by a gang of delinquents who had a need
for him. Impressed by the toughness of the older youths, the
future squad commander welcomed the invitation to join their
ranks.

The gang used Waldo's boyish, non-threatening appearance to
their advantage when preying on men seeking nocturnal
companionship. The youthful Waldo was the bait that drew a
targeted victim to a predetermined secluded area at night. Lying
in wait were gang members who, on cue, would then suddenly
emerge from their concealment and administer a pummeling to
their victim. After confiscating whatever valuables were to be
had, the delinquents would then flee, leaving their battered
victim on the ground.

Waldo also served as the gang's lookout during the
commission of commercial burglaries. If the police happened
by, it was Waldo's responsibility to alert the thieves by whistling
loudly. As he grew older, Waldo graduated to a more active role
in these crimes.

Waldo's luck finally ran out shortly after he turned seventeen.
He was nabbed for taking part in a warehouse break-in. It didn't
help matters in court when the law testified that they had found
Waldo behind the wheel of a stolen truck that contained the
stolen merchandise. Because of his age and the presence of a
teary-eyed mother, Waldo was given the option of spending his

time in the military or a jail cell. Waldo opted for the United States Army.

Surprisingly, Waldo took to soldiering. He enjoyed a number of aspects connected to the military. He found firing M-16 rifles, tossing hand grenades, and learning combat-enhancing skills to be pleasurable. Once controlled by forced discipline, Waldo earned a high school equivalency diploma. After receiving an honorable discharge, Waldo returned to his old neighborhood a supposedly reformed man.

Waldo took a job as a taxi driver while enrolling in night school. At school, he became friendly with an NYPD police captain who was teaching a course he took. The captain convinced Waldo to take the police entrance exam. Thanks to the captain, who took a hand in ironing out the wrinkles connected to Waldo's history, the former soldier got on the force. Those who had known Waldo back in the day simply couldn't comprehend how he had ever been accepted into the police fraternity.

Once assigned to a precinct, it didn't take long before Waldo regressed to his old ways. Armed with a gun and shield and having the law behind him made for easy pickings. The temptation to take advantage of his position was simply too great for Waldo to resist. He also took advantage of the opportunities to advance within the ranks of the NYPD by studying for the civil service promotional exams.

########

ATTIRED IN A CHARCOAL SUIT, white shirt, and cream-colored tie with matching pocket square, Lieutenant Reale responded to the Judge West crime scene. He looked more like a movie mobster than a squad commander. In his late fifties, the never-married Waldo did his best to maintain a trim physical appearance.

Waldo always selected the same detective as his driver when venturing out into the field. The squad commander's preference for the thirty-year-old Detective Lena Lesper had nothing to do with competence or compatibility. Waldo used the attractive

Lesper as window dressing. He wanted to give people the impression that he was doing well and was someone to be envied.

Waldo sat in the passenger seat as Detective Lesper drove. In the rear seat was Lesper's partner. After learning that the victim was a judge, Waldo knew to expect lots of public interest. Newsworthiness always meant that pressure would be applied from headquarters to solve the case.

"This is going to draw a lot of attention," advised the squad commander. Both detectives nodded their agreement. "Whose turn is it to catch this case?"

"Mine, Loo," answered Lesper. "I'll give crime scene a call." "Do that, Lena. Then round up whatever witnesses we got and have a radio car take them back to the office."

"What about notifying the homicide squad?"

"We don't need them. Just call up crime scene."

After notifying the crime scene unit, Detective Lesper and her partner went on to identify two witnesses, who were then transported to the precinct squad. In addition to Amos West, the judge's husband, there was a woman who had seen a man fitting the description of the shooter flee into a waiting car.

Leaving her partner at the scene with the crime scene unit, Detective Lesper returned to the precinct with her squad commander to interview the witnesses. The woman, who was a long time neighborhood resident who had been walking home from a friend's house, was the first to be interviewed.

"What's your name, ma'am?" asked Detective Lesper.

"I really don't want to get mixed up in this—do I have to give you my name?" asked the witness.

"It's just for the record."

"Who was it that got shot, Detective?"

"Judge Fatima West," answered Lesper.

"A woman....that really is terrible. Did she die?"

"I'm afraid so."

"Why was she shot?"

"Look, lady, let us ask the questions," injected Waldo, interrupting the flow of conversation. "Now, let's have your name," he barked. The edge to his voice was effective in gaining her compliance.

"Marie Provenzano," replied the witness.

"Get Marie some coffee, Lena," Waldo said, using a more civil tone once it was established that he was calling the shots.

"No, thank you. I don't want anything."

"Relax, Marie," said the squad commander, "have the coffee. There's nothing for you to worry about."

"Well, some people in this neighborhood—"

"Sure, I get it, Marie. Understand, though, we do this all the time, and nothing ever happens to our witnesses," assured Waldo. "Just answer Detective Lesper's questions, and we'll get you home." Marie nodded, indicating that she'd cooperate.

"So, Marie, what happened?" asked Lesper, after getting Marie's contact information.

"I was walking home when I heard what I thought was a firecracker going off or a car backfiring."

"How far away were you?"

"I was right around the corner from where it happened," she explained.

"How many pops did you hear?"

"I only heard one."

"You were standing in the street?"

"That's right. I was standing on the sidewalk across from where their car was double-parked."

"What kind of car was it?"

"It was a light-colored car, a Toyota."

"Go on....then what?"

"I saw a man run down the block from the boulevard and jump into the passenger seat. Then the car sped off."

"Could you please describe the man for us?"

"He was sort of large and had a prominent bald spot on the back of his head."

"About how old was he?"

"He was in his middle to late thirties, I suppose. He could have been older, maybe even younger."

"Was he tall?"

"He was about average."

"How was he dressed?"

"He was wearing dark clothes."

"Did you see him with a gun?"

"No, I didn't see any gun."

"Do you think you could recognize him if you saw him again?"
"I think so," the witness answered, adding, "I know that his name is Fats."

Detective Lesper did a double take at hearing this. "Do you know him?" questioned the detective.

"No, I never saw him before."

"Then how do you know his name?"

"That's the name I heard the driver call him."

"I see. Did you happen to get a look at the driver?" asked Detective Lesper.

"I did. When I crossed the street, I walked in front of her car."

"When was this?"

"This was like a minute before the shot rang out."

"Can you describe the driver?"

"Yes. She was thin-faced with long blond hair worn in a ponytail. She was quite pretty, but I could see that there was something not quite right with her eyes."

"What was wrong with them?" asked Waldo.

"They protruded."

"And you noticed that even though she was in the car?" questioned Lesper.

"I couldn't help but notice—the whites of her eyes just jumped out at me."

While Detective Lesper still didn't see how this was possible, she was in no position to dispute the account provided by the witness. She continued with her questioning.

"How old would you say she was?"

"She looked young. I'd say she was in her early twenties. Definitely no more than twenty-five," she added.

"Was she a white woman?"

"Yes, she was, and so was the man who jumped in the car."

"Do you think you could identify these people if you saw them again?" asked Lesper. The witness hesitated before answering. "She already said that she could," voiced the squad commander, answering for the witness.

"Well, I think that maybe I could recognize them if I saw them again."

"That's right," encouraged Waldo. "Go on and continue with your questions, Lena. Stay on track."

Although Lesper didn't appreciate Waldo's interference, she was in no position to launch any opposition.

"Could the man have had a gun in his hand?" asked the detective.

"I really don't know one way or the other, it all happened so fast."

"Let's get back to the female driver of the car, Marie. Describe her a little more for me."

"She had a long blond ponytail, and she was wearing a hat."

"What kind of hat was it?" asked Lesper.

"It looked like a dark baseball hat."

"Show her some pictures, Lena," directed Waldo.

Detective Lesper had the witness view the available precinct photographs of people fitting the descriptions she provided. This met with negative results. After Marie had seen all the photographs at the precinct, the detective took Ms. Povenzano home.

"We'll be in touch, Marie," advised Lesper. "We'll have to make an appointment for you to view more photos at headquarters at some point down the road."

###########

AMOS WEST SAT ALONE AT A DESK in the corner of the squad room. Still very upset, he worried about what tomorrow was going to be like without his wife.

Amos didn't notice Waldo until he was standing right in front of him. Amos looked up sadly. Coming face to face with the squad commander caused Amos to hastily sit up straight in his chair. Each man acknowledged the other with a nod.

"Thank you for your patience, Mr. West," said Waldo. "We're going to talk to you in my office. Please follow me."

The Lieutenant could see that Amos could use more time to gather himself. "I'll get you more coffee while we wait for Detective Lesper to return."

When Lesper returned, the squad commander instructed her to interview the first officer who had responded to the crime scene.

"You go do that, and I'll stay with Mr. West, Lena. Let's give him some time to have his coffee."

Detective Lesper's interview with the first responding officer was abbreviated. Her inquiry consisted of routine questions such as how the officer became aware of the incident, the identity of those present at the scene upon arrival, and whether or not the victim had said anything prior to death.

By the time Detective Lesper returned to the lieutenant's office, Amos had settled down somewhat. He indicated that he could definitely identify the man who killed his wife.
After getting the facts pertaining to the incident the detectives secured a detailed description of the shooter. They then had Amos view photos. After looking at the arrest photos of offenders on file at the precinct, a disappointed Amos advised that the shooter's photo was not among those he viewed.
"What if you saw him in person?" asked Detective Lesper.

"If I were to see him, I'd know him. I'll never forget that face."
"Don't you worry, Mr. West, we're gonna find this bastard who shot your wife," assured Waldo, "and when we do, I promise you that we'll nail his ass to the wall."

The witness s weakly shook his head in acknowledgment, putting forth a feeble smile. Although the lieutenant was oozing with confidence, Amos only half believed him. "Can I leave now, Lieutenant?"

"Sure. Detective Lesper will take you wherever you want to go," assured the squad commander.

9

Poachers Need Not Apply

IT WAS THE MORNING AFTER the Judge Fatima West homicide when Chief of Detectives Harry McCoy returned to his office. He had been out of town for several days. His puffed up face and the bags under his eyes were an indication that he wasn't at his best. The chief was physically worn down after having spent days dueling with relatives he hadn't seen in years.

At issue was the inheritance he was to receive from an elderly widowed aunt. The aunt, a long-retired nurse, had passed away unexpectedly at her home in Toms River, New Jersey. A search of the home uncovered a will that reflected the chief as the sole beneficiary of the late woman's estate, which included several properties. This created a problem in that the chief's many cousins felt entitled to a share in what was sure to be a substantial inheritance.

The chief was resting his head on his desk when Detective Silverlake tapped on his office door. The detective entered uninvited, as he usually did each morning. McCoy slowly lifted his head when the door opened.

"Well?" asked the chief.

"How about breakfast, Chief?" asked Silverlake, the chief's gopher and office receptionist.

"You can get me a bagel with cream cheese and a coffee."

"You want a little Irish in the coffee, Chief?"

"Is there any more of the Red Breast left?"

"We got plenty."

"Okay, and get something for yourself. You can join me," said the chief, who wanted a friendly ear to listen to his problems. Their breakfast was interrupted by the ringing of the phone. Seeing that it was the police commissioner calling, McCoy immediately distanced himself from the spiked coffee by pushing away from his desk. The chief then rose to his feet and put his index finger to his lip, messaging Silverlake to remain quiet. As if the commissioner was in the room, McCoy buttoned his suit jacket to give a formal appearance before answering the call.

"Hello, Commissioner," greeted McCoy, sounding livelier than he felt.

"What's the story with Judge Fatima West, Harry?" The tone of the commissioner's voice made it plain that the call was of a serious nature.

"I just got back in the office, Commissioner. Remember, I mentioned to you that my aunt died unexpectedly in Toms River. She had nobody, so I had to go down there to make the arrangements."

"That's right, I forgot. How did that go?"

"It's complicated. She left me everything because I was the only one who went to see her. Now I'm dealing with a million nieces and nephews looking for their end. They all think I pulled a fast one."

"That's the way it is with people, Harry."

"I suppose so."

"Now listen," said the commissioner, getting down to business. "This judge in Queens was shot dead, and I'm getting calls, so I need information."

"I'll get an update on the case and get right back to you, John," said McCoy, wondering why no one had notified him about it.

70

"Do that, Harry. When a judge gets shot and killed, well, *that's* big news."

"Sorry, I was tied up...."

"You already said that, and I get it. But the big cheese in city hall is looking for answers."

"I'll get a handle on it immediately, Commissioner," said the chief as he paced the floor nervously.

"Better put your A-team on it, Harry."

"No problem," replied McCoy.

Chief McCoy wasted no time in calling over to the office of Lieutenant Wright, who supervised the chief's special team of investigators. "What gives with the judge murder?" asked the chief.

The lieutenant had on his desk a short report prepared by the Queens detective squad that had caught the case. Wright apprised the chief of the facts to date by reading to him what was contained in the report.

"You should have notified me about this," said McCoy. "You left me exposed."

"I called you a couple of times last night, Chief. I left you two messages on your cell phone."

"Oh, I must have forgotten to check my phone. I was preoccupied with these money hungry relatives of mine."

"That's an old story when it comes to inheritances, Chief."

"Yeah, I suppose it is," agreed McCoy. "Send Markie and Von Hess over to Queens to pitch in on the Judge West case. And bring me over that report; I have to get back to the commissioner with something right away."

Lieutenant Wright promptly summoned his detectives after walking the report over to the chief's office. "It's official, Al, the chief wants you and Ollie to get out to Queens and see what can be done to further the Judge West homicide investigation."

"Who has the squad over there, Loo?" asked Markie.

"Lieutenant Waldo Reale," answered Wright. "Watch yourself around him, Al, he's got a reputation for being a tough guy to work with."

"Why is that?"

"I don't know. They say he's a control freak. Unless he's had an epiphany, don't expect him to be overjoyed at seeing you. He'll probably perceive you as an invader treading on his turf."

"It sounds like he is an egomaniac."

"He probably is."

"Do you know him, Ollie?" asked Markie.

"I only know him by reputation, Sarge. Everybody out there calls him Waldo the Boss."

"Now listen, I don't want you two banging heads with him," advised Wright. "Remember, you're out there to assist, not battle with a squad commander."

"No problem, Loo," said Markie.

##########

MARKIE AND VON HESS ENTERED the Howard Beach squad humbly. The two approached the desk of a police administrative aide who greeted those entering the squad room.

"May I help you?" asked the civilian aide.

"We're from the chief of detective's office," announced Von Hess, displaying his tin. "We're here to see the squad commander."

The aide rose from her desk after advising the visitors to stand by. She walked over to the squad commander's office to inform him that there were people to see him. Upon her return to the station, the aide pointed to Waldo's office, indicating that the visitors were free to proceed.

The detectives paused as they stared at the fancy gold lettering on the squad commander's office door.

Lieutenant Waldo Reale
Squad Commander and Top Gun

Markie looked at Von Hess and smiled crookedly. Von Hess could only shrug and say, "Now, this should be interesting."

"Talk about big egos," whispered Markie, "Who paid the freight on this? It wasn't the job, that's for sure."

"Waldo must have put the arm on somebody," presumed Von Hess.

"I should take a picture of this and show it to Chief McCoy." "If you did, Sarge, you'd probably make whoever painted that lettering a rich man. Every boss in headquarters would want their name on the door like that."

Markie tapped on the squad commander's door before slowly opening it. "Lieutenant Reale?" asked the sergeant softly.

"In person," replied the man seated behind the desk.

"We're from Chief McCoy's office. I'm Sergeant Al Markie and this is Detective Ollie Von Hess."

"What does the chief need?"

"He sent us here to lend support on the Judge West homicide."

"Is that a fact?" asked Waldo snidely. "And just what makes the good chief think I need support?"

"I'm afraid that's a question you'll have to ask him, boss."
"That's just what I intend to do," answered Waldo, snippily. "Stick around." The squad commander immediately telephoned Chief McCoy at his office.

"Chief of Detectives, Detective Silverlake speaking, how may I help you?"

"This is Lieutenant Waldo Reale; let me speak to the chief." "Hang on Loo," said Silverlake, who first checked with McCoy before transferring the call.

"Put him through," said the chief. "Chief McCoy on the line...." "Chief, this is Waldo Reale. Did you send a couple of your people over to my squad?"

"I did, Waldo. They're there to help you out."

"Thanks, but I don't need any help over here, Chief. The case is no big mystery. It was a robbery gone bad. The judge bit off more than she could chew and got herself killed."

"Are there any witnesses?"

"Yeah, we got a couple, and they can ID. So don't worry, I'll crack this case easy," assured Waldo.

"All of our squads are shorthanded, Waldo, so take the help

while you can get it," said McCoy, taking a diplomatic approach. "I've sent you capable investigators."

"But I don't need them, Chief. Why not send them to a squad that needs the help?"

"Your case is the newsworthy one, so I want them with you." "I appreciate that, Chief, but I reiterate, I don't need any help. I'm sending them back to you."

"Back up, Waldo," said McCoy, who was now becoming annoyed at the lieutenant's resistance. "Police Commissioner Randolph wants them involved, and so do I. We're looking for fast results."

"I'm sorry, Chief, but this makes me look bad, like I can't handle things."

"I know you can handle things," assured the chief. "Yeah, *you* know—but nobody else will if you send over reinforcements."

At this point Waldo overplayed his hand with McCoy, who reacted strongly by pulling rank.

"Listen, *Lieutenant, I'm* the chief—not you!" declared McCoy angrily. "Markie and Von Hess are working with you over there, and they're staying put until I say differently!"

"But, Chief—"

"Is Sergeant Markie there with you?"

"Yeah, he's here."

"Put him on the line."

Lieutenant Reale tossed the telephone on the desk. "The chief wants to talk to you," he said, with disgust.

"Yeah, Chief," said Markie after picking up the phone. "Listen, Sarge, get to work on the judge case. Get the skinny over there and then go your own way with it. Waldo can go screw himself, as far as I'm concerned. Just be sure that you keep him posted as you get results. If he gives you any crap, you get back to me direct."

"No problem, Chief."

"Put that stubborn asshole back on the line."

"The chief wants to talk to you, Loo."

"Yeah...." said the squad commander, after putting his ear to the phone.

"I'm giving you fair warning, Waldo. Don't make waves. Markie and Von Hess work for me, and they're assigned to help you. I don't want to hear of you abusing them. Do I make myself clear?"

"So now I can't call the shots in my own squad. Is that what you're saying, Chief?"

"Nobody is looking to usurp your authority, Waldo. You're still the boss over there. Can't you understand that I sent them there to support you?"

"Okay, Chief, no sense in me pissing in the wind," conceded Waldo, in a clearly frustrated tone.

"I'm glad you realize that."

"But I want you to know, I'm not happy about it."

"*You're* not happy?" asked the chief, whose agitation was rejuvenated. "I'm not in business to make *you* happy, Waldo. You're there to make *me* happy!"

"Okay, Chief, you're coming in loud and clear," said Waldo, looking to end the exchange.

"Now get this straight, Waldo, if you start getting cute with me it'll be at your own peril," warned McCoy. "I'll have your ass if you start shit-stirring. Do we understand each other?"

"Yes, we do."

After hanging up the phone the scorched lieutenant summoned Detective Lena Lesper to his office. It took all of Reale's self-control to purport himself professionally in the presence of Markie, Von Hess and Lesper.

"Lena," said Waldo, "say hello to these two. The chief of detectives wants them to assist us on the homicide of Judge West. Fill them in on what we know so far regarding the case."

"No problem, Loo, we can go into the field and do a really thorough canvass after I brief them—"

"Did I ask you to do that, Lena?" asked the squad commander snippily. "I said that you should fill them in on the facts. They'll do what they figure they need to do and will post me accordingly. Lets' get one thing straight—and I'm talking to all

75

of you—whatever information we gather has to come back to me in this office before it goes anyplace else."

All of the detectives, feeling the tension, left the office, presumably to do as directed. After gathering the facts relating to the investigation, Markie and Von Hess left the precinct. Once in their car they strategized regarding how to proceed.

"What do you want to do first, Sarge?" asked Von Hess.

"I want to have as little to do with that old bastard as possible," answered Markie, referring to Waldo.

"I hear you. Do you want to start by re-interviewing the witnesses?"

"They already interviewed the witnesses, so let's start by conducting a canvass in the vicinity of the crime scene. Let's see where that takes us."

"Waldo's pride is on the line, Sarge," observed Von Hess. "I figure he's gonna pull out all the stops to show that he's the top gun, as stated on his office door."

"Ahh, what the hell, Ollie, let's just play nice in the sandbox with him. If we come up with anything, we'll pass it along. As long as Waldo feels that he's leading the charge, he'll be happy."

"I think that's best, Sarge," agreed Von Hess, who wasn't into hostile relationships.

"Do you know what this might turn into, Ollie?"

"What?"

"It could turn into a competition to see who reaches home first."

"You're probably right."

"This reminds me of a movie I saw."

"What movie was that, Sarge?"

"It was about building tunnels. They start at opposite ends and meet in the middle."

"Is that how they do it?" asked Von Hess, going along. He had often heard Markie tell this story.

"Yeah, I learned that watching an old Victor McLaglen movie called *Under Pressure*. It was about sandhogs digging a tunnel. They start from opposite directions and wager on which crew climbs through the opening first when they meet up in the middle."

"Do you think that they still do it that way, Sarge?"

"Who the hell knows—and old Victor ain't around anymore to tell us."

10

Waldo Flexes His Muscles

LIEUTENANT WALDO REALE'S CONVERSATON with Chief McCoy bothered the squad commander to a point where he was unable to erase it from his mind. The more Waldo thought about the chief's interference, the more incensed he became. Alone in his office, the squad commander couldn't concentrate on anything other than what he felt was a challenge to his own personal fiefdom. The intrusion ignited a fire within him that caused Waldo to pace his office like a caged animal. The fuming squad commander clenched his teeth as he looked for a way to release his emotions. His bent elbows shook slightly, and his hands were balled into fists. Both were indications of someone about to explode.

Waldo's eruption finally came in the form of punching the coat that hung from a standing coat rack. Knocking over the rack wasn't enough to curb the squad commander's wrath. It took Waldo's kicking his desk until it became difficult to continue doing so that finally tempered his anger.

Although the ruckus could be heard through the closed office door by the detectives in the main room, no one seemed to be alarmed. Waldo's underlings were accustomed to his occasional violent outbursts.

Once the squad commander finally settled down, he sat at his desk to strategize. After figuring out what to do in order to scoop Chief McCoy's gumshoes, he opened his office door and called out to Detective Lesper as if nothing had happened.

"Go get the car, Lena," directed the squad commander. "We're taking a ride."

"Where are we going, Loo?" asked the detective, once Waldo had gotten in the passenger seat of the unmarked vehicle. "Drive over to Italo's Restaurant"

"You want to go eat something?"

"Yeah, that's right. I'm gonna take a bite out of their asses over there." Detective Lesper said nothing in response. She had no idea what Italo's Restaurant had done to irk Waldo. "You know that McCoy thinks he can call the shots while sitting on his fat ass over there in police headquarters. Well, we're gonna teach those sharpshooters over here a thing or two." Again, not knowing what to say, the detective remained silent. She simply nodded her head as if she understood.

When they arrived at the restaurant they were immediately approached by Italo, who recognized them as detectives from the local stationhouse.

"I'm Lieutenant Waldo Reale," announced the squad commander.

"Is everything okay, Lieutenant?" asked Italo. "I'm surprised to see you here."

"Why is that?"

"You're violating your own policy, aren't you?"

"What policy is that?" asked Waldo.

"I know all about you tagging my restaurant as being a corruption-prone location, right Lieutenant?"

Thanks to his relationship with a uniformed police officer assigned to the precinct, Italo possessed insights. In return for free takeout, the restaurant owner had a resource that kept him abreast of the goings on in the command.

The restaurant owner didn't respond to the question. "Are you here to eat, or do you have something else on your mind, Lieutenant?"

"I'm here on business, not to choke on that clothesline you peddle as spaghetti," answered Waldo, who used nastiness as an offensive weapon.

"So what's the business that brings you here?" asked Italo, ignoring the insult.

"You're gonna do me a favor, Italo."

"After what you just said, you're asking me for a favor?"

"You're gonna relay a message to that big shot relative of yours."

"Which one?" asked Italo, who was pretending to be unaware of whom Waldo was referring to. "I come from a big family."

"I'm talking about Ciro, your idol."

"Oh, you mean my cousin."

"That's right."

"I don't see Ciro all that often anymore. But if I do see him...."

"Cut the bullshit," said the squad commander abruptly. "You're either gonna go see him or get used to seeing me."

"My restaurant is run legitimately. I got nothing to hide from you or anybody else, Lieutenant."

"Maybe so, but do you call that casino you and your cousin run legit?" asked Waldo, accusingly.

Italo stiffened, never realizing that the detectives were aware of the gambling den he and his cousin operated. Sensing a shakedown, Italo was now more receptive to doing Waldo's bidding.

"I hear you, Lieutenant. What do you want me to tell Ciro?"

"You tell him it's gonna be bad for business if I don't find out who clipped Judge Fatima West. Killing a judge is the kind of thing that draws heat—on everybody."

Italo didn't let on that the judge and her husband Amos had had dinner at the restaurant just before the incident.

"Lieutenant, can I ask you a legitimate question?"

"Shoot."

"What's that judge got to do with me and my cousin?"

"Waldo dismissed the question. "Listen, all you need to know is that if I don't pinch somebody on the judge's case soon, both of your businesses will suffer. I can't make it any plainer than that."

"I really don't follow you—"

"You don't follow me?" asked the squad commander, who was now losing patience. "Then let me put it even plainer. You guys are gonna furnish me with the name of the person who bumped off the judge. If you don't, be prepared to put the out-of-business sign on that casino of yours. As far as this joint goes, every car that drives out of your parking lot is gonna be greeted by my detectives."

"What makes you think that we can find out who did it?"

"Your cousin is a made guy. He knows how to find out."

"I don't know if Ciro is gonna want to help you with something like this."

"He'll help," said Waldo confidently.

"I'll convey the message," said the restaurant owner soberly, aware that the lieutenant held the upper hand.

"I'll be expecting an anonymous call at the squad giving me a name. I'll take it from there."

"Have you got anything for Ciro to go on?"

"Yeah, two people were involved in taking out the judge. A guy named Fats and a young blond babe with an eye problem. The girl drove the getaway car. We think it's a Toyota."

As the detectives prepared to leave the restaurant, Italo addressed Detective Lesper, who had been silently standing by. "I see the lieutenant is doing pretty well for himself," said the restaurant owner with a snicker.

Waldo took exception to this remark and went on the offensive. "Hey—she's with *me*," he declared, giving the impression that Italo was treading on what was his.

Italo put his hands up defensively. "No offense, Lieutenant," he said, backing off graciously.

Detective Lesper remained stone-faced during the exchange. She didn't particularly appreciate the way she was being objectified. She'd also be less than truthful if she were to deny that she found Waldo's possessiveness to be somewhat flattering. Being teacher's pet did have a way of making her feel special.

##########

ALTHOUGH IT WAS WALKABLE, ITALO DROVE THE SHORT DISTANCE to his cousin's home. The front of the house displayed impressive holiday lights and decorations. A huge wreath could be seen hanging over the front door. Attached to the roof was an outline of Santa, his sled, and two reindeer in white, green, and red lights.

After ringing the bell, Italo let out a deep sigh. One would think he carried the world on his shoulders. Italo nervously tapped his hand against his thigh while waiting for someone to come to the door. When he was tired of waiting, he took out his cell phone and telephoned his cousin.

"Yeah?" asked Ciro, in a voice that sounded clearly thuggish. "It's me. I've been outside ringing the bell waiting for someone to come to the door," explained Italo.

"You're outside my house?"

"I think *we* got a problem. Are you gonna let me in?"

"Don't get your shorts twisted. I was taking a whiz. I'm coming now."

Ciro was a thin man well below average height. His black hair was parted on one side and neatly trimmed. The gangster was garbed in a black cardigan sweater, black turtleneck, black loafers, and black slacks. His eyes were cold and penetrating. The Rava family soldier was a man who rarely smiled, giving him an appearance that could easily be construed as cruel.

"Let's go downstairs," said Ciro.

Italo followed his cousin to the basement as directed. "Where is everybody?" he asked.

"My wife and kids are over my mother-in-law's place. It's somebody's birthday over there. What's up?"

"A couple of bulls from the precinct came by the restaurant."

82

"What did they want?"

"They wanted to know about what happened."

"How about you giving me a clue as to what you're talking about?"

"Sorry, Ciro, you know that judge that got shot and killed down the block from the restaurant?"

"Yeah, you're talking about Judge West. What about her?"

"They want to know who killed her."

"How should I know? It was a rip-off gone bad."

"They want you to find out who did it."

"Is that what they expect?" asked the stunned gangster. "What do they take me for, some kind of a stool pigeon?"

"This lieutenant is looking for an anonymous tip."

"What did you tell him?"

"What was I supposed to tell him, Ciro? He's got us by the short hairs."

"What do you mean?"

"He said that either we play ball, or our casino will go out of business."

"These cowboys," said Ciro, alluding to the stick up team, "deserve their asses handed to them."

"What's our play, Ciro?"

"Do you believe these bulls meant business?"

"No doubt about it. This lieutenant is the boss over there, and he ain't exactly a hayseed."

"Then we'll have to find out who these outlaws are. Did he give you anything to go on?"

"The shooter is a guy called Fats, and he said that the getaway car was a Toyota, driven by a woman with blond hair and messed up eyes."

##########

LIEUTENANT REALE RECEIVED THE ANONYMOUS tip he was after sooner than expected. The tipster, who refused to identify herself, was a woman. The caller advised that the person responsible for shooting Judge West was Fats Plummer, a man with an extensive criminal record.

The tipster described Plummer as corpulent and having a bald spot. Before Sarah Ince terminated the call, she provided the license plate of the getaway car used in the Judge West homicide. She neglected to mention anything about the person who drove the escape vehicle.

Ciro works fast, thought Waldo, who assumed that the anonymous caller was someone working for the Rava family soldier. The squad commander called Detective Lesper into his office, instructing her to bring along the telephone message logbook.

"Let me see that logbook, Lena," said the lieutenant.

The detective placed the book on the lieutenant's desk. Detective Lesper watched as Waldo signed his name beneath the logbook entry he had made. The notation reflected the information provided by the tipster.

"Ciro delivered, Lena," announced Waldo proudly. "We got us the name of the shooter, a description of the shooter, and the plate of the getaway car."

"Did we get anything on the woman who drove the car?"

"Nah, the caller gave us nothing on her."

"That seems kind of strange."

"Yeah, it does," agreed Reale. "Anyway, now you learned what can be accomplished under the right leadership," boasted the squad commander. "Go run the plate and let's see who it comes back to."

After a few minutes, Detective Lesper returned to the lieutenant's office. "The plate comes back to a man named James Plummer. He's got prior arrests for robbery under his belt, Loo."

"Do we have a photo of him on file here in the precinct?"

"No, I already looked, boss. But they got one of him over in the photo unit over at headquarters."

"Go there and get his photo. Then make up a photo array. We'll show it to the judge's husband."

"Do you want me to put the logbook back?" asked Lesper,

reaching for the book.

"No, leave it here with me."

"Should I post Sergeant Markie, Loo?"

"Forget that idea. Let the bright boy figure things out all by his lonesome."

After the detective departed, the lieutenant locked the logbook in his desk. He didn't want anyone, particularly Markie and Von Hess, to see the information contained in the entry he had made.

11

Markie Locates A Witness

THE CHILL IN THE AIR CAUSED THE LOCKSMITH to bundle up before stepping outside his shop. The red and black lumberjack hat he wore made him stand out. It seemed odd for such a burly man to be carrying a small broom and standing dustpan.

Once on the sidewalk, the locksmith paused to fire up the Macanudo that hung from his mouth. After several deep draws on the cigar, the light took hold. With the cigar wedged into the back corner of his mouth, he took an occasional puff as he began to sweep the front of his property.

As the locksmith swept, he heard the sound of flapping wings above him. When he looked up, he saw a dozen or so pigeons assembled on the edge of his roof. Like many property owners, he detested pigeons for their building-soiling ways.

The locksmith began chomping on his cigar as he ceased sweeping to watch the birds. A minute later, a half-dozen more birds joined their comrades on the roof after having found food on the ground below. When the second pack of birds arrived, another group flew off the roof in search something to eat.

"They got a damn system, these flying bastards," muttered the locksmith under his breath.

The business owner looked at his car, which was parked in front of his building. The thought of the nuisances possibly soiling his vehicle further upset him. When a brown pigeon walked the sidewalk near where he was standing, the locksmith monitored the bird searching for food. As the pigeon nibbled on things he picked up off the ground, the scowl on the face of the locksmith became pronounced.

What I'd give, he thought, *to fry up the lot of them.*

As the locksmith continued to sweep he noticed a rat in the street picking at a pizza crust. The sighting escalated the locksmith's irritation to the point of his taking action. He entered his building to prepare a horrendous treat for the rodent. He emerged from his shop carrying several comic book-size pieces of cardboard that he had liberally painted with heavy-duty tar. After placing the tarred cardboard squares just beyond the curb, he salted them with breadcrumbs. He then retrieved a folding chair from his shop and sat out front to watch his long-tailed prey partake in his offering.

As the locksmith relit his cigar, he noticed out of the corner of his eye two men in trench coats nearing him on foot. No one had to alert him that they were members of law enforcement. He could tell by the way they walked up to him that they were NYPD detectives.

The locksmith anticipated that he was about to be called out on his inappropriate response to the rat situation. Before Markie and Von Hess had the chance to speak, the locksmith went on the offensive in an attempt to justify his behavior. "Look, these damn rats are a friggin' nuisance," complained the locksmith. "And the same goes for these pigeons! Other than their baptizing my building with bird shit, what are they good for? It's the responsibility of the city to protect its citizens from public annoyances."

"Relax, my friend, we're not here to talk to you about those things," advised Von Hess.

"You guys are cops, right?"

"That's right. We're detectives. We're canvassing the neighborhood regarding the Judge Fatima West murder," explained Von Hess. "You must have heard about that, right?" The locksmith nodded in the affirmative. "Yeah, I heard about it. That kind of thing ain't an everyday occurrence around here."

"Do you live here?"

"Yeah, I live right here," answered the locksmith, pointing to his building, "and that's my locksmith shop."

"Were you home the night the judge was shot?"

"Yeah, I just missed seeing the whole thing go down by a minute or two."

"Do you remember seeing anyone on the street that might have seen something?" asked Markie.

"Yeah, there was this one guy walking his dog. He had to have seen what happened."

"Do you know him?"

"Not really, I just see him walking his Saint Bernard," replied the locksmith, adding, "That mutt stretches as long as a city bus. The guy should put a saddle on him."

The locksmith provided the investigators with a detailed description of a man and woman who regularly walked the Saint Bernard. With the information he sought now gathered, Markie addressed the tar traps that were left in the street.

"Did you put those out there?" asked the sergeant, pointing to the traps.

"Who, me?"

"C'mon, get that crap off the street. Somebody might step on them."

"What are you going to do about these rats and pigeons?"

"What do you expect me to do?"

"You're the law, aren't you? I expect you to do something," replied the locksmith. "How about you take them home to your house?"

The remark triggered Markie. "How about I run your ass in if you don't pick that stuff up?"

The locksmith mumbled something under his breath as he proceeded to comply with Markie's order.

########

WITH NO OTHER DOGS OF THAT BREED IN THE AREA, locating the owner of the Saint Bernard proved not to be difficult. After leaving the locksmith, the detectives canvassed local residents, which soon led them to the door of Cleopatra's owner.

The free-spirited girlfriend of Storm Wells was the only child of affluent parents. The multi-use adhesive her father had invented had made him a fortune. Despite his success, the inventor continued to live modestly with his family in Queens.

The inventor met his end from being run over by a drunk driver. His death was followed by his wife's passing the following year. Their daughter always claimed that her mother had died of a broken heart. It remained a mystery how she linked pancreatic cancer to the heart.

Storm's girlfriend was a trust fund baby with a penchant for art. Her passion motivated her to pursue an education in that field. After securing the teaching certifications necessary, she taught art at a high school in the East New York section of Brooklyn. While she didn't need to work, she did so out of her desire to educate others on the significance of things artistic. Faced with a challenging classroom climate, the sensitive teacher found her new position to be stressful. Pegged as an easy target for torment by unruly students, she was often unable to control her class. The final straw came when vulgar blackboard graffiti began greeting her whenever she entered her classroom. At this point, the teacher moved on to pursue other interests.

Storm's girlfriend next devoted herself to sculpting and painting. She also took an acting class. Spending summers at a beach house on Long Island and spending the month of February in warmer climates made for a good life.

In appearance, the former teacher preferred the casual look. She wore minimal make-up, kept her hair tousled, and favored faded jeans. Unlike Storm's father, she liked her boyfriend's beard, earlobe stud, and manner of dress.

Her only real vice was getting high. As a devoted aficionado of marijuana, she indulged in the weed on a regular basis. She came to rely on pot to serve as an enhancement to her everyday life. If intimacy was on the schedule, a joint or two was factored in along with the soft music and dim lighting that set the tone. Grass was also her remedy for things unpleasant. To combat the telltale signs of yellowing fingers, Storm's girlfriend relied on the use of tweezers to grasp the joint(s) she smoked. She had just finished smoking when Markie and Von Hess arrived at her front door unannounced.

The detectives identified themselves politely to the glassy eyed woman who was attired in a white tunic-length artist's smock with a shirttail bottom.

"Police, Ma'am," announced Von Hess, producing his gold shield.

Von Hess glanced at Markie after noticing the odor coming from inside the house. The sergeant missed his look. Markie was concentrating on the bare feet of the woman who came to the door. He found her long thin toes of interest.

"What can I do for you?" asked Storm's girlfriend.

"We would like to ask you a couple of questions, Ma'am."

"Well, come on in before we let all the heat out of the house." The two law enforcement officers looked at each before entering the home. They found the aroma of marijuana that permeated the air to be overwhelming.

"It's a little stuffy in here, isn't it, Ma'am?" asked Von Hess.

"I like it warm," answered the homeowner. "What are your questions?"

"Do you own a Saint Bernard, Ma'am?" Von Hess asked.

"Yes, I do—did the old man beside me complain again about the barking?"

Hearing voices caused Cleopatra to emerge from the back of the house. The presence of strangers in the house caused the dog to let out a series of woofs. The detectives took a step back as the massive animal advanced. Fearing attack, both Markie and Von Hess instinctively reached for their revolvers.

"Put away your guns!" the dog owner shouted, alarmed that the detective might start shooting. "Cleopatra's harmless!"

"Why don't you put *Cleopatra* in another room, ma'am," suggested Von Hess.

"She won't bother you."

"I'm afraid we're bothering her," said Markie. "Please, just put her someplace so we can talk for a few minutes."

"Oh, all right," the dog owner agreed, confining Cleopatra to another section of the house.

"Does a man sometimes walk your dog?" questioned Von Hess once the dog was removed.

"Yes, my boyfriend walks Cleopatra sometimes. Why?"

"I'll explain to you in a minute, but before I do, what's your boyfriend's name, ma'am?"

"Why do you want to know his name?"

"We have information that he was walking your dog when Judge Fatima West was murdered. For that reason, we'd like to talk to him."

"Storm didn't have anything to do with that!" she blurted out. In doing so she revealed the first name of the man she intended to shield.

"What's Storm's last name?" asked Von Hess.

"We just want to talk to him in the event he might have seen something," injected Markie.

"He didn't see a thing," she lied. "I'm not comfortable answering all these questions."

"These are just routine questions, Ma'am," advised Markie. "It's not like we're asking you something that could get anyone in trouble—like why this house stinks of pot."

Storm's girlfriend stiffened as she tried to figure out where she stood legally. Her worry wasn't over the aroma of pot. She feared that the detectives might discover her stash of recreational cocaine. Because she was treading on uncertain ground, her response came slowly.

"You guys really can't do anything without a warrant, right?" she asked, mildly challenging the detectives. Her reaction was revealing. It suggested that there was something within reach more substantial than marijuana.

"Ollie, can you believe that she doubts our ability to get a warrant?" asked the sergeant, looking to run a bluff.

Regret now existed in having made the mistake of letting the investigators into the house in the first place. *There's nothing to stop them from searching the house*, she thought, *and then claiming that the coke was left out in plain view someplace!*

"My boyfriend's an attorney," Storm's girlfriend declared, hoping that making this known would cause the authorities to back off.

"Your boyfriend lives here with you?" asked Markie, seemingly unfazed.

"Sometimes he stays here."

"Are you going to tell us who he is?"

"No, I'm not."

"Then I'm gonna put a cop car in front of this house until you do. And when your neighbors start asking the cops if anything is wrong, you can rest assured that your neighbors will be asked if they noticed any signs of narcotic trafficking going on in this house."

"You wouldn't dare—would you?"

"Try me," replied Markie, in all seriousness. Markie's bluff was convincing enough for her to believe that he'd carry out his threat.

"His name is Storm Wells," she finally revealed.

"You *are* aware that a judge was murdered on the boulevard, correct?" asked Von Hess softly, attempting to slip into the good guy role.

"Yes, I am."

"It was Storm who walked your dog that night, right, Ma'am?"

"I'm not sure. I can't remember."

"Well, who else would walk your dog besides you?"

"Yes," she conceded after some hesitation. "Storm walked the dog that night."

"Did he mention anything to you regarding what happened?"

"I....err....don't think so."

Her hesitation was enough to convince both investigators that Storm must have seen something.

"Tell you what, why don't you just give Detective Von Hess the contact information for your boyfriend," said Markie. As an inducement for her to comply, the sergeant began sniffing loudly as he scanned the room with his eyes. Markie intentionally made it appear as if he was looking for something. "All right," she said, fearing that the cocaine she kept in the kitchen cookie jar might be discovered.

After gathering the contact information for Storm Wells, the investigators set out to leave. Before actually doing so, Markie had one final question.

"Storm saw the shooting go down, didn't he?" asked the sergeant. Storm's girlfriend looked down and away without answering the question. She didn't have to. Her reaction was answer enough.

Once the detectives were gone Storm received a telephone call from his girlfriend. She apprised him of what had transpired. Not pleased at her having provided the detectives with his identity and contact information, the attorney hung up the phone in a snit.

########

WHEN STORM WELLS RECEIVED A CALL from his father advising that there were detectives in the reception area of the law firm looking to talk to him, he suddenly began to feel queasy.

"They're looking to talk to me?" he asked weakly.

"Yes, that's what I said, Storm," said the father from his private office. "What's this all about?"

"Tell them I'm out of the country on vacation," answered Storm, thinking it best to become scarce.

"Hold on a second," said the father. "Before you start running from the police, how about you first tell me what the situation is."

"I'm not sure what they want. Didn't they tell you?"

The father let out a deep sigh that made it clear to Storm that he was losing patience. "Stay by your phone," instructed the father, I'll call you back in a few minutes." After hanging up with his son, Storm's father called Markie and Von Hess into his office. "I have a call into my son. Do you gentlemen mind telling me what this is all about?"

"We just need to talk to him."

"I understand that, but I'd like to know whether or not my son requires representation. Do you intend to arrest him?"

"No, it's nothing like that," assured Von Hess, "We just need to speak to him about something he may or may not have witnessed."

"I see. So, you suspect that he witnessed a crime, I assume."

"We believe he may have."

"What kind of crime are we talking about, Detective?"

"Your son may have seen the robbery/homicide of Judge Fatima West go down," injected Markie.

"I see," replied the father, who remained poker faced. "Excuse me for a minute, will you?" After excusing himself Storm's father went to another office to call his son. "Look Storm, answer me straight, did you ever have anything to do with Judge Fatima West?"

"No, I never even met the woman."

"Well did you witness her killing?"

"After the lapse of a few seconds, Storm replied in a barely audible voice. "Yeah, Pop, I did."

"Naturally, you *can't* recognize anyone involved, right?"

"I can, it was that guy Fats. He's a client of the firm."

Storm's father let out a loud groan. *"This kid is brain dead!"* thought the father when Storm didn't get the hint he'd dropped.

"Pop, are you still there?"

"Get the hell into the office right now," ordered the father.

"But Pop—"

"Stop talking, just get in here!"

Storm's father returned to his own office to talk with the

detectives. "Why don't you boys get a bite to eat and come back in a couple of hours," he said, "my son will be here then. He's coming in from upstate." The investigators found this arrangement to be acceptable.

Once the investigators were gone, Storm's father convened with his law partner in their conference room. After he explained the situation to his half brother, the pair brainstormed.

"So, what do you think?" asked Storm's father.

"One thing is for certain," replied Storm's uncle, "we can't have your son give up Fats Plummer."

"That's for sure," concurred the father.

"We have to make sure that Storm doesn't get on his high horse and starts fingering a client of ours. He has to take the position that he didn't see a damn thing."

"We're in agreement. I'll drill that into his thick skull when he gets here."

##########

PARKED IN FRONT OF THE LAW FIRM, Markie and Von Hess passed the time drinking coffee and discussing the President Bill Clinton–Monica Lewinsky situation.

"Are you getting hungry, Sarge?" asked Von Hess. "Do you want to grab something?"

"No, let's just wait here outside the law office, Ollie. I don't trust these slippery ambulance chasers."

"I hear you."

"Do you think you could recognize Storm? There was a picture of him and his girlfriend on an end table."

"I saw it," said Von Hess. "He'll be easy to recognize with that beard, Sarge."

"That's what I figure. We'll intercept him when he gets here. If we let him get to his old man, it'll be like pulling teeth to get a word out of him."

When Storm arrived it was Von Hess who first spotted Storm. "I think this is him coming, Sarge," said Von Hess, recognizing his man as he walked toward the office building.

"They must have shot him out of a cannon to get here so quick," commented Markie.

The detectives approached the witness just as he was about to enter the building.

"Detectives," announced Von Hess, flashing his badge. "We need to have a word with you Mr. Wells."

"Uhh—about what?" Storm's not denying his identity made it clear to the detectives that they had the right man.

"Mr. Wells, just so you're aware, your girlfriend told us the whole story of what you saw the night Judge Fatima West was murdered," advised Markie, stretching the truth.

"I have no idea of what you're talking about," replied Storm. "If you'll excuse me, I'd like to get to my office."

The detectives continued to block the front door to the building. "You don't have anything to say?" asked Markie. "Is that going to be your position in front of a grand jury?"

The words "grand jury" terrified Storm, causing him to respond defensively. "But I didn't see anything."

Experience taught the detectives that a panicky person would likely weaken under sufficient pressure.

"Our conversation with your girlfriend was taped," fibbed Von Hess.

"And everything she said that you told her was memorialized and will be turned over to the district attorney," chimed in Markie, adding to the bluff.

His lack of familiarity with criminal law caused Storm's mouth to drop open. This was an encouraging sign to the detectives. It suggested they were making headway.

"Get smart, Storm. Do you really want to go in the ring and perjure yourself?"

Although no expert on criminal law, the young attorney knew that there were serious ramifications when a lawyer perjures himself. To do so could cost him his license to practice.

"I told you I have nothing to say....at this time," voiced the attorney, modifying his stance.

"Some people just gotta learn the hard way, Ollie," voiced Markie.

"I couldn't be sure who it was anyway," advised Storm, thinking he was helping himself.

The investigators perked up at hearing this reply. Storm's words were practically an admission that he recognized someone involved in the Judge West robbery/homicide.

"So, you did recognize the person who shot the judge."

"I didn't say that!" shouted the lawyer. "Don't put words in my mouth, Sergeant."

"Look, you're a lawyer, a law-abiding guy, everyone knows that," said Von Hess. "We'll keep what you say as confidential as possible."

"That's right, and the perps might cop a plea and your name wouldn't even have to come up," added Markie.

Storm found hope in these words. "You don't understand the price connected to my helping you. My father's firm represents clients that—"

"Listen, why don't we go sit someplace quiet and kick this around?" suggested Markie. "We'll find a way to make it work, a way that'll be amenable to everyone."

"Remember, your girlfriend already gave us the lowdown on the name you dropped to her," said Von Hess, being untruthful. "We just need to hear it from you."

"She told you?"

"Sure she did...."

Storm, feeling defeated, was close to conceding. "How can you possibly keep this confidential?" he asked.

"We may not even need you to testify at all," noted Markie. "Don't forget, you're not alone in this.
There are other witnesses. The victim's husband was right there when it happened. He'll definitely identify the shooter, once we firm up who he is."

"And then we got a woman who saw the getaway driver," said Von Hess. "We just need you to tell us what you saw. If all you could do is just put the perp at the scene, that'll work fine. If you saw the shooting go down that's even better. Whatever it is, we'll work with you."

At hearing this, Storm believed that he had some wiggle room. He agreed to cooperate. "All right, it was a client of the law firm who shot the judge," he said.

"Now we're getting some place. What's his name?"

"His name is Fats Plummer."

"There, that wasn't so terrible, now, was it?" asked Markie.

"You don't understand."

"Try me. I can be more sympathetic than you think."

"Fats Plummer is a maniac."

"Let's go sit down someplace and you give us the story from the beginning, Storm," suggested the sergeant. The attorney, now feeling that he had no choice, consented.

"We have a conference room in the law office," offered Storm.

"How bout we go to a diner instead," said Markie, wanting to avoid Storm's father and the law firm at all costs.

In Storm, the investigators identified an eyewitness who could attest to the fact that Fats Plummer had shot and killed Judge Fatima West. What all parties weren't aware of at this time was that Fats Plummer was being judged in another world before a higher authority.

Once through with Storm, the detectives returned to their headquarters office, where Von Hess conducted research in an effort to get a line on Plummer. It was then that they learned that James "Fats" Plummer was a small-time criminal with a long arrest history.

"So, we identified our boy," said Markie.

"I think so, but we got thrown a curveball, Sarge, which may actually turn out to be a good thing."

"What's the curveball?

"James "Fats" Plummer was found dead in his Toyota on Staten Island in what was believed to be a self-inflicted gunshot wound."

"What kind of gun was recovered at the suicide scene, Ollie?"

"The gun was the same caliber weapon as used in the Judge West homicide, Sarge."

"Well, what do you know about that," voiced Markie. "Let's get in touch with ballistics. We need them to determine if the bullet in the suicide and the bullet that killed the judge came from the same gun.

"You got it, Sarge."

"No, on second thought, hold up on that," said the sergeant, changing his mind. "Let's do this instead. Call Detective Lesper over at Waldo's squad. Fill her in on the witness we identified and what we found out. Tell her to request the ballistics comparison. If Lesper gets a hit, it'll make Waldo the Boss feel like he's done something. How's that for good politics, Ollie?"

"Very good, Sarge," complimented Von Hess. "How about we go get a photo of Plummer?"

"Yeah, let's do that. We'll put together a photo array on him and show it to the judge's husband."

"What about showing it to the lawyer?"

"I don't think we need to."

"Should we involve the Lieutenant and Detective Lesper regarding the photo identification involving the judge's husband, Sarge?"

"Nah, we have to show that we did a little something too. If we get a hit, Waldo's squad could run the lineup. That should be enough to appease the old crab-ass. If not, he can go screw himself."

12

Team Ciro

ITALO'S COUSIN CIRO WAS A MAN who had his thumb in many pies. Aside from his interest in the casino and restaurant, Ciro was behind a numbers and money lending business in the East New York section of Brooklyn. The Rava soldier worked in conjunction with Stefano's Sandwich Shop, an entity where a bet could be placed and money borrowed.

The sandwich shop was frequented primarily by neighborhood men and local workers in the area. They conversed, played cards, bet the daily number, and gambled on horse races. When they tapped out, losers could replenish their funds by securing a loan from the proprietor, who acted on behalf of Ciro.

The establishment had a large back room that was equipped with several tables suitable for playing cards. In addition to purchasing sandwiches and beverages, which were consumed while gambling, patrons could buy cigars, cigarettes, chewing gum, and other related items. In warm weather, the tables were set up in the backyard. When in the yard, the men had to be careful not to step on the egg-producing chickens that freely wandered about.

The owner of the sandwich shop was a man named Stefano who was known as Stef the Tailor. The story for public consumption was that Stefano got this nickname based on his proficiency at sewing on shirt buttons. There was no truth to this, however. It was Ciro who had coined the name after learning that Stefano had once sewed a man's lips together for informing his wife that he had a girlfriend on the side. This vile act went far in earning Stef the Tailor the respect of Ciro.

Stefano owned the four-story building that housed his business. He resided in the second-floor apartment over the store with his wife and elderly mother. The apartment on the third floor was rented to Stefano's longtime girlfriend, who also worked in the sandwich shop. The top-floor apartment, which was furnished, remained vacant. It was intentionally kept unrented so that it could be used to accommodate those willing to pay a premium for the space. Fugitive friends of Ciro who were hiding from the law qualified as renters. The apartment was also occasionally used as a temporary place to house stolen property.

As a courtesy to Ciro, the apartment on the top floor was always available to him at no charge. Whenever Ciro visited the sandwich shop Stef the Tailor couldn't do enough for him.

"Can I get you anything, Ciro? How about having a nice sandwich?"

"No, just some coffee, Stef. I need to use the apartment upstairs."

"Sure, go on up. The place is empty."

"Put some milk in that coffee, no sugar."

"It's coming right up."

"So, how is your mother doing?" asked Ciro when Stefano delivered the coffee.

"Other than her lumbago acting up now and then, she's got no complaints."

"They call it sciatica these days."

"That's right, that's what the doctor says she got."

"Well, take care of your mother, Stef. You only got one. Anybody else can be replaced."

"I know that well, Ciro."

"When Swatty gets here, send him up."

"I'll do that."

When Swatty arrived at the sandwich shop, he was directed to the top-floor apartment. Swatty's primary aspiration in life was to become a soldier in the Rava crime family. On the surface, it would seem that he possessed the intelligence and ruthlessness necessary to make that a reality.

As a member of Ciro's crew, Swatty continued to pay his dues by participating in whatever criminal activity demanded of him. He was ignorant of the fact that it was the very man he was serving who stood in the way of his being admitted into in the Rava family.

Ciro has no intention of proposing Swatty for membership into the family because he was afraid that in doing so, he might lose him as a member of his crew. Since Ciro liked the arrangement as it was, he only pretended to be sponsoring Swatty for membership, without actually doing so.

"So, what did you find out for me?" asked Ciro, wasting no time.

"There's a guy called Hugo Fatamore who just got out of stir a few months ago. They call him Fats," advised Swatty. "He went away for pushing pills."

"So?"

"So, I'm just saying."

"Has he got anybody behind him?"

"He's with a couple of brothers who come from down by the Navy Yard."

"Are they with anybody?"

"They're nobody to worry about, just a couple of local tough guys."

"That sounds like an opportunity for us," said Ciro, who was thinking of shaking down the brothers.

"Do you want me to go lean on them?"

"No, hold off on that. This business with Fats comes first. Did you go out looking for him?"

"Not yet. I just got a line on where to find him. I was gonna go run him down him now, but then I got your call to come here."

"Who are you taking with you?"

"I got Pinky Solomon waiting for me outside in the car," answered Swatty.

"Good, that guy can put a scare into anybody. Go do what you have to do. We'll talk later."

########

FATS FATAMORE SOLD PILLS from his car, which was usually parked somewhere on Kent Avenue, just east of the Brooklyn Navy Yard. As was his practice, the pudgy man waited for his customers to come to him. Fatamore put his head back and rested his eyes as he listened to holiday tunes on the car radio. His lack of diligence caused him to not notice the black Lincoln that pulled up behind him.

The drug dealer was awakened by a tapping sound coming from the back window of his car. As Fatamore proceeded to look over his shoulder, he was startled by the sight of a large man standing outside the driver's side door. The stranger's bent nose and thick neck caused Fatamore some concern.

Flashing a friendly smile, the stranger began circling his wrist, gesturing for the man behind the wheel to roll down his window. Although leery, Fatamore dropped the window down a couple of inches. "What's up?" he asked, looking up at the stranger.

"Your car is leaking," advised Pinky Solomon.

"It is?"

"Say, ain't you Fats?" asked Solomon, seeking to verify the identity of his man.

"Yeah—that's me," replied the man behind the wheel. "Do we know each other?"

"Sure, we were in the same can," answered Pinky, now smiling broadly. "You better get out and take a look at that leak." Fatamore, although he couldn't place Pinky, was nevertheless now put at ease. As he proceeded to the back of his vehicle, he suddenly felt himself being yoked from the rear. Pinky's forearm against his throat rendered the pill pusher helpless. Unable to put forth sufficient resistance, Fatamore soon found himself forced into the back seat of the Lincoln. His abductor assumed a position in the vehicle alongside his kidnap victim.

"What's this all about?" asked the abducted man, who thought that he was being targeted for robbery. "All I got in my stash is a hundred downs." The pill pusher's mouth trembled as the words passed through his lips.

"Stop squawking," ordered Swatty from the driver seat.
"The pills are in the car....where are we going?" asked Fatamore, who now began to realize that he was being snatched.

"Be quiet, I said!"
"Why are you guys snatching me? What the hell did I—"
In an effort to silence Fatamore, Pinky picked up a plastic hard hat off the floor of the car and placed it on his lap. "You heard the man, be quiet," he said, "or I'm gonna let one fly."

"You guys don't know who you're fucking with," conveyed Fatamore. "I got important people standing behind me." Pinky responded to the comment by viciously smashing his kidnap victim across the face with the hard hat. The blow temporarily silenced his man. Once the dazed Fatamore shook off the effects of the blow, he resumed his protesting.

"You guys are acting crazy! Tell me what I did—"
The request was answered with a second smash across the face. This time the impact of the blow drew blood from the assaulted man's eyebrow.

"Open your mouth again, and you'll get another kiss," warned Pinky, who was prepared to strike again.

This time Fatamore got the message. He remained quiet as Swatty pulled into a dead-end street that people used for a dumping area. Once parked behind a large mountain of trash, Swatty began to question Hugo.
"So, who was with you when you killed that judge?" asked Swatty accusingly.
"What judge—I never killed anybody!" exclaimed the victim, now certain he had been targeted for something he didn't do. "You guys are working off bad information!"

"Okay, have it your way," said Swatty, who nodded to Pinky.

The nod was a signal for Pinky to get physical.

Hugo Fatamore was dragged from the car by Pinky and thrown to the ground. Pinky began battering him mercilessly in an effort to get him to confess to a crime he didn't commit. After a barrage of blows, Pinky stopped to take a breather.

"We may have the wrong guy over here, Swatty," voiced the winded Pinky. "If this sucker knew something, he'd have spilled it. I don't know how much more of this he can handle."

"Ahhh, screw it, we must have the wrong Fats," agreed Swatty. "C'mon, let's get the hell out of here."

"What do we do about him?" asked Pinky, pointing to the victim.

"What do you want to do? Take him home with us? Leave him there."

"How many are we hunting, Swatty?" asked Pinky once they were back in the car.

"We're gunning for two people. We gotta find the right Fats and then beat the bushes for the blond bitch that drove the getaway car."

"Have we got anything to go on with the woman?"

"Yeah, she's young and supposed to have bulging eyes."

"Bulging eyes?" asked Pinky. "I have a friend who was just telling me about a blond hooker he banged like that."

"Her eyes bulged, and she was a blond?"

"She was a blond, and according to him, he had her peepers popping out of her head."

"Let's go find your friend."

########

AFTER VISITING SEVERAL HAUNTS, Pinky's friend was finally found standing at the bar inside a Woodside tavern. A slender man with a pockmarked face, he was drinking beer out of a long-neck bottle.

"Hey, what's doing?" asked Pinky. "I've been looking all over for you."

"I've been here," said the friend. "What's up?"

"Do you remember that hooker with the eyes that you were telling me about?"

"Which one was that? All the hookers I know got eyes."

"I'm talkin' about the young blond with the bulging eyes. You remember...."

"Oh, now I know who you mean. Her name is Sarah. What, did she rip you off?"

"No, it was nothing like that. We just need to talk to her. Where can we find her?"

"She works at the whorehouse on West 31st Street, off 8th Avenue in Manhattan. The joint is located next to the hat store. You can't miss it."

"What can you tell us about her?" asked Swatty.

"All I can tell you is one thing. She's worth the money, that's for sure."

"Yeah?" blurted Pinky, who was interested in such things. "Let me tell you—" began Pinky's friend before being interrupted by Swatty.

"Look, let's cut the shit," said Swatty. "We ain't got the time for that right now. Just tell us what she does besides turning tricks."

"All I can tell you is that she's a wild bitch," said Pinky's friend.

"Clarify for me what you mean by wild," said Swatty.

"To get to the point, she should have been born a man."

"Get a little more specific."

"She's a desperado. I got it on good authority that she's got a stash of guns. I *know* for a fact that she robs people."

"How do you know that?"

"My buddy's girlfriend is Sarah's best friend. The two of them are birds of a feather. Both of them are part-time hookers."

"Give me some names."

"Say, what's this shit all about?" asked Pinky's friend, now reluctant to provide Swatty with more information.

Swatty took out some money and held it up while responding to the question. "It's about you scoring a few bucks over here." The promise of a financial reward was an effective lubricant that loosened the lips of Pinky's friend.

"My buddy is Fats. We work together now and then. His girl is Greta. She's friends with Sarah."

"Fats who? There's more than one Fats running around."

"Jimmy Plummer, everybody calls him Fats."

"So, Fats and Sarah, these two know each other then?"

"They definitely know each other. You know, I just thought of something Fats once said about Sarah."

"What was that?"

"He said that Sarah was a Bonnie Parker, you know, like in the movie *Bonnie and Clyde*."

"Where can we find Fats?"

"I ain't seen him lately. I tried calling him on his cell, but he's not answering."

"Did you try his house?"

"He's got no house phone."

"You got an address for him?" Pinky's friend provided Swatty with the address he requested.

"Okay, here you go, pal," said Swatty, passing him money. "You earned it."

When Swatty and Pinky arrived at the apartment in question, they found Greta home alone.

"Who are you?" she asked. Since she was accustomed to occasionally servicing male visitors at her home, she wasn't particularly startled at strangers coming to her apartment.

"We need to see you," advised Swatty. "Let us in." A believer in the incentive of hard cash, he flashed some money for her to see.

"Come in," said Greta, misinterpreting why they were there. She quickly took the cash from her visitor and placed the money in the pocket of her jeans. "This will only cover one of you," she added.

"All we want from you is some information," conveyed Swatty.

"What kind of information?"

"We're looking for Fats."

"Why?"

"That's our business," shot back Swatty curtly.

Seeing that they were serious men, Greta explained that she was worried about her boyfriend, Fats, conveying that he seemed to have disappeared.

"I wouldn't be surprised if he took off for good," stated Greta gloomily.

"Where did he go?"

"I have no idea."

"What about Sarah with the bulging eyes? Did she go away with Fats?"

"No, of course not, Sarah's my friend."

Greta went on to reveal that she and Sarah had been working part-time in a Manhattan brothel. She conveyed that after Sarah got involved with some big shot's son-in-law, both Sarah and she were fired.

"Sarah's got something wrong with her eyes, right?"

"That's right."

"Who's the guy she got involved with?"

"His name is Mickey."

"What does he look like?"

"He has red hair."

Swatty winked at Pinky and nodded his head in the direction of the door, indicating that it was time to leave.

"You go ahead. I'll be down in a minute," said Pinky, flashing a half-smile. "I want to get your money's worth," he added, referring to the cash Swatty had given Greta.

Swatty looked at Pinky and then at Greta. "Okay, I'll be in the car. Don't take too long."

##########

SWATTY POSTED CIRO the following day at the handball court where Ciro took his exercise. The Rava family soldier, as usual, was dressed all in black. The sweat suit and sneakers he wore were of the finest variety.

"Jeeze, Ciro, you look like you've been through the wringer," said Swatty. "You look half dead."

"Handball's a strenuous game. You should try it. It'll keep you in shape."

"That's one game I never liked. The ball hurts my hand."

"You gotta wear a glove, dopey."

"I wore a glove, and it still hurt my hand."

"What can I tell you?" said the mob soldier. "Go play checkers."

"We made some progress after our setback."

"What setback?"

"We snatched the wrong Fats at first."

"Are you sure he was the wrong one?"

"Yeah, there ain't a doubt. Nobody would take the lumps that poor prick took without coming clean."

"What's the progress then?"

"The Fats we want is a guy named Jimmy Plummer."

"Are you sure?"

"We definitely got the right guy, Ciro. He's in the wind, though."

"That's a problem for the bulls, not us. You got any more for me?"

"Yeah, the driver of the getaway car was a hooker named Sarah. She used to work in a Manhattan brothel. She got canned for running around with some guy with red hair named Mickey." This information interested Ciro greatly. "Did you get a last name for this Mickey?"

"No, but supposedly he's married to some big shot's daughter." Ciro let out a long slow whistle after hearing this. "What?" asked Swatty, reacting to the whistle.

"Ruffy Shea's got a son-in-law with red hair named Mickey. I also know for a fact that Ruffy's in the flesh business."

"No shit—so how do you want to play this?" asked Swatty. The Rava family soldier shook his head in a way that suggested uncertainty. "I'm gonna have to think about this. So, for right now, we go leash and do nothing. I'll see you later."

"Okay, Ciro, whatever you say. Call me if you need me to do anything."

Ciro had already done all the thinking he needed to do. The

Rava soldier intended to execute a cunning plan. If things went well, Ruffy Shea would suggest to Philly Rava, the family boss, that Ciro would make an excellent capo. Such a promotion would mean big money for Ciro.

Ciro telephoned Stef the Tailor as soon as Swatty left.

"The sandwich shop," said Stef, after picking up the telephone.

"I want you to help me with something, Stef."

"Sure, Ciro. What do you need?"

"I need to find out about a whorehouse on the West Side of Manhattan that belongs to Ruffy Shea."

"I really don't know much about that kind of stuff anymore."

"Why is that?" asked the surprised Ciro. "I thought you liked going to cat houses."

"C'mon, you know I got my girlfriend in the apartment upstairs. Between her and my wife, that's enough for me."

"That makes things convenient for you."

"Yeah, I suppose it does."

"Listen, ask around and see what you can find out about Ruffy's son-in-law and a girl named Sarah. They're both hooked into the whorehouse. Get back to me right away. This is important to me."

"What's the son-in-law's name?"

"His name is Mickey, and he's got red hair."

By the following day, Stef had gathered the information requested. He was able to verify much of what Ciro had previously been told. In addition, Ciro was informed that the madam working at the West 31st Street bordello was Ruffy Shea's girlfriend, a woman named Queenie.

"Where did you get your information from, Stef?"

"A couple of guys who work out at the airport told me. They go there regular."

"And they knew this girl Sarah?" asked Ciro.

"Yeah, they knew her right away. According to them, you gotta duck so that her eyes don't poke you in the head when you're pumping oil."

13

Ciro Sends A Message

THE TIME HAD COME FOR CIRO to have a conversation with Ruffy Shea. Now suspecting that Ruffy may have had some involvement in killing Judge West, Ciro imagined a way to enhance his status in the Rava organized crime family.

Ruffy Shea's close relationship with the family boss was no secret to Ciro. In Ruffy, Ciro saw someone who could grease the wheels in his attaining the rank of family capo. Such a promotion would mean more money, more respect, and more power.

In order to gain Ruffy's endorsement, Ciro needed to do something special enough to warrant a return favor. Ciro believed that by exerting control over the witnesses in the Judge West case he'd be able to impress Ruffy. His intent was to show that he was protecting Ruffy and/or his son-in-law from potential prosecution. Ciro's brainchild was a no-lose proposition. Even if Ruffy and his son-in-law had had nothing to do with the homicide of the judge, Ciro would be credited for his effort to help a friend.

Moving ahead with his scheme, Ciro summoned his cousin to

his home. When Italo got to the house, Ciro moved their conversation down to the basement to ensure privacy.

"Are you still friends with that cop at the precinct, Italo?"

"Yeah, Ciro, we're pals for as long as I give away the free eats."

"See if he could find out who the witnesses are in the Judge West killing. I want their names and addresses."

"I'll ask, Ciro," said Italo. "I may have to sweeten the pot for the guy."

"Give the cop whatever you have to give him."

Italo returned to his cousin's house the following day to hand Ciro a sheet of loose leaf paper containing the requested information:

<u>Witness One</u>:   Amos West, husband, 69th Road, Forest Hills. West can identify the shooter.

<u>Witness Two</u>:   Marie Provenzano, 85th Street, Howard Beach. She can identify shooter and getaway driver.

<u>Witness: Three</u>: Storm Wells, Attorney, Wells & Marino ID's James "Fats" Plummer as the shooter.

Ciro was pleased with the information he received. "That cop gave you all this?"

"Yeah, Ciro," replied Italo. "The information came right out of the case folder."

"Did you grease him?"

"He wouldn't take it."

"That's surprising," commented Ciro, shaking his head. "I want you to go talk to these witnesses, Italo."

"No sweat, Ciro. We know them all."

"I know the husband Amos and the lawyer's father. But who is the woman?"

"She owns the bakery that we buy from. So, what should I say to these people when I go see them?"

"Tell them I said that they can't identify anyone to the cops, until they hear otherwise from me."

"The lawyer already fingered somebody."

"Yeah, well, tell him he's gonna have to change his mind about that."

"Sure, Ciro, whatever you say. But what do I do about the judge's husband? It would be only natural for him to wanna cooperate with the cops."

"Yeah, I suppose it would. See what you can do with him. If he balks, we'll have to use a little muscle."

##########

WITNESS MARIE PROVENZANO WAS IN THE shower when the doorbell rang. Hearing the bell, she threw on her bathrobe and hurried to see who was at the door. Peeking through the blinds, the forty-two-year-old woman saw a man standing outside her door. He was carrying what appeared to be a delivery of some kind.

Before opening the door she tightened the belt on her terrycloth robe and held both sides of its collar in one hand to cover her upper body. Marie was genuinely surprised when she came to realize that it was Italo standing in the doorway with a tray of food.

"Italo, what brings you here?" she asked. "Come in, it's freezing out."

"Me and my cousin heard all about you being questioned by the police," said Italo, once inside the home.

"Oh, that," said Marie, who was well aware of Ciro's reputation. "They just asked me what I saw regarding the murder of that poor judge."

"You know, sometimes, not getting too involved is a better way to go, Marie. I'm sure you get what I'm saying."

"I know. I tried telling them I didn't want to get involved. But you know how it is, when they start with the questions, they make it hard to—"

"Sure, I know all about it, Marie. But there are *other* people who can make it hard," he said, in a tone meant to intimidate. "Here, I brought you a nice tray of food."

113

Marie was now beginning to get the point. She nervously took the tray, fully aware that accepting gifts always came with expectations. Her face was twitching as she thanked him. Italo could see that he was effective in influencing Marie.

It was moments like this that invigorated Italo, who was, at best, a wannabe wise guy. He found that throwing a scare into people, even a woman, was gratifying. Such behavior was far removed from his usual role as the glad-handing restaurant owner who was tasked with catering to people. The interaction with Marie gave Italo the opportunity to be more like his cousin, a man who was feared— and thus someone who commanded respect.

"Too bad about that judge," said Italo. "She probably made the wrong choice. A long life is based on good choices, ain't that right, Marie?" Italo's veiled threat wasn't lost on the witness. "That's right."

"Sure it is. Take this judge business. How could you be sure of what you saw? It was dark out, wasn't it?"

"Yes, it was."

"And you wouldn't want to identify the wrong person, now, would you?" Marie shook her head. "No, of course you wouldn't. So why take the chance that you might hurt an innocent person? At least, that's the way me and my cousin feel about it. You feel that way too, don't you, Marie? You won't be identifying anybody, right?"

"How can I?" she answered weakly. "After all, it was dark, and I really couldn't be certain."

"Good," said a smiling Italo. "Just so you know, your husband is gonna be doing a lot more business with the restaurant. Tell him he could count on that, Marie. We know how to be good to our friends."

"What's in the tray?" asked Marie, trying to show that things were cool between the two by changing the subject.

"I brought you some lasagna."

"Thank you, but you shouldn't have."

"Don't mention it. I gotta go now, Marie. I have a couple more errands to run. And Marie," said Italo looking down at her bare legs and feet, "get dressed. You're liable to catch cold."

##########

WHEN ITALO ENTERED THE FOREST HILLS home of Amos West, he noted that some of the judge's clothes were resting on the couch. Also scattered about were cosmetic items such as lipstick, eyeliner, and rouge. He wondered why Amos didn't dispose of such depressing reminders.

"How you doing, Amos?" asked the restaurant owner as he handed the tray of food to him. *What the hell did he do with his wife's jewelry*, thought Italo. *That rock she wore on her finger must have been worth plenty. He's probably saving it, just in case he meets somebody.*

"What's all this, Italo?"

"Me and my cousin figured you haven't been eating right lately."

"Is that what brought you here?"

"Not entirely. Ciro wanted me to see how you're doing."

"Tell Ciro that I appreciate his concern. Tell him that I'm getting by."

"I'll do that. He'll be glad to hear it."

"You didn't have to go to the trouble of bringing me this food."

"You know, Amos, bad things happen in life, but there comes a point when you gotta just move on," advised Italo. "If you don't, you'll wind up getting yourself sick."

"I hear you, Italo. I'll tell you something, without seeing Fatima in this house I feel like a blind man with nothing to look at."

"Yeah, well, talking about being a blind man, Ciro needs you to do something for him."

"What's that?"

"Ciro told me to tell you that you shouldn't identify anybody to the cops until you hear back from him."

"For God's sake, why should I do that?"

Italo's look turned ominous. "Because Ciro said you should, Amos."

"C'mon, he can't expect me to go along with that. Besides,

115

why should he care what I do?"

"Amos, I wouldn't question this. You're dealing with people you don't want to be in the crosshairs of. Do you understand what I'm saying?"

Frustrated, Amos frowned sadly. "I'm trying to."

"Now, just get this through your head. You can't identify anybody. If you don't play ball, it's not gonna be healthy for you."

"I still don't get it," said Amos.

"You're gonna get it if you don't listen to me, Amos. I'm trying to help you, can't you understand that? I hope you do."

Amos had no choice other than to go along. With Ciro involved, he knew that there was little he could do. "Am I in any danger, Italo?"

"Not if you do what you're told, Amos. If you don't, it'll be a different story."

"I hear you, Italo. Tell your cousin that I'm on board."

"Good, now that's being smart." Italo could see that Amos was upset. "Relax, Amos. All you gotta do for now is just eat the lasagna. Okay?"

"I'll have it later, Italo."

"Listen to me, my friend. Maybe what you need is a diversion. I can send somebody over here to help soothe you, know what I mean?"

"Oh, no....no thanks. I got no interest in that sort of thing right now."

"Ciro also wanted me to let you know how bad we feel about you losing your wife."

"Tell your cousin that I said thanks."

After leaving Amos, Italo wasted no time in reporting back to his cousin.

"Good," said Ciro after receiving the update. That's two down. When are you going to see the lawyer?"

"I'm heading over to the law firm now."

##########

116

ITALO WAS NO STRANGER TO THE LAW FIRM where Storm Wells worked. He and his cousin Ciro had been a client of Storm's father for years. Italo entered the law office like he owned the place. His confidence was such that he saw no need to take along a tray of lasagna.

"How may I help you, sir?" asked the woman stationed at the reception desk.

"Hello, honey, do me a favor and tell your boss that Italo from the restaurant is here to see him."

"Which one of the partners do you mean?"

"Call both of them."

"Are they expecting you?"

"Just let them know I'm out here."

Upon receiving word that Italo was looking for him, Storm's father left his office to greet him.

"Italo! What brings you here?"

"We need to talk."

Believing that he was about to be retained on a matter, the lawyer invited their visitor into the conference room. "So, what can I do for you?" asked Storm's father. "Can I get you anything?"

"No, I'm good. Is your brother here? This concerns both of you."

"Is this something that serious?"

"It has the potential of causing a problem for you guys." Storm's father was taken aback by this statement. He immediately picked up the telephone and dialed the office of his half brother. "It's me. You'd better step into the conference room right away. It's important."

When all involved were seated, Italo explained the situation. The messenger needed no heavy-handedness to elicit the cooperation of the lawyers. Their firm represented too many members of organized crime not to go along with what was being proposed. It was clear to the attorneys that Storm's testifying against a hoodlum would do more than just alienate the firm's client base.

Storm's father assured Italo that they were on the same page. He conveyed that his son had no intention of cooperating further with the authorities.

"So, Storm is gonna understand that he made a mistake in his identification then?" asked Italo.

"Absolutely," voiced each law partner.

Once Italo left the office, the two brothers dropped their professional façade.

"How the hell could that dumb son-of-a-bitch son of yours identify a client of ours to the cops?" asked Storm's uncle.

"I don't know. What can I say?"

"That kid is an imbecile!"

"Don't rub it in, will ya? He's still my son, you know."

"So, what do you propose we do?"

"Storm is just going to have to say that he can't be sure at the lineup."

"That'll put us in worse than we already are with the cops, for sure."

"Well, what's the alternative?" questioned Storm's father. The two partners looked at each other in silence for a few seconds before each returned to his office.

14

The Enlightenment

RUFFY SHEA WAS AT THE Aqueduct Racetrack awaiting the arrival of Ciro, who had requested a meeting. Ruffy brought along his most trusted associate, Joe Bullets, who toted a small handgun in the side pocket of his sport jacket.

"I still don't get it, Ruffy," said Joe.

"Get what?" asked Ruffy, without looking up from the racing form he was studying.

"Why is Ciro all of a sudden calling you out of the blue for a meeting?"

"What do I know? Maybe he's looking for some kind of a favor," replied Ruffy. "Or maybe he's got a piece of work that he needs help with."

"Yeah, okay, that could be. But why is he coming here to see you? You know how those made guys are. They always expect you to come to them."

"I guess we'll find out what's on his mind when he gets here. In the meantime, what do you think of Fred's Folly in the next race?"

"That nag does better at a longer distance," answered Joe, who was familiar with the horse. "Anyway, getting back to Ciro, I'm ready for him if he tries something."

"*Over here*?" asked Ruffy. "He's not that crazy. Besides, what reason has he got to come after me?"

"The guy's a slippery snake. And that guy Swatty in his crew is no better."

"Why are you so down on them?"

"I just don't trust them," replied Joe. "Do you remember that guy who owned the gas station who they found off the highway, you know, by the dunes? The story is that the dead man was supposed to be going to meet them the night he disappeared."

Ruffy pushed aside the racing form. "You really think these guys are up to something?"

"All I know is that they can't be trusted, especially that Swatty. Him, I know a long time."

"It's a cinch they ain't doing anything in here, but maybe Ciro is up to something."

Ciro arrived as scheduled at the restaurant with Swatty. Ciro approached Ruffy's table respectfully. Ruffy's special relationship with crime boss Philly Rava warranted him such treatment. When Ciro cordially extended his hand, Ruffy took it. The mob soldier felt embarrassingly inadequate when Ruffy's large hand swallowed his own.

"Good to see you, Ciro," said Ruffy. "Have a seat."

"Thanks. How are they running for you?"

"I'm getting killed. I'd like to send half of these nags to White Castle for a cooking up."

"That's how it goes sometimes."

"So, what did you want to see me about?"

"It's like this, Ruffy. You heard about Judge West getting clipped, right?"

Ruffy nodded in the affirmative. "What about it?"

"I got the precinct bulls leaning on me over that. They know I'm vulnerable because I got the casino and all, so they come to me to find out for them who killed the judge. The squad commander in the precinct is threatening to shut my casino down if I don't deliver."

"Did you try greasing him? Maybe he can be bought."

"I never spoke to him directly, so I didn't get the chance. My cousin spoke to him."

"No disrespect, Ciro, but it sounds like your problem is not knowing how to cultivate a relationship with the precinct bulls." Ciro frowned, not appreciating the criticism. "Yeah, well, I'll have to work on that."

"So why are you telling me all this?"

"I'm here as a courtesy, Ruffy. While I'm trying to fix my problem, I found something out that has to do with you."

"Me?"

"Yeah….it's a *good* friend of your son-in-law who drove the getaway car in the judge's killing."

The expression on Ruffy's face immediately changed to interest. "Are you trying to tell me that Mickey was involved?"

"That's why I'm here, Ruffy," replied Ciro. "I don't know if Mickey or you were involved or not. I got to get that straight before I come up with an answer for the bulls."

"Well, get this straight," said Ruffy, "I had nothing to do with killing that judge."

"Okay, now I know. I just want you to know that I was looking out for you. I went out and neutralized all three witnesses just in case you were. They're not identifying anybody."

"Why did you do that?"

"I did it to protect your ass."

"So, you did this for me, Ciro?"

"Well, I didn't do it for me."

"I'm grateful for your consideration, but c'mon let's be honest with each other. What's your angle?"

"Look, I know that you and Philly Rava are tight."

"Yeah, we're real tight," acknowledged Ruffy.

"I'd like you to talk to Philly about getting me bumped up to capo."

"I see," said Ruffy. "But tell me something, who was it that did put the judge to sleep?"

"Some dunsky called Fats."

"Never heard of him," said Ruffy. "And you're saying that my asshole son-in-law knows him?"

"No, I'm saying that Mickey knows the getaway driver. She's a young broad."

121

Ruffy leaned in over the table toward Ciro, anxious to hear more. "Tell me more about this woman," asked Ruffy, not letting on about what he already knew.

"This ain't gonna make you happy, Ruffy. The bitch is your son-in-law's squeeze." Ciro watched closely for Ruffy's reaction. He could see that he was seething. Ciro then added some fuel to the fire. "The way I got it was that the girl works for you, Ruffy."

"Works for me where?" asked Ruffy, his words coming out through clenched teeth.

"She's one of the working girls in your cat house."

"That son of a bitch!" declared Ruffy bitterly, referring to Mickey. "Which one is she? I got a million women I'm running in and out of there."

"Not all like this one. This one has a gimmick."

"What gimmick?"

"She's got bulging eyes."

Ruffy did a double take. "You got a name?" asked Ruffy icily.

"Yeah, her name is Sarah."

Finally realizing that Queenie had hired his occasional bedmate to work in his brothel caused Ruffy to erupt. With a sweeping motion, he suddenly cleared the table with his hand. "Ooooo....what are you doing?" shouted Ciro. "Control yourself!"

The noise created by the falling plates and glasses silenced those in close proximity. The restaurant staff quickly appeared to clean up the mess. The time it took to do so provided ample time for Ruffy to regain his composure

"I heard enough," said Ruffy. "I appreciate you filling me in, Ciro."

"How about you go talk to Philly for me? Tell him that I'd make a good capo."

"Sure, I can do that. But for the record, my daughter threw that lowlife, miserable bum husband of hers out of the house. So, to me, he doesn't exist anymore."

Hearing this caused Ciro's eyes to widen. He leaned in closer over the table to whisper his proposal to Ruffy. "That could make things easy all the way around. I can clean the slate and

122

take out all of them. I'll get rid of the bitch, this guy Fats, *and* your son-in-law if you want. The bulls will be happy because the case will be solved, and everybody's problems will be gone."

"That's something I can't go along with, Ciro. A death sentence for Mickey is out of the question at this time."

"What do you give a shit—didn't you just say that Mickey's dead to you?"

"That son of a bitch is in the hole to me for a ton of money, and if something happens to him, I'm out the long green. The girl is something personal. I've got something special in mind for her. As far as this guy Fats, let's face it, who are we to say he ain't got a right to make a living?"

Ciro had no counterargument to offer. "No problem, Ruffy."

"As far as that bull, try offering him the money," suggested Ruffy.

"It's worth a try," said the crime family soldier, appeasing Ruffy. "Good luck with the races." The two men then shook hands and parted ways without incident.

Immediately after the meeting, Ciro instructed Swatty to place an anonymous call to the office of Lieutenant Waldo Reale. The purpose for the call was to inform the lieutenant of who was responsible for the Judge Fatima West homicide.

"Keep the message short and sweet, Swatty. And remember, let them know that the getaway driver is a hooker who works for Ruffy Shea and that she's screwing his son-in-law, Mickey. Then hang up. Don't stay on the line to answer any questions."

"Dragging Ruffy into this is liable to piss him off, ain't it?"

"Yeah, that's just too bad, Swatty. Anyway, make that telephone call. I want those bulls off my back."

########

SWATTY REHEARSED HIS LINES several times before calling the police detective squad. Unsure if the call would be recorded, he sought to disguise his natural speaking voice. After testing out several variations, he settled on using a clipped, low voice to convey his message to Lieutenant Waldo Reale. Waldo was at his office desk when he received Swatty's call.

"Let me talk to the detective boss," said Swatty, who placed his handkerchief over the phone when speaking.

"You're talking to him," advised the squad commander. "I'm Detective Lieutenant Waldo Reale. What can I do for you?"

"The man you're looking for is James Plummer. Everybody calls him Fats. He's the one who whacked Judge West."

"Who is this?" asked Waldo.

"Never mind," replied Swatty curtly. "The getaway car was driven by a blond woman who works in Ruffy Shea's whore house on West 31st Street in Manhattan. Her name is Sarah."

"Who is this?" repeated Waldo, just prior to the caller hanging up.

The lieutenant was puzzled as to why he received a second anonymous tip. *Maybe I've got two tipsters running around out there,* he thought. Waldo memorialized this notification as he did the first by recording it in the logbook. He then called Detective Lesper into his office.

"Did you make an appointment for Marie Provenzano to view photos over at headquarters on the Judge West case?" asked Waldo.

"Not yet. She keeps saying that she's busy when I call."

"Don't let her bullshit you, Lena. Go out and nail her down with a date."

"Will do, Loo. We have a new development on that case."

"What's that?"

"Fats Plummer turned up a suicide in his car on Staten Island."

"No shit, how did he accomplish that?"

"He shot himself."

"Who told you?"

"I just got the heads up from Detective Von Hess from headquarters."

"Von Hess?"

"Yeah, he said that the gun Fats killed himself with is the same caliber gun that was used in the Judge West homicide. I just got off the phone with ballistics and asked them to do a comparison."

"Why didn't Von Hess make that request himself?"

"I don't know, Loo."

"Don't let them fool you, Lena. They got a reason. Those mothers working for Chief McCoy are all for themselves."

"Well, at least this was a help to us, Loo."

"We don't need anybody's help!" snapped Waldo. "Go out and get photo IDs from our witnesses so we can close this case."

"Yeah, but we still got the getaway driver to find, and we don't know who that is, Loo."

"We do now. I just got another anonymous call. This time the information came from a man. The tipster said a prostitute named Sarah drove the car. You go make the appointment for the witnesses to view photos. I'll find Sarah for you. I know her boss."

##########

ON THE WAY HOME FROM THE TRACK, Joe Bullets could see that Ruffy was still steaming. They weren't in the car long before Ruffy began to vent.

"I'm gonna pay them all off in spades for this, Joe. We're gonna start with Queenie for falling asleep at the wheel."

"But Queenie might not have known anything about Mickey fooling around with one of the girls, Ruffy."

"Bullshit, Joe. She knew."

"What do you want to do about Mickey?"

"Like I already said to Ciro, I'm doing nothing for now. Mickey will get his comeuppance in due time. First, I gotta get my money out of him. After that, you could consider him a doomed man."

"How do you want to handle the hooker?"

"I'm gonna hunt her down and carve her up like a Thanksgiving Day turkey when I get my hands on her. I ain't killing her, but nobody's gonna want to pay a quarter to bang her when I'm through."

"This sounds personal, Ruffy. What did she really do? I mean, all she did was put out for Mickey."

"It is personal between me and her," admitted Ruffy. "That bitch made a chump out of me by going around behind my back with my son-in-law. You've known me a long time, Joe. No one gets away with making a chump out of me."

"I don't understand—"

"I've been doing Sarah on the side. I kept it in the shade to prevent Queenie from getting wise."

"I had no idea, Skipper."

"Like I said, I was careful to keep things under the radar."

"I get it."

"What would you do if you were me?"

Joe didn't flinch at the question. "When do we start hunting this blond bitch?" he asked.

Ruffy smiled. Like always, the two were on the same page. "We hunt her ass right after we pay a visit to Queenie."

##########

QUEENIE WAS READING A ROMANCE MAGAZINE while relaxing in her bubble bath. She ceased reading when she heard the door to her apartment open. She had left the door open for Ruffy, who had called to inform her he was on his way over. Queenie's spirits were high because Ruffy had told her that he had *something special* for her.

"You got here fast, honey," Queenie shouted cheerfully. "I'll be out in a minute."

Ruffy turned to Joe and flashed an evil smile. "You wait here in the living room, Joe. This won't take long."

"Is that you, Ruffy?" asked Queenie. "Who are you talking to?" When there was no response to her shout-out, she became concerned. "Are you there, Ruffy?"

When she saw her lover enter the bathroom, she let out a sigh of relief. "You scared the hell out of me! Why didn't you answer me, honey?"

Ruffy remained silent as he approached the bathtub.

Crouching alongside the tub, he ran his hand across the top of the warm water. When he removed his hand, he looked at the suds that stuck to his fingers and palm.

"Do you want to come in, honey? The water's fine," she said playfully.

Ruffy had no interest in joining her in the tub. He gently placed the palm on his hand on top of Queenie's skull. He then began stroking her head as if she were a puppy. When Queenie began to smile happily in response to the affection being displayed, Ruffy forced her head underwater.

Queenie's frantic efforts to rise above the water were to no avail. She was trapped, unable to break free from the grip that kept her head submerged. While desperately holding her breath, she saw her doom rapidly approaching.

Ruffy's cruelty remained unwavering as he watched the bubbles begin to surface. Finally, having gone as far as humanly possible, Ruffy lifted Queenie's head out of the water by her hair. He watched with a sadistic sneer as the nearly drowned woman coughed furiously. When she finally normalized, Ruffy began to question her.

"Why didn't you tell me that Mickey was screwing around with that blond whore you hired?" Ruffy demanded to know.

"What blond?" asked the terrified assault victim, who feared another dunking.

"I'm talking about Sarah, the one with the bulging eyes."

"She doesn't even work for us anymore," explained Queenie in a pleading way.

"No?"

"I got rid of her."

"Why?"

"I had a bad feeling about her. I only hired Sarah because one of the girls recommended her."

"Who recommended her?"

"Greta...."

"Where is this Greta?"

"I let her go too."

"Get up out of the tub and get me whatever information you

got on them."

After receiving the requested information, Ruffy was left to decide what he was going to do with Queenie. In the absence of concrete proof, he opted to believe that the madam was truthful in her claim that she knew nothing of the Sarah–Mickey relationship.

Ah, what the hell, thought Ruffy, *I got no time to find another Madam who can handle the business and screw like her.*

When Ruffy left Queenie's apartment, he and Joe proceeded to where Sarah lived. Finding no one home, he questioned the building super. The super advised that he hadn't seen Sarah that day.

"Call me when she gets in," Ruffy told the super, slipping him some money. He then gave the super the telephone number of his social club. "And not a word to Sarah about me," he added, "I'm looking to surprise her."

15

Amos Joins The Hunt

AMOS WEST WAS UNPREPARED for visitors on the evening Markie and Von Hess rang his doorbell. Attired in a knee length burgundy shawl collared smoking jacket, Amos had been drinking a scotch and soda while watching the news on television. Imbibing in solitude had become part of his routine since the death of his wife.

Amos threw his shoulders back and adjusted his paisley ascot before seeing who was at the door. Not recognizing the two men in the doorway, he waited for them to speak first. When the men identified themselves as detectives, Amos stepped aside, inviting the investigators into his home. The detectives conveyed that they were there to show the witness a photo array.

Amos expressed that he was under the impression that an appointment was going to be made by the precinct detectives for him to go to police headquarters to view more photos. He explained that on the evening of the incident he looked at the photos on hand at the local detective squad without success.

Foremost on the mind of the witness was how to express

himself, should the need arise to deceive the detectives. Scrambling to get his thoughts together, Amos excused himself by claiming that he needed to get his glasses, which were located in another room.

Once collected, Amos emerged from his bedroom, intending to heed the prior warning he'd received from Italo. He justified adhering to the wishes of Ciro by telling himself that sentencing someone to all the jail time in the world wasn't going to bring back the murdered judge. This rationalization aided in putting Amos at ease with his decision.

Detective Von Hess presented Amos with a photo array that contained six photos. Now faced with the decision to be truthful or not, Amos remained firm in his decision not to identify the killer of his wife should his photo be in the array.

From the perspective of Markie and Von Hess, the identification of the late Fats Plummer as the shooter in the Judge West homicide would solve the case without the fuss connected to arrests and court proceedings. This being the case, the detectives were very optimistic in getting the results they sought.

Amos looked to his left at Markie and then to his right at Von Hess. Being centered between the law enforcement officers gave Amos a trapped feeling. The serious expressions worn by the investigators didn't make things any easier.

Prior to looking at the photo array, Amos donned his reading glasses. He did this to give the impression that he was taking the identification process seriously. Amos lifted the photo array close to his face, which was another ploy to create the illusion of his intent to do the right thing. The response of Amos after seeing his wife's killer among the six people in the array was revealing to the investigators. Although he said nothing, Amos projected a changed look that suggested recognition. Adding to this was the fact that Amos immediately put his hand over his mouth upon seeing the array.

"Is the shooter one of the six men in the array, Amos?" asked the sergeant.

"Definitely not," Amos replied firmly. "I don't recognize any of these men."

"Not even maybe?" asked Von Hess.

"Not even maybe," replied Amos. His avoidance of eye contact with the law enforcement officers increased the existing air of skepticism.

"Look, Mr. West," said Von Hess, "if there is something holding you back from making an ID, some outside influence perhaps, that's something you need to tell us."

Amos was taken aback by the remark. "No, there are no outside forces involved," responded the witness without much conviction.

"Listen, Amos, you got nothing to worry about if you're concerned about making an identification," assured Markie. "All the men in this photo array are dead," noted the sergeant, who was being less than truthful.

"They are?"

"Every one of them is on the wrong side of the grass," advised Markie bluntly. "So there won't be any repercussions if that's what you're worried about. They'll be no lineup for you to view, no testifying in court, no nothing."

"The sergeant's right, Amos," injected Von Hess, "If the perp is here in this array, then all you have to do is just pick him out. Nobody's gonna be climbing out of a grave to come after you. If he's not in the array, well, then that's okay too."

"Are you sure these men are all dead?" questioned Amos.

"Dead and buried," assured the detective.

Markie could see that Amos was beginning to thaw out. "Look, Amos, just look at the photo array again," said the sergeant, "and cut the bullshit. You got nothing to lose."

Once convinced that all in the array were now deceased, Amos saw no downside to reversing himself. He bit down on his lip and took another look at the photo array. After a couple of seconds he tapped his index finger on the picture of Fats Plummer.

"Number four," announced Amos, "he's your man. He's the bastard who robbed me and shot my wife."

"You're sure, right?"

"I'm positive."

"When did you last see him?" asked Von Hess.

"When he robbed me and killed my wife."

"Now that was easy enough, wasn't it?" asked Markie.

"How did the bastard die, Sergeant?"

"It seems like it was suicide," advised Markie "Just so you know, you're not the only witness who identified the shooter."

"I wasn't aware of that."

"Let me ask you a question, Amos—do you think you and your wife were targeted, or was it a random thing?"

"I have no idea, Sergeant."

"Did you or your wife piss someone off, maybe?"

"Well, it is possible that the judge might have. After all, her business was sending people off to jail."

"What about you?"

"I have no enemies that I know of."

"You were carrying a substantial amount of money on you. Did anyone know that?"

"Not really."

"Well, answer this," injected Von Hess, "did anyone *see* you with the money?"

Amos thought for a moment before replying. "Well, there was just one woman who saw me carrying the cash."

"Who might that be?"

"This is going to remain confidential, right?"

"Certainly....who saw you with the cash?" asked Markie.

"A girl named Sarah that I know."

"When did she see you with the money?"

"It was on the day of the murder."

"Can you describe Sarah for us?"

"She is in her mid-twenties, I'd say, maybe younger. She's quite good-looking and has long, straight blond hair. She also has an eye condition, but that doesn't detract from her attractiveness."

"How do you know Sarah?"

Somewhat embarrassed, Amos went on to reveal his association with the sex worker. "We sort of hit it off and got

132

fairly friendly. I doubt if she would betray me if that's what you're thinking."

Markie looked at Von Hess after hearing this remark. "Do you know Sarah's last name?" he asked.

"I believe her full name is Sarah Ince."

"Ollie, make some calls and see if we can get a line on her," directed the sergeant. "This won't take long, Amos." A short while later Von Hess reported what he learned.

"I got her identified, Sarge. The eye condition made things easy. It's reflected on her arrest reports."

"What does it look like?"

"She took a few pinches. She even did time in the can."

"What was she sent up for, Ollie?"

"She went away for contempt of court. Apparently, she pissed off a judge."

"It was my wife who sentenced her to prison," injected Amos.

"Your wife sent her up?" asked the surprised sergeant.

"Yes, Sarah and I discussed this. She was cool about the whole thing."

"I think everything is starting to fall into place," commented Markie.

"You think so, sergeant?"

"Sure it is, Amos," replied Markie. "Your wife put Sarah away, right?" Amos nodded in the affirmative. "So that gives her a motive. She saw you carrying the bankroll, didn't she?" Again, the witness nodded his confirmation. "So, c'mon, it all fits like a glove."

"Yes, but—"

"Look, Amos, this Sarah fits the description of the getaway driver."

"She does?"

"Right down to the eyes." This last revelation was enough to convince Amos.

##########

AFTER THE INVESTIGATORS LEFT HIS house, Amos began to

rehash the entire situation in his mind. A ruthlessly competitive man in business, he wasn't used to being taken advantage of. Amos felt compelled to comply with the wishes of Ciro because he was in no position to oppose the mobster. However, he viewed Sarah Ince as a different story.

With revenge now consuming him, Amos considered taking steps to get even. He held Sarah as the person responsible for all his grief. *If Sarah didn't look to rip me off, Fatima would still be alive*, thought Amos. *Who knows,* she *might* even *have become mayor one day. The bitch cost me a small fortune on top of everything else!*

Amos looked up toward the heavens and addressed his late wife using the most serious tone possible.

"Fatima, I swear to you, Sarah isn't going to get away with it!" declared Amos. "The law down here on earth will be too good to her. I'm going to do whatever it takes to hunt her down and make her pay a severe price."

To take the edge off, Amos prepared a fresh drink for himself and then another. As he continued to fortify himself, he sat in his living room pondering what could be done about Sarah. Deep in thought, he became more ruthless than even he thought possible. Amos decided to reach out to a fellow attorney who would be able to help him achieve the satisfaction he now sought. He turned to Marvin Butterworth, his Friday afternoon bordello buddy, for help.

##########

DETECTIVE LENA LESPER worked on the Judge West homicide while continuing to catch new cases that came into her squad. When she finally got around to seeing Amos West, she had no idea that Markie and Von Hess had already shown the witness a photo array containing the photo of Fats Plummer. The array prepared by Lesper closely resembled the one previously presented to Amos by Von Hess.

"What's this?" asked Amos after letting the squad commander and his detective into the house.

"We'd like you to look at this array, Mr. West," advised Lesper.

"But I already looked at a photo array."

"You did?" asked the squad commander. "When was that?"

"Two other detectives came by yesterday."

"What two other detectives?" curtly asked Waldo.

"I forget their names. One was a detective sergeant."

"Was his name Markie?"

"Yes, that's it, that's who it was."

Unsure how her superior was going to act out, Detective Lesper made it a point to look in another direction.

"The lieutenant, with an edge to his voice, said, "Take a look at our photo array anyway." Once again, Amos identified the photo of James "Fats" Plummer. "Did you identify this person as the shooter to the other detectives?" asked the lieutenant.

"I did. It's the same photo in both arrays."

"I suppose they told you that the man you identified is dead."

"They said it was suicide."

"What else did they say?"

"Nothing else, Lieutenant," replied Amos.

"C'mon Lena, let's go," said Waldo abruptly.

##########

WHEN MARKIE AND VON HESS ENTERED Lieutenant Waldo Reale's squad, they did so bearing what they thought was good news. They approached Detective Lesper with nothing but the best of intentions.

"We were able to get a photo identification of the shooter in the Judge West homicide," advised Markie.

"We know all about it," said the voice from Markie's rear. It was Waldo, who seemed to have come out of nowhere. "We got our own ID. We're not asleep over here, you know. My detectives sometimes have to move a little slow because they continually get pulled away on new cases to investigate," he explained. "My squad doesn't have the luxury of concentrating on just one thing at a time like you guys."

At this point, Waldo knew he would have to modify his opposition to working with Markie and Von Hess. Working together cordially was the only way for him to remain abreast of all developments. With this thought in mind, the squad commander called all the detectives into his office.

"Everybody, take a seat," announced Waldo. "It's time we begin working as a cohesive team."

Most shocked by this statement was Detective Lesper, who could hardly believe what she was hearing. She was further appalled as her boss facilitating the exchange of all the information he and his squad had gathered to date.

When the detectives came to learn from the ballistics unit that their work had established that the gun that killed Fats Plummer was the same gun used in the judge's murder, all rejoiced. There was now no doubt regarding who the shooter was in the Judge West case. With this established, the only loose end remaining was the apprehension of the driver of the getaway car.

16

Hunting The Hunter

THE BUILDING SUPER WORKED OFF a simple formula. He extended himself only for tenants who took care of him during the holidays. Fortunately for Sarah Ince, even when funds were low, she believed in giving gratuities. Her consideration placed her among the super's favored tenants.

The super let no grass grow under his feet in alerting Sarah that two tough-looking men had come around looking for her. He made this notification face to face as soon as he knew Sarah was home.

"What did they want?" asked Sarah as she stood in her apartment doorway.

"The one guy who did all the talking didn't say. He just gave me some money and this number to call," advised the super, who then handed Sarah a piece of paper that reflected the number. "Did he say who he was?"

"No, he just said that when you get home, I should call the number and ask for the boss."

"That's it?"

"He told me not to mention anything to you about it."

Sarah didn't recognize the contact number. "What did he look like?"

Based upon the description provided by the super, Sarah suspected that the man in question was Ruffy Shea. This was verified when the super indicated that the man had a green shamrock tattoo on his hand.

"I saw the tattoo when he handed me the paper," advised the super. "What should I tell them if they come back?"

"Tell them that you haven't seen me," replied Sarah. "Here, take this," she added, giving the super some money for his trouble.

"What's going on?" asked Mickey, emerging from the rear bedroom in time to see the money being passed.

"We got problems, Mickey," announced Sarah after dismissing the super. "Your father-in-law came around hunting for me." "Why the hell would Ruffy be looking for you?" asked the disbelieving Mickey. "He's got it in for me, not you."

"Take a look at this," said Sarah, passing the piece of paper with the telephone number on it.

"That's the number to his club!" exclaimed Mickey. "What did you have to do with Ruffy?"

"It's a long story."

"Tell me...."

"I suppose that you might as well know. Your father-in-law and me are, or I should say used to be....*intimate*."

"What! How could you not tell me this before?"

"Because I knew you'd react like this."

"How do you expect me to react? Ruffy's a psychopath who's protective of what he sees as his. He might even kill you just for seeing me! I....I can't protect you from him if he comes looking for you."

Mickey's concern was touching to Sarah. While he was no tough guy, at least he was sincere, which earned him points as a novelty.

"Don't worry about me, Mickey. I know how to take care of myself."

"And how do you intend to do that?"

"We're going to fight fire with fire."

"You lost me, Sarah...."

"I'll explain later. First, we have to pack up and get out of here," said Sarah.

"Where are we going?"

"We're going to stay at Greta's place for a while."

Sarah hastily began to count the remaining money they had. She licked her thumb every so often as she flicked though the bills during the count. When she noticed that Mickey was fixated on what she was doing, she reminded him to go and pack their things. Mickey could hear Sarah mumbling to herself as he packed in the next room.

"How do we stand?" shouted Mickey from the other room. "We'll be okay for a while," replied Sarah, "but these payments to Ruffy make things impossible."

"Ruffy's never forgiving what I owe. Besides, if he's after you, we got no choice but to take off and start fresh someplace else," said Mickey.

"Where can we run to without a bankroll, Mickey?" asked Sarah flatly. "We're just gonna have to make a move against Ruffy. We have no choice." It was at this point that Mickey came to realize just how bad a woman Sarah was.

"C'mon, Sarah, get real. We're no match for Ruffy."

"Don't ever make the mistake of underestimating me, Mickey." "It's not a question of my underestimating you, Sarah. It's just that in Ruffy's mind I owe him the money, period! That ain't changing. He's hell-bent on collecting every nickel. That, in and of itself, will keep *me* alive. But I'm not so sure about you. So why take a chance? Let's play it safe and take off while we can." Sarah looked at Mickey and smiled. She saw him as unique in that he was unlike many of the other men she had known. Most men started out caring, but then, once they grew comfortable, they'd begin to take and put themselves first. In Mickey, Sarah had what she believed to be a rarity. Mickey was a giver who put others first.

"Ruffy has to go!" exclaimed Sarah adamantly. "Once he's out of the way, the debt will be erased and the threat gone."

The depth of Sarah's wickedness startled Mickey. "You don't really mean that we...."

"Don't worry, we aren't doing any of the real dirty work, Mickey," Sarah assured him.

"But killing?"

"You want the debt to die, don't you?"

"Sure I do, but you're not talking about just some guy. You're talking about Ruffy."

"Show me where it's written that this big shit is bulletproof," countered Sarah. "There is no other way, so that's it. Trust me, I have it all worked out."

Sarah's statement caused Mickey to be curious. "How exactly do you plan for us to take out Ruffy?"

"*We* aren't taking out Ruffy, remember?"

"Now you've lost me again, Sarah."

"Ruffy lives alone, right? His wife is dead—correct?"

"That's right. And Queenie is his girlfriend."

Sarah shook her head. "I don't know how I never figured that one out," said Sarah, straying momentarily. "Anyway, does Queenie ever stay over with him at his house?"

"No, nobody ever stays overnight at Ruffy's house as far as I know."

"That'll make things easier. Go grab our things; we're getting out of here."

"Where are we going?"

"Before we go to Greta's, we're gonna go see an old friend of mine."

########

SARAH'S OLD FRIEND WAS A CRIMINAL OPPORTUNIST who had fled West Virginia to avoid arrest. He made his way to the Big Apple, a venue where he believed that he could go about unnoticed among the city's vast population.

Sophisticated at committing burglaries, Leon Crabbe was a man with no redeeming qualities. Relying on money attained through criminal activity to get by, Leon was, more often than

140

not, in need of funds. When he was distressed financially, he was open to any form of illegal activity that would better his circumstances.

Leon traveled in a weathered 1970 white Volkswagen bus. He had inherited the vehicle from his deceased father. When he had made his trip east, he had successfully burglarized a liquor store, which provided him with enough spirits to fill up his bus. He used the intoxicants to barter with, thus offsetting most of his traveling expenses.

Once arriving in New York City, Leon had searched for a suitable place to live. He found what he was looking for in a desolate area near the South Brooklyn waterfront. The abandoned two-family building he took over seemed to be structurally sound. Leon tapped into the streetlight conveniently located in front of the house for electricity. The nearby fire hydrant and an old wrench gave him access to all the water he needed.

Leon furnished his home by scouring Brooklyn neighborhoods for things that had been put out for trash collection. Over time this effort netted Leon assorted items such as a beat up dresser, a king size mattress, a lamp, a battered recliner and a table and chair set. Since the abandoned building was on a street consisting primarily of factories, Leon had access to working men willing to purchase things from him without asking questions.

Leon rounded out his domestic scene by taking in an alcoholic woman who disliked the seedy hotel she lived in. The disability checks the woman received made the arrangement appealing to Leon in that her money would cover the purchase of whatever basics he wasn't able to pilfer.

Leon stood on the front steps of his digs smoking a cigarette. He looked suspiciously at the car that pulled up behind his VW bus. His concern vanished after recognizing the woman in the passenger seat.

Sarah smiled and waved at Leon. "Hey, Leon," she shouted, after exiting the car. "I knew you'd still be here."

"Sarah!" shouted Leon happily. "What brings you by?"

"I got something good, and I thought of you." Leon remained silent, reserving his interest until after he knew who the man with Sarah was.

"Who's your friend, Sarah?"

"Leon, say hello to my boyfriend, Mickey." The two men nodded their greeting, each a little wary of the other.

Leon had initially come into contact with Sarah when she and her friend Greta began hanging out in a waterfront dive hustling intoxicated seamen. Being of similar minds, Leon viewed Sarah as someone he could work with when performing an ancient scam. When propositioned, Sarah had agreed to form a loose alliance with Leon and the bartender, who resided in an apartment above the bar.

Their scam was the badger game, an extortion scheme in which Sarah would lure a married man to the bartender's apartment. Once the mark was in a compromised position, Leon would enter the apartment posing as the brother of the bartender. Leon would then threaten to notify his brother, whom he identified as Sarah's husband, unless compensated. Fearing that his wife would learn of his indiscretion, the philanderer usually agreed to pay up. The con only came to a close when it became too well known among the bar frequenters.

"C'mon inside the house, Sarah, so we can talk."

"I think you'll like this deal, Leon," said Sarah, as she followed him into the building.

"I'm always open to an opportunity," he commented.

The mattress that rested on the living room floor was just beneath the front windows. Atop the mattress and under several blankets slept a ruddy complexioned woman in a pink velour jogging suit. A stench of alcohol permeated the chilly room. It was obvious to both Sarah and Mickey that the woman was sleeping off a drunk.

"I see you're stepping up in the world. Who's your friend?" asked Sarah, referring to the sleeping woman. "Are you sure she's alive?"

"She's all right," replied Leon.

"It's awful cold in here," noted Sarah.

"You get used to the cold when you have to," answered Leon. "Besides, there are ways to keep warm," he added, pointing to the mattress.

"I suppose it's any port in a storm," conceded Sarah. "Anyway, here is the deal. I need you to get us into a house so that we can rip a guy off."

"A home invasion is a little out of your line, ain't it, Sarah?"

"That's why I need you. This drug dealer we know is holding a hundred thousand dollars in his house. All you have to do is get us inside."

"How do you know he's sitting on that kind of money?"

"I've been to his house," replied Sarah. She then added to her fabricated story. "He hides his cash in the drop ceiling of his basement. He may even have more stashed away in other parts of the house."

"Where does he live?" asked Leon.

"His house is over in Howard Beach."

"Where is that?"

"It's in Queens. Don't worry, nobody's gonna know you there" When there was no immediate reply Sarah grew impatient. "So, are you interested or what, Leon?"

"That depends. When do you plan on doing this?"

"As soon as possible, and we gotta do this in the middle of the night."

"What's the split?"

"We split up the money three ways," answered Sarah. "Okay with you?"

"Am I expected to go in heavy?"

"Yeah, that's why you're getting so much of the take."

"I got no gun."

"Don't worry about that. I'll have one for you."

"But the guy is gonna know you. So, how is that supposed to work?"

"Oh, then maybe we shouldn't leave behind any witness."

Leon laughed loudly. "Okay, Sarah, now I get why you really need me. I'll do the dirty work—but not for a third. My end is two-thirds, and you split the rest any way you like."

Sarah bit down on her lip for a second. She then flashed Leon a false smile. "Okay, Leon, whatever you say. I should've realized that there would be no outmaneuvering you."

"When do you want to do this?" asked Leon.

Sarah turned to Mickey for the answer to that question. "Mickey?"

"Sunday night. He's always home on Sunday night," said Mickey, responding on cue.

Once their agreement was solidified, Sarah and Mickey headed back to Queens. During their ride home, Mickey sought clarification. "I'm confused, Sarah," said Mickey. "What are we supposed to tell Leon when he finds out there is no hundred thousand dollars in the house?"

"We don't have to tell him anything. Leon's gonna be going out on the same train ride as Ruffy." Sarah saw the confusion on Mickey's face. Looking at her lover as if he was an innocent babe, she patiently explained her strategy. "The cops are gonna find *two* bodies and *two* guns. The gun that kills Ruffy is gonna have Leon's prints on it. The gun that kills Leon is gonna be the one we plant in Ruffy's hand. When the cops get there, how do you think they'll see things?"

"They'll see it as a falling out between thieves?"

"Exactly!" exclaimed Sarah excitedly. "The big boy gets a gold star on top of his paper!"

Sarah's paramour stood in wonderment at how Sarah's Mephistophelian mind worked. "You're unbelievable, Sarah," he finally voiced.

Proud of herself, Sarah gloated. "When they find the bodies, the cops are gonna be looking for a connection between Ruffy and Leon that don't exist. It'll be one dead end after another for them. After a while, they'll just stop trying to figure it out."

Mickey found Sarah to be diabolical. Her cunning was a warning to him that if he ever ran afoul of her, his life wouldn't be worth two cents. Any notion Mickey might have had about reforming Sarah was now gone.

"Got it," said Mickey, who wore a glum expression.

"What's wrong?"

"Nothing's wrong."

"My idea is no good?" asked Sarah, thinking that Mickey detected flaws.

"No good? You should be working for the CIA!"

"Maybe I should," agreed Sarah.

"So, where are we going now?"

"We're off to see Greta. She'll put us up for a while?"

"Has she the room for us?"

"Sure she does. Did you forget about Fats not being around anymore?"

Mickey looked straight ahead at the road without answering her. It was something he had put out of his mind.

17

The Long Arm Of
The Law

AS EXPECTED, SARAH AND MICKEY found Greta receptive to their staying with her. Offering the couple the spare bedroom, Greta escorted them to their quarters. After Greta left the room, Sarah took a seat on the edge of the bed as Mickey unpacked. When Sarah communicated, in a matter-of-fact way, that she was going to give some money to Greta for harboring them, Mickey ceased unpacking. Burdened with having to pay off the debt to Ruffy, parting with money had become a sensitive topic for Sarah's paramour.

"Greta's not gonna be expecting any payment from us once she understands the situation," voiced Mickey, who was hoping that he was right.

"We have to give her something," stated Sarah."

"Why? I thought you two were supposed to be such great friends."

"We are, but don't forget, she's putting herself at risk. If Ruffy finds out she helped us duck him, it won't go well for her," noted Sarah.

"I understand all that, but we're strapped for cash now," said

Mickey. There was a trace of annoyance in his voice.

"You can thank your bastard father-in-law for that!" Sarah barked, shifting blame. "He's the one bleeding us dry!"

"Okay, Sara, you're right," conceded Mickey. "So, what do we do now?"

"We need to go out and rustle up some money to give Greta."

"Right now?" asked Mickey.

"Yes, now."

"We don't have enough? How much do you intend to give her?" asked Mickey, who wasn't wise enough to avoid this topic.

"Don't start giving me the third degree!" snapped Sarah, jumping down Mickey's throat. "If you have a problem with how I do things, you can go pay off your own debt."

"Sarah, all I asked was—"

"You've asked enough! Just remember something, Mickey, I don't need you. You need me!"

Sarah's angry outburst was effective in stifling Mickey, who tried to smooth things over by explaining himself. "Don't get mad, Sarah. I'm not bucking you. All I'm trying to say is that we have to be a little careful right now."

Sarah rolled her eyes before responding. "Don't you think I'm damn well aware of that, Mickey? I know exactly what I'm doing."

Realizing that he'd never win with Sarah, Mickey aborted further discussion concerning finances. He waited for Sarah to cool off before again conversing. He chose a non-controversial topic to break the ice.

"Did Greta take the news of Fats's death hard?" he asked. "Greta doesn't know when she's got it good," replied Sarah, her voice sounding sour. "She actually believes she lost something in that loser."

"Maybe we should consider getting regular jobs someplace. We can't go on living like this forever."

Sarah bristled at the thought of honest work. She began to shake her head vigorously in the negative. She interpreted such a suggestion as a sign of weakness.

"We're not taking any jobs," she said firmly. We'll look out for ourselves just fine."

"Okay, okay, I was just saying. How about I pawn the watch and ring we got from the judge's husband to help hold us over?" Sarah refused to entertain such a suggestion. "C'mon, let's go, Mickey. Enough with all this talking. We've got fish to fry."

"What fish?"

"Go get the car."

Sarah directed Mickey to drive her to a bank she knew of in Bayside, Queens. As instructed, Mickey positioned the car so that they could observe those using the ATM machines.

"Here we go," said Sarah as she looked through the front glass of the bank. She drew Mickey's attention to a smartly attired woman who stood at the ATM machine. Her target fit the profile Sarah was looking for perfectly. The intended victim was old, walked with a cane, and didn't appear too sturdy. Her dress, as well as the way her hair and face were done up, smacked of affluence. The senior citizen was a perfect candidate for a rip-off.

"Keep the engine running, Mickey, and be prepared to take off when I get back."

Stepping up to the bank's window glass, Sarah was close enough to witness the intended victim count her withdrawal. Sarah was satisfied that a substantial sum of money had been withdrawn. *She must be going someplace with all that moolah*, thought Sarah, who wasted no time getting in position.

When the senior citizen stepped into the street, the strap on her pocketbook was wedged in the crook of her arm. The length of the strap made it an ideal target for snatching. Sarah approached the aged woman from the rear and yanked on the strap with velocity enough to cause the senior citizen to tumble to the ground.

The victim, who managed to hold on to her property, refused to capitulate. Their tug-of-war struggle finally concluded when the frustrated Sarah struck the senior citizen across the mouth with her own cane. As the crime victim spit out a tooth, Sarah gained control of the pocketbook. She then fled in haste to where Mickey was waiting in his car.

"C'mon, let's go!" Sarah ordered after jumping into the front seat. The adrenaline rush reddened her face.

"Where to?" asked Mickey, whose lack of awareness could be incredible at times.

"Just get moving," shouted Sarah. "We gotta get outta here!" As the duo made their escape, Sarah began going through the purse. After removing the cash, she conducted a quick count before stuffing the bills into her jacket pocket.

"We got us plenty," she announced proudly. Mickey just nodded without commenting. "Pull over for a second," instructed Sarah once they reached a safe distance from the robbery scene. "I want to dump this bag."

Sarah casually exited the vehicle to toss the purse into a residential garbage pail. Upon returning to the car, she let out a loud yawn.

"Are you okay?" asked Mickey.

"I feel great!" Sarah replied with great energy. "Let's find a nice restaurant and get something to eat. I'm famished."

##########

LEON CRABBE TOOK TIME TO WATCH the factory workers on his block as they prepared to leave for the day. He did this regularly in order to see what trash was being put out for collection. When he spotted two workers carrying out a metal closet, he darted over to where they were in order to claim the property. "You guys tossing that out?" Leon asked.

"Yeah," answered one of the workers. "You want it?"

"What's wrong with it?"

"Nothing, our boss got a new one," the worker replied. "So, do you want it or not?"

"Yeah, I'll be right back for it."

Leon returned to his home and rousted his lady friend from bed. "C'mon, get up out of there; I need you to give me a hand with something."

"What's the matter?"

"Just get up, will ya?"

The woman, after wiping her eyes clean with her fingers, focused on Leon. "You just interrupted a beautiful dream I was having," complained the woman.

"What did you dream, that you fell into a barrel of Coors Light?"

"Very funny. What do you want?"

"I need you to help me carry something into the house."

"What?"

"A closet—you'd like something to put your threads in, wouldn't you?"

"What threads have I got?" she answered.

"C'mon, get up," Leon repeated, his patience now running thin. The lady friend looked at the windowsill to make sure her beer cans were there. She used the chill coming from the slightly open window to keep the beverages cold. Seeing the beer stimulated her thirst.

"Okay, let's go get it," she said, adding, "what this place really needs is a refrigerator.'

"It'll come in due time, my little homemaker."

After they carried the closet into the abandoned building, Leon's lady friend rewarded herself with a brew. Leon joined her.

##########

AT 3:00 A.M., LEON ROSE FROM the mattress he slept on. Unable to sleep comfortably because of his lady friend's unusually loud snoring, he sat up in frustration. Between the chill in the room and what sounded like wood being sawed, he gave up trying to sleep.

Leon walked over to the pail of water he used for washing up. After dipping his fingers in the water, he dampened his face and ran his wet fingers through his hair. He then dried himself off with the tail of the shirt he had slept in.

Leon yawned as he changed clothes. Once attired in a flannel shirt, black sweater, jeans, brown boots, and a black ski cap, he was prepared to go to work. After slipping a flashlight into the side pocket of his black coat, Leon went outside to start his van. He was glad to see that he had plenty of gas. A full tank meant that he wouldn't have to siphon fuel from some vehicle parked on a nearby street.

Leon blasted the heat and returned to the abandoned building until the van was toasty. When he returned to his vehicle, Leon removed the black leather pouch that contained his lock picks from the glove compartment. He put the tools in the interior pocket of his coat.

Leaning back in the driver's seat with his shoulder pressed against the vehicle door, he got comfortable. Leon rolled down the window less than an inch and closed his eyes. He slumbered peacefully until awakened by the sound of tapping on the driver's side window. Seeing that it was Sarah, Leon shut off his engine and stepped out of the car.

"Are you ready to rock and roll?" asked Sarah, sounding exceedingly upbeat.

"Yeah, I'm ready," muttered Leon, who was still half asleep.

"C'mon, I got the artillery in the car for you."

"Can you put up the heat?" asked Leon, after getting in the back seat of Mickey's car.

"Here you go," said Sarah, passing back the handgun to him."

"How about turning up that heat?"

"Turn on the heat, Mickey," said Sarah. "Leon is delicate." When the trio arrived at Ruffy Shea's house, they observed a black sedan parked in the driveway.

"That's Ruffy's car," Mickey informed them.

"There is no need for all of us to be in front of the house," said Leon. "That might draw attention. Let me out, and you two go park up the block and wait for my signal. I'll shine my flashlight twice when it's time to go in."

"Okay," said Sarah, "we'll be waiting for your signal." Once parked, Sarah instructed Mickey to shut off the headlights and keep the engine running.

##########

THE OFFICERS ASSIGNED TO THE SECTOR had been working the overnight shift in Howard Beach for several years. Experience taught them that after three o'clock in the morning, anyone creeping around on the street was usually up to no good. The operator of the radio car made a routine swing through the block Ruffy Shea resided on.

"Kill the engine and duck down," shouted Sarah, spotting the prowl car. Mickey didn't have to be told twice. After shutting down the car he threw his body over Sarah's, where he remained for what seemed like forever to him. "Inch up," she instructed, "see if they kept going." Sarah soon grew impatient for an answer. "Well, c'mon, what do you see?"

"Wait a second, will ya? I'm looking...."

##########

"MY SIDE, AT THE END AT THE BLOCK," said the officer riding in the passenger seat of the police car. "Kill the lights, there's a guy by the front door of the white house."

"What's he up to?" asked the radio car operator, shutting off the headlights.

"It can't be anything good at this time."

The officers got just close enough to see their man tinkering with the lock on the entrance door. Convinced that they were witnessing a home intrusion in progress, the operator turned on the radio car high beams. He then ran the vehicle onto the sidewalk and up to the front door of the house.

Leon was startled by the blinding lights. Practically pinned against the building, he was unsure of what to do. The authoritative command "POLICE! DON'T MOVE!" echoed in the air.

What convinced Leon to remain in place was the sound of a gun being cocked, as opposed to the officer's order. The click sounded thunderous to him, removing any notion of his making a run for it. Where Leon came from a fleeing felon was fair game for an officer's bullet.

"GET THOSE HANDS UP!" instructed the booming voice of authority. Leon immediately complied.

Inside the house Ruffy Shea, a light sleeper, was awakened by the commotion going on outside his home. After removing an automatic from his closet, Ruffy went to the window to investigate. After seeing that the police had a man spreadeagled against his building, he returned the weapon to the closet. He then rushed to don his bathrobe and slippers before going downstairs.

"What the hell is going on?" asked Ruffy, who stood at the entrance of his home. The excitement rendered the gangster unfazed by the winter air.

"Stay back there," ordered one of the officers as their prisoner was being patted down.

"He's got a gun on him," declared the searching officer after finding Leon's weapon. "C'mon, asshole, let's go," the cop ordered, after rear-cuffing his prisoner.

Leon's face bounced off the edge of the police car roof in the haste to get him in the back seat. The mishap was a genuine accident. The impact caused a gash to Leon's right eyebrow, resulting in a stream of blood running down the prisoner's face. "Do you know him?" Ruffy was asked by one of the officers.

"I don't know....I'll have to get a better look at him."

"Come on over and take a look-see."

The rear door of the radio car was opened and one of the officers trained his flashlight on Leon's bloodied face. Ruffy squinted as he leaned his head into the police car, feigning that he needed to get closer.

"You're a dead man," Ruffy hissed, "unless you tell me who sent you here."

"Your aunt, Sadie," snottily answered Leon, who was unaware of exactly who Ruffy was.

Leon was a lot of things, but he was no snitch. He prided himself in knowing how to keep his mouth shut when questioned by the law. Right there, in the back of the police car,

Leon resigned himself to the fact that he was likely facing a stint in jail. To a seasoned criminal like Leon, doing a bit in prison was nothing more than an occupational hazard. The thought that he was wanted in another state never entered his mind.

##########

WHEN MICKEY SAW THAT THE POLICE nabbed Leon, he panicked. "They got Leon!" he shouted.

"Shhhhhh!" said Sarah, pulling her boyfriend down next to her. "Stay down!"

"What are we gonna do, Sarah?" whispered Mickey.

"Hold on, let me take a peek," she replied. Sarah, seeing that the officers were actively engaged with Leon, thought it best to leave the scene forthwith. "We can't wait. Leon may open his trap," said Sarah. Drive off now while the cops are busy," she ordered, adding, "Keep the lights off and slowly pull away. When you get to the corner, make a turn and put the lights on. Now get going."

"Get going where?"

"Stop with the questions and get us the hell out of here! If you don't start moving, we'll end up with Leon!"

When they were in the clear both Mickey and Sarah were able to once again breathe easily.

"So now what are we supposed to do, Sarah?"

"We got no choice but to try again," she answered.

"Are you crazy?" asked Mickey, amazed at Sarah's never say die attitude.

"We'd be crazy if we don't try again!" barked Sarah. "What do you think is gonna happen to us if Leon opens his big trap?"

"The cops will come after us?"

"It's not the cops we need to worry about, Mickey. If Leon shoots his mouth off, it's only a matter of time before Ruffy finds out, and you know what that'll mean. He's already hunting for me. This will only supercharge his efforts."

Mickey understood that Sarah was right. "So, tell me what to do...."

154

"Go back to Greta's. We'll be safe there. In a couple of days, I'll call the super where we lived. If nobody came sniffing around the apartment looking for us, it'd mean Leon did the right thing and kept his mouth shut."

"This is getting worse and worse for us, Sarah," voiced Mickey. "Let's get away from all this while we still can."

"Buck up, baby. We'll be okay."

"I hope so."

"I think we better start carrying a gun all the time now, Mickey. No sense taking any chances."

Mickey took a hard look at Sarah as she spoke. He was beginning to see his paramour as a female version of his father-in-law. "We're gonna be needing more money, aren't we, Sarah?"

"We'll get it."

"I'm afraid to ask you how...."

"We're getting it the same way we got it last time."

A sick look came over Mickey at the thought of committing more robberies. "But what do we do if Leon squeals and Ruffy does catch up with us?"

"That's exactly why we need to start carrying a gun." Sarah could see that her boyfriend needed bolstering. "Don't worry about a thing, Mickey. We'll get Ruffy before he gets us." Mickey's face projected a distinct look of worry. The very thought of Ruffy finding out that they were behind the home intrusion unnerved him. He eventually came to the conclusion that Sarah was right in wanting to kill Ruffy. It seemed to be the only way out of the mess they were in.

18

Sinister Alliances

THE PHOTO IDENTIFICATION OF FATS PLUMMER effectively put
to rest the great interest attached to the Judge Fatima West
homicide. Although the Staten Island authorities erroneously
concluded that Fats was a suicide, in the scheme of media
attention, that determination was of little consequence.

What was important was the presence of a common
denominator that linked Fats to Judge West. Determining that
the gun that killed Fats was the same one used in the homicide
of the judge led to the conclusion that Fats must have killed
himself after murdering the judge. In light of no evidence
existing to the contrary, this line of thinking made sense.

As is often the case when there is more than one perpetrator
involved, there was no urgency to apprehend the second piece.
In the Judge West case it meant that Sarah Ince was no longer a
law enforcement priority.

Prior to closing the case with positive results, Detective Lesper
went through the motions of trying to apprehend Sarah. She
and her partner responded to Sarah's last known address only
to find she was no longer residing there.

After speaking to the super of the building Detective Lesper
ascertained that the wanted woman hadn't left a forwarding
address. Now that the police were at his door, the super was

hesitant to get involved. He opted to keep what little information he had to himself. The detectives headed back to the precinct to confer with their squad commander.

"Do you want me to keep digging, Loo?" asked Lesper after apprising her squad commander of her negative results.

"No, I don't think we need to kill ourselves," replied Waldo, adding, "Next." The word was a common term used to indicate that it was time to move on to other cases. "Just put out a wanted card on Sarah. It'll only be a matter of time before she gets picked up on some bullshit charge. Once the wanted card drops, we'll scoop her up and hold her accountable for her role in the Judge West case."

At this juncture a decision was made by the chief of detectives that Markie and Von Hess were no longer needed to assist in the West investigation. They returned to headquarters to await their next assignment.

########

BEING A LIFELONG BACHELOR DIFFERENTIATED WALDO from most of the people he worked with. They had families to keep them busy. For them, there were always obligatory places to be and things to do, especially during the fast-approaching holiday season. Since Waldo had no wife, love interest, or children, there were times that he felt as if he were missing out on something. There were no toys or gifts to purchase and no preparing for festive holiday dinners. There were also no presents coming his way.

As Waldo sat in his one-bedroom apartment thinking about these things, he became depressed. To cheer himself up, he opened a bottle of rye. Drinking in solitude only furthered his state of despondency. He began to view everything in a negative light. Although the squad commander had no health issues, a recognition that he wasn't getting any younger caused Waldo to think of what life might be like for him post-retirement. *I could get sick,* he thought, *and if I do, who will take care of me? Even if I don't get sick, do I have enough money to see me through if I live to be really old?*

Waldo began to fret further when he considered the possibility of losing his mobility. The squad commander, who always took good care of himself, never denied himself anything. He took his meals out, so he usually ate well. Someone came in twice a month to clean. He wore clothes that were up to date and always drove a new car.

Waldo poured himself another drink when he considered how life would be if he were compelled to live differently. *What happens if I can't maintain anymore? Are my pension and social security going to be enough for me to live on if I need to take on an aide?*

Waldo went to work the following day with money on his mind. He saw having lots of cash as the only solution to his woes. The squad commander was determined to accumulate enough capital to live on regardless of his circumstances. To accomplish this he knew that he would have to step up his thieving ways.

Waldo was in his office reading the morning newspaper when Detective Lesper came to the door.

"They made a good collar on the late tour, Loo," advised Lesper, referring to an arrest made by members of the patrol force who worked the overnight shift. "They have the perp downstairs in the cell."

"What are the charges?" asked Waldo with mild interest. "They have one prisoner under for possession of a loaded gun, attempted burglary, and possession of burglar's tools."

"Was it residential or commercial burglary?"

"Residential."

"Nice, bust," commented Waldo.

"Guess who the owner of the house is?"

"How would I know?"

"Ruffy Shea," announced Lesper. "The cops on patrol didn't even know who he was!"

"Was Shea home?" asked the now very interested Waldo.

"He was sleeping in bed."

The squad commander removed a binder given to him by the

FBI. The binder contained information on known organized crime figures and their associates. After ascertaining Ruffy's date of birth, Waldo had Lesper check DMV records to see if the mobster was linked to the address of the attempted burglary. "It's the same Shea, Loo," advised Lesper after conducting the research.

Waldo noted that Ruffy Shea was documented by the feds as a high-level associate of Philly Rava, the boss of the Rava family. The squad commander asked Lesper to gather more details pertaining to the arrest.

Lesper learned that the serial number on the gun taken off the prisoner had been filed off. The detective further gathered that Ruffy made it clear that he didn't want to press charges. This left felony possession of a loaded gun as the major charge against Leon Crabbe.

"Let's get the perp up here," said Waldo.

"Where do you want him, Loo?" asked Lesper.

"Put him in the lineup room. You start the interview without me. I want to size him up from outside the room for a couple minutes before I join in."

The lineup room was constructed the same way in most of the recently erected police stations. The room doubled as a viewing room and a place to interview prisoners. The one-way glass that was embedded in the cinderblock wall made it possible to view what was going on inside the room. The glass was thick enough to make a conversation difficult, but not impossible, to hear through. When used for interviewing, the interior of the lineup room was sparse, containing only a metal table and three chairs.

Waldo watched quietly through the one-way glass as Detective Lesper engaged Leon in basic questioning. The squad commander managed to see and hear enough to be of the opinion that more than just one person was involved in the attempted burglary. He based this assumption on Leon's accent, which made it obvious that the prisoner was a transplant from out of town. If this was true, then Leon would have more than likely had an accomplice.

Somebody must have pointed this guy to Ruffy's house, thought Waldo. *He didn't just stumble upon a residence in Howard Beach by coincidence.*

The question now became whether or not Ruffy was targeted for robbery or something even more nefarious, like murder. Having gained his insights, the squad commander entered the viewing room to engage the prisoner.

"Was he read his rights, Lena?" asked the lieutenant.

"He was, Loo."

Once this was established, Waldo took the lead in interrogating the prisoner. "What were you doing with a gun, pal?" he asked.

"That wasn't my gun, sir," replied the prisoner. Leon's polite response was an indication to Waldo that the prisoner was a cutie.

"You can cut the *sir* shit. What's your full name?"

"Leon Preston Crabbe," answered the prisoner.

"Any relation to Buster?" asked Waldo sarcastically. He was referring to the actor who played Flash Gordon in the old movie serial.

"No, there is nobody named Buster in my family."

"Well, old Flash took a trip to Mars. You're gonna be taking one to Rikers."

Leon, who was a good deal younger than the squad commander, didn't know what to make of Waldo. He found him quite unlike the cops he was used to.

"I'm no stranger to jail, sir," replied Leon.

"Listen, pal, do you have any idea who owns that house you were breaking into?"

"I wasn't breaking into any house."

Waldo frowned. "What do they call a nighttime intrusion where you come from?"

"I wasn't looking to intrude in any house."

"Cut the crap," said Waldo, with a sharp edge to his voice. "You can float that bullshit with Sheriff Andy in Mayberry, but not over here with me. Where are you from, anyway?"

"West Virginia," replied Leon, now suspecting that the

exchange might get really nasty.

"What brings you to New York?"

Leon shrugged his shoulders. "I was never in New York before, and I wanted to see it."

"What made you pick that particular house to break into?"

"Look, Lieutenant, can I be honest with you?"

"Go on, that would be refreshing."

"I was just driving around with a friend in his car, when all of a sudden I had to use the bathroom," began Leon, trying his best to sound sincere. "I got out of the car to relieve myself."

"Who is this friend,"

"Just a guy I met. I don't even remember his name. I really wasn't even by the door. I was by the tree. I was just zipping up my fly when the officers jumped me. The dude I was with saw the cops coming and took off without me."

"Did you have your joystick out when the cops caught you working the lock to the front door?" asked Waldo.

"What was that?" asked the prisoner, not sure if he heard the question correctly.

"Did you have your pecker out when you were breaking in?" The question went unanswered. "Do you know who Ruffy Shea is?"

"I never heard of him, Lieutenant."

"He's a man who is close to the boss of an organized crime family," advised Waldo. "What do you think he's thinking, knowing that you were trying to get into his house armed with a roscoe?"

"I have no idea what he's thinking," replied the prisoner softly. Leon was beginning to get worried for the first time.

"Enlighten our friend here about how bad Mr. Shea is, Lena."

"He's a stone-cold killer," said Lesper, winging it. The remark caused the prisoner to sit up and pay attention.

"Is he some kind of a drug dealer?" asked the prisoner, trying to ascertain if he had been misled by Sarah Ince.

"He's no drug dealer, as far as I know." Leon's mouth dropped open after realizing that Sarah had gained his participation in the burglary via trickery. "Ruffy's going to think you went to his house to hurt him." pointed out Lesper.

"Me?" asked Leon, pointing his thumb to his own chest. "Why would I want to do something like that? I don't even know the man."

"Look, my guess is that you're in cahoots with somebody who had it in for Ruffy, and you're gonna tell us who," said the squad commander.

"Lieutenant, I've been around. If this Ruffy is all you say he is, he's not gonna press charges against me. He's gonna want me out on the street so he could take care of me himself. I know that much."

"I can't say you're wrong," agreed Waldo. "He'll look to take his bite out of your ass big time."

"If he doesn't press charges, I go free....right?"

"Not quite," answered Waldo. "You're forgetting that you have a felony gun charge to answer for."

"I think that maybe I want a lawyer," declared Leon, exercising his right to representation.

"Okay, smart guy, have it your way. But remember something, you're gonna answer to Ruffy whether you're in or out of jail. He's one guy capable of reaching you no matter where you're locked up."

Leon let out a deep exhale before responding. "Lieutenant, I got nothing more to say."

"I'm not asking you anything. I'm just wising you up. The only way out of the spot you're in is for someone to go talk to Ruffy on your behalf....and I'm just the guy to do that. But I gotta have something in return from you."

"You can do that?"

"Listen, after I talk to him, he'll see laying off you as in his interest. But before I do anything, I have to hear the full story. This brilliant idea to go up against Ruffy certainly wasn't yours." The prisoner thought hard about what the squad commander said. Feeling that he had been misled by Sarah, Leon's loyalty to her was now nonexistent. He decided to take his chances by throwing in with the law.

"If I cooperate with you, do I still go to jail for the gun?"

"That depends on what you bring to the table," replied Waldo. "We'll talk to the district attorney for you if you cooperate. That usually works out well."

"All right, so what do you want to know?"

"Do you still want that lawyer?"

"Nah, ask your questions."

"Go on, Lena…."

"Why don't we start by you telling us who you were with?" asked Lesper. "You had no car, so you needed a ride, didn't you?"

"I had a ride waiting for me."

"Who was in on this with you?"

"Some bitch I know named Sarah roped me in. It was her and her boyfriend, a guy named Mickey."

The squad commander and the detective looked at each other after hearing this revelation. "Is this Sarah a blond with an eye problem?" asked Lesper

"Yeah, do you know her?"

"Let us ask the questions," injected Waldo. "Go on and continue, Lena."

"What were you really up to at Ruffy's house?" asked the detective.

"Sarah just said he was a drug dealer," explained Leon. "She never told me who he was. She said that he had a hundred grand in the house. We went there to rip him off."

"So, it wasn't a planned hit or anything like that?"

"Nah," fibbed Leon, "it was meant to be just a rip-off."

"Where did the gun come from?"

"Sarah gave it to me."

"What is she the ringleader?" asked Waldo, who now took over the questioning.

"Yeah, she calls the shots. Her boyfriend ain't too bright."

"Did you know anything about Judge Fatima West?"

"I never heard of her."

"Did Sarah or Mickey ever talk about Judge West?"

"I never heard them mention the name."

"Let me ask you something, Leroy—"

"It's Leon, Lieutenant."

"That's right, my mistake. Tell me, Leon, how would you like to work for us officially?"

"That depends, Lieutenant. What's my gain?"

"Maybe we find a way to avoid jail altogether for you. We could wire you up and maybe you could get Sarah to talk about Judge West. The judge was killed during a robbery."

"I probably could do that, but how am I supposed to account for being back on the street?"

"Just say the arrest got voided because the complainant wouldn't press charges. People know Ruffy, so they'll buy it. As far as the gun goes, you threw it in the bushes and the cops never found it on you."

"Okay, Lieutenant, I suppose that'll work," answered Leon.

"Okay, now we're in business. Get the papers, Lena, and sign Leon up as a confidential informant."

This is gonna work out nice, thought Waldo, who now had ideas on how to help fund his retirement years.

##########

THE WAY FOR WALDO TO HELP ALLEVIATE his monetary concerns would require nerve to execute. Since he possessed the boldness necessary and believed the risk worthwhile, the squad commander rose to the occasion.

Waldo saw aligning himself with a major criminal like Ruffy Shea as a way to substantially supplement his income. Once an arrangement was established, he was confident that the flow of favors requested would come. Waldo referred to such opportunities as haymakers, and haymakers came with big price tags.

It was raining when the squad commander set out to see Ruffy at his home. On the drive over to Ruffy's house, Waldo was in such good spirits that he began whistling. He turned on the radio so he could croon along with his favorite vocalists.

As Waldo warbled his offkey rendition of *My Way*, he was consumed with the thought of the money he'd be making after coming to terms with Ruffy. At no time did the squad commander think that an arrangement couldn't come to fruition.

###########

THE SOUND OF THE RINGING doorbell bell woke Ruffy from the nap he was taking while seated on the living room easy chair. He slowly rose from his chair and went to the door to see who it was.

The caller flashed a badge and identified himself as Lieutenant Waldo Reale, the precinct squad commander. Ruffy was immediately suspicious because he knew that detectives traveled in teams. Ruffy, alone and unarmed, backed up a step. He took a defensive stance as thoughts of dashing for the nearest gun the house crossed his mind.

Waldo, sensing Ruffy's uneasiness, produced his police ID card to further prove his authenticity. Ruffy examined the credential carefully. Once satisfied, he engaged the squad commander. "Where did you say you worked, Lieutenant?"

"I'm the detective squad commander in this precinct," replied Waldo.

Ruffy now thought he understood why Waldo was at his front door. "Look, Lieutenant, I appreciate your interest. But, like I told the officers, it goes against my grain to press charges against the guy who tried to break in over here."

"I understand that," said Waldo. "That's your prerogative. But that's not my purpose for being here."

"Then why are you here?"

"I'm here because I figured that you might be interested in knowing who was responsible for targeting your home." This statement got Ruffy's attention.

You know who was behind it?"

"I do, you weren't exactly randomly selected, you know."

This bull has to have an angle, thought Ruffy.

165

"Since when do you guys work alone?"

"The business we have together is best conducted just between us."

"What's your game, Lieutenant?"

"I'm looking for an understanding with you," communicated Waldo, not mincing words. "I could be very helpful to you and your friends."

"Your help comes in return for what?"

"Ample compensation," replied Waldo.

Ruffy could now see he was dealing with a street guy. "Where are you from?"

"I told you, I'm the squad commander in the precinct."

"No, that's not what I'm asking. Where did you grow up?"

"I grew up in Manhattan."

"Give me some names." Waldo provided several names of low-level mob associates he was acquainted with. "Okay, Lieutenant, why don't you drop by tomorrow."

After Waldo left, Ruffy reached out to Miltie, who wasted no time in checking Waldo's references. When word came back that Waldo passed muster, Ruffy welcomed the squad commander back into his home the following day.

"Did I pass my test?" asked Waldo.

"You came out good," replied Ruffy. "So now I'm listening. Talk to me."

"For openers, I'll feed you the people who orchestrated the break-in over here. All you have to do in return is compensate me."

"How much compensating are you looking for?"

After working out the financials, the lieutenant conveyed to Ruffy everything he knew about the attempted break-in. This included Leon's connection to Sarah and Mickey. Judging by the way Ruffy's face began to twitch, it was clear to Waldo that he had triggered the mobster's homicidal side.

"I'm gonna—"

"Hold up, man," said Waldo. "What you *intend* to do, I don't need to share in."

"That's right," agreed Ruffy. "I'll get your money." Ruffy

returned to pay the lieutenant his fee in cash. "Let's stay connected, Lieutenant, but we can't be meeting face to face like this. Your contact with me will be through a guy named Miltie, he'll be in touch with you," advised Ruffy.

"He could be trusted?"

"No question about it. Miltie has been with me forever. He's gonna set up a post office box for us. Oh, and one other thing, I want Mickey to remain out on the street."

"What about his girlfriend and Leon?"

"You just tell me where I can find them."

"Leon is the guy who can take you to the girl," advised Waldo, providing the address of the abandoned building where Leon Crabbe was staying.

"Okay, Lieutenant, we're in business."

"Call me Waldo," said the squad commander with a friendly smile.

19

Leon Pulls A Houdini

PRIOR ARANGEMENTS WITH THE District Attorney's office resulted in the adjournment of Leon's case without bail having to be posted. When the defendant exited the courtroom he concealed his gloat. As he had hoped, his release presented the opportunity for him to abscond.

Detectives Lena Lesper and her partner, Scott Podell, were present in court for Leon's arraignment. After stepping out of the courtroom they escorted Leon to a private room on an upper floor of the courthouse where they returned his personal property to him.

"So, what happens now?" asked Leon, fishing for information that would facilitate his departure from New York City.

"You're going to give Sarah a call," advised Lesper. "You have her number, right?"

"Yeah, I got it. What am I supposed to say to her?"

"Tell her whatever you think she'll believe in order to get her to meet with you," replied the detective.

"Sarah's no dummy. She'll want to know how I managed to walk away from you guys. What's my story again?"

"Just say you tossed the gun before the cops reached you."

"That's right," injected Detective Podell. "Tell her that since nobody actually saw you holding the gun, the DA declined prosecution."

"Now, dial up Sarah," instructed Lesper.

Leon telephoned Sarah and to his surprise, after explaining himself, found her readily receptive to a meeting. Arrangements were made to meet, along with Mickey, later that afternoon at a Queens Burger King.

"Do I have to wear a wire for this meeting, Detective?" asked Leon, after hanging up the telephone.

"You'll definitely be wired for sound."

"I figured as much."

"You want to get them to talk about the Judge Fatima West murder," instructed Detective Lesper.

"And see if you can get them to talk about Ruffy Shea," added Detective Podell. "There has to be something more to it than the money for them to target him."

"Okay," replied Leon, thinking, *Fat chance to get me talking to them about us killing somebody.*

"Now, let's go get you cleaned up, Leon," said Lesper. "After that, Detective Podell will wire you up."

"I can make it home on my own, I'll call you and we can hook up when it's time to head out to the Burger King."

"Not a chance Leon, we aren't leaving you until after you have that meeting. Besides, you have to head the tape."

"What's that mean?"

"All it means is that you identify yourself on the tape and state the date, time and who you're going to be meeting," explained Podell.

When the detectives took Leon home to freshen up, they were shocked to see where he was living. The sight of the abandoned building of which Leon had taken control of brought safety issues into question. When he was informed that he was in violation of the law by living there, Leon seemed unfazed.

"Are you guys gonna find me someplace better?" he asked.

The detectives let the subject drop, not wanting to be burdened with such a task.

"We'll be waiting outside for you, Leon," advised Podell, thinking that the building might be unsafe structurally.

"We are not," voiced Detective Lesper emphatically, "we're going inside with him."

"Leon can freshen up without us having to hold his hand, Lena."

"C'mon, Scott, the building isn't going to fall down." Lesper then turned to Leon. "Is there anybody else living in there?"

"A lady friend may be inside."

"Okay, let's go in and get you cleaned up," said Lena. "And remember, don't try anything stupid."

"You got nothing to worry about with me," assured Leon, as he felt his pocket to make sure that he had the keys to his vehicle on him.

Detective Lesper noticed the poor condition of the pillows and blankets atop the weathered mattress that dominated the living room. She turned to look at Detective Podell to see his reaction to the living conditions. Podell, who had reluctantly agreed to enter the building, was shaking his head disapprovingly.

"My lady friend must be out someplace," commented Leon. Detective Podell looked at the empty trash barrel that, according to the address written on the barrel, belonged to a house on another block. The barrel, which blocked the staircase that led to the second floor, was half filled with empty beer cans.

"Did you drink all this beer?" asked Podell, addressing Leon.

"No, my lady friend likes her beer. She lives on it."

Podell's next question was put forth bluntly. "How the hell can you live in a dump like this?"

"Now you know why I signed on to pull that job with Sarah," replied Leon. "It takes money to step up."

"I suppose," voiced Podell. "And this lady friend of yours, just where does she fit in?"

"She serves a purpose for right now."

"I don't get it, Leon."

"Look, I'm not with her because of her beauty," revealed Leon. "It's those monthly checks she gets that appeal to me."

"Where do you wash up?" asked Detective Lesper, changing the subject. She found Leon's indelicate honesty to be bothersome.

"There's a bathroom right here on the first floor."

"You have a working bathroom here?" asked Podell.

"No, but I have plenty of water to take a birdbath."

"Where do you get the water from?"

"I get water from the fireplug outside."

"Show me the bathroom," said Lesper. After inspecting the bathroom, the detective gave Leon the go-ahead to wash up. "Just leave the door open," she said, "I'll be standing right outside."

"First, I have to go get some clothes to wear."

"Go on, get what you need, and hurry up about it."

After grabbing some clothes to change into, Leon returned to the bathroom. "No peeking," he said to Lesper before he began to cleanse himself.

The comment embarrassed the detective, who stepped away from the bathroom door. A few minutes later Detective Lesper's attention was drawn to the front room of the house after hearing voices coming from that direction. Observing her partner engaged in conversation with a large woman, Lesper made her way to the front room to see what was going on. Leaving Leon unsupervised was a tactical mistake.

"And now, who is this woman?" asked Leon's lady friend, who was carrying a case of the cheapest beer available.

"I already told you, we're detectives," answered Podell.

"Where is Leon?"

"Getting cleaned up," answered Lesper, entering the conversation.

"What's he supposed to have done?"

Once he realized that Detective Lesper's attention had been diverted, Leon seized his opportunity to slip away. He crawled from the bathroom unnoticed and retreated to the rear of the house, where he made his exit through a back window.

Once on the street, Leon took refuge inside the back of a truck that was parked in one of the factory lots on the block. He hid himself behind some cardboard boxes with the intention of remaining there until he felt it was safe to leave.

##########

WALDO ORDERED HIS DETECTIVES BACK to the squad when informed that Leon had slipped away. When they arrived, he feigned annoyance at their shoddy police work, when in fact he was delighted. With Leon on the loose, Waldo saw his chance to tap into Ruffy Shea's bankroll.

Waldo wasted no time in contacting Miltie, who was to notify Ruffy that Leon was more than likely on the loose somewhere by the South Brooklyn waterfront. Miltie was further told that Ruffy was now in a race with the detectives to find Leon. To give Ruffy an advantage over the authorities, Waldo held back his detectives for as long as he could.

"What do you make of this, Lena?" asked Detective Podell, when alone with his partner in the squad room.

"I don't know, Scott. I thought the lieutenant would be up one side of us and down the other."

"I did, too. I figured him to write us up for sure."

"He still may, if we don't find Leon. I got an idea, Scott."

"What's that?"

"I'm getting us some help."

Detective Lesper telephoned headquarters to speak with Detective Von Hess. After gaining the assurance of Von Hess that their conferral would remain confidential, she informed the senior detective of the entire Leon Crabbe development from the beginning. She then requested the assistance of Von Hess in finding Leon.

"Let me talk to the sergeant," said Von Hess after jotting down some of the particulars. He then went to fill in Markie.

"What do you think, Sarge?" asked Von Hess, after apprising the sergeant of what Detective Lesper told him.

"I can't understand how she and her partner could be so

172

careless," voiced Markie, critical of the detectives. "How could they take their eyes off him?"

"I don't know, Sarge. I guess they just made a mistake. Lesper and her partner got a lot of egg on their face over this. What do you say we give them a hand?"

"Yeah, I suppose we could help out. But to tell you the truth, I wouldn't blame Waldo for sticking a complaint up their ass."

Von Hess offered no opinion one way or the other. Once Markie posted his superiors, he and Von Hess went to their car. Much to their chagrin, they discovered their vehicle, which was parked on the street a few blocks from headquarters, had two tires slashed. Having to secure two new tires delayed their response to South Brooklyn.

As Markie and Von Hess tended to their car, Detective Lesper and her partner were seated outside their Queens precinct in their car. They were waiting for their squad commander to join them.

"What the hell is keeping him," asked Detective Podell.

"I don't know, Scott, but I do know that this procrastination isn't like him."

When Waldo finally joined his detectives, he directed Lesper to drive to Brooklyn. "Go back to the abandoned building. Maybe Leon went back there," said Waldo. "I'll go in," said the squad commander when they arrived at their destination.

"Okay, Loo," said Detective Lesper as she and her partner began to exit their vehicle.

"You two, stay in the car. I'll go in alone."

The bewildered detectives simply looked at each other. "What's that about?" asked Podell after the lieutenant was out of range to hear him.

"I got no idea," answered the equally puzzled Lesper.

Waldo walked into the abandoned building like he owned it. Seeing Leon's lady friend on the mattress, he wasted no time in approaching her.

"Who are you?" the squad commander demanded to know.

"Who am I? Who are you to bust in here?" asked Leon's housemate, who had been in and out of slumber.

"I'm Lieutenant Waldo Reale," announced Waldo, as if his name meant something.

"I was just leaving," she said, getting to her feet. Leon's lady friend was thinking the squad commander was there to take official action against her for trespassing.

"Leon's not here, right?" asked Reale.

"What do you want with him?"

"This is police business. Are you expecting him back?"

"All his things are here, and his wheels are parked outside. What do you think?"

The squad commander didn't reply. Satisfied, he turned around and exited the building.

Waldo returned to the unmarked police car and got in. "Take me back to the office, Lena. After you drop me off, check the hotels and see if you can come up with Leon. Maybe he checked in someplace."

"His vehicle is parked outside, Loo. I think maybe we should sit on the car—" suggested Podell.

"Did I ask you what you're thinking!" barked the lieutenant, annoyed at Podell offering his opinion.

"Do you want one of us to stay behind and sit on his car, Loo?" suggested Lesper.

"You too?" said Waldo gruffly. "He ain't coming back for his car. It would be too risky. Now get me back to the squad." Once dropped off at the precinct, the squad commander waited for his detectives to drive off. He then walked to the nearest pay phone to telephone Miltie, who was told to promptly get word to Ruffy Shea. The message conveyed was brief and to the point: "Tell your boss that Leon will probably be returning to where his vehicle is parked." Waldo then provided Miltie with the address of the abandoned building in Brooklyn.

########

LEON EMERGED FROM THE BACK of the truck that provided his shelter once he believed that the detectives terminated their search for him.

174

Taking catlike strides, Leon scooted to the abandoned building he called home, finding his lady friend sitting in a chair drinking a can of beer. Somewhat numb from the intoxicants she had consumed, she expressed no indication of surprise upon seeing Leon.

"The cops were here looking for you, Leon....what did you do?" she asked.

"They got me pegged for something I had nothing to do with," answered Leon dishonestly. "I have to make tracks until I can get this thing straightened out."

"But what are they accusing you of?"

"I got no time to waste talking about it. I need some money."

"I got no money for you," she replied, telling her own lie. "Look, sugar, it's time for you to pay some rent," Leon announced as he began to rifle her purse. "How much money have you stashed in here?"

"Hey, wait a minute," she protested, attempting to rise from her seat.

Leon shoved her back down into the wooden chair, causing one of its legs to collapse. As she struggled to get up Leon pushed his lady friend back down to the floor.

"Stay down there!" he ordered sternly. He then removed the cash that was contained in her purse.

"You bastard!" the victimized woman cried out, reaching up for the cash that he held in his hand. "That has to last me until next month."

"Relax, will ya," said Leon, smacking her hand away. "I gotta split for a while," he said, holding her at bay with an outstretched arm. Here, I'm leaving you a fifty."

"Where are you going?"

"Indiana," answered Leon, making up a destination. "I got a cousin there that's a lawyer."

"Are you coming back?"

"Sure, I'll be back as soon as I can, baby. You can stay here for as long as you want."

"You're heading out now?"

"First, I gotta get a couple of hours' sleep. I was up all night in a jail cell."

"You gonna sleep here?" she asked, hoping to get the chance to reclaim her money when Leon dozed off.

"It's too hot for me to stay here. I'll lay low at the foot of Atlantic Avenue. It'll be dead over there at this time."

"Do you want a couple of beers to take with you?" she asked, all apparently forgiven.

"Yeah, thanks," he said, taking six cans of beer. "Here, have some suds on me," he added, tossing her a cold can.

##########

WITH DELAY NOT AN OPTION, Sarah needed to formulate a plan to take out Ruffy Shea in a timely fashion. She knew that if Ruffy ever found out that she had masterminded the move against him, he'd come after her with an even greater vengeance. With things now having evolved into a dog-eat-dog situation, Sarah couldn't procrastinate.

"We can't give that son of a bitch a chance to ambush us," she declared adamantly. "We're getting Ruffy before he gets us, Mickey."

"Yeah, but what if—" began Mickey before being hushed. "You gotta stop with the hand-wringing, Mickey. You're distracting me from what I have to do!" she scolded.

"All right, Sarah, you tell me what you want me to do."

"The first thing is that we have to be careful when we leave this apartment. Even though nobody knows that we're staying with Greta, we can't let our guard down."

"Okay, Sarah, I hear you."

In an effort to bolster Mickey's confidence, Sarah gave him one of her guns. 'Here, take it," she said, passing the handgun to Mickey. "You'll feel better once you get used to packing." As was usually the case, Mickey succumbed to Sarah's will and agreed to arm himself with the revolver.

"Where the hell did you get all these guns, Sarah?" he asked after he glimpsed into one of her travel bags.

"One of my regulars gave them to me," she replied, referring to a man she used to service outside the brothel on her own time. "Too bad he died, he was a good guy….and there are no serial numbers on these guns," she added. "Stick the gun in your waistband, Mickey. Trust me, you'll feel like a new man."

Mickey practiced walking around the apartment with the gun tucked in his waistband. He surprised himself at how quickly he became acclimated to carrying a weapon. Once comfortable packing he stood in front of a mirror to observe himself. Mickey took out the gun and pointed it at his reflection in the mirror. Satisfied, he returned the weapon to his waistband.

As Sarah said, being armed had a transformative effect on Mickey. The ready access to a handgun went a long way in help easing his concerns of running into Ruffy or one of his goons on the street.

Bolstered by the equalizer Mickey assumed a strut as he traveled from the bedroom to the kitchen and then back again. In his delusional thinking, he began to see himself as an actual desperado. It was an attitude adjustment that didn't go unrecognized by Sarah, who chuckled at the transformation.

While Mickey still remained far from the hardened criminal Sarah wanted to mold him into, at least now she saw a man with potential in him.

Sarah informed Mickey that it was time to identify another bank with an ATM that was conducive to ripping off elderly withdrawers. As expected, Mickey went along without balking. Sarah sent him out to get his car, which was parked several blocks away from where they were staying.

"What about getting Ruffy?" Mickey asked.

"We need the money in order to move ahead with the plan I have for that bastard."

"Where do you want to start looking for a bank?"

"Brooklyn," Sarah answered. "I think it's best for us to keep moving around to different boroughs. It'll take the cops longer to detect a pattern."

"How do you know all this stuff, Sarah?"

Sarah was amused by Mickey's question. "I suppose I'm going

to have to teach you everything."

"What do you mean?"

"Never mind, Mickey, you'll learn. Go and get the car, I'll be outside waiting for you."

"Just give me a few minutes. The car is parked over by the school."

"Okay, but hurry up. Don't forget, we have a date with Leon later at Burger King."

"I know, but I still can't figure how he managed to get out of jail."

"We'll see what he has to say about that," voiced Sarah. "Go on. I'll be waiting outside for you."

"When is Greta coming home?"

"I have no idea. Sometimes I just don't know about that girl."

"What do you mean?"

"She still misses Fats. I don't know why. She didn't lose much."

20

Ruffy Gets Rough

EXACTLY HOW RUFFY SHEA GOT close to Philly Rava, the boss of the Rava organized crime family, was something not openly discussed. Their friendship came about because of an incident that occurred years prior. At that time, Ruffy was a young hoodlum seeking to find his way, while Philly Rava was a newly minted family soldier.

The two first crossed paths when Ruffy was driving home after an evening of barhopping. It was getting close to daybreak when he crept along in his car in search of a parking space. Ruffy's attention was drawn to a man standing in the street who appeared unsteady on his feet. As he drew closer, he recognized the man to be Philly Rava, a neighborhood gangster who he only knew by reputation.

Ruffy paused to watch as the obviously intoxicated mobster attempted to steady himself. Rava, who had a car key in his hand, was bouncing off the driver's side of a freshly waxed black Cadillac that presumably belonged to him. Seeing that the gangster was in no condition to drive, Ruffy decided to intervene.

Upon seeing Ruffy, the drunken man began raving incoherently. Ruffy managed to gather that the inebriated Rava was claiming to have just shot someone. At this point, Ruffy thought the crime family soldier was just talking gibberish. Thinking that it might benefit him at some point down the road, Ruffy decided to drive Rava home. *What the hell,* thought Ruffy, *he might remember that I put myself out for him.*

Ruffy managed to convince the organized crime soldier to let him drive him home. After traveling a block, Rava began babbling that he couldn't find his gun. Now taking Rava more seriously, Ruffy returned to where the gangster's car was parked to look for the weapon. He was of the belief that Rava might have accidentally dropped the gun because of his intoxicated state.

Ruffy commenced his search near where Rava's car was parked. Much to his surprise, he discovered the body of a dead man on the ground between two parked cars, located approximately 200 feet from Rava's Cadillac. The bullet hole in the murdered man's forehead made it clear that he had been executed. Next to the body was a .32-caliber handgun. Ruffy picked up the weapon and hurried to his own car, where he found Philly Rava dozing.

Ruffy quickly distanced himself from the crime scene. He pulled into the parking lot of a nearby all-night diner. Leaving Rava in the car, he entered the diner to pick up a container of black coffee for his passenger. After consuming the beverage, Rava finally began to come around. It was at this point that Ruffy ascertained his home address.

By the time they arrived at Rava's home, the soldier sobered up enough for Ruffy to give him back his gun. Rava took the weapon without saying anything. This incident garnered Ruffy a friend for life.

"You got steel balls, kid," said Rava finally, nodding his head approvingly. "What's your name?"

"Ruffy Shea."

A tired smile crossed Rava's face upon hearing the name. "What kind of name is Ruffy?"

"It's a nickname. My real name is Rufus."

"I think you better stick to Ruffy. Look, come back here

180

tomorrow, I'm gonna do something for you, kid."

Ruffy's criminal career took an upward turn thanks to the influence of his new friend. The two entered into a number of joint business ventures, with Rava always remaining in the background as a silent partner. As Ruffy prospered, the friendship blossomed to where there was nothing Ruffy wouldn't do for Philly Rava. This included being Rava's personal assassin. By the time Philly Rava became the boss of the family that came to bear his name, Ruffy's special status was cemented within the family.

########

RUFFY IMMEDIATELY CONTACTED Joe Bullet's, who was a reliable enforcer in his own right, after speaking to Miltie. "What's up, Skipper?" asked Joe, who was playing cards at the social club.

"Come over to the house, Joe," instructed Ruffy. "Bring a pair of Hush Puppies," he added cryptically. Joe understood that Ruffy was telling him to bring along two silencer-equipped handguns.

"They gotta be totally nuts," said Joe after Ruffy informed him of Sarah and Mickey's plot.

"They're gonna be more than nuts when I get through with them, I'll tell you that. Are you ready?" asked Ruffy.

"Lock and load, Skipper," voiced Joe without hesitation.

Just prior to heading out, Joe handed Ruffy one of the silencer-equipped guns. Ruffy slipped the weapon into the interior pocket of the long black overcoat he wore.

"Look at this shithouse," commented Joe after they arrived at the abandoned building believed to house Leon Crabbe.

Upon entering the unlocked dwelling, the last thing the men expected to find was a woman fast asleep on a mattress that covered the living room floor. Ruffy kicked at the snoring woman's feet a couple of times to wake her. When this met with no success, he grabbed her by her clothing and rolled her off the mattress. Ruffy then turned her on her back so that she faced the ceiling. Her mouth agape, she gave off a stink of beer that was nauseating.

"She's tanked up," commented Ruffy.

As Joe looked around the room, he noticed the barrel containing empty beer cans. "Jeeze, take a look at this," he said, pointing to the contents of the barrel.

"Go get one of those beers by the window," said Ruffy, "and pour some on her face."

"I should pour some down her throat," said Joe after fetching the beer.

"She'll probably like it," commented Ruffy.

Joe stood over the sleeping woman after opening the beer. After pouring beer onto the face of the sleeping woman, he then unleashed a brisk smack to her face in an effort to bring her around.

Ruffy began asking about Leon's whereabouts as she began to come to. When Leon's lady friend claimed not to know, Ruffy took matters to another level. He removed the leather belt that held up his pants. Even after he threatened to strike her with the belt, she remained steadfast in her denial of Leon's whereabouts.

Ruffy struck Leon's lady friend a vicious lick across her thigh with the belt. He was astonished to see that her only reaction was a quizzical stare. She was too numb to feel the hurt caused by the blow.

Ruffy wrapped the belt around the alcoholic's neck. Imminent strangulation proved effective. Once allowed to catch her breath, the assaulted woman became amenable to questioning. Ruffy was told that Leon could likely be found sleeping in a van parked somewhere in the vicinity of the waterfront, near the end of Atlantic Avenue. He was also informed that Leon's vehicle had out-of-state plates. Now satisfied, Ruffy returned to using the belt for the purpose of holding up his pants.

"I think it would be smart if you keep your trap shut about our visit over here, sister," warned Joe Bullets. "I don't think you really want to see us again."

The ordeal Leon's lady friend had gone through had left her

too weak to speak any more than she had to. As she held her throat with both hands, she nodded that she got his message.

##########

RUFFY AND JOE BULLETS LOCATED THE VEHICLE they were looking for on a side street just off Atlantic Avenue. They converged on the vehicle cautiously, finding it unsecured.

"If he left this shit box open, he's gotta be coming back soon," said Joe. "He's probably in one of the dives up the block on Atlantic Avenue. Do you know what he looks like, Skipper?"

"Yeah, I got a good look at him the night he tried to break into my house. Head over to the bars. Let's see if we can find him," said Ruffy. He soon spotted Leon coming out of one of the establishments. "There he is, on the left side, coming in our direction!" said Ruffy.

"You want us to take him now?"

"No, not yet, Joe. Stay with him. Let's see where he goes." Making a U-turn, Joe drove slowly behind Leon at a safe distance. They followed their prey as he proceeded to his parked van. Once Leon neared his vehicle, Ruffy drew his gun. "Get up on him, Joe," ordered Ruffy.

Once in close proximity, Ruffy fired a round from the car. The bullet struck Leon in the leg, causing him to collapse to the ground.

"You got him!" Joe announced enthusiastically.

"Kill the car lights and park, Joe," Ruffy directed, "and get me the tire iron from the trunk."

Ruffy dragged Leon to the sidewalk side of the parked van. When Ruffy held his hand out, it was a cue for Joe to hand him the tire iron. Ruffy proceeded to beat Leon about his head and torso.

"Ease up, Skipper," voiced Joe, unless you want to kill him without talking to him first." Ruffy backed off, passing the bloodied tire iron to Joe. "Let's get him in the van."

Once inside the van, Ruffy hovered over his victim, pointing his gun directly below Leon's belt. "What was the idea of coming to my house?" asked Ruffy.

"I....uhhh....stammered Leon, having difficulty getting the words out.

"You got exactly two seconds to come up with an answer before I shoot off your third leg," threatened Ruffy. "Now, what was it all about?"

"Sarah," answered Leon weakly, "it was her and her boyfriend."

"What's the boyfriend's name?"

"Mickey, I think....he's got red hair."

"What was the purpose?"

"They want you....dead." The response didn't phase Ruffy. "That little prick Mickey is smarter than I thought, Joe," said Ruffy, turning to his accomplice. "With me out of the picture he avoids having to pay me the money he owes me."

"What do we do with this asshole, Ruffy?" asked Joe, referring to Leon.

"I had no idea who you were, man," whined Leon. "Sarah told me you were a drug dealer."

"She said that?" asked Ruffy, gravely. "What else did she say?"

"She....she's the one calling the shots. Give me a play, will ya?" begged Leon, hoping that mercy would be considered.

"Sarah told you that I was a drug dealer?" asked Ruffy, who was unable to fathom how she knew of one of his darkest secrets. *How much else does she know?* Ruffy wondered. *Does she know about Philly too?*

"Yeah, I swear it....that's what she said. She didn't tell me anything else....give me a break, will ya?" Leon pleaded.

"Where can we find Sarah?"

"I don't know where she lives. All I got is a phone number for her."

"You want a break? Joe's gonna give you one. Go ahead, Joe, you do the honors."

Joe fired his gun once, putting a bullet into Leon's head.

"What next, Skipper?" asked Joe, as if nothing had happened.

"We have to go hunt down Sarah. She has to be someplace."

21

Mickey Breaks His Cherry

MICKEY WALKER HAD THE MISFORTUNE of running into a diligent police officer who took his work seriously. The officer's shoes were shined, his pants pressed and the gun he carried was well oiled. All this translated into a guardian dedicated to protecting life and property.

The officer was assigned to a school post in close proximity to a narcotics-prone location. His purpose for being there was to prevent a questionable element from congregating near the school. With things being quiet throughout the morning, the officer made his way over to the local firehouse to spend his meal hour. After having lunch with the firefighters, he returned to his post to find that a crowd had formed around two men embroiled in a nose-to-nose altercation.

After separating the combatants, the officer ordered everyone in the vicinity to disperse. Mixed among the onlookers was a man who had momentarily stopped to witness the argument.

Mickey Walker's lingering proved to be costly. After making eye contact with the officer, the armed Mickey suddenly appeared frightened. His apparent skittishness caused the officer to suspect that he was in possession of something illegal. "Hey, you," called out the cop, "hold up a second." The officer placed his hand on his gun as he approached Mickey. Not knowing what to do, Mickey froze in place. Although silent, his quivering lips spoke volumes. "Put your hands up against that car," said the cop, pointing to a parked vehicle.

Having no intention of going for the gun he carried, Mickey complied without question. When the officer patted Mickey down, he discovered the weapon. After taking charge of the handgun, the officer handcuffed Mickey, who offered no resistance. Although Mickey's eyes squinted in pain from the pinch of the tightly applied handcuffs, he never conveyed his discomfort.

"What are you doing with this gun?"

"I, err...need it," replied Mickey.

"Need it for what?" Mickey was unable to think of something to say. "Skip it, you might as well save your answer for the judge," advised the officer, who then radioed for a sector car to provide transportation to the precinct.

When the radio car arrived, Mickey was placed in the back seat, where he sat alongside the arresting officer. During the ride to the precinct the transporting officers chatted amicably among themselves about things that had nothing to do with Mickey or police work.

At the stationhouse Mickey nervously stood before the front desk. After the desk sergeant documented his arrest by making an entry in the command log, Mickey was processed. The booking procedure further entailed filling out forms, fingerprinting, photographing, and a strip search. Mickey was then removed to a room where he underwent questioning while cuffed to the chair he sat in.

"What is this, the first time you've been arrested?" asked the cop, noticing the depressed look on Mickey's face.

"Yes."

The officer could see by his demeanor that Mickey was far from a hardened criminal. "Relax, you're not going to the electric chair, you know," said the officer. "You don't seem like the type to be packing a gun. What gives?"

"It's a long story," replied Mickey.

"I got time."

"I'd rather not say, Officer."

"You know, the serial number being scratched off the gun is gonna make things a little tougher on you."

"How much time do you think I'll get?"

"That's hard to say, a lot depends on the judge."

"Can I make a call, Officer?'

"You're entitled. Who do you want to call?"

"I want to call my girlfriend."

"Let me have her full name, number and address and I'll call her for you."

"You need all that?"

"Do you want to call her or not?" The officer dialed up Sarah on a police department phone after receiving the requested information. "Is this Sarah?" he asked when his call was answered.

"Who is this?" asked Sarah loudly."

"That's her," said Mickey, who was able to hear Sarah's voice. "Hang on, Mickey wants to talk to you," said the arresting officer, who then passed the phone to the prisoner.

"Sarah?"

"Mickey!" exclaimed Sarah. "I've been calling you for an hour! Why didn't you pick up the phone?"

"I couldn't, I'm in the precinct. I got busted."

There was silence. Finally Sarah spoke. "Busted for what?"

"The cop caught me with the gun."

"Don't say another word. I'll be right there. Where are you?"

"I'm at the precinct near where we live."

At the precinct Sarah was able to speak with her boyfriend. "You shouldn't have come here, Sarah," said the prisoner. "It could be dangerous."

"No one knows about us in this precinct, Mickey, so don't worry. Just make sure that you keep your mouth shut," instructed Sarah.

"I know, but what do I do for a lawyer?"

"We don't need to pay any lawyer because this is only your first arrest. The court will appoint a legal aid attorney to represent you."

"What do I say to the legal aid?"

"Say that you found the gun on the street and that you were walking up to the cop to give it to him. Then say he arrested you without giving you a chance to explain. You have no record, so stick to that story and you should be okay."

"I understand," said Mickey, sighing loudly.

"Stay calm, Mickey. This is only your first arrest," advised Sarah. "Welcome to the club."

"The cop said that I may get time."

"Look at the bright side of it. This saves you from having to make any more payments to that bastard Ruffy."

"How do you figure that?"

"By the time you're back on the street the cemetery will have another tenant," advised Sarah, who was talking about Ruffy Shea. "I'll see to that."

Before Sarah left, she was given Mickey's phone and personal effects to safeguard.

##########

MARKIE AND VON HESS left for Brooklyn once they had their damaged tires replaced at the department repair shop. They proceeded directly to the abandoned building where Leon was living. Their hope was to find a clue as to where Leon might have gone.

When the investigators entered the building, they heard music coming from the small pink transistor radio that stood on the paint chipped mantelpiece.

Leon's lady friend was sitting in a chair dipping into a family size bag of potato chips that rested between her legs. She gently shook the can of beer in her hand to determine how much remained. She was happy to see that she still had a few sips to go before having to get up for a fresh brew.

Fearing another attack, Leon's lady friend recoiled at the presence of more men she didn't know. She reached for the wrench that she kept on the floor next to her chair. Determined not to be victimized a second time, she was psychologically prepared for intruders. She raised the wrench as the detectives moved closer to her.

"Stay back," she ordered, "or I'll part your hair!"

Markie and Von Hess, who ceased advancing, just looked at each other. Markie produced his identification and explained his purpose for being there.

"Are you all right?" asked the sergeant, noticing the bruising around the woman's throat and cheek. It was obvious to him that she had had a recent going over.

"What do you care?"

"I care enough," replied Markie. "Who roughed you up?"

"I know what you're thinking, but you're wrong."

"Tell me, what am I thinking?"

"You're thinking it was Leon who beat me, but it wasn't Leon," she replied. "It was two men who came by. I don't know who they were."

"Are you *sure* it wasn't Leon?"

"Leon only shoves. These were two real roughhouse men. I never seen them before, but I could tell that they were hoods. They were after Leon."

"Did they say why?"

"I don't know….I'd like somebody to tell me why everybody is looking for Leon all of a sudden?"

"I don't know about anyone else," answered Markie, "but the law needs to talk to him."

"Do you have any idea where Leon is?" injected Von Hess.

"I don't know where he went. He went out the back window when the other detectives were here. I never saw him again," she lied.

"Take a look around, Ollie," said the sergeant.

While Von Hess examined the first floor, he took note of all the empty beer cans in the trash barrel. The inspection of the premises conducted by Von Hess uncovered no clues as to where Leon might have gone.

"The people who beat you came by *after* Leon ran away from the detectives, right?"

"That's right."

"Look," said Markie, speaking softly, "why don't you just tell us where you think Leon might have gone?"

"I told you, I don't know," answered the woman.

"Look at me and listen," said Markie. " If you don't come clean, I'm gonna have to bounce your ass out into the gutter and have this place padlocked," he explained. "Now, you don't wanna sleep in the cold gutter tonight with the rats nibbling at your ass, do you?"

"It won't be the first time," replied Leon's lady friend, refusing to be swayed. "Besides, I have a place to go to."

"Who drank all that beer?" asked Von Hess.

"What, is it a crime to drink beer now?"

Markie knew it was time to switch tactics. "Ollie, give me the keys to the car. You keep our girlfriend company. I'll be back shortly."

Markie returned to the abandoned building carrying a brown paper bag that contained a six pack of Budweiser, a large bag of cheese doodles, a pint of cheap whiskey, and plastic cups. He removed the contents of the bag and poured two shots of whiskey.

"Do you want one, Ollie?"

"No thanks, Sarge."

The sergeant then opened a can of beer to share as a chaser. "Here's to you, kid," said the sergeant, raising his drink. "I know that you're a little mixed up right now, but we'll get you through this mess."

As they drank, Leon's lady friend became more amenable to conversing. Markie had found a way to speak her language. After the second round of whiskey, they became chums. "You're all right, for a cop," she said. "Why weren't you nice like this when you first came in?"

"What did those two louses want from you?" asked Markie, when he felt that the time was right. "Why did they rough you up?"

"The bastards came in here looking for Leon. When I told them he wasn't around, they started in on me. The one guy choked me with his belt."

"Do you need to go to a hospital?"

"No, I'm fine."

"Did they indicate why they were looking for Leon?" asked Von Hess, joining the conversation.

"They never mentioned why," she replied, gulping down her shot. "How about another shooter?" she asked, holding out her cup for a refill.

"So you told them where Leon was?" asked Von Hess, as Markie replenished her cup.

"Yeah, what else could I do? Those bastards would have killed me if I didn't tell."

"Do you know who these men were?"

"I never saw them before, honest."

"More beer?" asked Markie.

"I don't mind if I do. Say, ain't you getting kind of old to be on the force?" she asked, addressing Von Hess. Both Markie and Von Hess found her question to be amusing.

"So, now that we're old friends, why don't you tell us where Leon went?" asked Markie.

"You're a smoothie, you are," she said, pointing her finger at the sergeant. After a long slug of beer, she happened to think of the money Leon took from her. The thought prompted her to reveal what she knew. "Since you've been decent, I'll tell you. The last thing he said was that he was going to park somewhere by the foot of Atlantic Avenue. He wanted to get some sleep before leaving town."

"Where was he headed for?"

"Indiana."

"What kind of vehicle does he drive?" asked Von Hess,

"It's a van," she answered.

"Do you remember the color?"

"I can't remember. Maybe white, it was a light color. But I know it has out-of-state license plates."

After getting a description of her attackers, Markie and Von Hess proceeded to the foot of Atlantic Avenue. When they located the van in question, Markie checked the door to the van. Finding it open, he entered the vehicle and discovered Leon's body.

Von Hess telephoned Detective Lesper to tell her that they had located Leon. When Lesper called her office to inform Waldo that Leon was found murdered in Brooklyn, the squad commander displayed no reaction. Inwardly he experienced a sense of elation. Since Leon's body was found in another borough, far from his own jurisdiction, things couldn't have worked out better for the squad commander. Furthering his satisfaction was the money he was going to receive from Ruffy. Because of their cordial relationship with Leon's lady friend, Markie and Von Hess were asked to remain in Brooklyn to assist the local Brooklyn squad in the Leon Crabbe murder case.

Leon's lady friend was important to the investigation because she could identify the men who had been looking for Leon. To the dismay of the investigators, there wasn't enough booze in Brooklyn to convince her to try and identify the men who assaulted her.

22

Amos Reveals His Dark Side

MOST WOULD SAY THAT AMOS WEST had a lot of things going for him. Successful professionally, Amos was debt free, possessed a solid education and was happily married to a judge with a promising future. Unfortunately, things changed drastically after the passing of his wife.

In business, the graduate of New York University School of Law had gotten used to winning. His ruthlessness almost always gained him the upper hand during testy negotiations. Spoiled by his record of successes, Amos was a poor loser when things didn't go his way. Particularly disturbing to him was his having to comply with the dictates of a mobster against his will.

The visit to his home by Italo, on behalf of his cousin Ciro, left an irritation in Amos that required soothing. Being told that he wasn't to identify the killer of his wife was a humbling Amos never previously experienced. Consumed with the need to retaliate, Amos struck back at Sarah Ince, holding her responsible for all his woes. He justified his intent to do Sarah physical harm by convincing himself that the death of his wife needed closure.

Having no desire to personally take a hand in an act of violence, Amos turned to a trusted friend to provide him with a resource that was up to the task.

Amos was having lunch with Marvin Butterworth, a fellow attorney, at the 21 Club when he communicated his need for a goon willing to administer a beating. In reaction to learning the circumstances surrounding the surprise request, Marvin attempted to discourage Amos from embarking on such a dangerous path.

"Amos, listen to me," urged the older attorney. "Forget this nonsense. You have too much to lose to get involved in what you're proposing. Let it go."

"This woman needs to learn that she can't get away with doing something like that to Fatima," countered Amos.

"Fatima is gone, and she's not coming back, Amos, no matter what you do. If you hung this harlot from a tree in Central Park, all you'd be accomplishing is putting yourself at risk. Why do that?"

"I appreciate your concern, Marvin. But do you know of someone who can meet my need or not?"

"Well, I tried," said Marvin, conceding to the determination of Amos. "I think that I can introduce you to someone who might fit your purpose."

"Who is that?"

"He's a client of mine, an ex-detective."

"He'd be receptive to something like this?"

"I'm not exactly sure of that—he certainly doesn't need the money. He may help you as a favor to me."

"We can trust him?"

"He's trustworthy," answered Marvin. "He has to be."

"Why is that?"

"He's not without sin himself."

"Great, now here is what I want him to do...."

"Spare me the details, Amos. All I'm doing is facilitating a meeting. You work out the particulars with him."

########

194

FISHNET BUTTONED UP HIS COAT as he prepared to enter the backyard of the townhouse he had inherited. Armed with a plastic bag containing pond sticks, he ventured out into the cold to feed the colorful koi fish that dwelled in the pond. Fishnet found it fun to name the fish after people he knew. The first name of his late celebrity wife and some of her friends were among those represented in the pond.

The former detective looked down into the water as he dropped a singular pond stick into the drink. He did this in order to see the koi compete for the floating food.

"You're looking good, Sally," he called down to the fish he'd named after his late wife. "You're going to have to be a little quicker, Estelle," he said to the one he named after his wife's lover and fellow murder victim. "Are you two having threesomes with that gigolo Pascal down there? Is he dressing up like a fireman for you, like I did?"

After having his chuckle, the man who resembled Clark Gable noticed the menacing presence of a black cat standing atop the piles of jagged slate that surrounded the pond. This wasn't Fishnet's first run-in with a cat, the one animal he detested.

Fishnet stared at the feline suspiciously, getting the impression that the four-legged creature felt the same way about him. Fishnet rubbed the childhood scar he still carried on the back of his hand. The mark was a reminder of the price he paid for once attempting to yank on a cat's tail.

"Go on and scat," barked Fishnet, "before I slice you open and turn you into a pair of slippers."

Sensing a threat, the cat arched its back. The subsequent hissing was effective enough to give Fishnet pause. Believing that the feline was liable to go berserk and attack, the former detective slowly backed away.

Since the cat sported a collar and appeared well groomed, Fishnet assumed the animal belonged to one of his neighbors. Domesticated or not, Fishnet remained wary of the cat, whom he believed had intended to feast on the koi.

Determined to protect the fish, Fishnet retrieved the large, heavy duty net that rested against the fence not far from the pond. With the net in hand, he stepped toward the cat while bracing himself for a possible lunge by the animal.

"C'mon, you little son of a bitch!" challenged the former detective during their standoff.

Determined to destroy the cat, Fishnet advanced. Holding the net's long pole like a baseball bat, he took aim at the cat's torso. Fishnet swiftly swung the wide circular face of the net. Being struck by the metal that held the netting in place caused the animal to fall over into the pond. As the cat pawed furiously, the koi retreated to safety in the deepest corners of the pond.

Fishnet used the circular metal rim of the net to force the cat underwater. Pinned to the bottom of the pond, the feline furiously fought to get free. Unable to extricate himself, the cat ultimately succumbed.

Now concerned over the possible repercussions connected to killing someone's house cat, Fishnet looked up at the neighboring windows to see if anyone had been watching. With no indication of having been observed, he scooped out the dead cat from the pond. Taking the carcass down into the cellar of the house, Fishnet placed the cat into an empty five-gallon paint bucket. Bringing the bucket to the first floor, he filled it to the top with old newspapers, garbage, and rags. After placing a lid on the bucket, Fishnet then put it inside a black heavy-duty commercial trash bag, where it remained until later disposal.

It was late in the night when Fishnet proceeded to Restaurant Row with the dead cat. He casually placed his trash bag among the restaurant trash that awaited pick up by private sanitation. The following morning Fishnet noticed that messages were affixed to the trees and poles on his block. The postings were from someone named Courtney Meyer. The communication requested that neighbors keep an eye out for her beloved cat, Penny.

##########

AFTER PICKING UP THE PHONE, Fishnet frowned at hearing Marvin Butterworth's voice. Fishnet was never happy about keeping Marvin, his late wife's attorney, on retainer. He saw the lawyer as a pebble in his shoe that he was compelled to tolerate until the time was right for removal.

The former detective suspected that the attorney harbored the opinion that he murdered his wife Sally and her agent/lover. While Marvin never publicly voiced such speculation, Fishnet nevertheless believed that the attorney didn't buy the police findings that determined the deaths to be accidental.

Fishnet feared that Marvin, being an attorney, could raise questions that would resurrect the case that was closed by the Pennsylvania authorities. As it stood, the two seemed to have an unwritten understanding that guaranteed Marvin's silence as long as he continued to receive his inflated retainer checks.

This bird has a shelf life, Fishnet thought as the attorney spoke on the phone to him. Having the threat of Marvin's loose lips looming over him had become increasingly bothersome to Fishnet.

"Hello, my boy...." said the caller jovially.

"What happened, Marvin? Didn't you get your money this month?" asked Fishnet.

"No, no, no....nothing like that, my boy," replied the elderly attorney. "Our account is in order. But I would appreciate it if you would allow me to impose upon you for a small favor."

Here it comes at last, thought the ex-detective, *the big shakedown.*

"What kind of favor, Marvin?"

"I have a business associate, a very dear friend, seeking a remedy for a very sensitive matter that requires someone of your....let's say, resourcefulness."

"You know, there is one thing about you that never ceases to amaze me, Marvin."

"What might that be, my boy?"

"You always dance around before getting to the point. What is it that your friend needs done?"

"Perhaps...."

"What perhaps?" asked Fishnet, who had tired of the vagueness. "What's the story?"

"Very well, the long and the short of it is that my friend's wife was unfortunately murdered in Queens."

"So, what does he need me to do, find the guy who iced his wife?"

"What he needs to discuss with you is a private affair that's best left for him to explain. If you can find the time to speak to him, I'd be very grateful."

Butterworth's continued evasiveness made it clear that something unwholesome was afoot. Fishnet saw it in his interest to appease Butterworth.

"Tell you what, Marvin, as a favor to you, I'll meet with the guy."

"Excellent!" said Butterworth with great enthusiasm. "I'll let him know that he can speak frankly with you."

"Yeah, you do that, Marvin."

"I'll give my friend your number."

"No, don't do that," said Fishnet, who wanted no record of their communicating memorialized. "Just have your friend meet me at The Dancing Elf tonight at 7:00 p.m. It's on West 43rd Street, off 9th Avenue."

"How will he know you?"

"Are you kidding, Marvin?" asked Fishnet. "How many guys in the joint are gonna look like Clark Gable?"

"Point duly noted," conceded Butterworth, momentarily forgetting Fishnet's striking resemblance to the late movie actor. "My friend's name is Amos."

"Okay, Marvin, I'll be talking to you."

"Just a second, my boy, there is one other thing.

"What's that?"

"There is the question of a fee. Be sure to charge liberally for your services—and make it sizable enough to split with me."

##########

FISHNET ARRIVED AT THE DANCING ELF forty-five minutes early.

The venue was an old-school Hell's Kitchen tavern. Fishnet found room at the bar alongside a rum-worn couple who spent far too much time lapping up drinks.

Fishnet signaled the bartender, a gray-haired man of about sixty. The white long-sleeved shirt the bartender wore was crisp and clean, while his black tie was stained.

Recognizing Fishnet, the bartender nodded and walked over. "How are you, Mr. Gable?"

"Just call me Clark," said Fishnet, going along with the joke.

"What'll it be tonight?"

"Let me have an Old Grand Dad on the rocks," ordered Fishnet, who stood at the bar perfectly erect with his shoulders back. The thin mustache he sported, along with the long single breasted navy overcoat and white scarf, made him look more like the late movie star than ever.

Fishnet turned to look at the woman seated on the stool to his right. Her puffed jowls made her older than her years. She had on a long out of style gray tweed coat, brown scarf and a flower in her long salt-and-pepper hair. Fishnet wondered if the short, bearded, sinister-looking man in the newsboy cap standing alongside her was responsible for the two black eyes she sported. His long salt-and-pepper whiskers and droopy hound dog eyes made him appear as someone capable of beating a woman.

In his fifties, the woman's companion seemed to be a person of few words. Occasionally nodding, he seemed to be half paying attention to her chatter as he consistently perused the barroom as if looking for someone.

You gotta watch these quiet bastards, thought the one-time sleuth. *They're always up to something.*

The former detective then glanced to his other side, where a man of about forty-five stood. This fellow, a presentable sort in an immaculate white crew neck sweater, was well groomed. Noticing that Fishnet looked his way, the stranger didn't hesitate to initiate a conversation.

During their interaction Fishnet gathered that the stranger was a high school English teacher. As their conversation furthered it became apparent to Fishnet that the man was hitting on him. This became even more evident once the teacher began expounding on how much of a Clark Gable fan he was.

"Are you in the theater?" asked the educator, looking into Fishnet's eyes hoping to see something that wasn't there.

"No, not me," replied Fishnet, "that racket ain't for guys like me." The ex-detective purposely responded in an abrupt fashion to discourage the interested party. Fishnet underestimated the teacher's determination.

"Well, you certainly look like you could be a leading man. What did you say your name was?"

"Yeah, well, I think you've got the wrong impression of me, pal."

"I think not. You're the macho sort."

"Yeah, that's me," Fishnet said, turning to face the educator head on. Fishnet's manner was such that the stranger began to think that things could get ugly.

"See that waitress?" asked the teacher, pointing to a young woman with dark curly hair. He was attempting to divert Fishnet's attention elsewhere, once realizing that Fishnet could pose as a danger to him.

"What about her?"

"Do you like her?"

"What's not to like?"

"Would you like to meet her?"

"Who are you trying to kid, pal?" asked Fishnet, beginning to tire of the man.

"Seriously, I can help you with her. Give me a minute," said the teacher, leaving his station at the bar.

Fishnet simply shrugged his shoulders and said nothing. Fishnet watched as his new acquaintance engaged the waitress in conversation. When the man returned, he took a sip of his drink before turning to face the former detective. "She'll be by to say hello," he said confidently.

"What did you say to her?"

"I know her; she's a dancer looking to get into a show. So I told her that you were a very important man in the theater district."

Now seeing the teacher in a more favorable light, Fishnet smiled approvingly. "You're a pretty sharp cookie, my friend," he said, appreciating the man's ingenuity.

After a few minutes, the waitress stopped by to introduce herself. Fishnet listened as the young woman went on to explain her career ambitions.

"Maybe I can further your interests, sweetheart," said Fishnet, looking to take advantage of the false narrative the gullible woman believed to be fact. "Let's get together later to discuss things."

After stating this, Fishnet's mind drifted to his other world. He envisioned himself an impresario who was involved in a new Broadway production. He stood on stage before a line of young hopefuls like the woman before him. In his daydream, Fishnet had his pick of the chorus line.

"I said I have to get back to work now," repeated the young woman. "I finish at 10 p.m. when the kitchen closes. How about we meet up then?" When she received no response, she placed her hand on Fishnet's forearm to get his attention.

"What was that?" asked Fishnet, snapping out of his daydream.

"Are you okay?"

"Of course, I was just thinking of an opportunity that might fit you."

"I'm off at 10 p.m." she repeated. "Does that work for you? I'd *really* appreciate you taking the time."

Fishnet smiled as he placed his index finger on her nose. "Sure, baby, I'll be waiting for you right here. What's your name anyway?"

"Cheryl."

After Cheryl happily walked off, Fishnet turned to the teacher who arranged the introduction. He pointed his finger in the teacher's face as a sign of admiration and gave him a wink. "If I ever decide to switch teams, blue eyes, you're the one!" he said. "Hey bartender," Fishnet then called out, "set up my dear friend here with whatever he's having....his thirst is on me tonight."

"Are you joining me?" asked the now grinning teacher. *If I could get a few in him, he could be had*, thought the educator.

##########

AMOS WEST HAD LITTLE TROUBLE FINDING Fishnet when he entered The Dancing Elf. As was usually the case, Fishnet's resemblance to Gable made him easily identifiable.

"You must be Marvin's friend," said Amos, upon approaching Fishnet. "I'm Amos."

"Good to know you, Amos," greeted Fishnet. "Shepherd Fish is the name," he added.

Shepherd Fish was the alias Fishnet had invented for the purpose of scamming people. It was the alias he used when he met the wife he'd murdered.

"Get us a drink, Amos. I'll grab us a table where we can talk."

"What are you having?"

"The bartender knows."

Fishnet secured a small table located a short distance from where he had formerly stood at the bar. When Amos returned with the drinks, he commented on Fishnet's striking resemblance to the late movie star.

"Marvin wasn't exaggerating when he said how much you look like Clark Gable."

"Yeah, I get that all the time. The ladies dig that about me."

"I would think so."

"So, what's your problem, Amos?"

"Our mutual friend said that I could talk plainly to you, am I correct in assuming that?"

"Say what you came here to say, you ain't gonna be shocking me, pal," replied Fishnet. "And remember, I'm no cop no more, so nobody is gonna be looking to rat you out."

Fishnet's assurance made Amos feel better. Over drinks the attorney began to bring the former detective up to speed in connection with the Judge West murder. After being informed of the story to date, Fishnet could see no issue.

"I read about that case in the paper," said Fishnet. "So, your wife was the judge?"

"Yes."

"I can't see, other than you feeling bad that your old lady got clipped, what the problem is."

"I don't think you understand—"

"What's to understand?" asked Fishnet, genuinely seeing little to be concerned about. "You said that the guy who did the shooting is in the cemetery, so what more do you want?"

"Let me tell you. I want the strumpet who set me up to pay a severe physical price."

"The what?"

"The sex worker," clarified Amos.

"Oh, you mean the whore. So, explain to me the situation with this woman of the evening." Amos went on to explain in detail his relationship with Sarah Ince. "Now I get it," said Fishnet. "Okay, now that we established that, what kind of damage do you want inflicted? And how much money are you willing to cough up?"

"I'm willing to compensate you accordingly—"

"How bad do you want this hooker hurt?"

"I want her hospitalized."

"Let me ask you something, where do you go when you take care of business with her? Do you go to her house, a hotel or what?"

"She works in the Manhattan brothel that Marvin and I go to." "Marvin?" asked the shocked Fishnet. "That old buzzard goes to get his pipes cleaned?"

"Marvin remains quite capable."

"He goes with this whore too?"

"No, only I restrict myself to seeing just Sarah. Marvin likes variety."

"Friggin' Marvin, it's just like him to sample all the pies," commented Fishnet. "And you stick to the same chick every time?"

"Yes."

At this juncture a thought came to Fishnet in which he saw a way to benefit himself more than Amos. He began to set the stage for the plan he was mentally formulating.

"Let me give you a piece of advice, Amos. It never pays to do things half-assed. This woman, even if she didn't pull the trigger herself, killed your wife. I see this, as an eye-for-an-eye situation."

"You mean...."

"Yeah, your girlfriend should go bye-bye. Listen, even if she's hurt real bad, left alive she's in a position to fight another day. Why take the chance of her coming out for another round?"

"I'm afraid that murder is out of the question."

"Okay, okay, have it your way," said Fishnet, seeing that Amos was inflexible. "So, she gets a good shellacking."

"How much money do you want for this, Mr. Fish?"

"Forget the money. I don't want any money from you. All I want is for you to do me a small favor in return for my doing you one."

"I don't follow you. What favor could I possibly do for you?"

"My favor is along the same lines as yours. Since we're talking plainly, I'll put the cards on the table. I got it in for somebody the same way you got it in for Sarah."

"You do?"

"Yeah, I do. Tell me something, how close are you to Marvin?"

"We've been friends for years. We still do business deals together."

"Yeah, I gathered as much. The question is can you live without him for a while?"

"What are you driving at?"

"Simply this, sometimes Marvin can get too big for his britches. I'm thinking he needs humbling."

"I don't understand."

"Marvin needs to be taught a lesson, you know, just like Sarah needs one."

"You're suggesting that I play a role in hurting Marvin?" asked the stunned Amos.

"Nobody said anything about you hurting Marvin," conveyed Fishnet. "All I want is for you to lure him to a place where I can have someone throw a good scare into him. I promise, at worst he'll get a slap or two."

"Are you serious?"

"If you do this for me, I'll go as far with Sarah as you tell me to, no more, no less. How is that?"

"Marvin is my friend. I don't want to do anything against him."

"Yeah, well, that's my terms," said Fishnet firmly. "If you want me to scratch your back, then you gotta scratch mine. Marvin and Sarah are a package deal."

Amos couldn't believe his ears. While he wanted Sarah punished, he had no desire to see Marvin harmed. Now having second thoughts, Amos thought it best to play along for the time being.

"What's your timetable concerning Marvin?" asked the attorney.

"I haven't figured out the logistics yet, Amos. We got time with Marvin, so we could take care of Sarah first."

Seeing a way to have his cake and eat it, Amos did some scheming of his own at this point. "Maybe we could work something out…." said Amos.

23

New Deals

AMOS WALKED AWAY FROM his meeting with Fishnet with every intention of reneging on the agreement they had struck. Although his desire to get even with Sarah remained firm, there was no way he was going to engage in any activity that would be detrimental to his friend Marvin.

With his craving for revenge overshadowing caution, Amos chose to take a calculated risk by double-crossing Fishnet. Once Sarah was the recipient of her comeuppance, the late judge's husband aimed to alert Marvin Butterworth of Fishnet's desire to do him harm. Ever confident of Marvin's resourcefulness, Amos believed that his friend would have the wherewithal to derail whatever threat Fishnet posed. In this, he was putting too much stock in Marvin's often-repeated boast that he had the connections that enabled him to "play in the mud with the best of them."

Amos was under the impression that Sarah was still employed at the Manhattan brothel. When Fishnet proposed that he be taken to the bordello, Amos expressed reluctance to do so.

"Why do you need to go there?"

"I gotta see what this Sarah looks like," replied Fishnet, "don't I?"

"Won't my going there raise her suspicions?"

"Why should it?" asked Fishnet. "From what you told me, she should have no idea that you know about her involvement. By not going you might be arousing her curiosity."

"Well, I suppose you're right," acknowledged Amos. "Marvin and I would go there regularly after lunch on Fridays."

"So that's when we'll go. Now remember, when we go there you have to act like nothing happened. You're supposed to have no idea that she set you up."

"What about Marvin? He and I always go there together." "Call him and tell him you can't make it this Friday. Would he go without you?"

"Never, he always relies on me to pick him up and take him." Amos was visibly on edge the Friday that the two men visited the brothel. "Relax," said Fishnet, "you look like you're walking into the hot seat. I hope you ain't getting cold feet on me." "I'm here, aren't I?"

"All right, don't get your nuts in a twist. When we get inside, introduce me as your friend from Long Island."

"Come on in, boys," greeted the madam, readily admitting them after recognizing Amos. "Go in the parlor and get comfortable after you straighten out with me. We have some really beautiful girls working today."

"What about you?" Fishnet asked flirtatiously, finding Queenie to be attractive. "Are you on the roster?"

Amos did a double take after hearing Fishnet's remark. The madam reacted with a half-smile. "Now, aren't you the comedian," she commented.

"What do you expect when I'm looking at a rose among weeds."

"Where did you get him from?" asked Queenie, addressing Amos. Somewhat flattered, she turned her attention back to Fishnet. "You look very familiar to me. Have you been here before?"

"I'm the guy you've been dreaming about," said Fishnet, flashing a cocky smile. He knew that his looking like a fabled movie star of a bygone era usually went a long way with women.

"Yeah, that must be it," commented Queenie, who wasn't entirely put off by Fishnet's flirting.

When summoned, six scantily attired sex workers paraded out into the parlor. When they appeared Fishnet turned to Amos to ask, "Which one is our girl?"

"She's not there."

Fishnet turned to Queenie. "Is this the whole stable?"

"If you're expecting Sharon Stone, you're out of luck," the madam replied tartly. "It's her day off."

"Isn't Sarah working?" asked Amos, politely."

"She's no longer with us."

"What happened?" questioned Fishnet. "I was told she was the whole show."

"She moved on."

"Moved on where?"

"Look, are you here to see one of the girls or not?" asked Queenie, growing impatient of the questions.

Thanks to the money he came into after his wife's death, Fishnet had plenty to spend in order to influence outcomes. The ex-detective began to peel off hundred dollar bills from the ball of cash he carried.

"Maybe this will loosen you up, sweetheart," he said, passing the currency to the madam. It did.

After taking the money the madam turned to the waiting sex workers and declared, "False alarm, girls, go back inside and relax. I'll call you."

Queenie tossed her head in the direction of her desk, indicating for Fishnet and Amos to follow her. She took out a small notebook from her purse and jotted a telephone number down on a slip of paper. She then passed the paper to Fishnet. "Here is Sarah's number," said the madam. "As far as I know, she lives in Queens someplace. Just so you know, you won't find Sarah alone. She'll be with her boyfriend."

"And what is his story?" asked Fishnet. Queenie shrugged, making it clear that there would be no further information provided without additional incentive. "Here, take this," said Fishnet, passing her more cash.

"His name is Mickey Walker," answered the madam after taking the money. "I'd tread lightly if I were you, handsome."
"Why is that?"
"I'm just giving you a word to the wise."
"What, are you gonna leave me hanging?"
"Let me put it to you this way, I wouldn't want to be Sarah or Mickey right now."
"Somebody's after them?"
"Mickey used to have an interest here. You should remember seeing him," Queenie added, addressing Amos. "He was the young guy with the red hair."
"I never met him," voiced Amos.
"He used to be here at night."
"I only come here in the afternoon."
The madam went on to inform the men that Mickey Walker was the son-in-law of Ruffy Shea. "And if you know who Ruffy is, you'll know that he's no one to trifle with. Ruffy's got it in big time for those two. I think that's enough said."
Amos was uneasy after hearing all of this. He nodded his so long to Queenie and started for the door.
Fishnet took him by the arm to stop him. "Where ya going, pal? We ain't done here yet."
Fishnet made another play for Queenie. Seeing the potential for more greenbacks, the madam was receptive to his overtures. Before he left, she gave Fishnet another telephone phone number, one that her boyfriend Ruffy didn't know about.

########

FISHNET REACHED OUT TO A one-time colleague who was now employed in the security department of the telephone company. The retired detective was receptive to doing a favor for an old friend. For the price of a lunch Fishnet obtained the name and address connected to the two telephone numbers given to him by the madam at the brothel.
Fishnet proceeded to the address tied to Sarah. By checking the mailboxes, he discovered the name he was looking for.

Piggybacking into the building, Fishnet casually proceeded to the apartment in question. He put his ear to the door and listened. Hearing no sounds coming from within the apartment, Fishnet knocked on the door. When no one responded to his knock, Fishnet conducted an inquiry of those residing in the neighboring apartments. Finding one person home, he came to learn that Sarah hadn't been seen in a while.

The following morning Fishnet responded to the address that was linked to Queenie's telephone number. Finding the madam home, he immediately got down to business. Fishnet's liberal parting with his money was sure-fire in once again gaining Queenie's cooperation. The morning proved to be a productive but expensive proposition.

Queenie suggested that Fishnet speak to Greta, Sarah's best friend. She gave the former detective Greta's contact number. Before setting out to ascertain Greta's address via his friend in the telephone company, Fishnet had one other piece of business to conduct with Queenie. With their meeting of the minds behind them, all that remained was a meeting of the bodies.

##########

SARAH WAS ALONE IN GRETA'S APARTMENT when she answered the knock on the door. Armed with a gun inside her zip-up track jacket, she cautiously opened the front door a few inches. Peeking through the chain lock, she didn't recognize the stranger on the other side of the door.

Fishnet managed to see through the crack in the door that the blond haired woman had an eye condition. *This has to be her*, he thought. *Two people being here with blinkers like that ain't possible.*

"Hello, Sarah," said the ex-detective. He spoke in a smooth, almost calming voice.

Although the stranger did look somewhat familiar, Sarah couldn't understand how he knew her name.

"Do I know you?" she asked, thinking that he may have been

210

one of the Johns she serviced in the past.

"No, we haven't met," replied Fishnet. "But I know all about you, Sarah."

"What are you, a cop?"

"Relax, sweetheart. I'm no cop. Let me in."

"What do you want?"

"Where's Greta?"

"What do you want with her?"

"We're old friends," said the ex-detective, being untruthful. "I was one of her regular customers at Queenie's. I got a job for her. It'll mean big money."

"Oh, well, she's not home. What's the message?"

"I am planning a bachelor party. I thought she could help put it together. You know what I mean, right?"

"Let me have your telephone number. I'll give it to her when she gets in."

"Do you have a pen?"

"Wait a minute. I'll get one."

As Sarah began to close the door, Fishnet asked to use the bathroom. Believing his story, and since she was armed, she opened the door. Her visitor quickly stepped inside the apartment.

"Thanks, I really gotta go," he announced. "Where's the bathroom?"

Sarah pointed to where the bathroom was.

Once inside, Fishnet began to look about the apartment. At this point, Sarah knew she'd made a mistake. Satisfied they were alone, Fishnet confronted her. He was taken aback when he saw the gun that was being pointed at him.

"Back up, asshole," she declared. "What do you really want?" Instead of being alarmed, Fishnet was impressed. *She's got balls, this one*, he thought. In a strange way, Fishnet was developing an admiration for Sarah.

"Whoa, put that gun away."

"What are you after?" Sarah demanded to know.

"I just want to talk to you about what happened to Judge West."

"So, you are a cop!

"No, I'm not. I'm here on behalf of Amos West."

Sarah knew she had to hear him out at this point. "Sit at the table where I can keep an eye on you," she ordered. "Now let's hear it," she added, once Fishnet was stationary.

Taking no chances, Sarah kept her gun trained on Fishnet. As he faced the business end of the weapon, things began to take on a new wrinkle for Fishnet. In considering that his primary objective was Marvin Butterworth, Fishnet began to see in Sarah someone who would be easier to work with than Amos. In return for ample compensation, he was certain that Sarah was the sort who would be amenable to signing on with him. "My purpose has changed," answered Fishnet, honestly. "I assume you could use money, correct?"

"Keep talking. I'm listening."

"I've got a proposition for you," said Fishnet.

"What kind of proposition?"

Fishnet revealed that Amos West was out to cause her bodily harm.

"Amos is out to hurt me?" asked the astonished Sarah. "Why?"

"I think you know the answer to that, sweetheart."

"Well, have I got a surprise for that little shit!"

"You know Marvin Butterworth, right?" asked Fishnet.

"Are you talking about the old man?"

"That's the guy."

"What about him?"

"I see a way for us to help each other, Sarah. I got plenty of money to make it worth your time."

"Oh, you do, do you?" said Sarah. "Just who the hell are you, anyway?"

In order to sway Sarah to his side, Fishnet emphasized the extent of the wealth he had come into. As anticipated, learning of his worth got Sarah's attention.

"And you really expect me to believe that you own a townhouse?" asked Sarah.

"Yes, ma'am, believe it. It's all mine."

"Where is it?" she asked.

"It's in the best part of town," he answered.

"If you got so much money, then why do you need to waste your time with Amos?"

"Amos was important yesterday. Let's talk about today. I'm trying to tell you that we can help each other."

"How about we start by you helping me find a reason not to cap you," she said, testing his mettle.

Fishnet's macho calmness in the face of danger went a long way in winning Sarah over.

"You're not gonna do that, sweetheart, not without a reason. Besides, I'm gonna make you money."

"How do you propose to do that?"

"You're gonna kill Marvin for me."

"Are you serious?"

"I'm dead serious. If you're capable of handling a contract, as I think you are, you'll be making a huge score for yourself."

Sarah dismissed the question of her capability with a snicker. "What stops you from cleaning your own house....no stomach for it?"

Her statement gave Fishnet a laugh. "Don't worry about my stomach, sweetheart. I got reasons for contracting this job out. Let's just leave it at that."

"I'll need to know more."

Fishnet relented. He explained that Marvin's murder was sure to draw the attention of a certain detective sergeant, Markie, who was hell-bent on seeing him behind bars. With this being the case, Sarah understood the necessity for her visitor to distance himself from the proposed homicide.

"So, you see, Sarah, with you in the mix, my exposure is minimized."

"So, tell me, big shot, how much are you willing to pay me?" asked Sarah.

At this juncture, the two entered into negotiations. Since Sarah needed the money, they were able to come to terms swiftly.

"So, we're in business?" asked Fishnet.

"As long as I get my money up front, we are."

"Take it easy, sweetheart. I'll give you a third up front and the rest after the job."

"Okay," agreed Sarah somewhat reluctantly. "You do know I was prepared to kill you, don't you?"

"Sure I do, baby," replied Fishnet. "That's why I opened up to you about Marvin."

"You're pretty sure of yourself, aren't you?"

"And you love that in me, don't you?"

"What's your name anyway?" Sarah asked, not addressing his question.

"You could call me Shepherd Fish."

"What the hell kind of name is that?"

"It's one that'll do. You want to know something, Sarah?"

"What?"

"I could see things getting cozy between us." His words flowed in a way that caused Sarah not to disagree with him. "So tell me, what's the story with those peepers you got?"

"Maybe when you give me the money, I'll show you why my eyes are so popular."

"I got one question, though, Sarah. How much trouble have you got with Ruffy Shea?"

"Oh, so you know about that," commented Sarah. "That son of a bitch is hunting for me, so I gotta be real careful. Once I collect in full from you, I gotta think about what I'm gonna do about him."

Fishnet nodded approvingly. "Let's chop down one tree at a time, sweetheart," he advised. "Next time you see me, you'll have your third."

After leaving Sarah's apartment, Fishnet drove home to his Manhattan townhouse. During the ride, his mind drifted to his world of fantasy. He and Sarah were now the notorious Bonnie and Clyde. They had just robbed a bank in Missouri and were hiding out at a friend's home. The bandits were reclining on a bed of money when Fishnet, as Clyde, mounted Bonnie. In the midst of this mental high point, Fishnet's cell phone went off, destroying the momentum of his fantasy. The joy-killer was Amos.

"Yeah, Amos, what do you want?" asked Fishnet tartly, annoyed at being interrupted.

"I haven't heard from you, and I'm wondering what happened with that woman?"

"I got bad news for you, Amos. I changed my mind about our doing business."

"What am I supposed to do about Sarah?"

"I recommend you forget about her the way I did Marvin. Besides, I wouldn't get on the wrong side of her if I were you. She'll eat you alive."

"But you said—"

"I said, I'm done," declared Fishnet bluntly. "Go solve your own freakin' problems."

"That's it?"

"No, there is one other thing, Amos. I wouldn't say anything to Marvin about what we discussed. That wouldn't be healthy for you."

24

Political Priorities

THE DISTRICT ATTORNEY WAS A SEASONED prosecutor with a brilliant legal mind. He was also an excellent strategist. Since he was entering an election year, he understood the value of his office receiving as much positive media coverage as possible. Good press created a voter buzz that would further his reelection efforts.

The soft-spoken DA was an ardent student of Niccolò Machiavelli. Patterning himself after Machiavelli's "The Prince," he subscribed to projecting a truthful, merciful, religious image. He attributed his ability to acquire power, and hang onto it, to this formula. His running for office unopposed for many, many years would seem to prove his contention that Machiavelli knew what he was talking about.

Despite his best efforts at projecting a positive image, there were times when the DA, a man in his late fifties, puzzled people due to his aloofness. Those around him were unable to figure out if his cool reserve stemmed from shyness or arrogance.

The DA's distrust of ambitious people was the major contributor to his detachment. As a precaution he never surrounded himself professionally with such types. His thoughts on the matter never deviated from, *Why should I take a chance on someone who might undermine my position in order to further their own?*

Tim Gerard, an NYPD police captain, was a loyal and trusted childhood friend of the DA. The bond between them was strong enough for the DA to appoint his friend to the position of commanding officer of the DA's Office Squad, a unit consisting of a contingent of NYPD detectives who worked out of the DA's office.

Captain Gerard was a tall, thin man with glasses. A former Marine, Gerard saw his role as being protective of the DA. The captain carried himself in a way that led many to assume he was an attorney. The conservative pinstripe suits he wore further contributed to this presumption.

Gerard possessed a dark side that he cloaked well. Under his gloss of professionalism, existed a tough-as-nails, results-oriented man who would stop at nothing to enhance his friend the DA.

"With the election coming up we're going to need to generate some positive press, Tim," said the DA during a meeting in his office with the captain.

"Organized crime cases are always good copy, Chief. Do you want me to round up a few of the local wise guys?"

"If we can make cases against them, that would be beneficial," answered the DA.

"I can make some quick arrests for gambling and bookmaking. Or do you prefer protracted investigations?"

"As long as the crimes are being committed, let's do both."

"I have just the thing to start us off, Chief. I have an informant who has been telling me about a mob-run casino operating in Howard Beach."

"I leave it to you, Tim, you know what we need."

"No problem, Chief," assured the captain.

##########

CAPTAIN GERARD CALLED into his office Ronald "Damsel" Davis, a portly forty-four-year-old informant with fleshy lips. His street name stemmed from his likeness to a big-lip damselfish, a tropical reef fish noted for its large mouth and protruding lips.

"I have some work for you, Damsel," said the captain.

"What kind of work?"

"I want to knock over that casino operating in Howard Beach that you told me about."

"You're talking about Ciro's joint, right?"

"Yes, he's a made man, isn't he?"

"Yeah, Ciro's a soldier in the Philly Rava family. He's got a piece of that restaurant, Italo's, too."

"Do you still gamble in that casino?"

"When I got funds, I go there."

"They know you there, correct?"

"Yeah, I'm a familiar face both there and in the restaurant. I can take one of your people in with me with no problem."

Captain Gerard saw this as a step in the right direction. Taking out an organized crime gambling den and netting a Rava soldier would result in a decent headline for the office.

"When is Ciro at the casino?"

"Anytime I've seen him there it was early in the evening. The one who is there all the time is this other guy, Swatty."

"Is Swatty a made guy too?"

"I don't think so. The only juice he has comes from being with Ciro."

"I'll have one of my detectives go to the casino with you to gamble."

"No problem, Captain, just tell your detective not to start asking questions when we go in."

"Your job is to get us in, Damsel, my people will take it from there."

"I think our best shot is to start out at the restaurant and then ease our way over to the casino, Captain. It would seem more natural that way."

"And you get something good to eat."

"C'mon, Captain. Would I think like that?"

"No....not you," replied the frowning captain.

"Am I getting the usual compensation for this, Captain?"

"Yeah, Damsel, nothing has changed."

"You're gonna front me a decent amount of gambling money, right?"

"Yeah, you'll get money to gamble with," assured Gerard. "I'm gonna match you up with a female detective. I think that'll work best."

##########

THE DETECTIVE ASSIGNED TO work with Damsel was a three-year member of the police department. A one-time bank teller, she had entered the department to follow in the footsteps of her father, a deputy inspector. Thanks to the influence of her father, who was friendly with Captain Gerard, after two years on the job she was transferred to the DA's office. A year later, she received a gold shield. Although a promotion to detective for someone with so little time on the job raised eyebrows, nepotism prevailed.

Since the detective was spared the hardening that occurs after working years on the street, she lacked the cynicism often held by timeworn veterans of the force. The absence of jadedness made her an ideal undercover operative. With nothing cop-like about her, she was a logical fit to pose as the girlfriend of Damsel Davis.

The two began their investigation at Italo's. While waiting to be seated, Damsel began to feel the young detective out.

"If I put my arm around you," said Damsel, "it'll be to show everyone you're with me."

The detective's lack of experience didn't prevent her from seeing right through Damsel. Her look of disgust was evident. "I think we can do without that," the detective stated firmly, leaving no room for further discussion.

"Whatever you say," commented Damsel snippily. "Just don't forget, we're supposed to be a couple," he reminded. The detective cringed at the very thought of intimacy with Damsel. His fish lips making their way anywhere near her own was repulsive to her.

219

"How are you?" Italo asked cordially upon seeing Damsel, who he recognized.

"I'm doing okay," said Damsel. "Say hello to my girl."

"You're stepping up in class, Damsel," teased Italo. He then extended his hand to the undercover detective. "I'm pleased to meet you. I'm Italo. Are you folks up for a little action after dinner?"

"We definitely are," replied Damsel.

"That's just fine. I'll call over there for you when you're ready to head over."

After having an uneventful dinner, the undercover detective and the informer proceeded to the nearby gambling emporium. Upon being granted access they were immediately noticed by Ciro, who inquired as to who they were.

"Hey, Swatty, those two who just came in," said Ciro, "the guy with the fat lips, what's his name again?"

"That's Damsel. He comes in regular. I never saw the girl before."

"She's easy on the eyes. I wonder what she's doing with him." The informer and the detective were drawn to the buzz being made at one of the tables. "That's for us," said Damsel, heading toward a craps table. After purchasing chips, he turned to address the detective.

"You roll the dice and I'll place the bets," he advised.

Enjoying beginner's luck, the undercover detective went on to make multiple passes with the dice. Thanks to the betting acumen of Damsel, they were up two thousand dollars in a relatively short period of time.

"Let's go try and talk to Ciro," said the undercover detective. "No, not now, we're winning. Nobody leaves the game when they're on a hot streak." When their luck finally turned, they left the table while being well ahead.

"Where did Ciro go?" asked the undercover cop.

"It looks like he took off already. C'mon, let's play at another table."

"We got what we want, Damsel, we're leaving," said the undercover curtly.

"All right, keep your shirt on," said the informer glumly, counting up his chips. "I don't know what the rush is."

Once they were inside their car Damsel handed the detective half of their winnings. "Anyway, we made out okay," advised Damsel, looking at the bright side.

"Where is the rest of the money?" queried the undercover detective.

"What are you talking about?" asked the surprised Damsel. "I'm not holding out on you. I just gave you half the money we made, what more do you want?"

"The other half," replied the detective.

"You want my half?"

"Of course, I have to turn the money in, don't I?"

The informant's mouth dropped open. He was stunned at what he had just heard. "You have to be kidding me....we never turn any money in."

"No, I'm not kidding you. Now hand over the rest," ordered the detective.

"But nobody ever wins," insisted the informant.

"But *we* did."

Realizing he wasn't going to persuade the undercover differently, Damsel begrudgingly turned over the money.

##########

TO CAPTAIN GERARD'S DISAPPOINTMENT, Ciro wasn't present when a complement of twelve of his detectives stormed the casino. The captain had just missed nabbing Ciro, who had left the casino earlier than usual, by just minutes. The casino patrons and employees froze in place as they watched an invading force armed with guns, a warrant, and a few axes perform their duty.

Swatty, who was in charge of the casino in Ciro's absence, was caught totally off guard. He made the mistake of quickly raising his hands when confronted by an enthusiastic detective. His intent to signal that he was surrendering escaped the detective, who responded to what he perceived to be an act of aggression.

The roundhouse slap Swatty received came with enough oomph to knock him off his feet. Although dazed by the blow, Swatty shook the cobwebs out of his head and managed to rise to his feet unassisted.

"What was that for?" asked Swatty, as he held the side of his face in his palm.

"Don't try that again," warned the detective who struck him. "Now stand over against that wall," he directed, after frisking his prisoner. Swatty complied without hesitation.

Captain Gerard's voice could be heard loud and clear as he spoke through the bullhorn he held. While he proclaimed that a search warrant was being executed on behalf of the DA, the Captain's squad fanned out to separate the casino workers from the patrons.

The detectives diligently confiscated the gambling chips, equipment, and cash from the tables. Gerard made it a point to scoop up a healthy handful of one-hundred dollar chips. Just as a master would reward his dog, the chips taken by the captain were to be given to Damsel for a job well done. The informant would be able to use the chips when the casino reopened for business.

##########

CAPTAIN GERARD'S TEN PRISONERS were all transported to the squad room at the DA's office, where the arrests were processed. As part of their debriefing each of the apprehended individuals were queried in relation to their knowledge as to the workings of organized crime. As is usually the case, the authorities learned nothing new.

While his men photographed, fingerprinted, and debriefed the prisoners, Captain Gerard devoted his attention solely to Swatty, who was removed to the captain's private office for questioning. The two, when alone in the office, sat on opposite sides of Captain Gerard's desk.

The captain casually removed a pack of Kent cigarettes from his jacket pocket. After lighting up a cigarette for himself, he tossed the pack on the desk in the direction of where Swatty sat. "Feel free to take one," he said to the prisoner.

Swatty hesitated a moment before taking the captain up on his offer. With his look of defiance unchanged, Swatty removed a cigarette from the pack without saying thanks. He received his light from the captain without comment. After taking a deep drag, Swatty blew out smoke in the direction of the captain. The gust of smoke tickled the captain's nostrils. Not used to being disrespected in such a manner, Captain Gerard's face tightened. "If you want to be an asshole, I'll treat you like one," said the captain.

"Treat me anyway you like, Captain."

"You're taking this pinch personally," said Gerard, maintaining a calm voice. "We had a purpose for knocking over your joint tonight."

"What's all this about, Captain?" asked the perturbed mob associate. "And what am I doing in your office being treated like your star boarder?"

"You're here because you're special, Swatty."

"So, you even know my name," said the prisoner, who then began to shake his head.

"That's my business."

"Yeah, well your business ain't making me look too good in the eyes of my friends in the other room. They'll think we got something going"

"You're in here because you're the boss, everyone knows that."

"What everyone?" Swatty asked, lifting up his hand as he spoke. His fingers were gathered together as he moved his hand up and down. "Everybody knows that I ain't the boss."

"Then if you aren't the boss, who is?"

Swatty, after studying Gerard's face, concluded that there was nothing he liked about the captain. He found the squad commander to be too smooth to be totally trusted.

"I got nothing to say to you, Captain."

"You might want to rethink that, my friend."

"Look, Captain, we ain't ever gonna be friends. That's something you should get straight right off the bat."

"Are you forgetting the charges against you?"

"C'mon, you ain't dealing with no kid over here," said Swatty, dismissively. "What have you got, some bullshit gambling charges?"

"Am I correct in assuming that you've done time?" Gerard asked.

"You got all the answers, you tell me."

Captain Gerard nonchalantly lit up another cigarette. After taking a drag, he rested his cigarette in the ashtray. He then spun around in his chair to face the vintage combination floor safe located just a few feet behind his desk. After opening the safe, the Captain removed a large plastic bag containing white powder.

"Cocaine," announced the captain. "This stuff has no history, Swatty," advised Gerard holding up the plastic bag he was passing off as cocaine. It can belong to anyone—including you."

"What's that supposed to mean?" asked the gangster, who was now displaying signs of concern. The prisoner's open mouth signaled to the captain that he had his man worried.

"Weren't you the one who said that gambling was a bullshit charge, Swatty?"

"Yeah, but—"

"Well, now we got a serious charge."

This was the side of Captain Gerard that he concealed so well. Even the district attorney himself had no idea of just how vile his childhood friend could be in his effort to achieve results.

"Are you saying you're gonna flake me, Captain?"

Gerard shrugged in a matter-of-fact fashion before answering.

"That depends."

"You can't get away with this!"

"You've been pinched by the DA's office, Swatty. Think about that."

Convinced that he was about to be framed, Swatty's physical agitation was evident. "Why are you doing this to me? What did I ever do to you, Captain?"

"Let's talk about what you're going to do for me," replied the captain. "I want information, Swatty, and you're going to give it to me."

"What kind of information?"

"I want to know about whatever will make the DA look good in the headlines. This is an election year, so if you play ball with me, you'll walk out of here a free man. It'll be like you were never at the casino at all."

"What do you expect me to do, turn rat for you and give up my friends? That would mean my doom!"

"Don't get so dramatic, Swatty. It doesn't have to be as drastic as all that. All I want is something that'll look good to the public. You help me with that, and then you'll be free of this little inconvenience."

Swatty felt the offer to be tempting. "What is it that you need to know?"

"Anything that'll make for good press will work."

After giving it a moment of thought, Swatty came up with an offering. "How about I tell you who killed Judge Fatima West?"

"That ship sailed, Swatty. Everyone knows that the guy who killed her is dead. You'll have to do better."

"You got another cigarette, Captain?"

"They're right in front of you. Help yourself."

After receiving a light, Swatty took three consecutive long drags before speaking. "I know who drove the getaway car in that judge killing."

"Grabbing the second piece could be something valuable to me. Who was it?"

"Can I call somebody and talk privately, Captain?"

"Sure, if it'll help us advance. Who are you calling?"

"Do I have to say?"

"Not if you don't want to. Use the phone on the desk here. I'll step outside to give you privacy. I'm going to put a man on the door to keep a watch on you while I use the restroom."

Swatty took the opportunity to call Ciro when he received the okay from the detective assigned to watch him. Unbeknownst to the mobster, Captain Gerard was listening in on the call from an adjacent office.

"It's me, Swatty," said the prisoner, speaking in a whisper.

"What's wrong?" asked Ciro.

"The joint got raided. Everybody got busted."

"Where are you?"

"The DA's office, they were the one who raided us."

"Those motherless bastards," hissed Ciro."

"If I tell them what I know about the Judge Fatima West murder, they'll let me go."

"Tell them to kiss your ass. Where are they going with a gambling charge?"

"Look, there's more going on here than you know about. They got it worked out to fix me but good if I don't spill something. Do you get my drift?"

"Did you tip off that precinct bull?"

"Yeah, sure I did, just like you wanted me to."

"Then that son-of-a-bitch lieutenant in the precinct double-crossed us. He got his friends to raid us anyway."

"Look, they're gonna frame me over here unless I give them something."

"I don't buy that," voiced Ciro, "they're running a bluff. Did they get the Mona Lisa sandwiches?" Ciro was speaking cryptically. He was referring to the guns hidden behind a picture frame in the casino.

"No, they never even looked."

"Keep your trap shut then. I'll get you a lawyer."

"But I can walk out of here clean if I give them the girl who drove the getaway car in the judge killing."

"But they must already know who she is. You said that you tipped off the squad boss in the precinct, didn't you?"

"Apparently, that lieutenant didn't clue in this guy over here in the DA's office."

"You're sure that they'll let you go?"

"Yeah, I believe them."

At this point, Ciro saw no downside in giving up Sarah. "So tell them what they wanna hear. Just leave my name out of it."

"So, I can tell?"

"Yeah, go on. I don't get all this cloak-and-dagger bullshit with these cops. You'd think they would talk to each other."

"Politics, I guess."

"Yeah, I suppose that's it. Call me when you're in circulation again."

A few minutes after Swatty got off the phone, Captain Gerard returned to his office. Having secured permission from Ciro, the prisoner told the squad commander what he knew. Satisfied that he had his headline, the captain made good on his end of the agreement by cutting Swatty loose.

"So, I can go?"

"You can go," answered Gerard. "If you spot this Sarah anyplace, give me a call," said the captain. "It'll save me hunting for her."

"About that casino money you guys confiscated, do I get it back?"

"Keep walking, Swatty," came the captain's terse response.

"What about the others?"

"They're all getting booked on gambling charges. Somebody has to take the rap."

"I suppose that the raid will make the papers."

"That's the idea."

25

Sarah Gets Pinched

THE DISTRICT ATTORNEY TOOK NOTICE of the vast amount news coverage given to a domestic-violence-related homicide that had occurred in another borough. Recognizing the crime to be a hot topic got him thinking.

My office has put away more husbands than anybody else, he thought. Now seeing a way to boost his reelection campaign, he wasted no time in reaching out to Captain Gerard.

"Have you read about that woman who was murdered by her husband, Tim?"

"Yes, I did, Chief."

"I'll bet you didn't know that our office is responsible for more domestic violence prosecutions than any other district attorney's office in New York City, and it's been like that for years."

"I'm aware of that, Chief."

"We know it, but the public needs to be reminded of it. It would behoove us to get the word out there about our achievements in this area and the good work our office is doing."

"I could reach out to that cousin of mine. You know him, the newspaper reporter."

"That's the ticket. See if you could get him to do a story."

########

CAPTAIN GERARD VISITED HIS COUSIN at the reporter's Nassau County home one evening after work. The cousin, a police buff, had once aspired to be a police officer. Poor eyesight prevented him from achieving his ambition. The newsman had never quite gotten the police bug out of his system.

Gerard, as the older cousin, was someone that the reporter looked up to. Along with the authority that the captain held, his cousin had always been impressed by the gun the lawman carried on his hip. His fascination with the weapon never wavered.

"Hello, kid," said the smiling Gerard upon entering his cousin's apartment.

"Hey, Tim, how are you?" the cousin greeted him. "The place is a mess, you should have called and told me you were stopping by. Is everything okay?"

"Everything is fine," assured the captain. "I was in the neighborhood on something, so I decided to swing by and say hello."

"I'm glad you did. Do you want a beer?"

"Sure, thing. Are you joining me?"

"You bet."

"You know," began the captain, once settled in a chair. "I was wondering if you'd like to go to the police range up in the Bronx one afternoon and fire some of the weapons they got."

"I'd love to do that! You won't get in any trouble for bringing me, will you?"

"The DA's office never gets in trouble," answered Gerard with a laugh.

"When can we go?"

"We'll go as soon as you can do me a small favor."

"Oh, there's a catch," said the reporter. "I should have known. I still remember when you sold me that forged autograph of Babe Ruth when we were kids!"

Captain Gerard let out a booming laugh after recalling the incident. "What do you want? I taught you a good lesson."

Gerard was joined in laughter by his cousin, who also thought it funny how he was snookered.

"So, what is it that you need?" asked the reporter.

"Here's the situation. This is an election year and I'd like to see the DA's office get some positive press."

"Give me something to work with and I'll do what I can, you know that."

"We just knocked over an organized-crime-run casino in Howard Beach, how is that?"

"Did you take down any big names?"

"No, but it was a Rava family soldier-run operation."

"Sorry, Tim, but without netting the big fish, it means nothing. You've got to give me something to work with."

"Well, how about the fact that the office leads the league in domestic violence prosecutions."

"That might work, especially on the heels of that husband who butchered his wife."

"Work some magic, will ya? After all, it was me who gave you the inside track on that Queens bank heist that time. You came out smelling like a rose on that one."

"I'm not forgetting that," said the reporter, looking at his cousin seriously. He then suddenly brightened, believing he had found an angle to work with. "Say, wait a minute! Didn't you receive the Police Department's combat cross?"

"I did, I got that metal a hundred years ago though."

"What was the story with that again?"

"I shot the guy who shot my partner."

"That was on a rooftop, wasn't it?"

"You have a good memory. He was a burglar that we chased onto a factory roof that night."

"When was that?"

"In two weeks, it'll be ten years."

"The guy died, right?"

"Yeah, he took a header off the roof after I put one in his belly."

"And you were wounded, right?"

"Yeah, but mine was just a flesh wound on my cheek."

"Let me see," said the reporter, inspecting his cousin's cheek. "This is great. We can doctor that scar to pronounce it. That's the story....we'll play up the anniversary of the shooting."
"Hold on, it's not about me. You gotta squeeze the DA in there."
"Was the guy you killed married?"
"Yeah, he had a junkie wife who later died of an overdose."
"Okay, so we'll make him a wife beater. I'll write that the DA chose you specifically to join him in his effort to combat domestic violence. I'll put in a picture along with the story that'll show you and him working side by side in the office. Off that, I can ease into how you guys are also focusing on the mob, citing the recent casino bust.
"I owe you one for this, kid," said the appreciative Gerard.
"I know you do. So, when are we going to go shooting up at the range?"

########

THE DISTRICT ATTORNEY WAS QUITE PLEASED with the newspaper coverage he received. He felt the attention drawn to his office by the article would go far in favorably influencing the voting public. The DA called Captain Gerard to his office to discuss what could be done as a follow-up to the story reported. "Your cousin did an outstanding job for us, Tim," praised the DA. "Now we need a quick follow-up piece, can you think of anything?"
"The second piece in the Judge West case is still at large, Chief. Since the getaway driver was female, that might work."
"Do you think that the precinct detectives are diligently looking to find her?"
"I doubt it. They just don't have the time, Chief. They're constantly catching new cases every day."
"Well, then, see if you can find her."
"The squad commander over there isn't exactly an easy guy to get along with, Chief."
"Assure him that his people can make the arrest. Tell him we'll

announce it as a joint investigation. His people can even do the perp walk in front of the cameras."

"I'll do that, Chief. But Waldo Reale can be a difficult customer."

"If that's the case, then tell Waldo he can say a few words before the television cameras."

"That would probably appease him, Chief. And my cousin, the reporter, we have to do something for him."

"Tell him that he'll get the inside scoop on all our newsworthy cases. He'll get to leave his competition in the dust."

########

CAPTAIN GERARD DIDN'T SHARE with the district attorney his personal history with the precinct squad commander. Gerard's relationship with Waldo had been strained ever since an incident that had occurred when both were young police officers.

Waldo had been at a house party of a fellow cop with the woman he was engaged to. Scheduled to work the midnight shift, Waldo was compelled to excuse himself from the party early, leaving his intended in the company of her sister. Present at the party that evening was Tim Gerard.

After Waldo left for work, Gerard triggered a spark in Waldo's intended wife. As it turned out, she left the party with Gerard. The subsequent rumors that circulated, although never substantiated, were disturbing enough for Waldo to call off the wedding. This was the basis for a continuing grudge.

Gerard arrived at the precinct to meet with Waldo with two of his more physically imposing detectives. He relied on the presence of these men to help maintain a professional climate. Also present were Detective Lena Lesper and her partner, Detective Scott Podell. It was no secret to those there that bad blood existed between the two squad commanders.

After the initial tension subsided, the captain and the lieutenant convened privately in Waldo's office.

"The district attorney's office has an interest in the Judge West case, Waldo," advised Gerard.

"It's solved," stated Waldo tartly.

"The second piece is still out there," reminded the captain. "We got a want card out on the getaway driver. She'll turn up eventually."

"The DA would rather not wait, Waldo."

"Is that a fact?" asked Waldo, taking exception.

"It's an election year. Nabbing the second piece will give the DA a boost."

"So you guys want to stick your finger in my pie," commented Waldo, "and play the big shot off the back of me and my squad."

Captain Gerard's face conveyed his frustration. "Look, Waldo, nobody is looking to cut you out."

"That's bullshit, and you know it!"

"Listen, *Lieutenant,* do you really want me to start pulling rank on you?"

Waldo held his tongue after being reminded of his place in the police department's pecking order. He recognized that in a paramilitary organization, it was all about rank….and Tim Gerard was a captain.

"You got the upper hand on me, *Captain,*" conceded Waldo, "so I'm not gonna start pissing in the wind. You're holding the aces. Enlighten me as to your intentions."

"Now you're talking sense. If we work together, we'll both make out."

"We already tried to find her. She's in the wind, so, like I told you, we put out a want card."

"If the warrant drops on her, I want you to be sure to notify my office, Waldo. In the meantime, let's try and figure out what more we can do to come up with her."

"I have to ask you something," said Waldo, looking to get what was bothering him off his chest. "How can you expect me to roll over and play dead when you come to my squad and take over in front of my own people?"

"Take it easy, Waldo," replied the captain. "Nobody is taking over. All we want is to show the public that the DA's office is in the game pitching. It's all about the press conference," explained the captain.

"So, the DA intends to do a press conference?"

"With you, Waldo, after your people make the arrest....now that's reasonable, isn't it?"

"I'm gonna be part of that press conference?"

"You're gonna be right there when those cameras roll," assured the captain."

"So, I'm there to hold the DA's valise and look like a valet. Ain't that swell!"

"Jeeze, Waldo, stop it, will you? You'll be speaking to the press too, and it'll be before the cameras." This concession went far in settling Waldo.

"Okay, that works. Let's get the show on the road then," suggested Waldo.

At this time, all of the investigators were called into Waldo's office for a team meeting. During the briefing, it was noted that the ballistics report reflected that the gun used in the death of Fats Plummer was the same weapon that killed Judge Fatima West.

"So, we got the shooter in the judge case nailed down," announced Waldo. "Now we want the getaway driver."

"So, Plummer was a suicide on Staten Island," noted Captain Gerard.

"That's right."

"Any chance that it wasn't suicide, Waldo?" asked Gerard. "Are you trying to say it wasn't a suicide?" asked Waldo. The scowl on Waldo's face was telling.

"I'm just asking," answered the Captain. "There could've been a falling out among thieves. It's possible that the gun could have been planted, couldn't it?"

"That's a good point, Cap," voiced Detective Lesper. "We never thought of that."

Waldo looked at Lesper as if she were a mutineer. Her voicing support for the captain's observation was interpreted by Waldo as extreme disloyalty.

"Jesus Christmas, Lena!" thundered the lieutenant, unable to control himself. "Why are we complicating this?" he asked. "Fats Plummer went down as a suicide. He killed himself using the same gun that killed the judge. End of story. If that don't put the cork in the bottle as to who killed the judge, nothing will." Captain Gerard covered his mouth to hide his snicker. "Waldo's right," finally said the captain. "Let's just concentrate on finding the woman." Gerard had successfully concealed his glee at seeing Waldo lose it.

##########

AFTER THE MEETING, DETECTIVE LESPER took it upon herself to discreetly contact Detective Von Hess at his office over in headquarters. She let it be known that the DA's office expressed an interest in the Judge West case, noting that a diligent effort was now underway to find Sarah Ince.

Lesper's reason for keeping Von Hess in the loop was self-serving. She was using Von Hess to ingratiate herself with Markie. Her hope was that she might be able to finagle a transfer into the sergeant's team at headquarters. Working out of the office of the chief of detectives was considered a choice assignment and one that would eventually lead to a promotion in grade.

After thanking Detective Lesper for the heads up, Von Hess posted Markie.

"Why are the DA's people sticking their nose in?" questioned Markie after being apprised of the situation.

"That's the question," replied Von Hess.

"Maybe it is best that we go back out to Queens and get a handle on things. Chief McCoy is a man who doesn't like surprises."

"Very good, Sarge, I just have a question. How involved do you want us to get in Brooklyn?"

"What's in Brooklyn?"

235

"That hit on Leon Crabbe happened in Brooklyn. Are we sticking close to that?"

"No, forget Brooklyn," answered Markie. "None of the brass is gonna give two shits about Leon Crabbe. And Ollie, it would be good for us if we could come up with that getaway driver. Are you up for a little hunting?"

"Let's do it, Sarge. Where do you want to start looking?"

"My guess is that Sarah Ince will probably be close to wherever that boyfriend of hers is. Let's start by doing a little research, Ollie. Let's see where that takes us."

"The boyfriend wasn't hard to find, Sarge," announced Von Hess a short time after commencing his research. "Mickey Walker is in the can."

"What did he do?"

"Possession of a loaded gun," answered Von Hess.

"Who made the pinch?"

"A uniformed cop in Queens made the arrest."

"That's a start. Let's go talk to the arresting officer, Ollie." The subsequent conversation with the arresting officer resulted in the investigators gathering all the information they needed to find Sarah Ince. The cop conveyed that Mickey, when arrested, had exercised his right to make a phone call and telephoned Sarah. The officer memorialized the telephone number called on the arrest report and in his memo book. Also recorded was Greta's residence. Mickey had foolishly informed the officer where he and Sarah were currently living.

"Let's take a drive over to this address, Ollie," directed Markie. "After that, we'll give a courtesy call to Waldo the Boss in order to bring him up to speed."

"I'm sure he's gonna love hearing from you, Sarge."

##########

SARAH SAT AT THE KITCHEN TABLE in Greta's apartment smoking a cigarette. She was having second thoughts about aligning herself with Fishnet, the former detective. With Mickey's incarceration being the deciding factor, she eventually justified her decision. It came down to her needing financial support to carry on with her plans.

If Fishnet was being sincere in his claim of wealth, he presented a means to amass capital enough for Sarah to assemble a crew of lawbreakers that would do her bidding. All it would take was for her to figure out a way to wrest control of the former detective's fortune. If she could accomplish this, she'd be able to go eliminate the threat that Ruffy Shea posed. Sarah's concentration was broken by the sound of a knock at her door.

"Detectives," announced Von Hess through the closed door. *What the hell is this place*, thought Sarah, *Times Square?* "Who is it?" she asked, gripping the gun she carried on her person. "Detectives," advised Von Hess, open the door.

"What do you want?"

"We want you to open the door."

Sarah opened the door a crack. She peeked over the chain that prevented entry. "Let me see your badge." Once satisfied, she advised them, "Wait a minute." She then closed the door. Sarah quickly hid the gun she was carrying. After doing so, she then let the detectives in the house.

"So, what do you want?" Sarah asked.

"You're Sarah Ince, aren't you?" asked Markie, remembering her eye condition.

"Unless somebody's been fooling me, I am."

"C'mon, let's go, sister. You're taking a ride with us," advised the sergeant authoritatively. "Put a coat on." The sergeant's grasp was firm, making it clear to Sarah that he was all business. "Hey, easy with the rough stuff," protested Sarah. "What are you, some kind of caveman?" she asked. Her question fell on deaf ears.

Once on the street, Von Hess took charge of Sarah. As the detective was placing her in the rear seat of his car, Markie telephoned his office to apprise his superiors that he had picked up Sarah Ince. His second call was to Lieutenant Waldo Reale. "What?" Waldo asked, answering his phone.

"We're bringing her in now, Loo," apprised Markie.

"How did you know where to find her?"

"Good police work," replied the sergeant, not giving anything up.

"All right, just get her in here," said Waldo abruptly.

Waldo prepared to conduct a lineup at his squad. He sent Detective Lesper and her partner out to rustle up the female witness in the West case. He then placed a call to Captain Tim Gerard over at the DA's office. It killed Waldo to do it, but he had no choice other than notify the district attorney's squad that Sarah was in custody.

##########

SARAH ARRIVED AT THE PRECINCT rear cuffed and snarling, looking very much like the outlaw that Waldo expected her to be. After an unfruitful interview, she was placed in a cell by herself. She remained there while arrangements for the lineup were underway.

Waldo stood staring at Sarah through the cell bars. It was as if he were watching a caged animal in the zoo. Captain Gerard and his detectives arrived at the squad in a timely fashion. Gerard walked up to Waldo to let him know he arrived.

"So, this is who we've been looking for," Gerard said.

"In the flesh," commented Waldo.

"You got fillers for the lineup Waldo?"

"Not yet." The squad commander then called out to Detective Lesper. "Lena, check and see if we got any females in the precinct with blond hair. We need fillers for the lineup."

"I know that there is at least one, Loo," answered the detective.

"Is she about the right age?"

"She's close enough."

"Tell her to put on civilian clothes and get up here. Then see if you can find another body."

"You have your witness ready to come and view the lineup, Waldo?"

Waldo resented being questioned by the captain. "Yeah," he replied curtly.

"How is she?"

"How the hell do I know? According to Lena, the woman seemed scared shitless."

26

Cold Feet

SARAH'S EYE CONDITION DIDN'T POSE as an insurmountable obstacle when gathering lineup fillers. Since the lineup was being viewed through a one-way glass that was a substantial distance away, the consensus was that the eye discrepancy wouldn't be noticeable to the witness viewing the lineup.

Two police officers who were assigned to the precinct were recruited to participate in the lineup. Both women sufficiently resembled the suspect, but not to the point of creating confusion. One officer welcomed the opportunity to participate in the lineup because it got her off the street on a cold winter day. As instructed, she reported to the squad room in civilian clothes. As the first filler to arrive in the squad room, when told to stand by, she knew she had lots of time before the lineup would be underway. She prepared herself a cup of tea before making herself comfortable while she waited. She used the time to catch up on current events by reading the newspaper.

The second precinct officer designated to stand the lineup was less agreeable to the disruption in her day. The sour look on the officer's face expressed her displeasure. The lineup conflicted with an event being held at the local VFW post she planned on visiting.

"Lena, what's her problem?" Waldo asked, pointing to the unhappy officer.

"She wanted to poke her head in at an event being held at the VFW Post, Loo," replied Detective Lesper. "A friend of hers is receiving an award."

"Was she getting an award?"

"I don't think so."

"So what's she crying about? Make sure she wipes that puss off her face when she sits for the lineup," instructed the squad commander. "We don't need her drawing attention to herself." Waldo received a telephone call from Markie. Miffed at Markie having brought in Sarah Ince, he sent the sergeant and Von Hess out looking for lineup fillers to get the detectives out of his sight.

"What's the problem?" asked the squad commander when Markie called from the field.

"There's no problem, Loo. I'm just calling to find out how many bodies you need."

"We got two. Dig up three or four, and make sure they're blonds."

"Got it," stated Markie. He then turned to Von Hess. "We have to come up with three or four blonds for this miserable jerk, Ollie."

"What about the DA's squad, Sarge? I thought they were supposed to be helping out."

"I don't know, I guess Waldo's looking to stick it to us." Markie and Von Hess drove around in search of suitable women who would stand in a lineup. With only a small stipend to offer those willing to sacrifice their time, finding takers was not the easiest of tasks.

When Von Hess spotted a young blond woman who took up residence on the street next to a movie theater, he stopped the car. "What do you think, Sarge?" he asked, pointing to the woman.

"I don't know," replied Markie. "She's probably mentally ill." "She doesn't look it, Sarge. I mean, look at her, she appears very clean."

"All right, go talk to her. As long as she's stable maybe we could use her."

The down-on-her-luck woman was relegated to homelessness after losing her job as a counterperson in a pharmacy. Unable to adapt to the negatives connected to shelter life, she opted to sleep on the street. She protected herself from the elements by taking shelter inside a large industrial cardboard box that served as her quarters. She found sufficient warmth inside a red sleeping bag that rested atop several quilts.

The woman's personal belongings were contained in plastic crates that were stacked on an old hand truck positioned just outside the box. A long jump rope was used to connect her ankle to the hand truck while she slept at night.

The street person maintained herself hygienically by returning to the shelter every other day to clean up. Whenever the sun was out, she could be seen painting her nails or combing her hair as she sat on her sleeping bag.

This unhealthy lifestyle was possible thanks to a number of sympathetic neighborhood residents who contributed to her nourishment by providing food and drink. There were also those who occasionally donated money to her cause.

"I'll be right back, Sarge," said Von Hess, exiting the vehicle. "Forget about it if she smells, Ollie. We don't wanna stink up the joint." Von Hess nodded, indicating that he understood. "How are you doing? Von Hess asked, as he approached the woman. Now up close to her, he was surprised to see that she was actually attractive.

"I'm fine," replied the homeless woman. "Do you have a dollar you can lend me?"

"I can do better than a dollar. How would you like to make a few bucks?"

"Doing what?"

After establishing that she was lucid, the detective explained what she was needed for. The woman expressed a willingness to participate in the lineup for the allotted monetary compensation. However, her availability came with one provision. Von Hess had to sweeten the pot by throwing in a buttered bagel and a cup of hot cocoa in order to seal the deal. After picking up the food, the woman was transported to the precinct squad.

After depositing their find in the lineup room alongside the other fillers, Markie and Von Hess resumed their search for additional bodies. They got lucky when they came across a young college student who had been walking on the street. Finding the opportunity to get involved in a police lineup to be exciting, the criminal justice major happily agreed to participate. The final filler turned out to be the student's mother, who had become inquisitive when her daughter called to tell her she'd be late arriving home. When questioned as to how late, her daughter explained that she couldn't be sure because the detectives were still in need of at least one other filler. Since the student's mother was relatively youthful looking and blond, her daughter talked her into participating in the lineup. The mother's presence rounded out the number of fillers to five.

########

BOTH THE CAPTAIN AND THE LIEUTENANT WATCHED QUIETLY as the detectives arranged the armless metal chairs side by side in the viewing room. Sarah was stationed in the fifth position from the left as she sat among the other fillers. Each woman was holding a yellow manila folder that reflected a numerical designation. The supervisors nodded their approval as they observed the lineup through the one-way glass.

"It looks like we're good to go," declared Waldo.

"Don't forget to take a picture of the lineup, Lena," reminded the captain. Waldo shot Gerard a dirty look. "She knows," said Waldo.

After taking the photograph Detective Lesper telephoned her partner, who had been babysitting the witness in an office. The time had come for Marie Provenzano to view the lineup.

Marie's downturned mouth made it apparent that she was faced with an unpleasant task. All she could think of was her husband's parting words prior to her leaving for the precinct with the detectives. His reminder of the hazards associated with going against the wishes of Ciro, a soldier in the Philly Rava family, was unnecessary. Ciro's partner and cousin, Italo, had made that point clear enough.

"Don't be nervous, Marie, no one can see you," advised Detective Lesper. "Just look through the one-way glass and tell me if you recognize anyone." The detective then lifted the green shade covering the glass. "Do you recognize anyone, Marie?"

Marie looked for several seconds before turning her head away. "No, I don't recognize anyone," she answered."

"Take a good look, Marie."

"I took a very good look," answered the witness, sharply. "It was dark that night, I can't be sure." Detective Lesper was disappointed, but not surprised.

Sarah's triumphant look was on full display when informed that she was free to leave the precinct. As she exited the squad room, she intentionally walked with a strut to rub in her victory. The smirk on her face earned her the wrath of Waldo, who took such things personally.

I'll have her squashed like a bug, thought the squad commander, who had every intention of providing Sarah's new address to Ruffy Shea.

As far as Captain Gerard went, he too was disappointed. Returning to the district attorney with negative results wasn't going to be pleasant for him. The captain departed the precinct squad without bothering to say goodbye to Waldo the Boss.

Markie and Von Hess took the setback in stride, their philosophy being that you win some and you lose some. They made their goodbyes and returned to their headquarters office.

##########

WHEN SARAH RETURNED TO GRETA'S apartment, she found her girlfriend in an excited state. Greta had been waiting to share with Sarah the news she had heard about Leon Crabbe.

"Did you hear that they found Leon murdered?" Greta asked excitedly.

Sarah could hardly believe it. "They did?"

"Yeah, could you believe it?"

"How do you know Leon?"

"What are you getting senile, Sarah? I was with you when we met him at that waterfront bar we used to go to," explained Greta. "I was there the night you ripped off that guy with the one leg. I tried to talk you out of it because I felt sorry for him, remember?"

"That's right, I got little mixed up. Things are starting to move real fast for me. What else did you hear?"

"They said that the detectives found him in his van beaten and shot," informed Greta. "Leon really must have pissed somebody off real good."

"Yeah, he must have," agreed Sarah, who could only think that the hand of Ruffy Shea had played a role in the homicide. When Sarah thought of what Ruffy would do if he ever caught up with her, she started to panic. "I gotta get out of here right away, Greta."

"What's wrong?"

"I just got back from standing in a police lineup. The cops know I've been living here with you. Once the cops get wind of something, then everybody knows."

"What were you doing in a lineup?"

"It was on the Judge case. They let me go once the witness said that she couldn't be sure it was me."

"Where are you going to go?"

"It's better that you don't know, Greta."

"Will I hear from you?"

"Of course you will. But for now, I gotta concentrate on hiding from Ruffy Shea until I can make plans to do something about him."

"Be careful, Sarah," warned Greta. "I'm here when you need me."

A cold chill came over Sarah as she imagined how Leon must have suffered. *Ruffy had to have made Leon talk,* she thought.

"I have to get moving, Greta, and don't worry, I'll be in touch."
Sarah now saw Shepherd Fish, a.k.a. Fishnet, as a lifeline
because he was in a position to harbor her. The question
became whether or not the former detective would be willing
to extend himself. Sarah knew that to get the one-time sleuth to
sign on would require her to incentivize him. There was only
one way at her disposal to accomplish that.

The hunted woman reached out to Fishnet, indicating that it
was urgent that she see him. She steadfastly refused to provide
a reason over the telephone. Not wanting to jeopardize their
agreement calling for Sarah to murder Marvin Butterworth,
Fishnet relented. He gave her the address of his townhouse and
told her to come by.

Sarah's belongings were contained in two suitcases. Among
the items packed were three handguns. Before leaving to see
Fishnet, she took great pains to beautify herself. She was
counting on her desirability to influence Fishnet.

When Fishnet's came to the front door he was surprised to see
her arriving with packed bags. Unsure as to what she was up to,
Fishnet nevertheless let Sarah into his home.

Once inside the house, Sarah began tugging on her eyelid. She
was feigning that she was trying to get something out of her
eye. The maneuver was successful in getting Fishnet to take
notice of what she oddly considered to be an asset. Fishnet saw
through her ploy, wondering what Sarah had up her sleeve.
Pointing to the suitcases, he asked if she was taking a trip.
After being apprised of the latest developments with Ruffy
Shea, the ex-detective pondered his options. After some
deliberation, he permitted Sarah to stay at his home. Fishnet's
graciousness came with the strict provision that the house guest
remained indoors so that no one would know that she was
staying with him. Concern for Sarah's well-being had nothing to
do with Fishnet's decision. His only reason for harboring Sarah
was to avoid disruption of his plan to rid himself of Marvin
Butterworth.

##########

MARKIE AND VON HESS RETURNED to their duties at police headquarters. The first time the sergeant crossed paths with the chief of detectives, he was corralled into having a conversation about Lieutenant Waldo Reale.

"How did you find working with Waldo, Al?"

"It could have been worse, Chief."

"It must of have gone well, because I received no blowback on this end. I guess I humbled old Waldo enough to keep him in line."

"I suppose you did, Chief. Unfortunately, the getaway driver in the case slipped through the net."

"That's no big deal," said McCoy. "As long as the shooter was identified and we cleared the case with positive results, we're good."

"Yeah, but the getaway driver—"

"Let it go, Al, and remember our primary focus. Do you know what that is?"

"What, Chief?"

"To keep the folks at the top of the pyramid satisfied—and as it stands now, they are. So, relax. We're batting a thousand. There is no room to improve on that batting average. If we return to the plate, we run the risk of screwing something up, and that'll put us in the shithouse."

While Markie didn't necessarily agree with Chief McCoy, the insight provided gave the sergeant a good idea why McCoy had made it to the rank of chief of detectives.

27

Money First

UNDER DIFFERENT CONDITIONS, Ruffy Shea would have immediately passed a death sentence on his son-in-law for his treachery. It was Ruffy's love of money that saved Mickey from meeting the same fate met by Leon Crabbe. What Mickey didn't realize was that once the debt was satisfied, Ruffy had every intention of killing him.

When word reached Ruffy that Mickey was arrested for possessing a loaded gun, he found it hard to believe. In one sense, Mickey earned a degree of respect from Ruffy by his having backbone enough to arm himself.

Another part of Ruffy lamented that a jail term for Mickey would mean that he wouldn't be able to collect his money until Mickey was set free. All Ruffy could do under the circumstances was wait and see how things played out in court.

If Mickey avoided prison, Ruffy could continue to look for his weekly cash payments. If Mickey was sent away to jail, then the payments would have to be placed on hold until Mickey was free again.

While Mickey received a temporary reprieve from Ruffy's style of punishment, such consideration was not extended to Sarah. On the contrary, hunting the sex worker had become a priority. No longer targeted for a basic maiming, Sarah was now marked for death. Ruffy's decision to kill Sarah came as easily as eradicating a careless house mouse foolish enough to step into the light.

##########

RUFFY AND JOE BULLETS WERE having a quiet dinner at Italo's. The fact that the restaurant was doing a brisk business didn't go unnoticed by the thugs. Things turned serious when the topic of Sarah came up.

"Do you think Queenie might know where to find Sarah, Skipper?" asked Joe.

"We don't need to involve Queenie in this," replied Ruffy. "I already know where her new hideout is."

"You do?"

"I got tipped off by the same bull who put me wise to where I could find that guy Leon. Sarah's been staying with her girlfriend."

"That lieutenant came through?"

"Yeah, Joe, me and him are on a first name basis now," said Ruffy. "To me, he's Waldo."

"That's funny."

"I'll tell you what's really funny….Waldo's got it in for Sarah himself," revealed Ruffy. "But I have to give that bull credit for one thing."

"What's that?"

"He's smart enough to let somebody else do the dirty work."

"And you don't mind that, Skipper?"

"Not when it comes to Sarah. When the time comes, she's one mission I'm gonna fly on alone."

"I hear you."

"Are you around tomorrow?"

"When ain't I, Skipper?"

Joe drove Ruffy over to Greta's apartment the following day. After gaining entry into the building, they located the apartment in question. When no one answered his knock, Joe put his shoulder to the door and pushed forward. Feeling some

249

give, he believed he could force the door open without causing too much of a disturbance. Before doing so, Joe checked to see if the neighboring apartments on the floor were occupied. After establishing that no one was at home in the other apartments, Joe tried forcing Greta's front door open by throwing his shoulder into it. Having failed, he tried again. After his second unsuccessful attempt, Joe backed up a step and thunder kicked the door with such force that the door flew open.

Once entry was gained, they walked through the apartment. They discovered nothing to indicate that Sarah had been there. "Looks like we got a bum lead, Skipper," commented Joe. "Yeah, maybe," replied Ruffy, who then opened a closet door. "Look at this shit," he declared, pointing at the clothes in the closet. "Those are Mickey's clothes. We'll come back in a couple of days. If she ain't here then, we'll start asking around." Not allowing his disappointment to stand in the way of his appetite, Ruffy decided that they should return to Italo's for dinner that evening.

##########

RUFFY AND JOE BULLETS COULDN'T GET OVER the amount of business Italo's was doing. The restaurant bar was lined with people having drinks while they waited to be seated. The clientele at the eatery consisted of customers of all ages.

"Jeeze, this place is jumping," commented Ruffy as he scanned the room in search of the owner. He was looking to circumvent the line and be seated expeditiously. Upon spotting Italo he smiled broadly and waved him over.

"Hey, Italo, what's going on in this place?" asked Ruffy. "What are you dishing out over here? The interest Ruffy exhibited was unusual for him.

"Just good food," replied Italo. "Welcome back, you must have no complaints with our food."

"It's the best. How about getting me and Joe seated?"

"No problem, follow me," replied Italo, who immediately ordered his staff to find room for an extra table to be placed.

"So, I'm glad to see that everything has been good with you," voiced Ruffy, once seated.

"Yeah, things are going along fine. I have to go take care of some people who just came in now," explained Italo, excusing himself. " I'll be back to see you guys later. Enjoy."

After Italo left both Ruffy and Joe watched him. They envied the amicable interactions Italo was having with his patrons. More importantly, they envied the imagined money he was likely pulling out of the restaurant.

"He's got a nice setup over here," said Joe.

"Yeah, it sure looks like he's doing all right with this joint," concurred Ruffy, "and no credit cards in this dump."

"You can't beat a cash business. It's the only way to beat the tax man."

When Italo returned to check on their table to see how they were getting on, Ruffy posed a few questions. "You never take credit cards, right Italo?"

"Sometimes I have to, but we try to encourage cash."

"But it's mostly cash you gotta be pulling in, right?"

Italo shrugged his shoulders. "Well, I suppose," he admitted shyly, not eager to acknowledge this.

"You gotta stop by my new cat house in Manhattan," said Ruffy, referring to his prostitution business. "It'll be my treat."

"Oh, I don't know….," answered Italo. He was reluctant to become obligated.

"Sure you do—give him the address, Joe." Joe jotted down the address on a matchbook cover. "Initial it, Joe, and mark it OTH (on the house)."

"Here you go, Italo," said Joe, handing the signed matchbook cover to Italo. "Now you're officially a guest."

"Ask for Queenie when you go," added Ruffy. "She'll take good care of you."

"Thank you," said Italo. Well, it's been nice seeing you boys again."

"Hey, where are you running to?" asked Ruffy. "Take a seat and have a glass of wine with us."

"Sure," said Italo, seeing no way out of it. Ruffy was known to be well connected to the Rava family boss, and thus, someone not to be denied. "What would you like, red or white?"

"Give us the red."

Italo summoned the waiter, instructing him to bring a bottle of one of the better red wines. "You'll like this," advised the business owner when the wine arrived at the table.

They were well into the bottle when Ruffy began probing further into Italo's business. "You know, I never imagined you pulling in crowds like this on a weeknight."

"Yeah, business has been exceptionally good," admitted Italo.

"What do you attribute that to?"

"A lot has to do with our new chef. The guy's brilliant."

"Where did you get him from?"

"We got him from the other side."

"Are you telling me that all these people are here just because of the chef?" asked Joe skeptically.

"Well, to tell you the truth, it's not just the chef."

"I didn't think so," commented Joe, feeling validated.

"So, what's the secret?" questioned Ruffy.

"Things really picked up once we opened the other place," whispered Italo. He then shook his hand as if he were shaking dice. "People come in to eat and then go over to the other place to do a little gambling. Sometimes it's the reverse, especially if they've won."

"You're to be complimented, my friend, you got a good thing going."

"I know how to steer the right people over there," boasted Italo, as the wine began to loosen his tongue further.

"It's just you and your cousin who are partners here, right?"

"Yeah, Ruffy, we're partners right down the middle, both in here and over there. I run the restaurant, and Ciro oversees the casino."

"It's all in the family, eh, Italo."

"Yeah, it works out good for both of us."

"I can see that. Send Ciro my regards."

"I'll do that, Ruffy."

There came a point during the conversation when Italo finally came to realize he had been talking too freely. He gracefully excused himself from the table by announcing that he had to get back to work.

"Ciro's got it easier than his cousin," pointed out Joe, after Italo walked off.

"How do you figure that?"

"I know for a fact that Ciro delegates a lot of the casino responsibility to his man, Swatty," explained Joe. "Over here, it looks like Italo does all the work himself."

"These cousins got a good thing going," noted Ruffy," stroking his chin. The gesture made it evident that he was thinking. "Are you getting ideas, Ruffy?"

"I'm wondering if my dear friend Philly knows just how good these guys got it over here. I'm thinking that maybe I see an opportunity for us, Joe."

"Are you looking to buy in?"

Ruffy looked at Joe and smiled. "I got in mind something along those lines."

"If you're thinking of muscling in, don't forget that Ciro is a made guy."

"It'll all depend on what Philly Rava wants to do. Here, have some more wine," said Ruffy, filling Joe's glass.

"This could start a lot of trouble, Ruffy," cautioned Joe. "Philly is the boss, so don't worry about a thing, Joe. I know just how to work it."

"Jeeze, good luck if you can pull it off."

"We'll pull it off once we get the green light."

"We?"

"You're in for a piece, Joe. Tell me something, have you ever been inside that casino?" asked Ruffy.

"I've been there," Joe replied. "Did you know that they got raided?"

"They did?" asked a surprised Ruffy. "When was that?"

"Not too long ago, but things are up and running again."

"You know this guy Swatty, right?"

"Sure, Swatty is Ciro's man. He was the guy who showed up at the track for the meet with Ciro."

"How well do you know him?"

"Well enough, why?"

"Would you say he's ambitious?"

"No more or no less than anybody else, I guess. I know that he's chomping at the bit to get his button."

"And his boss is doing the same to make capo," reminded Ruffy. "Is Swatty ambitious enough to listen to a proposition?"

"If it meant a way to advance in the family he would. Let me put it this way, Swatty would cross his own mother to become a Rava soldier."

"Go feel him out and see if he'd consider doing business."

"He's gonna ask me what kind of business...."

"Just tell him it's an opportunity with me. And Joe, emphasize how I stand with Philly Rava. Let him know that I may be able to help him get that button he wants so badly."

"This could be risky," Joe cautioned gravely.

"Since when are you worried about taking a risk?

"I ain't worried. I'll go see Swatty right away, Ruffy."

"No, wait a day. I want to go see Philly first and get his blessing."

##########

PHILLY RAVA RESIDED ALONE in a large house in Toms River, New Jersey. The never-married Rava was a thin man of average height. He wore his silver hair slicked down with a high part. The crime boss could be exceedingly clever when it came to achieving goals. This was proven by his rise in the family which now bore his name.

At seventy-five, the years had settled the family boss, who now carried himself in a relaxed fashion. With his carousing days long behind him, he never seemed to get excited or break into a sweat. His only physical activity consisted of shuffling a deck of cards.

During the summer months, Rava could usually be found lounging by his pool in his sleepwear, which he restricted to monogrammed silk pajamas that he wore beneath a matching silk bathrobe on cooler days. In the winter, he relaxed indoors while attired in the same apparel.

Wednesday afternoons were set aside for Rava's captains to visit his home. At these meetings, his underlings discussed business, met their monetary obligations, and joined the boss in feasting on the finest of foods. Since Ruffy Shea wasn't of the right ethnicity to be a made member of the family, he wasn't invited to these Wednesday meetings. However, as the pet of the crime boss, he socialized privately with Rava.

Rava was a stickler for holding members of the family accountable when it came to following the rules of the organization. Being a hypocrite, he never addressed his own lack of adherence when it came to family laws.

Involvement in narcotics was a no-no. It was prohibited out of fear that those caught selling drugs would cooperate with the authorities rather than face long prison sentences. Violators of this ban on drugs faced a death sentence.

Due to the profitability connected to drug trafficking, the crime boss entered the narcotics business as Ruffy's silent partner. Ruffy, as a non-inducted member of the family, was under no restrictions.

It was early in the morning when Ruffy visited Philly Rava at his home. As was always the case, the two men sat at the kitchen table while Rava cooked breakfast.

"Here you go, Philly," said Ruffy, holding out a cash-filled envelope.

"Just put it on the table. I'm making us a Swiss cheese omelet with sausage, mushrooms, and red peppers," announced Rava. "Do you want some orange juice?"

"No, the coffee is just fine."

After sitting down to eat, Rava examined the envelope between bites. He smiled approvingly as he held up the envelope in his hand.

"You're a good boy, Ruffy," Rava complimented. "You've proven yourself a better earner then any two men I have in my family. I only wish you were Italian so I could propose you for membership and make you my underboss."

"Thanks, Philly. I'm grateful for our friendship. I can only do what I do because I got you behind me. After all, it was you who took me under your wing at the beginning when I was young floundering punk."

"You're wise to recognize that, Ruffy. You'd be surprised at how many people have short memories once they begin making a little money. The stupid ones forget who helped them achieve their riches."

"Not me, Philly. I'm loyal."

"I know that. You mentioned on the phone that you had something you wanted to discuss."

"I've had my eye on Ciro's casino and restaurant operation."

"Ciro, who is a friend of mine?"

"Yeah, Ruffy, that Ciro."

"Is he causing problems for you?"

"No, it's nothing like that."

"Then what is it?"

"I think that he may be holding out on you."

"Explain."

"Do you have any idea how much money him and his cousin are pulling in between that casino and the restaurant they got?"

"From what I'm receiving, I'd say he's making a living."

"That's what I figured, Philly, so I did some homework. Let me tell you, that casino is pulling in the green hand over fist. That Ciro is a cutie pie who wants to keep all the gravy for himself."

"What about his cousin, Italo? Is he the same way?"

"My guess is that Italo doesn't know a thing about the actual casino take. He's probably happy with whatever Ciro gives him."

"This is interesting," said Rava.

"Listen to this, it gets better. Ciro came to me asking for a favor. He wants me to talk you into promoting him to capo."

"You're that friendly with him?"

"No, I hardly know the guy. He's too slippery an eel for my

money. Anyway, I thought you should know, Philly."

"I assume that you have an idea as to what should to be done."

"I do have an idea, Philly."

"Go on, let's hear it."

"With your blessing, me and Joe Bullets will take over both the casino and restaurant for us. But you'll have to give me the okay to take out Ciro."

"What do you propose to do with Italo?"

"We'll keep Italo at the restaurant as a partner."

"Is there enough money to go around?"

"I think so."

Rava nodded, indicating that he would go along. "Keeping Italo in the mix is smart. Without him the other family members would begin to have questions."

"That's the way I figured it. What are you going to do about Ciro's other business interests?"

"My capos can take over whatever else he has going"

"We could start a rumor that Ciro turned rat, Philly. That would explain his getting canceled out."

"Yes, that'll work. I'll let it be known to my family that you and Italo are now partners. You know, Italo's family comes from the same little town in the old country as I did."

"No wonder he's a decent guy," commented Ruffy, browning up the boss.

"You have my permission to move on this, Ruffy. But remember, I need to remain in the shadows," stipulated Rava. "It must never be known that I'm involved in a move against a member of my family."

"Naturally, you'll remain strictly in the shade, just like all our other business dealings."

28

The Big Surprise

SWATTY WAS CHAIN SMOKING in an effort to steady his nerves. He was chauffeuring Ciro and Italo to Bayonne, New Jersey, which for one of them was to be a one way ride.

The men in the back seat were too absorbed in their own conversation to pay any attention to Swatty. The driver tilted his head back to rectify the difficulty he was having in hearing what his passengers were saying when they lowered their voices.

Swatty gathered that Ciro and Italo were discussing the opening of a second restaurant and casino. It seemed, as of yet, they weren't certain where to plant a flag for their new venture. "What about Staten Island, Ciro?" asked Italo, who preferred a not-too-distant locale.

"That's no good," Ciro replied. "We have to be far enough away to be under the radar."

"Well, then, how about New Jersey?"

"No, that's still too close. I'm thinking maybe we start up under a new name in Pennsylvania or Ohio."

"That's very far away, Ciro...."

"We got no choice. Anytime Philly Rava gets wind of somebody in the family making an buck, that vulture looks for his taste."

"You mean you don't intend to tell him about it?"

"Why should I? As it stands, he's getting plenty out of us already," answered Ciro.

"But what if he finds out later?"

"He won't, as long as we're smart. We'll install a front man as the face of the restaurant and open up under another name."

"So you figure that we'll do things the same way as we do in Queens?"

"That's the formula. We get the restaurant up and going, and then the casino follows. I'm thinking that we could put my wife's cousin in to run the restaurant. You know him, the guy who works for the Transit Authority."

"Do you think he'd want to do it?"

"I'm sure he would. He's been looking to retire from his Transit job, so he'd be up for it. We'll get him to work with you for a while so that he understands the business. Once he does, we'll set him up out of state."

"What about the casino?"

"When the time comes, I'll send Swatty to get the casino up and running. The crew we got in place can handle the Queens operation with me, so we could afford to let Swatty go."

Swatty's ears perked up after hearing his name mentioned. *These bastards are making plans to ship me out without even asking me,* he thought. Swatty was perturbed enough to begin puffing on his cigarette furiously.The smoke inside the car caused Ciro to begin coughing.

"Hey, put that thing out! You're killing us back here!" complained Ciro.

'Sorry," said the driver who rolled down the window to toss the butt out.

"What's your wife expecting a baby?" asked Italo jokingly. "You're smoking like a chimney."

"Yeah, what's wrong with you today?" questioned Ciro. "You'd think you were the one getting bumped up, instead of me."

"I just don't want you to be late for your own promotion," said Swatty.

Swatty pulled up in front of a one story building that housed a small restaurant. There were no lights visible in any of the windows.

"The place looks closed," voiced Italo. "Are we gonna be able to get in?"

"I was told that the back door would be left open," replied Ciro. Now remember you guys can't go in with me. Philly wants this done real private like. He said that he only told a couple of capos that I was being moved up."

"Why is that?" asked Italo.

"Philly don't want to hear any squawking from anybody claiming that they're more deserving. He even ordered me to keep this whole thing a top secret and not to discuss tonight with anyone in the family."

"Swatty's day should be coming soon, right?" asked Italo.

"He didn't make it this round," replied Ciro, who then reached forward to pat Swatty's shoulder. "Don't you worry, Swatty, I'll be pushing for you big time now that I'm getting a boost."

"I know, Ciro, I know," answered Swatty, sounding disappointed.

"Okay, here I go, boys. Next time you see me I'll be a capo!"

Or a corpse, thought Swatty.

Ciro walked around to the rear of the building. As expected, he found the door unlocked. Bursting with pride he opened the door where he expected to be met by family bosses awaiting his arrival. Instead, his greeting committee consisted of Ruffy Shea and Joe Bullets.

"SURPRISE!" shouted Joe, as he placed Swatty in a bear hug. While Joe held Ciro, Ruffy looped a rope around his neck. Each assassin then held one end of the rope and proceeded to garrote their victim. Ciro's desperate struggle to prevent strangulation was to no avail. Once he was gone, his murderers let his body fall to the ground.

After catching his breath, Joe stepped outside to signal Swatty, who was waiting in the car with Ciro's unsuspecting cousin. Joe's wave meant that Swatty and Italo should enter the building.

"Come on, they want us inside," announced Swatty.

"What's he doing here?" asked Italo, who was a bit wary since Joe Bullets wasn't a member of the fraternity.

"I don't know. I guess we'll find out."

Once inside the building, Italo stopped short after seeing his cousin's body on the floor. He then looked at the three men around him. Their emotionless faces caused the color to drain from Italo's face. Believing that the time of his doom had arrived, Italo made the sign of the cross and began to pray.

The restaurant owner was too numb to feel Swatty's hand on his shoulder. When he finally turned to face Swatty, Italo realized who betrayed his cousin.

"Relax, Italo," said Swatty. "No one is gonna hurt you. You're among friends."

When no response came from Italo, Ruffy spoke more assertively. "Do you understand what Swatty just said? You're in no danger. You're gonna be part of the new management."

Italo turned to look at Swatty. Wanting to say something, he found himself unable to express himself. Understanding Italo's upset state, Swatty placed his hand gently on Italo's face. "Buck up, Italo," he said, "things are gonna work out okay for us. This move was just good business."

At this point Ruffy stepped up to Italo and callously declared that his cousin Ciro had put up a valiant fight before succumbing to the rope.

"The son of a bitch made a good account of himself," Joe chimed in. "I didn't think he had it in him."

Italo came to accept that he was going to have new partners in his restaurant and casino. There was no mention of Philly Rava having a secret interest.

"But Ciro was a soldier in the family...." uttered a perplexed Italo, to no one in particular. "There are gonna be repercussions."

"Yeah, well let me worry about that, Italo," said Ruffy.

"What am I supposed to tell people when they start asking me about Ciro?"

"You tell him that Ciro left his wife and kids to run off with his girlfriend to Portugal."

"What girlfriend?"

"Just say that he had a whole other family on the side and that's all you know about it."

Italo glanced down at his dead cousin's body on the floor and shook his head sadly. "So, who am I supposed to be with now?" "From this day on, you, me, Joe and Swatty are all gonna be partners in the casino and restaurant business," answered Ruffy. "When I get Philly to formally induct Swatty into the family, we'll make the necessary adjustments."

"What happens to Ciro's body?"

"Joe and Swatty are gonna take care of that."

Italo looked at Swatty with sadness. Sensing Italo's disappointment, Swatty felt compelled to speak.

"Take it in stride, Italo," advised Swatty. "You gotta just make the best of it."

"But you were Ciro's friend."

"Sure I was, but he would have made the same play if our positions were reversed."

Italo couldn't argue the point, especially after Ruffy voiced loudly that he didn't want to hear another word about it.

29

Another Notch For Sarah

FISHNET WAS SIPPING COGNAC WHILE seated at the piano in the main room of his townhouse. Having no knowledge of how to play the percussion instrument, he randomly tapped at the keyboard with his index finger. This was something he often did when immersed in thought.

The former detective paused when he reached a sequence of notes that sounded familiar to him. He recognized the *dum-de-dum-dum* sound as coming from an old television show called Dragnet. As he recollected the show, his mind entered the concocted world he frequently traveled to.

In this fantasy he imagined himself as Joe Friday, the fictional LAPD detective sergeant. As Friday, he was charged with investigating Marvin Butterworth, an axe murderer who preyed on the Hollywood set. As his storyline unfolded Fishnet simultaneously put words to the tune he played. He began to utter, *"Dum-de-dum-dum .... Go-and-axe-one."*

"Who are you talking to?" asked Sarah, who entered the room. She thought someone was in the house other than Fishnet.

"WHAT?" Fishnet asked, annoyed at his fantasy being interrupted.

"I just asked who you were talking to...."

"I was talking to myself. I was working out something in my mind."

"What were you working out?"

Fishnet couldn't bring himself to reveal his Joe Friday daydream. Instead, he thought it time to go over the bizarre plan he had in store for Marvin Butterworth. He conveyed that he intended to duplicate an autoerotic death he once investigated.

"Autoerotic death....I gotta be honest, I still don't get what's the hell that's all about," commented Sarah.

"You don't have to. Marvin's gonna be discovered in a hotel room while attired in the underwear of a woman. You're gonna put self-degrading comments, printed in red lipstick, across his chest," advised Fishnet, adding, "a lot of people go that way," As Sarah listened she began to seriously doubt Fishnet's mental state. Having experienced a variety of strange people during her tenure at two bordellos, she had never come across anyone as quite strange as Fishnet.

"This is nuts," said Sarah, not knowing when to hold her tongue.

"What makes you say that?" replied Fishnet, who wasn't happy with her remark.

"I'm just saying, we don't need to go through all this extra bullshit if you just want him dead."

"I'm orchestrating this, sweetheart, not you. I want the old man's death to go down as being accidental, and autoerotic asphyxiation is the way to go."

"Who is this Marvin anyway?"

"That's my business, Sarah."

Fishnet's tart response caused Sarah to back off. With the threat of Ruffy Shea being on the hunt for her, Sarah didn't want to alienate her host. She couldn't risk doing anything that would disrupt the safe environment that Fishnet provided.

Sarah had little choice other than to go along with Fishnet's plan, regardless of how bizarre.

"How am I supposed to overpower this Marvin?" asked Sarah. "It'll be easy," replied Fishnet. "He's an old man with a bad back. You'll have no trouble with him once you kick him hard in the back," assured Fishnet. "He'll fall apart like a cheap suit."

"I think I know an easier way that'll be much simpler—"

"I want it done exactly the way I explained it," insisted Fishnet, who had become increasingly frustrated with Sarah. The onetime detective issued Sarah an ultimatum. "Listen, there's the door. If you want out, use it and take your chances on the street."

"All right, you don't have to get that way. I'll do it whatever way you want. How am I supposed to get to the hotel?" "Don't worry I'll get you there and see to it that you get back here safely. All you have to do is follow my instructions." "Say, what's your name again?"

"Shepherd Fish," answered Fishnet, sticking to the alias he had established when first meeting his late wife. "Now remember, the best way to take Marvin down is from behind. Just kick him in his lower back."

"Okay, I got it."

"Once you got him down, keep him on his belly by sitting on him. Then finish him off by putting the plastic bag I'm gonna give you over his head. Just make sure you got the plastic bag handy so you don't have to get up off him. What do you do next?"

"Then his clothes come off, and I put the panties on him." "And then what?"

"Then I draw a big pecker on his body with red lipstick and scribble some curse words on him."

"Don't forget to leave behind the lipstick. This has to look like Marvin did this to himself."

"I got it."

"Good, now let's have a drink."

Sarah looked about the room as Fishnet poured a drink. Impressed by the affluent surroundings, she regretted not having asked for more money for the murder she agreed to commit. "So, this house is all yours?" she asked.

"Yeah, baby, all mine, lock, stock, and barrel," he answered. "So, what did Marvin do to piss you off so much?" she asked, again succumbing to her curiosity.

"Never mind about that," Fishnet replied curtly. "I'll call him in the morning and get the ball rolling,"

"I've been thinking. I got no problem doing what you want, but with all this other stuff it's turning out to be a lot more work." "So?"

"So how about giving me a little more money?" asked the hired killer straight out.

"You want more money?" asked the astonished Fishnet.

"Be a sport, handsome—you got it."

"Are you forgetting that on top of what I'm paying you, I'm hiding your pretty little ass out?" countered Fishnet. "Ain't that enough?"

"It's good, but don't forget, I'm earning my keep upstairs too," answered Sarah, referring to the bedroom. "I don't think you've been disappointed in that department."

Since he had no intention of paying Sarah anyway, Fishnet wasn't about to quibble. "All right, Sarah, I'll sweeten the pot with a bonus once the job is done," said Fishnet. He then smiled to give the impression that all was cool between them.

"Now you're being a sweetie!" Sarah said happily, reaching over to hug and kiss him. "Can I ask you just one question that I've been curious about?"

"Go on...."

"Why is that sergeant after you?" she asked, referring to Sergeant Markie.

"That's a fair question," conceded Fishnet. "To tell you the truth, I really don't know why. I even did the guy a favor once, and from what I know he's still got it in for me." Fishnet then drifted off to the private world he frequently visited.

Sarah could see that the ex-detective assumed that faraway look. She studied him as she wondered what his thoughts were. She had no way of knowing that Fishnet envisioned himself

266

standing over her and Marvin as they sat back to back, tied down in connected chairs. The two were on the ground high on Mount Blanc, which borders France, Italy, and Switzerland.

When Fishnet saw himself pushing the bound couple off an icy cliff, Sarah was able to see a smile forming on his face. As the ex-detective imagined the bound pair bouncing off the ice ledges, his smile broadened.

"Hey, where are you?" Sarah finally asked.

"What was that?" asked the startled Fishnet.

"Where is your mind?"

"On those eyes of yours," replied Fishnet without missing a beat.

Sarah smirked before replying. "Oh, so that's what you were thinking of. Let's go upstairs," she invited. "You could watch them do the bunny hop."

###########

THE FOLLOWING MORNING SARAH slept late. Having spent the night in Fishnet's room, she was awakened by his voice as he spoke on the telephone. Listening to just one side of the conversation, it took her awhile to realize that Fishnet was talking to Marvin, their intended victim.

"No, I'm serious. I have a good opportunity for you."

"Well, thank you for thinking of me, my boy," said Marvin Butterworth.

"I thought of you because I wanted to show you that there are no hard feelings on my end regarding your friend," advised Fishnet. He was referring to Amos West. "His situation was something I didn't want to be involved in."

"Whatever business it was that you discussed with Amos was strictly between you two." *Cagey as ever, this old buzzard,* thought Fishnet.

"I'm glad to hear that you're not ticked off, Marvin."

"I make it a policy never to take things personally, my friend. Now what was it that you believe to be in my interest?"

"There's this gal I know who is married to a much older rich man who is on his last legs. He owns all kinds of properties in Manhattan. Since he has kids from a previous marriage, the wife needs to figure out a way to get the old man to sign over everything to her before he cashes in his chips. I think you could walk away real fat if you could help make that happen."

"How much of a fee do you think she'll agree to?"

"She's no businesswoman, so I'd go in high and ask for half the works."

"By all means, I'm interested, my boy," said Marvin, now sounding very chipper. He began to lick his lips at the thought of such an opportunity. "When can you bring her around to the office?"

"Forget the office, Marvin. She wants to meet you at the bar in the Bixby Hotel the day after tomorrow. Does that work for you?"

"The Bixby works fine. What time?

"Figure on 7:00 p.m."

"Are you going to be there?"

"No, Marvin, I don't want to get in the middle. I'll do what I can from the background. It'll just be you and her."

"How am I supposed to know her? Give me her phone number." Fishnet ignored his request for Sarah's number. "Don't worry, she'll know you. Besides, you can't miss her. She's a hot, good-looking young blond."

"Yeah?" expressed Marvin.

"Down, boy, you don't want to have a heart attack. I could tell you more about her, but I'd be wasting my time on an old fart like you."

"You'd be surprised, my boy. Do I need to compensate you should this come to fruition?"

"Nah, I don't need any money, Marvin. This is my gift to you for being such a good guy."

"Well, thank you very much."

You lucky murdering son of a bitch, thought the attorney after hanging up the phone. Marvin couldn't let go of his suspicion

268

that Fishnet murdered his wife, and her agent, in a Pennsylvania quarry.

"Okay, Sarah, we're all set," advised Fishnet, turning to the woman in his bed. "You're gonna meet Marvin at the Bixby Hotel bar at 7 p.m. the day after tomorrow. There'll be a room in Marvin Butterworth's name waiting for you."

"How is that gonna work?"

"Don't worry; you'll have the room key before you go into the hotel."

########

IN ORDER TO SECURE A ROOM at the Bixby Hotel in Marvin's name, Fishnet needed an accomplice. Wanting to make it appear as if Marvin himself had checked in, the former detective thought that No Tax Johnny Layton would fit the bill perfectly because the two looked alike and were roughly the same age. The only downside to consider was that No Tax suffered from dropped head syndrome. The affliction prevented him from lifting his head in an upright posture, giving him the appearance of someone with no neck. Since Marvin was stooped, Fishnet was sure that people wouldn't be able to tell the difference between No Tax and Marvin if shown a photo. Fishnet wasted no time in heading out to the Brooklyn OTB parlor that No Tax was known to frequent.

As expected, Fishnet found No Tax at his regular hangout. The elderly gambler was leaning against a mailbox in front of the betting parlor. He was holding the racing form in one hand and, in the other, the magnifying glass that he used for reading the small print. Absorbed in his handicapping, No Tax was oblivious to the Mercedes that parked at the curb. It was only after Fishnet had approached him that he took notice.

"Hey, No Tax!" greeted Fishnet energetically. "How the hell are you?"

The old man could only twist his body and lift his eyes upward to see who it was. "Hey, look who it is, Sherlock Holmes," said the senior citizen. "They said you ended up a vegetable in a hospital someplace."

"You believed that? C'mon, the bullet wasn't made that could keep me down, pal," said Fishnet cockily.

"Tackling a guy like Red Harris took a lot of balls. That guy was a stone killer."

"Yeah, well, like they say, the strongest oak must fall."

"Everybody on the street thought you were nuts for trading lead with him."

"But not you, No Tax, you didn't think that. You were betting on me."

"I wouldn't have given you a chance," stated the old man frankly. "Are you here for me to cash a winning ticket for you?"

"No, it's nothing like that. I'm here because I got a way for you to make some easy money."

"I could use it. Things ain't been so good with me," complained No Tax. "Since I don't pay taxes, I make my money when I can cash tickets for big winners who want to avoid the tax bite. The problem is, nobody's been winning big lately. Funds are getting low."

"This will give you some relief, old timer."

"I hope so....how much relief?"

"I'm figuring you got a grand coming to you on this deal."

"For a grand, you got yourself a man."

"I figured you'd be interested."

"What do you need me to do?"

"I want you to take a room at the Bixby Hotel in Manhattan under the name of Marvin Butterworth."

"All the way over in Manhattan?" balked No Tax, playing up the inconvenience. "I don't know, that's a big trip for me in my condition."

"Don't worry about that. I'll pay for your ride to and from."

"I suppose that I'm gonna need phony identification under that name."

"Can you take care of that?"

"It depends. When do you need this done?"

"I plan on doing this tomorrow."

"You're gonna have to take a haircut in order to acquire the identification on such short notice."

"I understand that."

"You're lucky that I know somebody who can take care of this for you."

"Okay, here, take this," said Fishnet, passing money to the senior citizen. "This should cover it, right?"

No Tax counted off the bills he received. "Yeah, this is good," said No Tax. "What do I do about checking in money?"

"Here is some more cash to cover that," advised Fishnet. "What, did you hit the Lotto?" asked No Tax, impressed by how freely Fishnet was parting with his funds.

"Let's just say I married well, No Tax. Make sure the name on the ID is correct."

"What's the name?"

"Marvin Butterworth."

"What the hell kind of name is Butterword?"

"It's *Butterworth*, not Butterword! Fishnet corrected. "Wait a second, I'll write out the exact name and address to use. Give me that racing form."

"You gotta get the marbles out of your mouth, so you can be understood," shot back No Tax. "Write big so I can see it." Fishnet shook his head as he wrote.

"Now listen, once you get the room, you're gonna give me the key and room number. I'll be outside in my car waiting for you." "Then what happens?"

At that point, your job is over. You get your grand and you're done. We got a deal?"

"You got a deal."

The following day No Tax ran into some opposition at the Bixby Hotel when trying to check in as Marvin Butterworth. The issue was No Tax not having a credit card. In answer to the senior citizen's loud proclamation that he was an American citizen and disabled veteran, the hotel manager was called in to arbitrate the dispute. In light of the age of No Tax, the manager made an exception and agreed to accept cash at check-in.

"Remember, you're paying to get me back to the OTB," reminded No Tax after turning over the room key to Fishnet. "No problem. Here," said Fishnet, handing No Tax cash, "This will cover it."

As Fishnet looked for a taxi, he began to think about what he was going to do about No Tax, the man who never paid his taxes. He held some concern that the octogenarian might shoot his mouth off one day down the road about taking the room. With this on his mind, he stopped what he was doing to ask No Tax a few questions.

"How old are you now, No Tax?"

"I'm gonna be eighty-seven in April."

"That's a long run you've had."

"Yeah, I've been around a long time now."

"How's your health? Do you think you're gonna make it to a hundred?"

"Not a chance, I may look good, but I'm in the last inning over here," said No Tax glumly.

"Are you sick or something?"

"The sawbones over at the VA hospital said I got pancreatic cancer. That means curtains in any man's language."

"Sorry to hear that, old timer," said Fishnet. Actually, he wasn't. Fishnet saw the revelation as a relief that spared Fishnet from having to kill the old man. *Why bother*, thought Fishnet. *How long has he got?*

##########

ARRIVING EARLIER THEN HER SCHEDULED meeting with Marvin Butterworth, Sarah made her way to the room at the Bixby Hotel unchallenged. Once she'd gained entry, she placed the small travel bag she carried on top of the dresser. Contained within the bag was the paraphernalia necessary to set the stage for detectives to conclude that Marvin's death was due to autoerotic activity.

Sarah, out of caution, remained in her room until it was time to meet Marvin at the hotel bar. Just prior to leaving the room, she checked her appearance in the bathroom mirror. Confident that she was alluring, she proceeded to the hotel bar.

When Marvin and Sarah met up, both were taken aback. Their acquaintance originated from Ruffy Shea's brothel. Sarah had to think fast.

"What's this all about?" asked Marvin, demanding an explanation.

"It's a long story. I can explain—"

"I'm listening," said Marvin, who suspected that Sarah was trying to pull some kind of con on Fishnet, his client.

"Look, I have a room here. How about we go upstairs where we can talk?" she suggested, hoping to lure Butterworth to the room. "There are some things you need to know.'

"Let's do that, my dear," agreed Marvin.

Sarah found Marvin to be a very confident man. She still couldn't help but wonder what Butterworth might have done to warrant a death sentence. However, her curiosity didn't deter her from carrying out her mission.

Once behind the closed door of the room, Sarah put the room key next to the television remote control device. As soon as Marvin turned away from her, Sarah launched a forceful thunder kick to his lower back. The blow collapsed him, just as Fishnet said it would.

With the attorney downed and in pain, Sarah was easily able to flip her victim off his side and onto his stomach. Sitting on Marvin's back, Sarah clasped her fingers and placed her palms against his chin. She then clutched his head back until she no longer felt resistance. Sarah could have easily ended things then and there, but instead, she adhered to the wishes put forth by Fishnet.

Sarah dragged the semi-conscious Butterworth over to the bed. After hoisting him onto the mattress, she removed a plastic bag from her pocket. After positioning her victim onto his stomach, she again mounted him. Listening to Marvin's feeble mutterings began to excite Sarah. She felt a sexual rush as she placed the plastic bag over her victim's head.

When she was finished, Sarah removed the plastic bag. She then placed the small mirror she had removed from her purse under the dead man's nose. When she saw nothing on the mirror, she was comfortable that Marvin had joined the ranks of the deceased.

The assassin again placed the plastic bag over the attorney's head. She stripped Marvin of his clothes and began to further follow the instructions Fishnet gave her, adding a few touches of her own. She removed a small rubber ball from her bag, slipped it under the plastic, and wedged it in Marvin's mouth. She then affixed a spring clothespin to each of his nipples. Using red lipstick, Sarah wrote the words "slut" and "slave" next to the penis she drew on his chest. Finally, she placed a pornographic magazine that featured sexually explicit acts on the floor next to the bed.

Satisfied with her handiwork, Sarah cleaned up after herself. For a second, she was tempted to take all the cash out of the dead man's wallet. She ended up just taking half, not wanting it to appear as if a robbery occurred. The murderess left the room with her valise in hand. As planned, she met Fishnet a block from the hotel. She was then safely returned to the townhouse. When Fishnet was informed of the grisly details, he lavished Sarah with praise for her resourcefulness in persuading Marvin to go to the room with her. He was so profuse with his accolades that Sarah didn't mind obliging Fishnet's later request for a round of eye-popping passion.

###########

WHEN NO TAX JOHNNY LAYTON passed the newspaper stand on his way to the OTB, as was his routine, he stopped to pick up a newspaper. Scanning the headlines as he walked, he noted that a prominent attorney had been found dead in a room at the Bixby Hotel. He paused to read a few lines.

When No Tax learned that the identity of the deceased man was Marvin Butterworth, his mouth dropped. He had just one thought: *Well, I'll be a son of a bitch!*

30

Markie Gets Short
Circuited

FINDING THE DEAD BODY OF A PROMINENT LAWYER LIKE
MARVIN BUTTERWORTH under autoerotic circumstances was
the kind of gossipy news that traveled fast in the police
department. When word reached the ear of Detective Ollie Von
Hess, he immediately remembered Butterworth as being the
attorney he and Markie had gone to see in connection with the
death of Fishnet's wife. The detective wasted no time in
apprising Markie of the attorney's unusual end.

Markie wasn't about to discount anything that had the
remotest connection to Fishnet. Regardless of how distanced
Fishnet seemingly was from Marvin's death, the sergeant
expressed an interest in knowing more.

Since Markie strongly suspected Fishnet of being responsible
for killing his wife and her lover, he viewed Butterworth's death
as an opportunity to possibly unearth information that would
shed new light on the Pennsylvania deaths. To satisfy his thirst
for justice, Markie, along with Von Hess, ventured off to see the
detective assigned to investigate the Butterworth death.

When they arrived at the Manhattan precinct, they found the detective seated behind his desk. He was snacking on black licorice while cleaning out his pipe. Raised in the South, the transplanted precinct detective was nothing like an average New Yorker.

When Markie flashed his badge and identified himself, the detective slowly lifted his lanky frame from behind his desk to politely greet his visitors. Spotting the bag of candy, Markie found himself unimpressed by the detective. There was something about his folksy manner that signified lackadaisicalness to the sergeant. The less critical Von Hess knew his boss well enough to see that he was underwhelmed. "Feel free to help yourselves, gentlemen," said the detective, pointing to the open plastic bag on his desk that contained the black licorice. "Have some licorice. It's my only weakness."

Markie, being an old movie buff, was automatically reminded of the scene in *The Bride of Frankenstein,* when Doctor Pretorius said, *"Do you like gin? It is my only weakness."*

Markie politely declined the offer. Von Hess, who liked licorice, helped himself.

The squad detective gladly explained why he arrived at the conclusion that Marvin Butterworth had met an accidental death. "That old boy died while engaging in a perverted solo sexual act, Sarge," he declared confidently. "No doubt about that."

"Doesn't an autoerotic death seem rather odd when considering Butterworth's age?" asked Markie.

"Oh, now I wouldn't exactly say that, Sarge," replied the detective. "He probably took some of that there Vi-agra."

"I suppose that's possible," acknowledged Markie. "But why did he need to go to the expense of renting a hotel room to take care of business?"

"Oh, well now, Sarge, remember, there are different strokes for different folks.

At the end of the day, the detective made it known that his boss was just fine with the way the case was closed. He further made it known that he hadn't heard anything contrary to his findings from the medical examiner.

"Was the hotel room in Butterworth's name?"

"It sure was."

"Was a credit card used?" asked Von Hess.

"No, cash on the barrelhead. A lot of old timers don't use credit cards."

"You don't think it odd that a big shot attorney didn't use a credit card?" The squad detective offered no reply. "Did you speak to the person who checked him in, detective?" Markie asked.

"We saw no need for that, Sarge."

"So, you don't know if the deceased checked in alone?"

"No one said he wasn't alone."

"He could have had a visitor. Did you ask around to see if he was seen with anyone?" queried Von Hess.

"Look here now. If you have a problem with how I handled this, maybe you better talk to my boss, who happened to sign off on my report."

"Relax, we're not looking to make waves," assured Markie. "It's just that we know this dead man from another caper," explained Markie. "You say that your squad commander is on board with the findings?"

"Certainly, he responded to the scene with me. I mean, c'mon, it was really pretty obvious how the guy died, Sarge. He had a penis drawn on his chest in red lipstick, for heaven's sake."

"I suppose it was," commented Markie.

"Do you mind if I ask what the big interest in this is, Sarge?"

"No big interest. Like I said, we just knew the deceased from an old case. Anyway, thanks." Markie then turned to face Von Hess, "Come on, Ollie, we're out of here."

Once they were on the street, Markie voiced his true feelings to Von Hess. "I can't see how an old geezer like Butterworth does this kind of crazy shit, Ollie," commented Markie. "It just doesn't sit well with me. That friggin' detective in the squad leaves a lot to be desired."

"He didn't know the history as we do, Sarge," reminded Von

Hess.

"Did you see him cleaning that pipe?"

Von Hess laughed. "It could have been worse, Sarge. He could have been whittling a piece of wood."

"Okay, joke if you want, but I still smell a rat."

"So, do you want to go by that hotel?"

"Not without the green light from the Chief of D's office, Ollie. Let's go see what they say back at the office."

############

BACK AT POLICE HEADQUARTERS, things were quiet, which made the timing good for Markie to bring up the Butterworth death to Lieutenant Wright, his superior. Not surprisingly, the sergeant was met with little encouragement as far as his delving deeper into the lawyer's death.

"Look, Al, you have nothing to support your suspicion. How could you suggest that the lawyer died any other way, other than what was determined by the squad that investigated the case?"

"I know, Loo, but—"

"It is a stretch to think a connection exists between Butterworth's death and those deaths in Pennsylvania. Besides, you were already told to back off once."

"Just give us the okay to talk to the people who work at the Bixby, Loo."

"No dice, Al, so let it go. Enjoy the down time or find someplace else to devote your energy."

"Okay, Loo, whatever you say," stated Markie. The disappointment in his voice was evident.

Lieutenant Wright, sensing that Markie was frustrated, tried to cheer him up with a compliment. "You guys did a nice job on the Judge Fatima West case. All the bosses around here are happy right now, thanks to you and Ollie. So take the kudos while they're coming and quit while you're ahead."

Markie had little choice other than to go along with his superior.

"Cheer up, Sarge, don't let it get to you," said Von Hess, upon learning that his boss was denied.

"Someday that fucker is gonna slip up, Ollie," said Markie, referring to Fishnet. "And when he does, I'm gonna be right there with the bracelets."

"That's right, Sarge. With a guy like Fishnet, it's just a matter of time."

########

DISILLUSIONED OVER HIS INABILITY TO gain permission to probe deeper into the death of Marvin Butterworth, Markie felt the need to unwind. He sought relief by stopping for drinks after work at Fitzie's.

Upon seeing Markie, Fitzie stepped around to the customer side of the bar to embrace the sergeant.

"Where have you been hiding?" asked Fitzie. The one-time prizefighter genuinely considered Markie to be a friend. "I've been worried about you."

"The job has kept me a little busy, Fitz."

Fitzie signaled his new bartender to take their drink order. As she approached, Markie took notice. At fifty, Fitzie's new employee retained enough of her youthful form to still turn heads. As the bartender approached, she brushed back her long black hair with her fingers. The threads of gray gave her something of an exotic look.

"Bring us two shots of Jameson, neat, and a couple of short beers," said Fitzie. "These drinks are on the house."
"Coming right up," answered the bartender.

"She's an old squeeze of mine from years ago," whispered Fitzie. "We go back over twenty years."

Markie turned to take a closer look at the bartender. After getting a good gander, the sergeant crunched his lips and nodded approvingly. "How much mileage has she on her?"
"She's a lot younger than me," replied Fitzie. "I suppose she's gotta be in the neighborhood of fifty now."
"She keeps herself nice."

"You should have seen her back in the day."

When the drinks arrived, Fitzie introduced the object of their conversation to the sergeant. After a few friendly words, the bartender returned to her duties.

"She seems kind of shy, Fitz."

"That means she probably likes you."

"You still involved with her?"

"To be perfectly honest, at my age, I ain't got the ability no more."

"C'mon, I don't buy that. If she gave you the green light, you'd jump her bones."

"Don't bet on that, Al. I got so much pain from this damn arthritis that I can't get comfortable long enough to fulfill my end of the bargain."

Finding the conversation now awkward, Markie changed the subject. "There's talk about making a movie about the Cinderella Man, Fitz."

Markie had spent enough time around the bar owner to know that he knew the nickname of James J. Braddock, the heavyweight boxing champion of an era long past.

31

Like-Minded People

AFTER KILLING MARVIN BUTTERWORTH, Sarah was given the money she was entitled to. She held out her hand and counted along with Fishnet as he slowly placed each bill in her palm. Noticing the ease with which he parted with his money led Sarah to think he had plenty on hand. *He must have a stash of cash hidden someplace in this house,* she thought.

While money was no longer an issue for Fishnet, thanks to his inheritance, there was a darker reason behind his largesse when it came to Sarah. Since she remained in hiding and he intended to kill her in the near future anyway, there was little chance of Sarah spending any of the money.

Fishnet encouraged Sarah to stay with him so that he could keep an eye on her, at least until he could figure out the best way to dispose of her. As was the case with No Tax, the retired detective harbored concerns that, out and about, Sarah might get into trouble with the law. Faced with prison, there was a chance she would implicate him in the Marvin Butterworth homicide in an effort to lighten her sentence.

Unlike No Tax, who was dying, Sarah posed a greater threat because she was healthy. While it unlikely that she would talk, the possibility nevertheless existed. *Why take chances*, thought Fishnet.

Extending Sarah's stay at his town house also came with domestic advantages, since he had not yet fully tired of Sarah in a romantic sense. The manipulative detective considered using Sarah's sanctuary dependency to his further benefit. As he thought of this his mind drifted.

Fishnet's trip to his imaginary world saw him as a cult leader along the lines of Charles Manson. In Sarah, Fishnet saw someone to mold into his first slave. When Fishnet eventually emerged from his fantasy he came to dismiss the notion of Sarah ever being his slave. Even in Fishnet's wildest dreams, that wasn't going to happen. Sarah was far too strong-willed to fall victim to his brainwashing.

##########

AS SHE BECAME ACCLIMATED TO LIVING WITH FISHNET, Sarah grew covetous. The luxurious townhouse, the jewelry, his bottomless pit of ready cash and what she managed to gather of his portfolio all stimulated her envious side.

Sarah decided that she would make it her business to find a way to remain in the townhouse indefinitely, or at least until she could figure out a way to abscond with some of what Fishnet had. To accomplish this end, she knew that she needed to ingratiate herself with Fishnet to a point where he wouldn't want her to leave.

Sarah relied on the time-tested power of flattery to see her through. Her puffery commenced with her praising Fishnet for his brilliance in masterminding the Butterworth execution. She also liberally put forth compliments concerning the former detective's handsomeness. Fishnet found such accolades easy to get used to. Sarah came to believe that her strategy was effective after Fishnet extended her stay at the townhouse without her having to ask.

"You don't have to move out right away," said Fishnet. "Why not stay until this business with Ruffy Shea blows over."

"You know, I was hoping that you would say that," she confessed. "We get along good, and I really feel safe here with you."

"Sure, sweetheart, stay here with me. I have plenty of room. Nobody would think to look for you here in Manhattan."

Fishnet's honeymoon with Sarah came to a halt when it became evident that his houseguest was relentlessly poking into his affairs. Their cohabitation had evolved into something where distrust overshadowed convenience. Things finally came to a head when Sarah began questioning Fishnet's goings and comings.

The streetwise Sarah was able to sense the cooling. Anticipating that Fishnet was going to ask her to leave the townhouse, she now knew enough about him to put into play her own treacherous plan of action. Sarah's initiative was an exceedingly bold one that involved her assuming control of the townhouse, and her host, by force.

Sarah intended to hold Fishnet captive long enough to acquire as much of his assets as possible. She banked on gaining his compliance by breaking the former detective down both physically and psychologically. For Sarah, there was just one other alternative to this diabolical plan. *If I could get the son of a bitch to marry me,* she thought, *I'd be legally entitled to a share of whatever he has.*

After further reflection, the practical side of Sarah reigned supreme. *I've got no shot at wedding bells,* she thought. This being the case, Sarah reverted back to her initial game plan.

###########

SARAH COMMENCED HER MORNING STRETCHING in her bedroom as usual. While doing so, she heard a voice coming from the backyard. Peering through a window that faced the rear of the house, she observed Fishnet standing over the pond looking down. She watched curiously as he spoke to the koi while feeding them. Unable to clearly hear what was being said, she shook her head. *This guy is a friggin' nut!"* she thought.

Realizing that Fishnet's conversational engagement with the fish was turning into a lengthy affair, Sarah took the opportunity to snoop around. She commenced her search for valuables as if on a treasure hunt. She hit pay dirt in Fishnet's bedroom. Sarah gently bit her lip when she came across a gem filled jewelry box that once belonged to Fishnet's late wife.

Sarah fingered the baubles before finally taking the emerald ring with a diamond halo. Placing the ring on her finger, she was elated to see that it fit well. She stretched her arm out to admire her acquisition from afar. The thrill of feeling such an expensive piece of jewelry against her flesh gave Sarah a rush. With some difficulty she managed to control her avarice, limiting her acquisition to the one emerald ring.

Sarah then engaged the remaining jewelry no differently than Fishnet's one-way conversation with the koi. "You'll all be coming home to mama soon," Sarah said softly to the valuables. She then turned to address the emerald ring. "Don't worry baby," she said, "your family will be joining you later."

When Sarah heard a noise coming from the first floor, she froze. She listened intently. Recognizing the sound of Fishnet's steps, Sarah hastily returned the jewelry box and tiptoed to her own bed. She slipped the emerald ring inside the pillowcase and curled up beneath the covers, where she pretended to be fast asleep. The blankets that covered her body provided a sense of security for her.

Sarah waited and listened patiently. During her idleness, she began to wonder where other valuables might be kept. Of particular interest was the cash that Fishnet seemed to have an abundance of. *The money he paid me off with had to come from right here in the house,* was a thought that persisted. *He's probably got a safe tucked away someplace. And what about his guns?*

When Sarah heard steps on the staircase her concentration shifted. When Fishnet arrived on the second floor, he looked in on Sarah, as was his way. After poking his nose into her bedroom, he began to shake his head disapprovingly. *Look at this lazy thing. She'll sleep all afternoon if I let her*, he thought. "C'mon, it's time to get cracking," Fishnet announced loudly. Faking a yawn, Sarah stretched out her arms. "What time is it?"

"It's time for you to do something new, sweetheart."

"What's that?"

"You're gonna get up and cook me breakfast."

This is something new, thought Sarah, who was appalled that Fishnet expected her to cook his breakfast. *Who does he think he's talking to? The crazy son of a bitch should be cooking me breakfast!*

Sarah saw his demand to be catered to as evidence that she was losing status. She steeled herself to take whatever he had to offer without complaint until she was prepared to tilt the scale in her favor. Remaining on good terms with her host was paramount until it was time to strike.

"How do you like your eggs, handsome?" Sarah asked, trying to sound pleasant.

"On a plate, sweetheart," he replied.

Smart ass, she thought. As Sarah scrambled eggs, she dwelled on how much she'd love to put rat poison in his food. *Maybe I could get away with putting a little in each day without killing him, just to see him bellyache*, she thought.

Over breakfast Sarah put forth what she believed to be a convincing argument as to how happy she was to be staying at the townhouse. Fishnet countered by elaborately conveying how delighted he was to have her as his guest. Both parties were equally adept at being untruthful with a straight face.

After breakfast, Sarah showered. While she was occupied in the bathroom, Fishnet entered his bedroom to put away the clothes he had picked up from the laundry the day prior. As he unpacked the laundry bag, he smelled the neatly folded garments to make sure that they had been properly tended to. Once satisfied with the results of his sniff test, Fishnet began placing the clothes in drawers.

Somewhat of a neat freak, Fishnet attended to his unmade bed. After he finished straightening out his room, he entered the room where Sarah bedded down. After making her bed, he began to smooth out the wrinkles in the pillowcase. When he felt something hard contained within the pillowcase, he looked to see what it was. Fishnet was hardly surprised by what he discovered. He returned the emerald ring to the pillowcase as if it belonged there.

"This cuts it. The last round up for you is right around the corner, baby," Fishnet hissed, under his breath.

"What did you say?" called out Sarah as she emerged from the bathroom with a towel wrapped around her head.

"I said hurry up, baby," he replied, thinking fast.

"Are we going someplace?"

"Yeah, I got plans for us."

As he waited for Sarah's hair to dry, Fishnet traveled to his fantasy world. He envisioned the two of them at Breivika Beach, located in northern Norway. It was late in the evening, and they were resting on a blanket atop the sand after enjoying a swim. Fishnet was stroking Sarah's damp blond hair as she rested her head lazily in the pocket of his shoulder. He took a moment to glance around at his surroundings. Other than a cliff and a few houses in the far off distance there was nothing for him to fear in terms of someone witnessing his planned execution. Fishnet took a firm hold of Sarah's hair.

"Not so rough," protested Sarah, making it clear that she disliked such treatment.

Seeing Sarah's open-mouthed look of astonishment inspired Fishnet. Taking a handful of sand with his free hand, Fishnet began jamming granular substance into her mouth. As his victim endeavored to spit out the first mouthful, Sarah simultaneously began to fight for her life. Fishnet was too strong for her. Reaching for more sand, he packed her mouth. He then began to plug her nostrils. Shortly afterward, with satisfaction, he inhaled the cool sea breeze. The Sarah in his fantasy was unable to do likewise.

Sarah noticed the silly smile Fishnet had on his face. "What's so funny?" she asked.

"Oh, nothing, I was just thinking of something fun I'd like to do," he replied.

Fishnet realized that the beach in Norway was a stretch. As he watched Sarah dress, he arrived at a practical alternative. *Hey*, he thought, *the sand at Coney Island is good enough for her*.

##########

SARAH HAD SPENT SUFFICIENT TIME WITH FISHNET to have learned a few things. She came to realize that he was a loner who had no family. She was also aware that he usually carried a gun.

Sarah found it interesting that the same delivery person rang the front doorbell on a regular basis to give Fishnet an envelope. She made it her business to later retrieve the empty envelope from the trash. The printing on the envelope depicted the identity of an accounting firm. At this juncture, it seemed more than likely, that this was where Fishnet's cash was coming from. Unable to resist confirming her suspicion, she impulsively acted on what she observed.

"I wish I had your mailman," Sarah commented.

"What do you mean?" asked Fishnet, taken by surprise at her statement.

"C'mon, you know what I mean."

"What big eyes you have, Grandma."

"The better to see you with," voiced Sarah.

"My accountant sends me my spending money. It saves me from having to go to the bank myself. I call him up, and he sends me what I need."

"You gave him the authority to do that?"

"Sure, why not? He pays all my bills and sees to it that I got enough walking around money. I only see the guy about once a year."

Sarah was astounded to learn that all interactions between the accountant and his client were conducted telephonically. She further gathered that when Fishnet wasn't at home, the envelope containing the money was left in the mailbox for him. Armed with these revelations, which fit perfectly into Sarah's plans, her scheme to take over grew legs.

Since Fishnet was far too formidable to take on alone, Sarah required support. She telephoned her best friend Greta, who, as expected, readily signed on. For muscle, Sarah relied on Greta to come up with someone.

Greta came through with her current flame, one Judo Edwards. Judo was a sometime martial arts instructor with a fondness for cocaine. Greta assured Sarah that Judo, who had several arrests in his portfolio, was big, tough, and a martial arts expert. In short, he was more than enough man to handle Fishnet.

What cinched making Judo an acceptable crime partner was Greta's assurance that Judo had no connection to organized crime. This meant that her whereabouts wouldn't reach the ears of Ruffy Shea or any of his cronies. The promise of easy money was enough to lure Judo into Sarah's web. A meeting between the three was set on a day when Fishnet was scheduled to go for his annual physical. The trio met at Tio Pepe's on West 4th Street in the West Village.

"Sarah, this is my friend, Judo," said Greta. Sarah nodded her greeting, preferring to size up Greta's new boyfriend before getting too friendly.

"Hi, Sarah," greeted Judo. Aren't you warm in here with that scarf around your face?"

"I have reason to conceal myself," replied Sarah, who was satisfied with whom she saw before her.

"What is somebody after you?"

"Yeah, I'm being hunted, so I have to be careful."

"Is that why you need me?" asked Judo, adding, "I got a lot of money troubles, so for the right price, I'm your boy. You can count on me to do the right thing because you're Greta's friend."

"I got a deal going that can give us all big-time relief, Judo, but it's gonna take nerve."

"Nerve I got, money I don't. What's the proposition?"

After explaining her situation with Fishnet, Sarah outlined a scheme that called for Judo and Greta upend Fishnet at the townhouse. Sarah's plan called for holding Fishnet captive by chaining him to one of the posts in the cellar. She explained to her crime partners that they could then take up residence in the townhouse while they fleeced their victim for all they could. "We're gonna pluck this sucker like a chicken," conveyed Sarah. "We'll force him to make calls to his accountant and get him to do whatever we want," related Sarah. "It'll take a little time to figure things out, but time we'll have. We could even sell off some of the junk he has in his house," she added.

"But what are we supposed to do with this chump after we get what we're after?" asked Judo. "He'll be able to identify us, you know."

"We'll have to see about that," replied Sarah. "Our man is really in no position to run to the cops, that's for sure. Besides, with his money, he could stand the loss."

"If he's that flush, why don't we just snatch him and hold him for ransom?" asked Judo. "Then we'd be done with it. Do you think he'd pay up?"

"I don't like that idea," said Sarah. "We gonna do things my way. You got a problem with that?"

"No, like I already told Greta, I'm okay working for you. I was just concerned that your way, the guy could go running to the cops later."

"Judo's got a point, Sarah," injected Greta.

"If that's what you two are worried about, then we can just kill him once we get what we want," said Sarah, in a matter-of-fact fashion.

Both Judo and Greta shrugged, indicating that they were not opposed to the idea.

"You know what, Sarah," said Greta, "maybe that's best. Let's go all in."

"Okay, end of discussion then. The pigeon goes bye-bye."

"Do you have any plans for afterward, Sarah?" Greta asked.

"You already know the answer to that. I've got to take care of that guy who is hunting for me," advised Sarah. "Once that's done, things will probably get too hot for me to stick around. I'll probably head down south and wait for my boyfriend to get out of jail."

"Have you heard from Mickey?"

"No, I haven't. We worked it out before he went away that that he shouldn't call me. He knows I'll reach out to him when the time is right."

"How will you where he is by that time?"

"He'll be in jail someplace, I'll find him."

"You know, Sarah, we got nothing holding us here. How about me and Judo tag along with you?"

"Sure, you two can help me get rid Ruffy. Once that's done, we can all take a breather from this town."

"That sounds good," said Greta, "what do you think, Judo?"

"I'm in," he replied.

"Then it's a deal," confirmed Sarah. "But one thing, if we're going to be working together, I call the shots."

32

Waldo Proves His Worth

RUFFY SHEA WAS AT HOME when his cell phone started ringing. He glanced at his phone to see who was calling. Since it was his late brother's wife, who lived nearby in Howard Beach, he took the call. Experience taught him that a call from his sister-in-law usually meant there was a problem. This time was no exception. Amid the hysterics on the other end of the line, Ruffy was able to piece together what the issue was. It seemed that his nephew, who lived with his mother, was actively engaged in an altercation with someone. Judging by the shouting in the background Ruffy could tell that the situation was getting out of hand.

"Oh, my God!" suddenly shouted Ruffy's sister-in-law into the phone. "My son is going upstairs with a bat!"

"Sit tight, I'm on the way over," said Ruffy, hanging up the phone abruptly.

Ruffy telephoned Joe Bullets and instructed him to meet him at his sister's house forthwith. Armed with one of the guns he kept in his house, Ruffy then headed there himself.

"What's up, Skipper?" asked Joe, once the criminal associates met up in front of the house.

"My nephew is having a beef with somebody in the house. Let's go in and see what it's all about."

"I'm not heavy...."

"Don't worry about it, Joe. I got a piece on me."

When they entered the house, they could see that Ruffy's sister-in-law was worried. Remaining silent, she pointed upward to the top of the staircase, where groaning sounds could be heard. When they reached the upper floor, they found a downed man in one of the bedrooms, writhing in pain. The injured man was holding one of his legs, which appeared to be fractured. Standing alongside him was Ruffy's twenty-three-year-old nephew, who was holding an aluminum baseball bat in his hand.

"What's going on here, kid?" asked Ruffy. His tone was neutral, which the nephew knew could translate into further violence.

"I caught him in my room stealing," replied the nephew.

"Who is this guy?"

"He's a friend of mine who needed a place to stay, so I let him stay with us for a while."

Noticing the jailhouse tattoos on the injured man's hand and neck caused Ruffy to suspect that the dispute might be drug related. His suspicions were confirmed after he raised the man's shirt sleeves. The visible track marks told the tale of drug addiction.

"You gotta have something wrong with you," scolded Ruffy, turning on his nephew. "How do you bring a dope fiend into the house to live?" Unable to conceal his embarrassment, the nephew looked down at the ground as he feebly attempted to answer the question. "Save the cock and bull story for your mother," said Ruffy with disgust.

"But I caught him going through my things," said the nephew, trying to justify his actions. He was still holding the bat he used to smash his friend's leg.

"He's lying! We're partners," whined the injured man who was looking up from the floor.

Joe Bullets kicked the tenant in his injured leg in an effort to silence him. The blow had the opposite effect, causing the man to howl in pain.

"What do we do with this asshole, Ruffy?" asked Joe, attempting to move things along.

After assessing the situation, Ruffy turned to address his nephew. "Go downstairs and tell your mother to go out and take a walk for herself while I figure out what to do with your friend here."

When the assault victim heard this, he became terrified. Thinking the worse, he began screaming at the top of his lungs for the police. The very idea of calling in the authorities so enraged Ruffy that he lost all self-control. He removed the handgun from his coat pocket, put it to the injured man's temple, and fired once, thus ensuring the victim's silence.

"You didn't have to kill him!" shouted the nephew, who rushed back upstairs after hearing the shot.

"Shut up," barked Ruffy. "Next time, clean up your own mess! Did your mother leave?"

"Yeah, she's gone."

"We could take him out of here in a rug, Ruffy," proposed Joe, who was used to such outcomes.

"No, we better let the cops find him right where he is," said Ruffy, wiping his gun clean of his fingerprints. He then placed the gun in the victim's hand.

"My mother's gonna flip out," declared the nephew.

"Don't underestimate your mother, kid," said Ruffy. "Just call 911 when she gets back."

"What am I supposed to tell the cops?"

"Tell them you heard the shot and came upstairs to investigate. Remember to say that your friend was very depressed lately, so you took him in to cheer him up," instructed Ruffy. "You got that?"

"Yeah, I got it."

"C'mon, Joe, let's breeze."

"You guys are leaving?"

"We can't stick around here, kid."

293

"All you have to do is tell the story the way your uncle said to tell it," Joe interjected. "And don't add anything."

"Yeah, sure, I got it. But what about the gun…."

"It was his, period."

"That gun belonged to a guy long dead," advised Ruffy, "so don't sweat it."

########

DETECTIVE LENA LESPER and her partner were called by the patrol force to respond to the home of Ruffy's sister-in-law. Once confirming that a death had occurred, Lesper notified her squad commander, requesting that he respond to the location. When Waldo arrived at the scene, he took note of the entry wound caused by the bullet. The star-shaped wound made it clear to him that the bullet was fired from a gun pressed to the dead man's head. This indicated that the shot could have been self-inflicted. Noting the gun in the dead man's hand, he gave a knowing look to Detective Lesper.

"It looks like this guy checked himself out," announced the squad commander.

"That's what I thought at first, Loo. But look at his leg." Waldo took a closer look at the dead man's leg. He could see that it was broken. "How the hell do you suppose that happened, Lena?"

"That's what I'm wondering."

"Why do you suppose his sleeves are rolled up?" Waldo asked. He then examined the arms of the deceased. "This guy's a junkie. Look at these track marks. Do we have him identified yet?'

"Yes, the landlord's son told me who he is."

"Is he anybody important?"

"I don't think so."

"Check and see if the stiff's got an arrest record, Lena."

After making the inquiry Detective Lesper reported back to her commanding officer. "He's got several priors for narcotics, Loo."

"All right, let's see what these people downstairs have to say."

Once downstairs, the squad commander had Detective Lesper commence the questioning of Ruffy's sister-in-law and nephew. "Do you folks have any idea why he would want to kill himself?" asked Lesper.

"He was depressed," voiced Ruffy's nephew.

"What was depressing him?"

"He had a drug problem."

"Were you home when this happened?"

"I was down here when the shot rang out," explained the nephew. I went running up to see what happened and found him dead on the floor. That's all I know."

"Is that right?"

"That's the truth."

"Did you hear the shot too, Ma'am?"

"Who me?" asked Ruffy's sister-in-law. "I wasn't here when it happened."

"Where were you?"

"I was out taking a walk."

"In this weather you took a walk?"

"I like to walk," replied the older woman.

"Did you people know that he was on drugs?" Both mother and son nodded that they did.

"He was a sick boy," stated Ruffy's sister-in-law. "My son felt sorry for him."

"What's your name?" asked Detective Lesper, addressing Ruffy's nephew.

"My name is Roger Shea." Upon hearing the name, Waldo did a double take.

"And you, ma'am?"

"Mary Shea."

"Is Shea your married name?"

"Yes, my husband died a few years back."

"I see," said Lesper, who saw no reason to delve further along these lines. Did you—"

"Hold it a second, Lena," said the squad commander, interrupting to ask a question. "Are you folks any relation to Ruffy Shea?"

"He's my brother-in-law, but we have nothing to do with him," answered Ruffy's sister-in-law.

"How about you, son—do you work?" Waldo asked, addressing Ruffy's nephew.

"I'm waiting to take the test for the sanitation department."

"That's a good job, good luck," said the squad commander. The civility in the lieutenant's tone was noticeably unusual. "Well, it is what it is, Lena," stated Waldo. "It's cut and dry. The guy killed himself and did us all a favor. Finish up here and let's go back to the office."

"But the leg, Loo—"

"What leg?" abruptly asked Waldo. "What are we, doctors now? This is a straight case of suicide."

Before Waldo left, he had a word in private with Ruffy's nephew. "I want you to make sure that you tell your uncle that Lieutenant Waldo Reale took care of this situation over here personally."

When Ruffy Shea later learned how things went with the detectives, he couldn't have been more pleased. He talked over the matter with his friend, Joe Bullets.

"What do you make of that, Joe?" asked Ruffy.

"It looks like you got a friend, Skipper."

"Yeah, and he's worth every penny."

"He still hasn't delivered Sarah yet," pointed out Joe.

"Don't worry, he'll deliver. That's why I'm not killing myself looking for her. He'll come up with her for me."

"I guess that bull really is worth the money."

"He is, Joe. I want you to give this money to Miltie," instructed Ruffy, handing Joe currency he removed from his billfold. "Tell Miltie it goes to the bull, and to put this money in the box for him."

33

Ruffy's Long Reach

RUFFY SHEA WAS HAVING LUNCH at the racetrack restaurant with Joe Bullets and Swatty. His handicapping expertise was failing him, and he wasn't in the best of moods. For race after race he could be heard cursing the horses he wagered on as he tore up losing tickets. His losses could be measured by the tickets that began to clutter the table.

"The Shea Method just ain't working today," complained Ruffy. "What's The Shea Method?" questioned Swatty, who only recently began spending time with Ruffy and Joe.

"He always bets on the gray horse," quipped Joe.

"Very funny," commented Ruffy. "So, tell me, what does the financial picture look like this week at the casino and restaurant, Swatty?"

"We're doing okay."

"We're doing just okay?"

"Well, to tell you the truth, business has been a little off," advised Swatty, who had learned fast that any admission of exceptional business would result in Ruffy and Joe raiding the register. To avoid further discussion Swatty excused himself from the table. "I'm gonna go make a bet," he said. "There's a gray horse running in this race coming up."

"I'm still not sure about that guy," commented Joe after

Swatty had walked off.

"What are our spotters telling you?"

"All I'm hearing from them is that the casino and restaurant are both doing a booming business."

"There ain't a chance that Italo is holding out on us, Joe," said Ruffy. "He ain't got it in him to get cute. It's gotta be Swatty."

Joe thought for a second before replying. "You may have something there. I can't forget how fast Swatty was to cross Ciro. If he did that to a made guy, what stops him from doing that to us to too, Skipper?"

"Do we know enough to operate the casino without him?"

"It's not that complicated, all we need to do is put someone in there we can trust."

"Then maybe we have one partner too many, Joe."

"I'm thinking the same thing, Skipper. What about your nephew, the wannabe sanitation man?"

"He might work out at that. I just have to talk to Philly about this."

"Do you think he'll go along?"

"As long as I keep feeding him those envelopes Philly's not gonna care."

The content of their conversation shifted once Swatty returned to the table.

"Let's see what this gray horse can do," announced Swatty. "Hey Ruffy, how did your son-in-law make out in court?"

"The little prick got sent up. He's doing his time in Sing Sing," answered Ruffy. "Which reminds me, Joe, I need you to drive me up to the Bronx tomorrow. I have business up there." Ruffy then turned his attention to Swatty. "Swatty, go get me a pen, mine is running out of ink."

"Sure, Ruffy," said, Swatty, heading off on the errand.

"I didn't want to say too much in front of him, Joe," said Ruffy in a low voice. "I'm gonna arrange to have my Bronx friend look out for Mickey in jail. He has the connections to the people who run the can Mickey's in."

##########

RUFFY MET WITH HIS FRIEND in the office of a crooked Bronx-based reverend. The collar wearing flimflam artist made his living, in part, by shaking down large corporations. The entities were given the option of either hiring workers from the reverend's pool of job seekers or face disruptions at their jobsite.

This extortion was particularly effective with large construction companies, who went along because they were able to pass on the additional expense to their clients.

The hired workers, in return for their job, agreed to kick back a portion of their wages to a not-for-profit operated by the reverend. Half of these proceeds were funneled to Snow Johnson, the reverend's muscle and partner.

Johnson, a drug trafficker, was in charge of collections. Workers who were foolish enough to renege on the bargain they struck with the reverend found themselves answering to Snow and his squad of goons.

"Welcome, Mr. Shea," greeted the reverend when Ruffy arrived at his office. "Mr. Johnson awaits us in the conference room."

When Ruffy entered the conference room, he found Snow seated at the head of a long table. The empty bottle of water he held in his left hand brought attention to the several silver rings that adorned his fingers.

"How ya been, Snow?" asked Ruffy, extending his hand.

"Hey, big man," replied the drug trafficker rising to take Ruffy's hand.

"Nice threads," said Ruffy, referring to the suit Snow wore. "Like they say, you gotta dress for success. Everything's going smooth with the shit we've been sending your man, right?"

"Yeah, Miltie said it's all good. I'm here because I need a favor." Ruffy went on to explain exactly what he wanted.

"So, you want your son-in-law protected while he's serving his sentence in Sing Sing, right?"

"That's right."

"No problem, man. My wife's brother runs the joint in

Ossining," said Snow, "and he got another five years to do."

"I also want you to put him to work when he gets out, that way he can earn and square the debt he owes me."

"That makes it two favors you want from me," noted Snow. "Ruffy's face took on a scowl. When I bankrolled you when you got out of the can, I also went to see certain people to protect you from getting shook down," reminded Ruffy.

"I squared that loan, man. You've been getting your shit all along at a discounted rate, man."

"Yeah, I got no beef in that department. But that was *two* favors I did for you, wasn't it?"

"I suppose it was...."

"If I add in those two they fished out of the Hudson River, then it comes to me doing you four favors."

The broad smile that crossed the face of Snow revealed several gold teeth. "Easy man, I was just playing with you. I'll find a place in the organization for your son-in-law when he gets out." Ruffy returned to his car where Joe had been waiting patiently. When he got inside the vehicle Joe thought it was time to clear the air. "Say, Ruffy, are you in business with these people up here?" he asked.

Ruffy turned serious. "What if I am, Joe? Is that a problem?"

"C'mon, Ruffy, we go way back together. I'm just curious."

Ruffy smiled at his most trusted friend. "Yeah, Snow supplies the coke Miltie distributes for me."

"But how is this gonna sit with Philly?"

Ruffy smiled. "Do you think I'd get in bed with people in the drug business up here without Philly being partners with me?"

"He's involved?" asked the surprised Joe Bullets.

"He's my partner in everything," revealed Ruffy. "Now that you know, you should also know that what I just told you ain't for everybody's ears."

"You don't have to worry about me, Ruffy."

"I know I don't, Joe. You're like me, we both understand consequences."

##########

EVERYONE DOING TIME IN the Ossining prison adhered to the mandates of Zorro's Raiders, the gang that controlled the inmate population. Their leader, Zorro, was the brother-in-law of Snow Johnson.

Mickey was in the prison yard when he was approached by Zorro, a burly man with a ten inch scar that ran down one side of his face. Mickey, when confronted, didn't know what to expect. He backed up a step as a precautionary measure. Without having any alliances, Mickey was well aware that he was vulnerable to being shook down or targeted for deflowering.

"Hey, man, from now on, you're with me," declared the deep voiced inmate.

"I don't understand...." said Mickey, nervously. He was unsure as to the context of the remark.

"It means you're with Zorro's Raiders, man, and I'm Zorro. Anybody gonna be messing with you in this joint, is messing with me and the rest of the Raiders."

Mickey was astounded to learn that it was Ruffy who arranged for his protection. He questioned Zorro as to why Ruffy would bother to look out for him.

"They want you healthy, man. You got a debt to pay off, and you gotta be in one piece to do that." Zorro could see that Mickey was naïve. Taking pity, he offered some advice. "Let me put you wise, man. As long as you keep paying, you'll be okay."

"Oh," said Mickey. "I should have known, my father-in-law is just protecting his own interest."

"C'mon, man, what did you think? You can't be a chump and expect to survive in this joint."

"What do you mean?"

"You gotta toughen up. You're gonna start lifting weights and learn how to kick ass. There ain't room for no weaklings in Zorro's Raiders, man."

As the two men got to know each other better, Zorro came to appreciate that Mickey possessed a certain number of organizational skills. Zorro, who recognized this as an asset, found use for Mickey in keeping track of the things he had going with other inmates. In time Mickey explained to Zorro how his relationship with Sarah had caused him to run afoul of Ruffy. "Woman will bring you down every time, man," declared Zorro, as if he were an expert on relationships. "That's why you gotta wear the pants from the beginning."

"You don't know Sarah like I do. I'd put her up against any man."

"Have you heard from her since you're in here?" asked Zorro.

"No, I haven't heard anything yet."

"She didn't come see you or write you, did she?"

"I tried writing her, but my letters were returned."

"Did you call her?"

"No, she didn't want that. She insisted that we don't talk on the phone."

"So you never called her?"

"Once I did call her number, she didn't pick up the call."

"So, what does that tell you, man?"

34

Swatty Gets Sneaky

THE PILFERING OF FUNDS FROM THE CASINO BY Ruffy and Joe Bullets had become increasingly more problematic for Swatty. The tipping point came when the two showed up at the casino unexpectedly. They remained on site until closing in order to be present for the counting of the proceeds.

Swatty placed the money on the desk in his office. Before he started the count, he was called away by Ruffy to discuss an operational matter on the casino floor. When Swatty returned to commence counting the money, he noticed that there was substantially less cash on the desk. Although infuriated, Swatty could do little under the circumstances. Exercising good judgment, he looked hard at Joe Bullets, but held his tongue. Feeling that the time had come to put an end to such bold thievery, Swatty approached Italo to test his willingness to take a stand. While Italo wasn't happy at being taken advantage of, he lacked the intestinal fortitude to enter into a conflict with Ruffy and Joe.

With bitterness, Swatty accepted that he would have to take action alone. Further fueling his determination to take steps was Ruffy's reneging on his promise to talk to Philly Rava about Swatty being proposed for membership into the family.

Swatty's calculated that if he could figure out a way to shake loose Ruffy and Joe, he'd have direct access to the family boss. By being the one passing the tribute money to Philly Rava, Swatty would have the necessary face time to cultivate the family boss. Having this avenue was sure to enhance Swatty's chances of gaining membership into the family, or so he believed.

One major hurdle facing Swatty was his lack of the muscle necessary to take on Ruffy and Joe Bullets. Unable to call on the regular family enforcers without permission from a made member of the family, placed Swatty at a disadvantage. Swatty had but one reliable tool at his disposal, his craftiness.

"These bastards are gonna learn," thought Swatty. *"I'm gonna chop the legs out from under them!"*

Trying to identify vulnerabilities, Swatty began to work on Miltie by feeding him drinks whenever he showed up at the casino. Swatty caught a break when the loose-lipped Miltie let it slip that a detective lieutenant named Waldo was on Ruffy's payroll.

Swatty remembered Waldo as the precinct squad commander who put pressure on Italo and Ciro to identify those involved in the Judge West homicide.

Possessing this knowledge empowered Swatty in that he saw the law as a mechanism to seize full control of both the casino and restaurant. While feeding Miltie drinks, Swatty pumped the drunken Miltie for all the particulars concerning Ruffy's relationship with Waldo.

Swatty decided to keep Italo in the dark as to his plans. Italo's price to pay for his lack of backbone was going to be a smaller percentage of ownership.

##########

SWATTY STOOD ALONE ON THE SIDEWALK opposite the district attorney's office. Waiting for Captain Tim Gerard to depart work, he lifted the collar of his brown tweed overcoat to protect against the gusting wind. He held onto his hat in order to avoid the topper flying off his head.

Where the hell is this guy? I'm freezing my ass off over here, Swatty thought, as he puffed on the cigarette that dangled from his mouth. Swatty had smoked enough cigarettes that the foulness of his own breath began to bother him. In an effort to alleviate the unpleasant taste in his mouth he munched on the breath mints that he carried.

When Captain Gerard finally exited the building, he gave Swatty a discreet nod of recognition. As a signal for Swatty to follow him, the captain poked a finger in the direction he was heading in. Swatty followed the law enforcement officer to a nearby office building. The man at the lobby desk, a retired police officer, directed Swatty to the elevator where the captain was waiting for him. The two men took the elevator to the lower level where they made their way to a small office.

"So, talk to me," said Gerard, who was curious as to why Swatty was willing to provide him with information.

"Like I said on the phone, Captain, I got information that you'll want to hear."

"Why are you being so thoughtful?"

"I come to you because you held up your end of the bargain when you busted me on that gambling rap. Besides, by me helping you, I'm helping myself."

"How is that?"

"I got partners in that casino who are robbing me blind."

"Okay, now it's starting to make sense. I assume that you want me to put them out of circulation, correct?"

"That's it in a nutshell, Captain."

"Let me hear what I get out of it," said Gerard, expecting to be bribed.

"I got the headlines you want." Gerard was caught off guard, not expecting to hear what he heard. "I can fill you in on a certain crooked detective lieutenant named Waldo who is on the payroll of Ruffy Shea. Does that tickle your fancy?"

Gerard remained stone-faced, displaying no overt reaction.

305

"Ruffy Shea is the partner you want ousted?"

"Yeah, that's right, both him and Joe Bullets."

The expression on Captain Gerard's face now showed great interest. "I like what I'm hearing, Swatty," replied the captain. "Unearthing a police corruption scandal is votes in the bank for the district attorney during an election year."

"That's what I was figuring."

"Explain to me again how you intend to benefit?"

"I benefit by you putting Ruffy and Joe in the can for a long, long time. That, and there is one other thing."

"Which is?"

"I want your word that you'll lay off my gambling joint," propositioned Swatty. "You guarantee me that, and I'll supply you with all the information you'll need on that squad commander and Ruffy."

"So full control of the casino is your end game?"

"That's right."

"I see. What about the restaurant?"

"I got a piece of that too, but just so you know, that restaurant is mostly run legit."

"Do you expect payment for your information?"

"That would be nice, Captain, but it's no deal breaker."

"If you want money, I'll have to put you on record," explained Gerard. "That means signing you up as a confidential informant."

"Then forget the money, Captain. I don't want my name on paper. You don't have to pay me squat as long as you lay off the casino and get rid of my partners. So, I got your word that we got a deal, right?"

"You have my word."

Swatty went on to reveal the primary way in which Ruffy interacted with Waldo.

"Everything goes through this guy Miltie. Miltie feeds a post office box that's used to pass messages and money," explained Swatty.

"Who are the key holders to the box?"

"Waldo the lieutenant has a key, and Miltie has a key."

"Who is Miltie?"

"He's in Ruffy's crew."

"What's his last name?"

"I don't know. I only know him as Miltie."

"How did you find all this out?" asked Captain Gerard.

"When Miltie drinks, he shoots off his trap."

"What does the lieutenant's end amount to?"

"I don't know the exact amount. All I do know is that Miltie leaves money in the post office box for the lieutenant."

"What exactly does Waldo do to earn this money?"

"I don't know, Captain….just favors," replied Swatty.

"That's important for me to know, Swatty."

"He can shit cans cases, cover up a crime, that kind of stuff," said Swatty, who was now winging it. "I'm pretty sure they got something going right now, Captain."

"What's that?"

"Miltie told me he had to make arrangements in Atlantic City for him and Waldo. The trip is a reward for Waldo doing Ruffy some kind of solid."

"You got pretty chummy with this Miltie. Why is that?"

"Miltie's a degenerate gambler. He comes to the casino, gets drunk, and I extend him credit, so he loves me."

Captain Gerard removed a pack of cigarettes from his desk. After handing a smoke to Swatty, he gave him a light and then lit his own.

"This might put a lot of people in jail," advised Gerard, "not just the people you want to see hurt."

"Good riddance, as far as I'm concerned," said Swatty. "How long will they go away for?"

"That depends on what else you can tell us."

"Can you put together a RICO case against Ruffy and Joe Bullets if I tell you about their other crimes?"

"RICO is for the federal courts, but we got something similar in the State. But understand something. Now you're talking about putting people away for a *very* long time."

"Yeah, ain't that a shame, Captain?"

Captain Gerard could now see just how desperately Swatty wanted Ruffy put out of circulation. Swatty's zeal to achieve this end heightened Captain Gerard's wariness. He had to be careful that Swatty didn't begin to fabricate information just to strengthen the cases to be made.

"How about I send out for a bottle of scotch and some Chinese food, Swatty?"

"You really know how to live large, don't you, Captain?"

"What, you don't like Chinese food?" asked Gerard, sounding somewhat put off.

"Take it easy, Captain," answered Swatty. "I'm good with Chinese food. I eat it every Chinese New Year."

Besides having a buzz on, Swatty left the meeting with Captain Gerard feeling positive. If things fell according to plan, Ruffy and Joe Bullets would soon be a memory.

The following morning Captain Gerard proceeded to reach out to the district attorney to report the agreement he entered into with Swatty. The district attorney saw the police corruption case as a steppingstone to something much grander. His goal was to take down Ruffy Shea in order to get to a much bigger fish, namely Philly Rava, the family boss.

The DA decided that the police corruption matter would best be undertaken as a joint investigation conducted by his office and the police department's internal affairs bureau. As far as initiating a more sweeping probe, that decision would be made at a future date based on the evidence gathered. Working in conjunction with the feds in putting together a RICO case, with the ultimate target being Philly Rava, was a definite consideration.

Regardless of the path chosen by the DA, one thing was for certain. Swatty's casino was to operate unbothered.

###########

THE COMMANDING OFFICER OF INTERNAL AFFAIRS reassigned two of his investigators to temporarily work out of the district attorney's office under the direction of Captain Gerard.

The detectives initiated their investigation by monitoring Waldo during his normal working hours. Other than confirming that the squad commander occasionally visited a post office box, the investigators gathered nothing of substance. The wheels in their probe were finally greased when Captain Gerard was contacted by Swatty.

Swatty informed the captain that Miltie had stopped by the casino to gamble the evening prior. He indicated that he saw to it that Miltie consumed enough alcohol to loosen his tongue. Miltie came to convey that he was preparing to spend the weekend in Atlantic City with "the cop." Based upon this information, Gerard ordered the internal affairs detectives to conduct a weekend surveillance of Waldo's home. He also instructed the investigators to be prepared to stay overnight in Atlantic City.

It was mid-morning on Saturday when they observed, through binoculars, Waldo the Boss exiting his residence. The squad commander was carrying an overnight bag.

"It looks like the information was solid," noted one of the detectives. "Do you think we should notify Captain Gerard?"
"Not yet. Let's wait and see what he does," replied the detective's partner.

When a black stretch limo pulled to the curb, Waldo got in the back without hesitation. The subsequent rolling surveillance took the detectives south. When they got beyond Toms River, it seemed more than likely that the limo was heading to Atlantic City.

##########

MILTIE WAS A CHUBBY little man of middle age. He looked anything but the one-time accountant he claimed to have been. His being a member of that profession was something Waldo found quite doubtful.

The shine on Miltie's double-breasted gray suit, his use of a black pocket square, and the carnation attached to his lapel were hardly the garb of a CPA. Miltie's greasy gray comb-over,

309

his crooked smile, and the black rings around his eyes also didn't fit the profile of a professional man.

The one thing Miltie had going for him that gave him some degree of accounting credibility was his extensive vocabulary. When met with skeptics, Miltie made it a point to sprinkle his conversation with terms such as balance sheet, expenditures, marginal cost and cash flow forecast.

During the ride south, Miltie fueled himself with periodic slugs of whiskey taken from a silver flask. As he grew more comfortable, he admitted to Waldo that he had served a spell in jail for embezzlement and criminal impersonation. He failed to mention that he had once been sent up on a federal narcotics conviction.

"So, what's on the agenda in Atlantic City?" asked Waldo. "Ruffy's appreciative of how things are working out with you," advised Miltie. "He told me to treat you to a big time, so plan on having a blast. We'll check in, freshen up and then do a little gambling. Later we'll grab a steak dinner. After that, the real fun begins."

"What real fun is that?"

"We're gonna meet up with a couple of working girls I know."

"That's it?" questioned Waldo, sounding disappointed.

"You don't like women?" asked Miltie, picking up on Waldo's lack of enthusiasm.

"I like them fine, but what about spending money?"

Miltie chuckled. "Don't worry about that. You're gonna be a big winner at craps."

"Beautiful. Be sure to tell Ruffy thanks and that he can count on me for whatever he needs," declared Waldo.

"He knows that," Miltie assured, "and Ruffy's the kind of guy that's willing to pay big for your help."

Waldo smiled as he began patting Miltie's hand. "I think maybe you and me are gonna be good friends, Miltie," he said.

"Let me ask you something, Lieutenant. Do you ever get high?"

"I only drink booze."

"How about expanding your experiences?" asked Miltie.

"What do you have in mind?"

"How about you try a little blow? The girls we're gonna be hooking up with are crazy for that shit."

########

THE INTERNAL AFFAIRS DETECTIVES WERE careful to maintain a safe distance from the two men they watched on the casino floor. From afar, they witnessed Miltie pass Waldo casino chips at the crap table.

Enlisting the help of the hotel security director, a retired New Jersey State Trooper, the investigators ascertained that Miltie had registered at the hotel under the name of Milton Kassoff. They further learned that Miltie was a regular at the casino. His status as a high roller enabled him to receive transportation, lodging, and meals courtesy of the hotel.

The internal affairs detectives took notice of how their subjects began to loosen up as they partied with the hookers at one of the casino lounges. Their excessive drinking caused Miltie and Waldo to behave recklessly, as if invisible to others.

After having their dinner the group of four stepped out onto the boardwalk. Seemingly oblivious to the cold, the group indulged in cocaine use while seated on a boardwalk bench. Using a newly invented device that was called a mobile videophone, the detectives were able to capture photos of the group snorting cocaine off the flat surface of a newspaper. The surveillance ended for the evening when Miltie and Waldo retired to their suite with the young women.

After this weekend Miltie and Waldo became great friends. As the two began to spend lots of time together, Waldo grew accustomed to the good times when engaging in Miltie's vices. As their friendship blossomed, Waldo began renting out the power of his police shield whenever Miltie felt he could use the squad commander's support during drug transactions. These outings gave the detectives tailing the lieutenant more than enough opportunity to gather sufficient evidence to put the squad commander behind bars for a long time.

35

Kill Or Be Killed

IT WAS LATE AFTERNOON and Sarah appeared to be watching a crime drama on television. As she sat on the loveseat twirling her long blond hair, she was actually consumed with thoughts of her own crime drama, one in which she intended to play a starring role. In her production Fishnet was the intended victim. Fishnet, who was seated at the piano, glanced over at Sarah. He mistook the expression on her face to be one of boredom due to being cooped up indoors. He saw this as the right time to execute his own wicked plan.

Fishnet rose from his seat to retrieve an expensive bottle of cognac. With the bottle in hand, he called over to Sarah. After getting her attention, Fishnet held the bottle up and gestured for her to join him in a drink. Sarah readily accepted his invitation while flashing a false smile. The owner of the townhouse wasted no time fetching two clean glasses. After opening the bottle, he poured two drinks and assumed a position on the loveseat beside Sarah.

After consuming his first swallow, Fishnet shifted his body to be closer to Sarah. He began to tenderly pet her long blond tresses. After a few strokes, he began running his fingers through her hair with an earnestness that she found to be both soothing and arousing. Whatever ill will festered within Sarah was temporarily neutralized thanks to the comfort that came with drink and his caresses.

When the affectionate touching had run its course, Sarah began to question why Fishnet was being so nice. *What all of a sudden brought this on?"* she wondered. *If he wanted some, he would just come and take it, like he always does. No, there is something behind this other than his being horny.*

"What brings all this on?" Sarah finally asked, her curiosity getting the better of her.

"What do you mean?"

"Why so lovey-dovey all of a sudden," she asked.

"What can I say? You're starting to grow on me," he replied. Fishnet then began to assure Sarah that she had nothing to fear while he was around to protect her.

"What do you mean? I have everything to fear. I can't leave this house without looking over my shoulder. I have to constantly worry about getting ambushed."

"You can go out as long as I'm with you," said Fishnet. "Now that's a comfort, isn't it?"

The time has come at last! Sarah thought, seeing a chance to put into play her plot.

"Yeah, it is," she acknowledged. "Do you know what I'd really love to do?"

"Name it, sweetheart."

"I'd love to go out to dinner someplace," said Sarah.

Fishnet could hardly believe his luck. *She's making it too easy for me*, he thought.

"I'm afraid that going to a restaurant might still be too risky," said Fishnet. "But I have an idea. Let's go to the beach on a winter picnic," he said with spirited enthusiasm. "We can leave once it gets dark."

"It's freezing out," said Sarah, who was cool to the idea. "Who goes to the beach in December?"

"That's just the point. No one does. It'll be safe because nobody will be around."

"But the cold...."

"It won't be so bad where I intend to take you. Don't worry.

I've done this before. I know a cozy spot under the boardwalk."
"You want to go under the boardwalk? Are you nuts altogether?"

"Think about it, when was the last time you went to Coney Island? We'll stop at Nathan's to pick up some food. You must like Nathan's...."

"Of course I like Nathan's," said Sarah. Her fondness for Nathan's hotdogs went a long way in persuading her. "I haven't had their hotdogs in ages."

"We'll bring along blankets and a bottle of Remy Martin. We'll feast on Nathan's hotdogs and fries."

"Well, I suppose it could work out."

Sarah's real reason for relenting was not her desire to eat hotdogs. Being away from the townhouse for a couple of hours allowed her to proceed with the nefarious plan she worked out with her accomplices.

"I wish we had a little coke to take along."

"You got it, Sarah. We'll do some coke if you like."

"You do coke?"

"Sure, I do," fibbed the former detective.

The chance to get Fishnet outdoors for a couple of hours, coupled with his returning to the townhouse high, was perfect for what Sarah had in mind. To reduce her concern about running into the wrong people, Sarah reassured herself by intending to take along one of her guns on the excursion. "Okay, you're on, handsome. What time do you want to leave?" Sarah asked.

"We'll head out once it gets dark."

"Would you mind doing me a favor?"

"What"

"I feel like smoking a cigarette with my drink—I'm out. Could you go get me a pack?"

"Here, take one of mine," offered Fishnet.

"No, I only smoke filtered cigarettes—do you mind?" "Not at all, whatever you want," agreed the former detective. In Fishnet's brief absence, Sarah was able to telephone her accomplices, Greta and Judo, to inform them that the time to act was at hand. She conveyed that the front door to the townhouse would be left open for them.

When Fishnet returned with the cigarettes, he poured another cognac for the two of them. After clicking glasses, the happy twosome smiled at each other artificially, each believing that their own devious plot was progressing nicely.

Sarah put a cigarette in her mouth and asked Fishnet for a match. The detective found her an old book of matches that he had written his telephone number on when posing as Shepherd Fish. Not noticing the number, he gave the matches to Sarah.

After a sip of his drink, Fishnet leaned over to kiss Sarah gently on the cheek. As he did this, Sarah smiled, thinking that she had ignited Fishnet's passion for the very last time. Little did she realize that as Fishnet performed this act of affection, he was fantasizing that he was legendary mob kingpin Vito Genovese giving the kiss of death to underling Joe Valachi when both shared a prison cell.

##########

AS PLANNED, SARAH LEFT THE FRONT DOOR to the townhouse unlocked. She visually scanned the street in an effort to see her accomplices. Feeling relieved after spotting Judo Edwards leaning up against a parked car, she calmly waited in front of the building for her pickup.

When Sarah drove off with Fishnet, Judo telephoned Greta, who was standing by around the corner awaiting word,

After gaining entry to the townhouse, Judo proceeded directly to the loveseat in the living room. He lifted the cushion and retrieved the gun that Sarah had left for him. Judo decided that since the front door opened inward, he would position himself so that he could overtake the unsuspecting Fishnet from the rear when he arrived home.

Greta and Judo did their best to make themselves comfortable while they waited to bushwhack Fishnet.

##########

FISHNET DOUBLE-PARKED outside Nathan's. The heater in the car was set high, keeping the vehicle toasty enough for Sarah to remove her coat. Preparing to step into the cold, Fishnet wrapped his red scarf around his neck snugly before buttoning up his overcoat.

"I'll jump out and get four hotdogs and two fries....all right, Sarah?"

"That's fine. Bring some beer too."

"You sure you don't want anything else?" Fishnet asked, opening the vehicle door.

"Shut that door!" shouted Sarah. "You're letting all the heat out of the car!"

"Okay, okay," said Fishnet shaking his head. Her tone of annoyance was going to make his dirty work a pleasure. Sarah's hooded down coat rested on her lap, as did her mittens and hat. The gun she carried was secreted in the zippered side pocket of her coat.

"Did you get ketchup, relish and mustard," she asked, upon Fishnet's return.

"I did. It's all in the bag."

Feeling the coolness that came from the open door chilled Sarah. "Why don't we just have our picnic in the car?" she suggested.

"No, we can't do that. It'll spoil everything."

"What do you mean? Spoil what?"

"You'll spoil the whole specialness of the experience."

Sarah, now remembering not to appear contrary, managed to produce a smile. "Sure, I get it. It's something we can tell our grandchildren about."

"Well, let's not get ahead of ourselves." *Fat chance of that happening*, thought Fishnet.

"How about we crack open that bottle?"

"Sure, why not," said Fishnet, reaching into the vinyl bag that rested on top of several blankets in the back seat. "Here, knock yourself out," he said, handing Sarah the bottle.

Sarah had consumed two blasts of the cognac by the time Fishnet parked the car. Her imbibing was fine with Fishnet, who encouraged her drinking. He figured that her being intoxicated would make his vile work easier.

"How about that coke?" asked Sarah.

"Let's do that once we're settled under the boardwalk," replied Fishnet, who had no cocaine or intention of getting any. By the time they made their way onto the beach, Sarah had taken several more swigs of the cognac. With flashlight in hand, Fishnet led her to what seemed to be the darkest place under the boardwalk.

The ex-detective's dirty work was over in just minutes. Sarah was so overwhelmed by the sand sandwich that was being forced down her throat that she never had time to withdraw the gun from her coat pocket. Fishnet, who had no idea that Sarah was armed, departed the beach carrying everything except the blankets. He used those to cover Sarah's body.

Once back in the car, Fishnet ate the hotdogs and a few fries. He was appalled at how much was missing from the cognac bottle and shook his head before taking a swig himself. Feeling too exhilarated to go home, Sarah's killer decided to stop off at The Dancing Elf in Manhattan.

Fishnet was hoping to hook up with the waitress he had promised to do things for professionally. When he found out that his love interest wasn't working, he went to her nearby apartment. Fishnet found her receptive to his unplanned visit once he conveyed that he had a job in a play arranged for her. Before he headed home the following morning, Fishnet promised the young waitress that he would get back to her in a couple of days concerning the work he promised. The former detective was sincere in this offering. Fishnet's late actress wife had introduced him to enough theater people that he believed himself to be in a position to open a door or two.

##########

JUDO AND GRETA REMAINED at Fishnet's townhouse until daybreak. Not hearing from Sarah caused them to believe that something must have occurred to alter their plans. With things now gone awry, they rushed to clean up after themselves before departing the townhouse.

When Judo later heard on the news that a woman named Sarah Ince had been found murdered under the Coney Island boardwalk, he immediately went to see Greta. The news stunned Greta. After considering the matter over, they ultimately came to the understanding that silence was golden. In the end the hunt for Sarah had concluded with none of her pursuers having the satisfaction of catching up with her. With the only people having insights into Sarah's homicide remaining mum, the case was destined to go unsolved.

As for Judo and Greta, the dark secret they shared tightened their bond. Unsure of the circumstances surrounding Sarah's death, they believed it wise to leave New York City and start anew elsewhere. Passing themselves off as a married couple, they settled in Branson, Missouri, where they maintained a low profile. Determined to get beyond their checkered past, they made a concerted effort to turn their lives around. Judo found employment in a martial arts school, while Greta took work in a theater selling tickets.

As it turned out, once they had secured legitimate jobs, they found domesticity within a wholesome setting to be appealing. Since no one knew them in Branson or had reason to challenge them, their fictionalized history held up. Judo eventually went on to open a boutique martial arts school, which proved to be successful. When Greta became pregnant, the two married. The addition to the family further solidified their commitment to reform. They never again looked back at the life they left behind.

###########

SARAH INCE'S BODY WAS DISCOVERED BY a police officer assigned to the boardwalk post. His attention was drawn to the corpse by the loud barking of a dog. When he looked onto the beach, he saw an Irish setter yelping wildly as if suddenly spooked. The dog was pointed at something under the boardwalk that he apparently found irritating.

The officer noted that the hound's red coat was well groomed and that the dog wore a black leather collar. Having a way with animals, the officer managed to calm the dog. With no one in sight, the officer was baffled as to how the dog had gotten separated from his owner.

The dog, again irritated, resumed barking while looking toward the area beneath the boardwalk. The officer, thinking that perhaps the dog's owner had taken sick there, decided to investigate. It was then that the body of Sarah Ince was discovered under several blankets. Seeing the caked sand in the mouth and nostrils of the dead woman made it clear that a homicide had been committed.

Realizing that nothing could be done to help the victim, the officer made the dog his priority. He alerted the division dispatcher that he had found a lost dog. Once a pickup for the dog was arranged, the officer requested the response of the patrol supervisor.

After seeing Sarah's dead body, the responding sergeant called the Coney Island detectives to the scene. Among the property recovered from the victim's coat was a loaded handgun, a red wallet, a pack of cigarettes and a book of matches. The detectives were able to identify Sarah by the identification she carried in her wallet.

Back at the precinct the detective who caught the case decided to smoke one of the recovered cigarettes. He used the related matches to light up. When finished he stored the cigarettes and matchbook in the center drawer of his metal desk. Had he been more observant, he would have seen a telephone number written on the inside flap of the matchbook cover.

##########

THE MEMBERS OF LAW ENFORCEMENT who once had an interest in Sarah Ince now couldn't care less about her. Captain Gerard of the DA's office had set his sights on bigger fish, namely Philly Rava. Lieutenant Waldo Reale's interest in Sarah didn't extend beyond his trying to find her for Ruffy Shea. To Waldo, Sarah had been nothing more than a dollar sign.

The only person with some interest remaining in Sarah was Markie. Since things quieted down for the squad working out of headquarters, Markie grew bored. He decided to find out more about Sarah's homicide strictly out of curiosity.

"What do you say we go over to Brooklyn and check out the progress being made on the Sarah Ince homicide, Ollie?" asked Markie. "I'm curious to see what the story is."

"Sure," Sarge, replied Von Hess. "With her, it could have been anything, so I'm curious myself."

When Markie and Von Hess arrived at the precinct squad room, they sat down with the detective who had caught the case. As they went over the case particulars, the squad detective reached into the center drawer of his desk to retrieve a cigarette from the pack that had belonged to Sarah.

"You don't mind if I smoke inside, right, Sarge?" asked the detective, taking the matches that were with the pack. "They got that silly law now about smoking indoors."

"Knock yourself out, it's your lungs," replied Markie.

After the detective struck the last match in the book, he flipped the used up matchbook on the desk. When the three detectives finished going over the case, they were in agreement that there were no solid leads to pursue, just lots of backtracking to do regarding Sarah's life.

"What do you think, Sarge?" asked Von Hess.

"There is nothing we can do to help at this point, Ollie. God only knows what kind of jam this Sarah got herself into. It looks like these folks here in the Coney Island squad will have to figure this one out."

"We'll try not to kill ourselves doing it," said the squad detective, making it clear he wasn't about to lose any sleep over the mystery.

After Markie and Von Hess departed the squad, the assigned investigator began cleaning up his desk. It was at this time that he noticed something written on the inside cover of the matchbook he discarded. The squad detective looked at the flap and saw the telephone number.

"Well, what do you know about this," said the detective aloud.

"What?" asked his partner, who sat at a nearby desk.

"I got these matches from the jacket of the dead woman. It's got a phone number written on it. I never noticed before."

"Are you talking about the DOA under the boardwalk?"

"Yeah," answered the detective, who then proceeded to dial the number. "There's no answer," announced the detective.

"Check out the number with the phone company."

"Yeah, I'm gonna have to do that."

Not having a contact in the phone company, the squad detective needed a subpoena to acquire the information on an unlisted exchange. It was a process that took some time.

When the detective received the results, he learned that the unlisted number came back to a cell phone belonging to someone named Fieldstone Remington. The address on record was a post office box that was later determined to come back to the same person. Efforts by the detective to gather information on Remington proved negative.

The squad detective telephonically reached out to Markie over in headquarters to see if the name meant anything to him.

"So, you guys never heard of a guy by the name of Fieldstone Remington, Sarge?" asked the squad detective.

"That name never came up with anything we worked on," replied the sergeant. "I'd have remembered a name like that."

"Thanks anyway, Sarge. I'll keep you posted if we make any headway."

Unbeknownst to the detectives, the telephone number on the matchbook cover actually belonged to Fishnet Milligan. When in the business of scamming affluent citizens, Fishnet did so under the alias of Shepherd Fish. When portraying Fish, the ex-detective played the role of a do-gooder seeking charitable donations for those in need overseas. Fishnet put the phone he used when posing as Shepherd Fish under the name Fieldstone Remington in order to blur his trail. In doing so, once again Fishnet managed to slip through the net.

36

The Hammer Falls

WHILE ARRESTING A CORRUPT squad commander, was newsworthy, it paled in comparison to the media splash connected to taking down the boss of a mafia family. With this in mind the district attorney's office decided to aim high. The DA instructed Captain Gerard to concentrate on building a case against Philly Rava, boss of the Rava crime family.

Tasked with taking down Rava, Captain Gerard considered his options. He concluded that he would have to put the screws to Waldo as a first step on the road to implicate Philly Rava in criminal activity.

Gerard coordinated with the commanding officer of internal affairs in order to orchestrate the arrest of the corrupt squad commander. The goal was to get Waldo to cooperate with the district attorney's office.

Gerard's game plan was to use Waldo to help build a stronger criminal case against Miltie Kassoff, one serious enough that would induce Miltie to join the good guys in return for a reduction in jail time.

If successful, Captain Gerard intended to use Miltie as a bridge to Ruffy Shea, the man who was in a position to lead the law to Philly Rava.

LIEUTENANT WALDO REALE was always in good spirits when he visited the post office box. In anticipation of the bribe money he expected to find, he failed to take notice of the men and women in business attire closing in on him. The detectives who surrounded him were being led by Captain Gerard of the DA's squad. In addition to Gerard's investigators, also present were investigators from internal affairs.

Waldo's concentration was finally broken when Captain Gerard cleared his throat. When Waldo turned around he was startled to see the emotionless Gerard standing behind him. The captain seemed unusually distant, which made it clear to Waldo that this wasn't merely a social call.

The precinct squad commander stood helplessly by as his postal box was emptied. A pain came to his stomach at the sight of his funds being confiscated. Waldo offered no resistance when the detectives relieved him of his gun and shield.

"Sorry it had to come to this, Waldo," said Captain Gerard, once the precinct squad commander was rear cuffed.

Waldo responded with defiance. "Do me a favor, save the hearts and flowers," he spat out. "you're getting off on this, you cheese-eating rat."

"Put him in the car," ordered Captain Gerard stiffly, opting not to respond to Waldo's remark.

Not totally convinced that he would be convicted by a jury, Waldo stood firm in his refusal to entertain the captain's overtures that he turn informer. Later, Waldo's optimism would fade. When it came out that Miltie was going to be taking the witness stand to testify against him, Waldo was crushed. By that time, it was too late for deal making. The defrocked squad commander was going to jail to serve a lengthy sentence and he knew it. Just before trial, the squad commander copped a plea in return for a less then generous sentence. He did this to spare himself the expense of what he knew to be an unwinnable trial.

##########

FACED WITH WALDO'S ADAMANT REFUSAL TO COOPERATE, Captain Gerard had little choice other than to focus on Miltie Kassoff. He ordered his detectives to conduct extensive research on Miltie. The results attained established that Miltie was the president of a Manhattan-based entity known as TTJT (Thrill-Time-Joy-Time) Associates, a concern that distributed pornographic magazines and videos. Business records revealed the owner of the property that housed the entity to be 118 Walworth Street, Inc.

Recognizing 118 Walworth Street as a Brooklyn address, the investigators dug deeper. They ascertained that the owner of the 118 Walworth Street property was S & K Enterprises. Captain Gerard correctly suspected that S & K stood for Shea and Kassoff.

Miltie's criminal history proved to be exactly what Captain Gerard was hoping for. Miltie had been arrested and convicted on various charges on more than one occasion. Among these was a federal narcotics conviction for smuggling large consignments of heroin from New York City to other cities in the United States. This conviction netted Miltie a 7 ½- to 15-year sentence in the penitentiary.

The most recent records on file at the police department's intelligence division revealed that Miltie, who hailed from the Midwood section of Brooklyn, and Ruffy Shea ate breakfast together at a Queens County diner weekly. Miltie was also documented as a regular visitor to Ruffy's social club.

Based upon the information gathered, Captain Gerard dispatched a team of detectives to conduct an early morning surveillance that was to commence at Miltie's home. This monitoring resulted in detectives tailing Miltie to a Bronx bicycle shop. Eyebrows were raised when Miltie exited the shop carrying a small shopping bag. One of the investigators shadowed Miltie on foot while his partner followed in their car. Miltie, who was heading to his car, turned to his rear while walking. This was an old habit of the drug dealer. When Miltie noticed someone who looked like a detective walking behind him, he put into play his testing mechanism. Miltie picked up his pace and then spun around quickly, in time to see the man to his rear abruptly halt. Miltie was now convinced that he was under law enforcement surveillance.

Now desperate, Miltie quickly ducked into a bagel store, where he quickly placed the shopping bag containing kilos of white powder on the floor in a corner. He then distanced himself from the bag by getting on the customer line as if to place an order. The detective on foot followed Miltie into the store while his partner double-parked his vehicle.

The detective in the store noticed the discarded bag. As he opened it to determine its contents, Miltie hurriedly made his way to the exit. Intercepted by the second detective, he didn't get far. When informed that he was under arrest, Miltie groaned loudly. As he was led from the store in handcuffs, his expression was zombie-like. Miltie was sophisticated enough to know that he was now facing a lengthy period of incarceration. As Captain Gerard was hoping, Miltie had no desire to go back to jail. Shortly after being booked, Miltie made it known that he was receptive to cooperating in order to avoid prison. While interviewing their newly minted informer, the investigators gained the insights pertaining to Ruffy Shea that they were looking for.

In addition to Ruffy's drug trafficking involvement, Miltie provided the details of how he was present when Ruffy murdered two Bronx-based hoodlums as a favor to a drug kingpin. The authorities couldn't have been more delighted in learning from Miltie some details pertaining to Ruffy's involvement with crime boss Philly Rava. Miltie's cooperation earned him a minimum sentence, after which he relocated to another state under another identity.

##########

JOE BULLETS IMMEDIATELY PULLED HIS CAR over at the sound of the police siren coming from the unmarked car. Since he was adhering to the rules of the road, he was puzzled as to why he was being pulled over. Seeing all the detectives emerging from two vehicles, he knew that this was something more than a routine traffic stop.

"What's the problem?" asked the gangster through the vehicle's open window.

"Out of the car," ordered one of the detectives.

"Jesus," said Joe, remaining in his vehicle. "You guys got the whole army over here!"

"I'm Captain Tim Gerard of the District Attorney's Office Squad," declared the captain stepping forward and flashing his badge. "Now, step out of the car."

"I'm honored," commented Joe sarcastically. "So, what is this, a pinch?"

"I said to step out of the car," ordered Gerard, signaling two of his detectives to assist in the process of removing Joe from his vehicle.

"What are you guys rousting me for?" questioned Joe. "What did I do?"

"You best just pipe down and start listening, pal," said the burlier of the two detectives, who physically removed Joe from his car.

Realizing that he was outmatched, Joe straightened his clothing and threw up his hands defensively. He was made to stand spread-eagled across the fender of his car as the detectives searched him and his vehicle.

"You got a warrant?" Joe finally asked over his shoulder. His question was ignored.

"Look what I found, Cap," one of Gerard's detectives said after finding a dozen Rolex watches in the trunk of the vehicle. "What are you doing with these watches?" asked the captain. "What watches?" Joe replied.

Captain Gerard didn't bother to argue the point. "Listen, Joe, I want you to convey a message to Ruffy Shea for me," said the captain.

"Who is he?"

"Cut the crap unless you're looking to get pinched for those swag watches."

"That's no swag...."

"You want to show me the proof of where those watches came from?"

"What's the message, Captain?" asked Joe, changing his tune. "Tell Ruffy he's got to turn himself in to me," said Gerard handing Joe his business card. "You tell him that the district attorney wants him to surrender to the DA's office squad with his lawyer."

"That's it?"

"Yeah, that's it. And by the way, just so you know, you're one lucky son of a bitch."

"Oh, yeah, how is that?"

"You slipped through the net this time, but your boss wasn't as fortunate." Quitting while he was ahead, Joe remained silent after hearing this.

"What about these watches, Cap?" a detective asked.

"Put them back in the trunk where you found them," replied the captain.

##########

AFTER JOE BULLETS RELAYED THE MESSAGE, Ruffy immediately reached out to his lawyer. Without knowledge of what the charges were going to be, the lawyer recommended that his client surrender to the district attorney's office squad as requested.

When Ruffy and his attorney walked into the squad room at the DA's office, they knew they were in deep trouble after seeing that the district attorney himself was on hand waiting for their scheduled arrival.

"Brilliant move, genius," said Ruffy, who angrily turned to his mouthpiece. "They got the head honcho himself here waiting to take a piece of me." Once Ruffy learned that Miltie would be testifying against him, he realized just what a precarious position he was in. "Miltie has enough on me to bury me," lamented Ruffy.

"Easy, Ruffy, they still got to prove whatever charges they got," noted the attorney.

"Do you think they ain't got proof enough? If they didn't, that little shit wouldn't be here," said Ruffy, who was referring to the DA. "Forget about it."

"Do you want me to try and cut a deal?" asked the attorney. "I can talk to the DA direct right now."

"I don't know...." replied Ruffy, who was unsure of what to do.

"There's always a chance I could get you off if we go to trial. Or, if you don't want to take that chance, I could try to make a deal for you."

"Go see what you can do about a deal."

"Okay, but before I do that, what do you think Miltie can tell them?"

"He could sing a song of drugs and murder. Is that enough?"

"Stand by while I go talk to the DA."

After having a conversation with the DA, Ruffy's attorney returned to inform him that things didn't look good. "He's looking to lock you up and throw away the key unless you roll over."

"He expects me to turn rat?" asked Ruffy as if such a suggestion was preposterous.

"That's what the man wants. What do you want to do?"

After thinking a moment, Ruffy responded. "Tell the DA I can deliver Snow Johnson to him. He's got a huge drug operation out of the Bronx. He's in cahoots with some shady reverend up there."

Ruffy's attorney left to confer with the DA. He returned a few minutes later with more bad news.

"The DA said that he isn't interested in any Bronx drug dealer or shady reverend," advised the attorney bluntly.

"What the hell does he want then?"

"He wants information to sink Philly Rava. "I'm telling you, Ruffy, the guy is adamant. He'll only deal if you give him Philly Rava."

"I should've thrown that little son of a bitch Miltie in the drink along with the other two!" mumbled Ruffy to himself in anger.

"Your only chance is to give them what they want, Ruffy. I know this is not what you want to hear, but it's your only shot at receiving a break."

"I'm not ratting out Philly," declared Ruffy unwaveringly. "I'd do a million years first!"

"But Ruffy, it's Rava who they really want, not you. And to get him they need you. Can't you see that we can get a good deal out of the DA. It'll mean light at the end of the tunnel for you." Ruffy's response was short and to the point. "No way am I going against Philly, so don't mention it again."

Ruffy's determination not to snitch on mob kingpin Philly Rava guaranteed his receiving a lengthy sentence if convicted at trial, which he was.

Ruffy entered prison with the right attitude. He was determined to serve his sentence one day at a time. Having resisted all attempts by law enforcement to get him to cooperate, Ruffy entered jail with the respect of the inmate population. No one was more appreciative of Ruffy's decision to take his medicine without implicating others than Philly Rava and Joe Bullets, who both escaped prosecution.

Although serving an exceedingly lengthy sentence, Ruffy nevertheless looked ahead to the future as he counted off the days until his freedom. Thinking he would live forever, Ruffy approached life as someone having something to look forward to. The thought of one day being able to even the score with Miltie, Sarah Ince, and his son-in-law Mickey kept him going.

##########

WITH JOE BULLETS MANAGING to escape prosecution, Swatty was beside himself. Since Joe was now officially representing Ruffy's interests, Swatty was left no further along in freeing himself of their abuses. Returning to the drawing board, Swatty now had to figure out another way to eliminate Joe from involvement in the casino and restaurant.

Since Joe Bullets was a notorious shooter in his own right, Swatty knew he had to be careful. Since the matter was a complex one, Swatty needed to convince Italo to help come up with a way to rid them of Joe. All of Swatty's worry turned out to be for naught. As things stood, Joe was too busy engaged in another battle, one more lucrative than the casino, to bother with Swatty and Italo.

##########

WITH RUFFY AND MILTIE REMOVED FROM THE EQUATION, Snow Johnson no longer saw it necessary to maintain an allegiance to Ruffy Shea, who he considered now to be a toothless tiger. Besides, Snow thought that things were simply too hot to take any chances by continuing to do business with Ruffy's crew.

When Joe Bullets went to the Bronx to try and salvage what was once a lucrative business relationship, it was made clear to him by the drug dealer that their love affair was over. Outmatched, Joe had no alternative other than to accept Snow's verdict.

Joe was too embarrassed to face Ruffy due to his dismal performance in attempting to put the pieces back together with Snow. He grossly blundered by taking it upon himself to visit the home of crime boss Philly Rava for guidance and support. Feeling vulnerable, Rava exploded at the unannounced visit. After scolding Joe mercilessly, Rava ordered Joe out of his home.

Several days later the police found Joe Bullets at Kennedy Airport in the trunk of his car with a bullet in the back of his head. Other than Ruffy Shea, few people cared. Ruffy, who had no idea that Joe had gone to the home of Philly Rava, swore revenge. He was convinced that the only people who stood to gain by Joe's death were Swatty and Italo. The two were added to Ruffy's revenge list, right up there alongside Miltie, Sarah and Mickey.

Those in law enforcement viewed Joe's demise as good news in that there was one less criminal on the street to worry about.

37

The Smoke Clears

AFTER RUFFY WAS CONVICTED, Miltie was free of his legal entanglements. Although he might have been without friends, fortunately, he was not without funds. Miltie had been slicker than most criminals in that he squirreled away lots of cash in preparation for the day he might need to disappear. His finances were such that he was able to start anew elsewhere under an assumed name and live comfortably.

Miltie relocated to Santa Claus, Indiana, a venue where he learned to live without hookers, gambling, booze, drugs and double breasted suits. Also missing from his life were thoughts of engaging in criminal activity. His was a lifestyle that took some getting used to, but in the end Miltie managed to embrace legitimacy.

Miltie opened a small convenience store in Santa Claus. He made his living quarters in the back section of the store he rented. The profitability of his business, like many businesses, fluctuated.

While toiling in his store, Miltie became friendly with a customer who was the wife of a much older minister. A tall woman with excellent posture, everything about her seemed taut. Her smile revealed no teeth, just lips that formed a sealed straight line. When she spoke, her sentences came out concisely through a mouth that barely moved. Even the clothes she wore seemed to hug what Miltie considered to be a shapely figure. Something about the chestnut haired minister's wife caused Miltie to see her as a challenge.

Miltie finally acted on his impulse to test the waters after learning that the minister dropped dead of a heart attack during one of his more fiery sermons. He began his pursuit of the widow with small gestures that conveyed thoughtfulness. She would sample the candies he sold and seemed to show a sincere interest when he spoke about his business. This led to extended conversations whenever she entered his store.

Miltie began to share tales of the charitable work he did when he lived in New York City. Her receptiveness to his fabrications encouraged Miltie to build upon his false narrative. Things progressed well enough for the two to marry. Unfortunately, not long after they officially wedded, things began to unravel. Trouble began to brew once Miltie's bride took an active hand in his business. A dedicated workaholic, she came up with innovative ways to enhance business. Miltie began to grumble at having to now put in longer hours to meet the demands of the enterprise.

With a track record of success behind her, Miltie's wife became obsessed with expanding the business. Her unbridled ambition began to take a toll on Miltie.

Although Miltie welcomed financial success as much as his wife, the price he was paying physically was steep. Since his spouse tended to be tightfisted when it came to spending money, Miltie found himself doing much more work than he was accustomed to. His suggestion that they take on help was discouraged.

At this point Miltie was beginning to feel trapped. He was reluctant to divorce his wife because he was afraid of receiving publicity that could potentially expose him for who he really was. Until he was able to figure out the best way to get out of the marriage, all he could do was complain to anyone willing to listen. Miltie openly began referring to his spouse as a widow-maker who wouldn't be satisfied until she worked him to death.

Although it's been said that there is no substitute for hard work, this principle proved to be fatal to Miltie. A couple of years into his marriage, the former snitch dropped dead of a heart attack while stocking one of his refrigerators. When it came to husbands having heart attacks, the woman Miltie called the widow-maker had a perfect record of 2 dead and 0 survivors.

##########

INCARCERATION BECAME Waldo Reale's hell on earth. With nothing to do other than dwell on his confinement, the former squad commander lapsed into a deep depression. He woke up each day a little more diminished. The iron bars that caged him were a cold reminder of the freedom he lost. His pension was gone and his savings were practically exhausted due to legal fees. Perhaps the worst aspect of his situation was that Waldo was alone, without family or friends to visit or correspond with.

Thanks to his association with Ruffy Shea, Waldo was embraced by those inmates with organized crime ties. This provided some relief in that Waldo had people to associate with. In jail, eating at a table with the mobsters was something to be thankful for.

Waldo's tribulations continued to mount, as did his bouts of melancholy. His decline made it clear to all that he was having difficulty doing his time. This condition, in the eyes of the inmate population, made him appear weak.

Waldo gradually became disconnected from others. He ventured out into the prison yard less frequently and declined the opportunity to engage in activities. His lack of interest in mingling gradually alienated him from even those who took him into their fold. Things only degenerated for the worse as Waldo grew lax when it came to hygiene. Soon after, his body began to fail him.

When Waldo was finally released, he emerged from prison a pathetically broken man. His gray hair was now sparse, and his look was gaunt. With ill fitting glasses, that were now too big

334

for his face, Waldo faced his freedom with the aches and pains that eventually befall almost everyone.

Waldo made his way to St. Augustine, Florida, where he took a job as a desk clerk in a motel. While the wages he received were far from handsome, the job did come with a rent-free room and free breakfast.

Waldo took to solitary drinking, which eventually caused him to die alone in his room. His body was discovered by a cleaner who found him lying on his side in bed. He was apparently on the telephone when he gave out. A deep impression caused by the phone could be seen on the side of Waldo's face.

Mysteriously, Waldo's death mask projected a snarling look. It was conjectured that in Waldo's last seconds, he was either perturbed due to a verbal dispute or he was in pain, calling for assistance. No one cared enough to find out which.

##########

VISITING DAY AT THE PRISON was always something that Ruffy Shea looked forward to. His company always came with tidbits about developments on the street. These bulletins kept Ruffy connected to the outside world.

The first sign that Ruffy's mind was declining came when he began to lose track of current events. He spiraled down to where he consistently repeated himself while mentally trapped in a time long past. Enacting revenge on his enemies had been the lifeblood that strengthened Ruffy's will to go on.

Ruffy's cognitive capacity dwindled, with his attention span, recall, and mental processing all waning. Even Ruffy's ability to navigate the prison came into question at times. Luckily, he managed to remain in the general population thanks to fellow inmates who extended themselves by lending him assistance when necessary.

Finding it too painful, Ruffy's daughter ceased her visits when her father no longer knew who she was.

"Where the hell is Joe Bullets?" Ruffy could be heard muttering from his cell after lights out. "Wait until I get my hands on that Sarah and Mickey!" he'd blurt out in agitation. This behavior lasted as long as Ruffy did.

##########

PRISON LIFE AND EXPOSURE TO Zorro's Raiders effectively desensitized Mickey Walker. Influenced by the coarseness attached to the prison system, Mickey gradually came to accept dysfunctional behavior as the social norm. Even the homicide of Sarah Ince was something he came to trivialize as being "just one of those things."

Mickey readily recognized the value in having Zorro, a jailhouse honcho, looking out for him. Since Mickey knew his place and efficiently carried out whatever tasks were assigned to him, Mickey remained on Zorro's good side.

By the time Mickey completed his sentence, the two men had become close enough for Zorro to put in a good word for Mickey with drug trafficker Snow Johnson. Snow, who no longer honored his agreement with Ruffy Shea, nevertheless found a place for Mickey in his drug organization. Ironically, by the time the jailed Ruffy began to suffer from Alzheimer's, Mickey had established himself as a genuine asset in Snow's criminal network.

Mickey's drug trafficking success had lots to do with his presenting a less intimidating figure than his criminal associates. This attribute went far in his infiltrating the hottest nightclubs in town. After building a clientele of affluent weekend cokeheads, Mickey was able to springboard to those in the theatrical and sporting worlds who loved to party. The access Mickey gained to celebrated personalities enabled him to penetrate deeper into Snow's inner circle. Plainly put, Mickey took Snow into an arena that the drug kingpin could never access on his own steam.

Since Mickey's red hair was a rarity among his drug dealing cronies, he was perceived as something of a novelty. When one of Snow's nieces began to show romantic attention toward Mickey at a holiday function, he was susceptible to her overtures. This initial interaction was followed by a courtship and then marriage. By this time, the groom's recollection of Sarah Ince had been reduced to less than a very distant memory.

########

SWATTY AND ITALO VIEWED the homicide of Joe Bullets as a gift. They discussed Joe's killing one Sunday night after cutting up proceeds from their enterprises. Italo, who was subservient to Swatty, voiced no resistance to the 60–40 split his partner came up with.

"I wonder what Joe Bullets did to get himself whacked?" asked Italo innocently.

"Nobody knows," replied Swatty.

"How are we supposed to kick money upstairs to Philly now that Joe's gone?"

"Don't worry about that, Italo. One of Philly Rava's boys will come around to let me know how that's gonna work," answered Swatty. "I'll handle it."

"Is that what they said?"

"Nobody said a word to me yet, but I'm the logical choice. Who knows, they might straighten me out once I start fattening the envelope with a few more fazools for the old man," speculated Swatty, referring to his becoming a made member of the family on the strength of his paying Philly Rava increased tribute money.

"You think so?"

"Sure, why not? That's how things work."

Swatty overestimated his position. Reality set in once word came down from a family messenger that Philly Rava wanted to see Italo at his home.

"He wants to see us?" asked Swatty.

"The old man made no mention of wanting to see you, Swatty," said the messenger. "He just wants to see Italo."

########

ITALO COULDN'T HAVE ENTERED THE HOME of Philly Rava more respectfully. Attired in a suit and tie for the occasion, he brought along a tray of sausage and peppers.

"Put the tray on the table," said the crime boss, nodding approvingly. "You're a good boy, Italo, you understand the meaning of respect. Sit down, have some vino."

Italo took a seat in the easy chair as directed. He watched nervously as Rava poured red wine. After wishing each other luck, the two men drank.

"We mustn't be strangers, my friend," said the family boss, finally getting down to business. "I've just learned from my sister in the old country that the Rava and Pissiano families are now united in marriage."

"They are?"

"Yes, they are."

Rava informed Italo that his sister's grandson had married one of Italo's cousins in the old country. This news greatly pleased Italo, who understood what such a family alliance could mean to him. After ninety minutes of chatting, Italo was permitted to depart the Rava home. He was leaving with the knowledge that he was now Philly Rava's protégé. As such, moving forward, Italo had the inside track on visiting Rava's home regularly to fork over envelopes of money.

"Are things going well with Swatty?" asked the crime boss as he walked his guest to the door.

"It's okay."

"Why is it just okay?"

"The split hasn't been exactly even."

"Aren't you equal partners?"

"Well, we're supposed to be. But...."

"I see. There is no need to explain. Things will soon change, my friend." After thinking a moment, Rava revealed more than he originally intended. "I've always been a silent partner with

Ruffy, and this is to remain our secret. Let me explain to you the breakdown of the profits...."

Italo's newly acquired access to the top man in the Rava crime family came with greater leverage than he thought possible. Italo had been elevated to dominant partner status in both the casino and restaurant. Swatty's enlightenment as to the new arrangement came when he was visited at home by a well-respected Rava family capo.

"I'm here to let you know how Philly wants things handled."

"What are you talking about?" asked Swatty defiantly.

"Make no mistake about one thing, Swatty. Italo has the greasy thumb now. He's in charge of the money."

"No problem," replied Swatty, biting down hard. "I'll bring Philly his end like clockwork."

"No, you ain't."

"I'm not?"

"No, Philly only wants to see Italo."

"Italo?" asked the bewildered Swatty.

"That's the way Philly wants it," advised the high-level messenger. "Oh, and a couple of other things you have to get straight—Italo calls the shots in the casino and restaurant. And from now on, the split is 60–40, Italo's way....after the old man gets his."

"I don't understand—what did I do wrong?"

"The only thing you did wrong was not marrying into Philly's family."

Swatty realized that he couldn't buck an order coming from the boss of a crime family. He meekly nodded his agreement. Much to the displeasure of Swatty, Italo was proposed for membership in the Rava family. The day after Italo took the blood oath, Swatty went on a bender. He was never without a vodka filled flask on his person again.

##########

THE VERY SCARED HUSBAND OF JUDGE FATIMA WEST made the decision to relocate after the death of his friend Marvin

339

Butterworth. Based on his history with mobsters in the aftermath of his wife's death, and then having had to deal with Fishnet, Amos West convinced himself that his own life might be in jeopardy.

Taking no chances, Amos chose to distance himself from the entire situation by packing up and retiring to Mexico City. Thanks to his financial solvency, he was able to create a new life for himself in a vibrant expat community.

At first, memories of his late wife and Marvin Butterworth continued to haunt him. However, once he began making new friends and interacting with wholesome people, Amos was able to suppress these unpleasant reflections. With the focus of Amos now on creating new memories, eventually, even thoughts of his late wife Fatima began to fade.

The new life Amos thrived in was filled with enjoyable pastimes. His participation included great restaurants, evening walks, dances, fitness classes, card nights, membership in a book club, and the company of women.

Aside from investment updates, Amos had no interest in learning what was happening to those in the land he left behind. Such knowledge would have run the risk of upsetting the tranquility he had now come to savor. Fortunately, thanks to his self-imposed exile, Amos lived happily and free from fretting.

38

The Baby Machine

MARKIE STOPPED BY FITZIE'S place for a drink after work. As he made his way toward his usual spot at the far end of the room, he noticed two women sitting at the bar having a drink. Of the two, the fair-skinned woman with the blond highlights in her hair caught his eye. Once he heard her voice, he thought that she sounded familiar, like someone he might know. When the sergeant came to notice the space between her upper center teeth, he was able to place her. She had been a bridesmaid at his wedding many years prior.

Feeling awkward, he didn't know whether or not to say hello, since she was his ex-wife's girlfriend. Finally, after giving it some thought, Markie approached her.

"Karen?"

"Al!" she answered with surprise, after turning upon hearing her name. The broad smile on her face indicated that she was happy to see him. "It's been so long! How are you?"

"I'm fine," replied Markie, who was struck at how well his ex-wife's girlfriend had kept herself. "Gilda, say hello to Al. We've known each other forever," said Karen. "I was in his wedding party."

Markie's eyes darted a sneak peek at Karen's cleavage as she turned to introduce her friend. His roving eye didn't escape the attention of Gilda or the woman behind the bar serving drinks.

"Pleased to meet you," said Gilda politely.

"It's my pleasure. Can I buy you two a drink?" asked Markie, signaling the bartender by raising his finger. "Give these two ladies whatever they're having."

The bartender, although less than pleased by the attention Markie was affording the two women, simply nodded her acceptance of the order. A veteran when it came to men who didn't live up to expectations, she knew how to deal with disappointment.

As Markie and Karen reacquainted, Gilda began to feel like a third wheel. In answer to her feeling of alienation, Gilda tried to move things along.

"I'm famished," announced Gilda, "I'm ready for dinner."
"Oh, do you have to go?" questioned Karen, confident that Gilda would get the hint. The two had been out enough times for Gilda to recognize her exit cue.

"Yes, I have to run," answered Gilda. "It's been very nice meeting you, Al."

Markie wasn't sorry to see Karen's friend go. "It's been my pleasure, Gilda."

"You know, I haven't seen or heard from Florence in long time," said Karen, carrying the conversation once alone with the sergeant.

"I haven't seen her much either, not since she hooked up with that dentist she works for."

"Oh, I didn't know about that. What about your kids, Al? How are they?"

"They got no time for me. We touch base by phone, mostly."

"I'm sorry to hear that," said Karen.

"That's the way it goes, I guess. How about you? I heard you got divorced."

"Yeah, we broke up. It took five kids for me to realize that we weren't suited for each other."

"You have five kids?" asked the astonished Markie.

"Yes, all girls who live with me."

"That's amazing."

"What can I say? I get pregnant shaking hands."

"You're a regular baby machine."

"Well, my baby-making days are over. After the fifth, I had my tubes tied."

"How do you handle five kids?"

"I'm lucky that my father is retired and my sister still lives at home," said Karen. "We all live together in my father's house, so I have help."

"So, you returned to the nest after you split up?"

"I had to. It was the only way I could get by. With five kids, I have to work."

Markie reacted by simply nodding his understanding. "Let's have another round," he said, not wanting to proceed with the topic being discussed. Having his own headaches, he didn't want to hear about the struggles of someone else.

Having found each other, it didn't take too much work for Markie to convince Karen to call and let her father know that she'd be late. When Markie finally took her home everyone in her house was asleep.

"I'll call you," advised Markie, just before Karen got out of his car. His words were what she wanted to hear.

########

WHEN KAREN DIDN'T HEAR FROM MARKIE, she began dropping into Fitzie's in the hope of running into him. One night her timing was right, and she was able to spot Markie from afar before he noticed her. He was sitting at his usual station at the bar engaged in conversation with the bartender.
Pretending not to see the sergeant, Karen casually slid onto a stool mid-bar.

Upon seeing the newly arrived customer, the bartender's mouth dropped open. She reacted by remarking, "Oh." She then turned to Markie to inform him that, "You're friend is here." The bartender went on to take Karen's Martini order with a coolness that suggested that the customer wasn't wanted.

343

While her drink was being prepared Karen made her way to the ladies' room, a trail that that would take her past Markie. Determined to appear nonchalant, she walked by the sergeant expecting to be acknowledged first. She wasn't disappointed. Markie's delight in seeing Karen equaled her happiness to see him. It seemed the natural thing for them to sit together while enjoying their cocktails.

Fitzie, who had a trained eye when it came to barroom interludes, knew that his bartender would be unable to compete with the younger woman. Feeling sympathetic, Fitzie whispered to his employee that she shouldn't take things personally. He explained that Markie still hadn't gotten over the death of the woman he was to marry, as if that was a good excuse for his insensitivity.

An experienced hand when it came to men, the bartender took things in stride. "You don't have to worry about me, Fitz," she said, adding, "I'm used to assholes." The remark gave the bar owner pause, as her onetime lover, he wondered if he was on that list.

When Fitzie noticed that Markie and Karen began to get touchy-feely, he left to prepare his apartment above the bar. Upon setting the stage, he left the door to the apartment open. When he returned to the bar, he discreetly signaled Markie by pointing to the ceiling. This was the sort of courtesy that Fitzie was known to extend to those he liked.

With alcohol having fueled their mutually amorous emotions, Markie and Karen eventually found themselves upstairs in the apartment tearing into each other. They never noticed the two shots of whiskey that were left out for them atop the small bar in the living room.

##########

IT DIDN'T TAKE LONG BEFORE word got around that Markie had a girlfriend. His ex-wife was happy for him until she learned who his new love interest was. The sergeant's children remained indifferent to their father's romances.

Curious was the wife of Ollie Von Hess, who learned of the existence of Karen from her husband over dinner one evening. "So how did Al meet this woman?" asked Mrs. Von Hess.

"I don't know, I didn't ask," replied Von Hess.

"Let me tell you, these men waste no time getting over things," declared Mrs. Von Hess.

"What are you talking about?" asked Ollie between bites. He had been half listening.

"I'm talking about your friend—the woman he was going to marry isn't even cold yet, and he's got a replacement!"

"C'mon, life goes on."

"Oh, does it? Would you be out looking so fast if something happened to me?"

"I wouldn't have to look," replied the detective. Attempting to be funny, he added, "The line would be around the block with women looking to jump in your shoes."

"Oh sure," commented his wife, "and they'd have to put up police barricades to control the crowd."

"Now, ain't that the truth."

"C'mon, Ollie, be serious. Was he seeing this new girlfriend all along on the side?"

"How should I know?"

"Wouldn't he tell you?"

"What he does on his own time is none of my business. I don't probe when it comes to things like that."

"Are you going to tell me how he met this new girlfriend or not?"

"I'm telling you, I got no idea. We don't talk about that stuff."

"Well, what do you two talk about all day?"

"Police work, what do you think?"

Mrs. Von Hess persisted in her questioning. "Well, when you don't talk about police work what do you talk about?"

"We talk about old movies. Al loves old movies."

"That's it?"

"Okay, you want to hear something few people know about Al?" asked Von Hess.

"Of course....what?" asked Mrs. Von Hess, who was always anxious to hear a juicy tidbit.

"You know those old gangster movies he loves to watch on television?"

"Yes...."

"Well, Markie roots for the bad guys to come out on top."

"Get out of here, Ollie."

"No, it's the truth, honest to God."

"Is that normal?"

"C'mon, let's finish dinner," said Von Hess, not wanting to go there. He'd seen so much over his long career that the difference between normal and abnormal had become blurred.

39

The Maestro
Comes Through

FISHNET MILLIGAN FOUND THE MAN HE WAS LOOKING for sitting under the bright sun on a bench in Washington Square Park. It had been a while since he last saw the Maestro. A brilliant, but complicated man, the octogenarian had been a friend of Fishnet's late actress wife.

The old crab-ass hasn't changed much, thought the former detective. *He still looks like a penguin.*

As the former detective perused the goings on in the park he spotted Pascal, the Maestro's significant other, talking to a man in his early twenties. *There's the other one*, thought Fishnet. *What the hell is he up to with that kid?*

The ex-detective's trained eye suggested to him that Pascal was in the market to cop drugs. As he watched the transaction unfold, Fishnet shook his head. *Probably cocaine*, he thought. Fishnet waited until Pascal returned to where his partner was seated. Once the two men were sitting side by side, Fishnet sucked in his stomach and threw his shoulders back. This is what he usually did when he approached people with the intent to intimidate them.

The couple ceased conversation at the sight of Fishnet, who they perceived to be a homophobic beast. The concerned look on Pascal's face suggested fear, which indicated to Fishnet that Pascal remembered the beating he received at the hands of the former detective. Fear was an advantage, Fishnet believed. "How are tricks, boys?" asked the Clark Gable lookalike. Fishnet's tone was typical of a wiseass.

His question received no immediate response, just wary eyes that conveyed concern. The smirk on the former detective's face made it obvious that Fishnet's presence was not of a wholesome nature.

"That's a very nice fur coat you're wearing, Pascal. Is it keeping you warm and comfy?"

"It serves its purpose," replied Pascal in a clipped voice.

"Did the Maestro buy it for you?"

"What do you want with us?" questioned the Maestro, injecting himself into the conversation. "State your business and leave us alone," he barked. "We have no time for your nonsense!"

Fishnet took exception to the elderly violinist's tone. "Calm yourself, Maestro. No need to get uppity. I didn't say the coat was made of skunk, you know."

"We find you an exceedingly boorish man with whom we want nothing to do," said the Maestro, raising his voice. "Is that put plain enough for you?"

The Maestro's taking a stand triggered Fishnet's sadistic side. "Do you find this boring, Pop?" asked Fishnet, grabbing the old man's nose between his index and middle fingers. The Maestro let out a yelp as Fishnet began twisting his nose.

"Now cut that out," shouted Pascal, jumping to his feet in defense of his companion.

With a brisk one-handed shove, Fishnet sailed Pascal back down onto the bench.

"You boys are starting to really piss me off," warned the former detective. as he looked down at the two men humbled before him.

The Maestro sat silent as he held his aching nose. The shaken

Pascal was breathing heavily as he tried to compose himself after being roughly treated. Both victims conceded that they were no match for Fishnet physically.

"What do you want of us?" finally asked Pascal weakly.

"Is the coat mink or beaver?" asked Fishnet, who was genuinely curious. When he received no answer, the aggressor repeated the question, this time using a sharper tone. "I asked you a question. Now, what is it, mink or beaver?"

"It's red fox," answered Pascal, who warily looked up at Fishnet from the bench.

"Please, just tell us what it is you want and let's be done with this," voiced the Maestro, whose nose continued to ache.

"All right, Pop. Let's get down to cases," advised Fishnet, seeing no purpose in prolonging things. "I'm here because I need you to do me a favor. A friend of mine is looking for a job in the theater, and I want you to help get her one."

"I know of no one in the theater anymore," said the Maestro, letting out a deep huff. "I'm far too removed from all of that."

"My friend's got plenty of talent, Maestro. I can attest to that, if you get my drift."

"I'm sorry, but I have no friends who could—"

"Cut the bullshit," snapped Fishnet. He again revealed his ugly side by reaching out to twist the Maestro's nose again.

"Maestro, please," pleaded Pascal, who was concerned that things would again turn violent. "Just pick up the phone and put an end to this."

"Pascal is talking sense. Listen to him, Pop."

"Stop calling me Pop!" shouted the Maestro, losing control of his temper. "And Pascal, be still. I'll handle this."

"Okay, Maestro, you handle it. What's your play?" asked Fishnet.

"I'm calling the police!"

"Yeah, what for—to do a line of coke with you guys?"

"Never mind," responded the Maestro defiantly.

"Now listen, cocksucker," said Fishnet, "you're gonna make that call, or I'm gonna fracture your skull for you," threatened Fishnet, who was on the brink of backhanding the Maestro.

"Please, Maestro...." again pleaded Pascal.

"You better wise him up fast, Pascal," warned Fishnet.

"Maestro, please," pleaded Pascal. "Just do what he wants, so we could be done with this."

Maestro's continued refusal to comply caused Fishnet to take a handful of the loose flesh that hung from the old man's throat. All it took was a couple of quick yanks to get the Maestro to finally relent.

"Who is it that wants the job?" asked the assault victim after catching his breath.

"That's better. My new girlfriend's name is Cheryl."

In the end, the Maestro secured stage employment for Fishnet's waitress friend in an upcoming off-Broadway production.

##########

ON HIS WAY HOME FROM Washington Square Park, Fishnet stopped off at a pet shop to purchase two koi. Excited to unite the new koi with the existing ones in his pond, he wasted no time rushing to the yard of his townhouse. Once there, he released the koi from their water-filled packaging and dropped them into the pond. He smiled as he watched the tiny fish swim freely.

"Say hello to Sarah and Marvin, folks," he said, speaking happily to the fish in the pond. "C'mon now, you two girls be nice to them," added Fishnet, speaking to the koi he named after his late wife and her girlfriend.

After watching the koi in amusement, Fishnet was set to face the rest of the day in an exceptionally good humor. He decided to call on Cheryl and ask her if she wanted to go ice skating in Rockefeller Center. The former law enforcement officer thought it would be a novel idea to break the good employment news to her while on the ice.

40

Fore!

IT WAS EARLY MAY WHEN MARKIE received a call from Lieutenant Wright advising him to report to his office. A meeting with the lieutenant either meant new work or trouble. The sergeant was happy to learn that he was receiving a new assignment.

"I have a job for you and Ollie," advised the lieutenant.

"Homicide, Loo?"

"No, it has something to do with some big shot plastic surgeon that belongs to one of those fancy private clubs in midtown. It sounds like a harassment matter to me."

"We're taking on harassment cases now, Loo?"

"I'm really not sure what the hell it's all about. All Chief McCoy told me is that the police commissioner plays golf with this guy, and he has to be taken care of. So, talk to him and see what his problem is. If you can do something to help him, do it."

"No problem, Loo. Should I call him to make an appoint to meet with him?"

"No, it's all set. He's coming here. Actually, he's on his way."

"He's coming here?"

"Yeah, Chief McCoy said he was never in police headquarters. I guess it'll be a thrill for him."

"No problem, Loo."

Markie returned to his office and informed Von Hess that they'd soon be conducting an interview.

"What kind of caper, Sarge?"

"Some rich doctor is getting harassed. We have to take care of him."

"If he's getting harassed, he must have pissed somebody off, Sarge."

"I'd say so. Anyway, we'll be finding out the story soon enough."

Markie had no way of knowing that the man he and Von Hess were to interview on a seemingly minor matter would lead them on a journey involving murders, illicit love and an introduction to the world of country club golf. The matter would one day be remembered as *The Case of the Amorous Caddy*.

-THE END-

ANTHONY CELANO is a former Detective and Detective Squad Commander who served twenty-two years in the NYPD. His expertise in organized crime led to assignments in the Queens District Attorney's Office Squad and the Colombo Organized Crime Task Force during the Colombo Wars of the 1990's. Other assignments included the Organized Crime Control Bureau, the Drug Enforcement Administration Joint Task force and several detective squads in Manhattan and Brooklyn. He was also a special investigator for the Office of the Special State Prosecutor-Nursing Home Investigation. Mr. Celano was the Co-Founder/Owner/CEO of Full Security Incorporated, a Midtown Manhattan based investigative firm, for seventeen years. After retiring from his business he began devoting his time to creating a series of Sergeant Markie Mystery novels, with this, The Case Of The Hunted Woman, being his fifth offering in the series. In 2019, Mr. Celano, along with Flagstar Bank, began hosting monthly Author-Wordsmith Networking lunches in Manhattan to assist authors, aspiring authors and business people to establish mutually beneficial contacts.

Visit the author's website, anthony-celano.com, for further information.

www.ingramcontent.com/pod-product-compliance
Lightning Source LLC
Chambersburg PA
CBHW072316020726
47501CB00002B/527